LEONARDO'S CHAIR

A NOVEL

LEONARDO'S CHAIR

A NOVEL

John DeSimone

RIVEROAK®

Good News in Fiction

COOK COMMUNICATIONS MINISTRIES
Colorado Springs, Colorado • Paris, Ontario
KINGSWAY COMMUNICATIONS LTD
Eastbourne, England

RiverOak® is an imprint of
Cook Communications Ministries, Colorado Springs, CO 80918
Cook Communications, Paris, Ontario
Kingsway Communications, Eastbourne, England

LEONARDO'S CHAIR

Published in association with Hartline Literary Agency, Attn: Janet Benrey,
123 Queenston Dr., Pittsburgh, PA 15235.

This story is a work of fiction. The events are the product of the
author's imagination.

First Printing, 2005
Printed in the United States of America
1 2 3 4 5 6 7 8 9 10 Printing/Year 08 07 06 05

ISBN: 1589190319

To Mark and Susanna.
Dreams do come true.

The painter paints himself.

—Leonardo da Vinci, *Notebooks*

Prologue

Florence, Italy 1542

Pierino da Vinci stood in the courtyard of his father's Florence palazzo, biting his lip, as the cardinal studied him from his seat on a nearby stone bench.

"So you are the nephew of Leonardo?" the gray-bearded cardinal said.

"Yes, Excellency," he said, lowering his eyes. He could hear his father's shoes clicking across the tiles as he paced behind the cleric.

The cardinal stood, his brocaded white tunic rustling in the gentle summer breeze. He fingered the lad's long blond hair, then put a bony index finger under his chin, raising it so Pierino's eyes rested on the shiny golden medallion of the Papal Nuncio around the cardinal's neck. "Your hair is like his, and your face has a resemblance." He took up the boy's left hand and examined his long fingers. "I take it you paint with this hand," he said.

"And write, Excellency."

He dropped the boy's hand. "They say you are another Leonardo. Is this true?"

"Please, Excellency," his father interrupted. "It is not for him to say such things. His brush speaks for him."

"You are right, Bartolomeo," he said, eyeing the father. "We have heard enough rumors in Rome. I have come to judge for myself. Let me assure you, I know Leonardo's work." He fingered the medallion as if reminding those present who had sent him.

"Your Excellency," Bartolomeo said. "I have also seen my brother's work."

"Very well. Let us see the young man's then." The cardinal returned to his seat.

Bartolomeo snapped his fingers, and from the shadow of the hall behind him, two servants brought out a painting covered with a green cloth. Another servant brought a simple wooden easel. The men gently placed the painting on the easel. The cardinal rose and waved them away. The sun made its way toward noon, and the sunshine poured into the courtyard in buckets of gold.

The lighting will be perfect, thought Pierino. *He will see my greatness.*

The cardinal, with a skeptical look, caught Bartolomeo's eye. He lifted the green cloth to reveal a portrait of a woman. His face turned red; he clenched his jaw. "This is outrageous."

"Your Excellency?" Bartolomeo said, taking a step toward him, his hands clasped together.

"This is Leonardo's. I am sure."

"Not so."

"Do not lie to me," he said angrily, tightening a fist.

"Your Excellency. This is a portrait of the boy's mother. I am a notary of the city of Florence. My word is my life. I watched him paint it myself." Bartolomeo motioned to someone in the hall, and a woman in a yellow silk dress stepped forward into the sunlight, her blonde hair tightly twined in braids over her head. She bowed her head demurely to the cardinal.

"Cardinal Tourimi, may I present Constanza, my wife and mother of Pierino."

The cardinal, unsmiling, studied her face, then the portrait.

"The maestro has been dead for over twenty years," Bartolomeo said. "The portrait is as you see Constanza today, because this," he waved toward the painting, "was completed just a few weeks ago."

The cardinal raised his eyebrows and looked at the boy. "Pierino, please come here."

The boy strode over to the cardinal. The cleric put his hand on his shoulder. "Did you paint this?"

"Yes, Excellency. I've also completed several sculptures, and I'm working on a new painting. Would you like to see them?" Pierino said.

The cardinal's eyes moistened, his lips trembled. He took Pierino's head in his hands and kissed first one cheek, then the other, then his forehead. "Praise the holy God, he has given us another Leonardo. This is truly a miracle." He lifted the medallion and its heavy chain over his head and put it around Pierino's neck. "His Holy Father commands your presence in Rome, my son. He wishes to meet you himself."

The next day, as the whole household busied itself preparing Pierino for his journey, Bartolomeo took his son into the chamber where they kept the special gift from Leonardo, the delicately hand-carved chair of the maestro's own handiwork. He explained again how Leonardo had personally given it to Bartolomeo, his favorite brother.

Pierino, from his youth, had sat in it hour after hour, drawing or reading or listening to his father tell him stories of his famous uncle. Today, running his hand over the intarsia work on the thick wooden arms, Pierino could feel the spirit of the great maestro. His gift had become Pierino's gift. How? He did not know. His father only said Leonardo had given the chair to him to keep his gift alive. Such a thing only the genius of Leonardo could accomplish.

Bartolomeo put his hands on his son's slim shoulders and spoke directly to him. "Remember my words. The gift is in the chair, not in you. You must keep it with you at all times."

"But why, Father?" he asked, fingering the medallion.

"Leonardo spent his whole life consumed with his talent, and it wasn't until late in life he realized his astonishing gifts were from God. Thus he told me that the one who used the chair should never be far from it. It reminds us that our talents are but gifts."

Pierino nodded. He'd heard this part of the story many times before, but he knew his father left some of it unexplained. "What is this curse that Uncle Leonardo spoke of?"

"Stay humble. Never let the pride of greatness lift you up. And the curse will never touch you."

"I will obey, Father."

Bartolomeo pulled his son close to him. "Do not ever be far from the chair."

⚜

Pierino stood at the window of his studio overlooking the fountain in the piazza of his residence. Water poured in gentle arcs from the mouth of a dancing stone fairy into a round marble bowl settling into a calming pool of glass. He pushed his window open to let in the soothing sound of the tumbling water. His stomach felt as if he'd eaten a bad bowl of oysters, yet he hadn't eaten oysters in months. The fresh breeze and pleasant rhythms no longer comforted him the way they had when he first came to Rome. Two years of incessant demands for portraits; patrons showing up at his door at ungodly hours, gold ducats bulging their leather purses; always gold; always the best for their mistresses, their wives, their sons. Everyone looking for immortality in paint.

He closed his eyes and rubbed his forehead with his fingers. The burning inside grew into a shooting pain under his heart. He was nothing more than a rich men's slave. This house and its splendor had become his prison. A gilded prison, but still a prison. He turned and glanced at the far corner of the room, past the unfinished portrait of a duchess on his easel, to the chair. The one his father said he should never be far from. His father's kind smile formed in his mind.

Home. That is what he missed the most. Rome was not his home. He made his decision quickly, lest he dwell on it and reconsider the possible consequences of an impetuous departure. He was in the middle of a commission for the pope, the imperious man and his pompous cardinals would not be pleased. Be that as it may, in the morning he would journey home—to Florence. And that big wooden thing sitting in the corner was staying here.

I, Pierino da Vinci, no longer need it, he thought.

Before the sun brightened the sky with its streaks of red and purple the next morning, Pierino sat alone in his comfortable coach as it jostled and rolled toward Florence. He brought just one piece with him that he wished to finish and show his father before handing it over to the Holy Father. Late that afternoon the carriage came to a halt for the night at an inn, a two-story stone building with a red-tiled roof, set alongside the road outside the walls of Pisa. Stepping into the dimming sunshine, he saw the valley behind the inn bursting with yellow, magenta, and blue flowers. A freshness came over his spirit. One he hadn't felt in a while. He smiled to no one but himself.

He had to paint.

He swaggered into the large dining room and strode among the wooden tables filled with eating travelers, searching for the right light to work in. He stopped by a long table near the far corner under a window overlooking the valley. Two bearded men sat eating slowly off pewter plates. One tore a leg off a roasted game bird and gnawed at it. Pierino slapped the table with his palm and glared at them until both men stood and moved away to another table.

"Porter," he called, "unpack my paints. I will work here."

"Sir, but the other guests," the rough looking man said.

Pierino stared at him, then motioned with his hand toward the window. "Here is the light I need."

The servant frowned but trudged back and forth with several trunks of supplies. The last piece the porter carried in was the heavy wooden panel of Pierino's unfinished painting covered carefully in white lines. He went about setting up the young man's easel, unwrapped the unfinished painting of a Madonna and child, while Pierino mixed his paints, and began to work.

The light streaming in the window had the same golden hue as what he envisioned for the highlights of the Madonna's face. He could feel the yellowish glow of the late afternoon sun cascading down the folds of her gown in rivulets of soft gold. What he saw in his mind flowed through him onto the wooden surface in perfect strokes of genius. He worked deftly, lightly, with a control that delighted him.

The fiery sunset waned and twilight waxed in thickening blue filling the window, slowing his progress. He called to the porter across the room.

"Porter, bring a lamp," he demanded.

The man shuffled across the room and placed an oil lamp at the end of the table a few feet from his easel. Pierino studied the effect of the light. It was not enough.

"Bring the other lamps. This is not enough."

"But the other guests, my lord," the man remonstrated.

"Can't you see I'm working on a painting for the Holy Father?" he said with a scolding voice.

The porter sighed and collected the three other lamps, leaving the others in darkness, and placed them in a circle on the floor around the young painter and one on the table adjacent to the easel. The darkened room filled with murmurs of disgruntled voices but Pierino ignored them. *They are nothing but ignorant fools,* he thought. The room gradually fell silent, and he only heard the steady stream of scuffing of feet on the wood planks as the guests trundled up the stairs to their rooms. When he heard the porter slide the heavy iron bolt in the door for the night, he knew he was alone and could finish his work undisturbed. Deep in the quiet morning hours he slumped down, exhausted but finished, on the end of the wooden bench and admired his artistry.

A masterpiece fitting of Leonardo. The Holy Father will see this paint-ing and ask me to decorate his private rooms in the Belvedere. I will be the greatest artist ever to have worked in Rome.

Smiling to himself, he flexed his weary legs in front of him and accidentally kicked over one of the oil lamps, smashing the glass ball filled with liquid. The oil splattered over the wooden floor and ignited. He hopped up onto the bench and yelled for help.

The flames licked up the far wall, so he jumped to the floor and ran to other side of the room, calling for the porter. In a moment of far deeper panic he looked back: His masterpiece stood untouched in the center of the fire. He ran between the tables to try to reach it, but the flames blocked his way. He leapt onto a table next to his easel, reached over one of the oil lamps and grabbed his painting. Clutching it, he pulled the heavy wooden panel toward him. In his eagerness to rescue his masterpiece his elbow tipped over the lamp next to him. The glass shattered as it hit the rough planks, dumping oil in a stream away from him, but the liquid splashed his tunic. The table exploded in flames, jumped to his tunic, turning him into a human torch.

He screamed and furiously stamped his feet and slapped at his clothes with the painting, refusing to let it go. The flames raced up his torso catching the sleeves. He leapt to the floor, ran to the stairs yelling over and over for the porter. The flames flew to the paint-ing igniting the face of the Holy Child cradled in Mary's arms. *My masterpiece!*

He tried to drop the panel but the flames had caught the wood and joined his hands to the panel in a union of agony. He fled to the door, banging his fiery painting futilely against the door as he screamed and writhed in excruciating pain. He slid down the bolted door, hit the planks, and gave out his last breath.

The greater the sensibility, the greater
the suffering—much suffering.

—Leonardo da Vinci, *Notebooks*

1

---

*J*acob Stein came to a stop in front of the hilltop Laguna Beach home of Vincent LaBont. He cut the motor and killed the lights. For the past two months, he had charted the LaBonts' every move to prepare for tonight's job. In fifteen minutes, he would have the item he'd come for wrapped in furniture pads in the back of his van. Every detail had fallen into place so perfectly it scared him. Its rightful owner had assured him that the ancient curse had more than likely disappeared. But even if it hadn't, with all that rode on its return to Savoy, Stein had to swallow his uncertainty and focus on his job. He glanced at his watch. It was only 7:55 p.m. He had plenty of time.

Grabbing his clipboard and flashlight from the seat, he studied the attached Thompson Movers work order. An alarm code was written across its face. Folding the paper, he stuffed it in the top pocket of his crisp, white overalls. He patted his breast pocket for the lump of his small tool kit, retrieved his Tazer from the glove compartment, and clutched two furniture pads and a cloth tie under his arm and opened the door. He knew no one would be home before midnight, but he always worked prepared.

He chose to disguise himself as a mover, because workmen had been transporting paintings in and out of the house all week. If any of the neighbors questioned him, he would just shrug and say he was moving the chair down to the gallery. But this was California. Neighbors didn't pay much attention to what was going on around them.

Stein strode briskly through the darkness to the porch. There was no need to rush. Right about now Mrs. LaBont was probably serving caviar and Dom Pérignon to their guests at young Paul LaBont's inaugural art exhibit. The young man would be explaining his work to prospective clients, while the elder LaBont schmoozed the critics and gallery owners.

During his preparations for tonight, Stein had even dated their maid. She had unwittingly helped him with the layout of their home, the family schedule, and their habits. The challenge had been the prized alarm code. He'd found her weakness: a low tolerance for alcohol. One evening, after a bottle of expensive wine and too much dancing, she fell into a sound sleep on the way home. Before carrying her into her apartment, he rummaged through her purse for the code. Tomorrow she'd awaken with nothing more than fond memories of the sweet taste of a bottle of Grand Cru Chablis and a night of sweaty salsa dancing.

At the front door, he donned a pair of kid leather gloves. Picking both locks, he entered the marble foyer. A tiny red light blinked, the alarm beeped its forty-five second warning. He punched in the code. The light turned solid green, the beeping fell silent.

He panned the dark rooms with his flashlight. The home looked exactly as he expected—a miniature art gallery of valuable original art. Before he came to work for the Duke of Savoy, he would have cleaned the place out. But his only job tonight was the recovery of the chair stolen during World War II from his boss. It was scheduled to leave Los Angeles International freight terminal at midnight for Milan. He intended to have it on that flight.

Moving cautiously up the stairs, he paused on the third-floor landing. He played the thin beam in an arc. The space facing the street had been turned into an elegant sitting room furnished with French antiques. Two perfectly restored Louis XVI armchairs in yellow silk patterns with a round matching table between them sat under the window. A bookcase with glass doors from the same period stood against the wall. A Renaissance-period cupboard nestled next to the bookshelf. But the chair he came for wasn't here. He breathed a sigh of relief. The stories the duke had told him about the premature deaths of the ancient users of the chair had chilled his bones like nothing he had ever heard. At first, he considered such tales as fables until he saw art like da Vinci's, created by men who merely sat in the chair's grasp. How could this be? Ordinary men did not paint like the maestro. But then the fiery deaths of the men who used the chair flashed through his mind. He had assured Stein that simply touching it would not harm him. But could anyone be so certain? He scoffed at his fear—*it's just a chair!*

Turning around, he faced the ocean side of the house. The hallway ran from right to left in front of him. Running the beam of light down the hall to the right, he saw a door that he knew led to the studio near the end of the corridor. Directly in front of him was the entrance to the library, where the maid had told him the chair was kept most of the time. Once inside the darkened room, he flipped the light switch.

The oblong room was lined with mahogany floor-to-ceiling bookshelves on both walls, while the far wall was a solid window reaching up to the vaulted ceiling. The room was bare of furnishings except for two pieces at the far end of the expanse of a thick Oriental carpet that covered a polished hardwood floor. The chair sat against the window, directly facing him like a throne waiting for its king. To its left was a French provincial writing desk with a lamp on it.

Stein imagined how many hours the LaBonts had spent sitting in the hand-carved masterpiece of the maestro. He smirked, wishing he could see the LaBont's shocked faces when they came looking for a ride tonight. Would the curse befall them once the chair disappeared from their home? The duke was certain it wouldn't. Stein had no way of knowing the truth of the matter, nor was it a great concern to him. He had no intention of sitting in it. The only reason he had agreed to retrieve it for the duke was his promised share of the sale of a lost da Vinci that would miraculously be found in the ancient castle of Savoy. The reward far outweighed the risk.

Crossing the room, he studied the chair. A few pre-World War II photos and a copy of the only extant drawing of the chair from Leonardo's own hand found in the University of Madrid Library in the late '60s had not had not prepared him for its exquisite workmanship.

It was fashioned out of rich walnut and styled in the straight-backed, rectangular style of a Roman throne chair, a popular style in da Vinci's time. He wanted to run his hand across the high back, covered with the type of intarsia work Italian Renaissance craftsmen were famous for, but he could only stare. The large square surface of the back was inlaid with ivory and tortoise shell, designed into perfect miniaturized renditions of four of his masterpieces. *The Last Supper* in the upper right-hand corner, the *Mona Lisa* in the upper left, the *Virgin of the Rocks* in the lower right, and the *Madonna and Child* in the lower left. In the center was a rounded marble Pietra Duma, made of inlaid marble, with a barely distinguishable figure of the maestro himself etched in exquisite low relief. Arabesques were carved along each arm, ending in a lion's head.

Stein held his hand above the arm, then touched it with his index finger, not feeling anything. He slowly rubbed his palm along the arm. There was not one surface that hadn't been decorated with intricate designs by the maestro.

What would it be like to enjoy a tranquil moment in the chair? Painting had been a passion of his when he was young, but he had soon learned he was better at stealing it than creating it. He turned and started to seat himself, then hesitated. Would its power suddenly seize him? Would he become so distracted he wouldn't be able to finish his job? The chair had to make its way to Savoy tonight. But something called to him, like a father to a long lost son. What harm would a moment sitting on it do? He lowered himself into the deep, velvet seat and lightly rested his hands on the lions' heads. They were cool to his touch. A clarity and simplicity of thought came over him, then a shot like a burning fire rammed through his chest. He jumped out of the chair, landing on his feet.

He didn't dare touch its smooth skin again. He took a deep breath and calmed himself. He would bring the chair home to Savoy; he would help sell the painting when it was finished, but he would never sit in it.

He covered it with the furniture pads then wrapped the cloth tie around it like a belt. Grabbing the arms to lift it, he noticed a sparkle of light glinting off a piece of glass. It was from the lamp on the writing desk. It looked familiar. Setting the chair down, he stepped around to the side of the desk. The lamp was about two feet tall with a clear, delicately hand-blown globe seated on a brass base. Stein stooped to scrutinize royal signets painted on two sides of the globe. He didn't recognize the signets as De Medici or Sforza, but the exquisite lamp could be from the House of Este, which would indeed be a rare find. It appeared to be from the same high-Renaissance period as the chair. If it were authentic, such a piece would bring a handsome sum.

Picking it up to examine it, he supported the heavy brass base with both hands. The large globe had originally been designed to hold oil, but had been converted to electricity. From the looks of the frayed cord by his feet, the alterations had been made some time back. Carefully turning the piece over to see if he could find a craftsman's signature, he was disappointed that the bottom was worn smooth. Various guilds signed their creations in different places, but Stein only had time for a cursory inspection. He scolded himself for getting distracted.

Cradling the lamp with both hands, he turned it back over and shifted his weight. As he placed the brass base gently on the desk, his right foot came down hard and mashed the brittle electrical cord into the thick carpet, half pulling it out of the socket. Blue sparks arced from the plug, startling him. He gingerly backed off, only to find that he had cracked the cord, nearly severing one of the double strands. He swore under his breath and reached down for the plug; but again a blue spark leapt from the socket, as if trying to bite him. Instinctively he recoiled. He felt terrible about leaving the lamp in this condition, but he had a schedule to keep.

Stein hoisted up the heavy chair and then froze in midstride when he heard a door slam downstairs. *It couldn't be the LaBonts.*

Marcella LaBont's green Ford Explorer jerked to a stop in her garage a little after eight o'clock. She had sped through the back streets of Laguna, making it home in record time. Driving like a crazy woman wasn't one of her bad habits, but taking her anger out on the accelerator was a poor substitute for taking it out on her husband.

She entered the house and slammed her purse on the granite

kitchen counter. She hadn't wanted to leave Paul's show early, but during an inpromptu sparring match with Vincent, in front of all of their guests, she started having the blurry vision with the flashing lights that presaged a migraine. Now her head throbbed on the right side and soon it would be pounding mercilessly unless she took her medication and lay down. Marcella found her Fiorinal in the cabinet and chased down two tablets with a full glass of water. Soon the pain would dissolve into a faint memory, and nothing would wake her until morning.

She frowned at the thought of not being with her son during his hour of triumph. Paul would learn to deal with the art critics on his own, even though it was like throwing him to the wolves. The sooner he got his share of bites and claw marks in his artistic hide, the better. She feared their argument had embarrassed him on such an important night. It wasn't like her to blow up in public, but she just couldn't stomach Vincent's rude remarks anymore.

Vincent will rue the day he said my watercolors are for Gypsies and street vendors.

She kicked off her heels and then picked them up and trudged up the wide staircase to the master bedroom to ready herself for bed. On the second-floor landing, she dropped one of her shoes. Bending over to pick it up, she thought she heard a familiar noise from upstairs—one of those squeaky twinges of an oak floor plank when you stepped on it just right. But she knew everyone was still at the show. She cocked her ear. Her head was throbbing; maybe she was just hearing things. Turning toward the stairwell leading to the third floor, she could see a glint of light coming from upstairs. *It wasn't like Vincent to leave a light on.*

The wrapped chair turned into a piece of lead in Stein's hands, but he didn't dare move a muscle. He had heard someone tromp up the stairs. Whoever it was, from all the noise being made, apparently didn't suspect he was in the house. The footfalls weren't heavy ones like a man would make. It was more like a woman or the young LaBont. No, he thought, it must be LaBont's wife. Paul wouldn't come home early from his own show. Stein had lost track of her sound, and if he didn't soon hear her closing doors then she might suspect something. Fear always froze people. He'd been in homes too many times when the owners came home. These situations could get out of hand quickly if he wasn't careful. Whatever happened, he did not intend to leave here without this chair. If she started up the stairs to the third floor, he'd have to act fast. He was glad he brought his Tazer.

On the second-floor landing, Marcella could see light slanting out of the library door. She had left around lunchtime today and movers had been in and out of the house all day. Anyone could have left it on. She stood perfectly still and the house took on its customary quietness. It was probably just a settling noise she periodically heard. Her head continued to pound. She had to get ready for bed before her medication kicked in. Once in the master bedroom on the second floor, she changed and settled under the covers. With the darkness caressing her like a warm blanket, she could feel the Fiorinal kicking in. She smiled at Paul's enthusiasm over his successful show. It reminded her of her passion for painting that had dried up to an almost unnoticeable trickle over the years. She'd made the choice not to paint any longer for the sake of her marriage. She had concluded long ago that Vincent couldn't stand anyone competing with him in his own house. That was what made her so proud of Paul tonight. He had stood tall and handsome, basking in his artistic accomplishments. He was well on his way to becoming his own person and an accomplished artist.

Tomorrow she would go back to her not-so-secret studio in the Gillespie Gallery and continue her painting. Marcella smiled in the darkness. Vincent wouldn't like it. She would figure out what to tell him if she had to sit in front of her workbench all day. The pleasing thought of painting again, like a tonic for her troubled soul, helped her drift off into a deep sleep.

Stein thought his arms would explode, sweat dripped down his forehead, stinging his eyes, but he stood like a statue even after he heard a door close. It sounded like she had gone into her bedroom; he waited to see if she came back out. He would stand there until she went to sleep if he had to; but if she came home early, anything could happen. He had to get out quickly. Tiptoeing across the library, he hesitated at the top of the stairs. All was quiet. He took the stairs one at a time. The second-floor landing was vacant. He hustled noiselessly down the stairs to the first floor. She had set the alarm, so he couldn't open the door without it going off. He set the chair down, punched in the code, and the light blinked green.

Once outside, the cool breeze chilled his sweat-soaked body. Bundling his load into the van, he secured it with tie-downs so it couldn't move. In the driver's seat, he checked his watch: 8:26. He was ten minutes behind schedule. His next stop was LAX.

He fired up the engine and drove away with the casualness of a man heading down the hill for a leisurely evening of dinner and drinks. The tension from his close call drained away, but he wouldn't be able to completely relax until the chair was crated and on its way home to where it had spent nearly the last four centuries—in the castle of Savoy. With its return, Stein was certain, the genius of Leonardo da Vinci would make him fabulously wealthy.

In the third-floor library, a spark from the damaged lamp cord smoldered in the wool carpet, filling the room with smoke. It crept up the wall of books, making its way toward the smoke detector high up on the vaulted ceiling. Though the detector was new, it was too high in the dead-air space close to the peak of the vault to speak its warning.

The fire below devoured the green wool yarn, then the tan, finally the delicate flower embroidery, all the way to the other end of the library. It gained strength from the wood floor underneath, eating through five coats of varnish. The floor burst into a sheet of flames, leaping up the walls of books, consuming paper and ink.

The thick, noxious smoke slipped under the library door and curled its way down the stairs. The stream sought for openings under doors along the second-floor hallway. It crawled under the master bedroom door, and continued its trek down the long hall. When it reached the smoke detectors on the hall ceiling, they both went off with a wail.

As Marcella slumbered, a black stream of hot air wrapped itself around her bed in the spacious master bedroom. She tossed fitfully, agitated by a disturbing dream. Paul's show was a great success, and she drove to the bank to deposit the receipts. Entering the bank, her ears stung with the nerve-wracking metal jangling of an alarm. The bank manager approached her; an addled look contorted his face. Wringing his hands, he asked why she was there. Marcella's chest tightened, she labored to breathe. She turned to leave, but he grabbed her arm. Her body dripped with sweat. She struggled for air. The bag of money dropped to the shiny speckled terrazzo. Checks and bills floated around the room. She tried to run. But a paralyzing fit of coughing came over her.

Hacking and choking, she jolted awake from her deep sleep. Furiously she gasped for air and then screamed. Instead of a fresh draft of air, a dark finger of hot smoke shot down her throat, scalding her as if she had swallowed a cup of boiling coffee. Clutching her throat and clamping her eyes shut, she knew she would die in her own bed unless she remained calm. Groggy from the Fiorinal, she could hear the unmistakable roar of fire above. She rolled off the mattress onto the floor, wrapping the covers over her head, and crawled along the floor toward the door. She fought to ignore the searing pain in her chest.

Keep calm. Breathe slowly. Oh, God, help me get out of here alive.

⚒⚒⚒

Paul LaBont didn't know which was brighter, the gleaming moon that hung full and silvery over the Pacific Ocean or his future as an artist. Promptly at eleven, his first art exhibition had closed. Not too much later, he and his father rode home along Pacific Coast Highway, the spring air cooling Paul's flushed face. He knew few artists enjoyed such attention on their first show as a professional.

"Some show, huh, Dad?" Paul asked, smiling. He brushed his hand through his black hair and smoothed it down.

"I've never seen a first show sell out like that," Vincent said. "Even that Cubist portrait sold."

Paul propped his elbow on the window frame and let the air ruffle his shirt-sleeve. He glanced over at his father. Vincent's gray eyes, usually full of energy, looked tired, with deepening lines down his cheeks and creeping crow's feet around his eyes.

"It surprises you people like different styles, doesn't it?"

"Nothing really surprises me anymore. It's just ..." Vincent nervously smoothed down his mustache.

"You don't understand why someone would do a portrait in any style other than classical, huh?"

The road wound through a series of hairpins as it climbed the home-filled hillside.

"Don't knock me for sticking to what's worked well," Vincent said with firmness in his voice.

Paul stared out the window at the glassine ocean, its iridescent waves crashing on the white sandy beach below. The view of the

Pacific expanded north and south as scattered blinking lights on the water blended with the star-studded sky. Tonight wasn't the time to pick a fight. He'd put off talking to his father all week about his plans, and now was as good as time as ever to tell him that he was moving out of the house on Monday. "You're the best there is at portraits. That's why all the big people come to you. But doing portraits all the time in the same old way just isn't for me."

"Don't lose your perspective because of the flattery of a few modern art critics."

"I know all that. I just don't need any more lectures about art theories."

"You did enough experimenting in college; it's time to grow up. Your abilities are superior to sentimental beach scenes or splashing paint on a canvas with a spatula."

Paul jerked his head toward his father. "So, is that what you said to Mom that made her stomp out of the show?"

Vincent gripped the steering wheel tighter. "You knew about her studio at the gallery, didn't you?"

"I think she's a talented painter. She loves watercolors. I don't understand why she has to do it secretly."

"I never said she has to do anything secretly. All I'm saying is that with the talent our family is blessed with, why not concentrate on its highest and best use?" Vincent tapped the steering wheel with the palm of his hand as he spoke.

"Why not concentrate on what you enjoy?" Paul said. "Watercolors are what Mom enjoys. What's the big deal?" He fought the urge to tell his father that he was tired of classically composed portraits. He was tired of princes and princesses, senators and congressmen. He was tired of shaking their hands and listening to their egotistical stories. He wanted to paint anyone besides the rich and the famous, their bratty kids, and their stuck-up wives.

As soon as I get home, I'm packing my bags and leaving. I'm not taking this anymore.

"The big deal is," Vincent said, turning to Paul with a confident grin, "we can accomplish what lesser talented artists will never achieve."

Paul had heard this argument so many times. He didn't think his father would ever see things differently. It was time for him to get out from his father's prodigious shadow and the sooner the better. Now he just needed to break the news.

"I saw you talking to Richard Kraemer for a long time. What did he want?" Vincent asked.

"He's hosting some shows at his gallery in San Francisco," Paul said, wondering how much of the conversation he should share with his father. "He was looking for landscapes." He rested his arm on the open window and waited.

"So what did you tell him?"

"I told him I'd do it. He wants me to send at least fifteen canvases by the end of April."

"The Crown Prince of Kuwait is coming into town in April. You promised to help me out. He wants portraits of all his wives."

"Fine! But they'll be the last of any classical portraits I'll paint. And I plan on keeping my commitments to Richard Kraemer."

Vincent gave a short guttural laugh.

"Don't start telling me this is just a phase and I'll grow out of it. I'm not saying I'll do landscapes the rest of my life, but I want to do this show with Kraemer."

"So do it," he shot back, shrugging his shoulders.

The car rounded another curve and the top of the hill came into view. *Now's the time to stand up. I'll work with him, but not for him.* "Dad, I've decided I'm going to move ... hey, what's that?" Paul asked, observing a glow in the sky above the row of houses along the rim of the hill. "Stop the car!"

The Mercedes jerked to a halt in the middle of the deserted road. Paul squinted out the window. Flames dancing against the dark sky illuminated the top of the hill. One of the houses lit up like a giant bonfire silhouetting the row of expensive homes along the moonlit ridge.

"Dad! That's awfully close to our house."

He punched the accelerator and the Mercedes responded smoothly through the tight turns.

Paul kept the home in view, as the car zigzagged up the hill. The sight of the burning home looked like an iridescent torch against the starry sky. He shivered thinking about his mother. He knew she was upset when she left. She had done so much for him, and tonight she had outdone even herself. He hoped she wasn't in one of her deep sleeps because of her migraine medicine.

Paul clutched the dashboard with both hands as the Mercedes roared up the winding road.

※※※

The wicked taste of ash lay thick on Marcella's tongue. With the comforter over her head, she crawled toward the door. The smoke stung the soft lining of her throat. The hollow beat of her pulse throbbed through her temples as she clawed her way on all fours across the room.

Vincent, where are you when I need you?

The Fiorinal made her feel confused. She had to fight the urge to simply lie down and go back to sleep. Groping blindly, she reached out with her hand, wanting desperately to feel the doorframe. If she took an innocent wrong turn, she wouldn't have the energy to find her way out. She kept imagining herself rolled up in a fetal position in the closet; or a falling, fiery beam smashing her, turning her body into warm ash. But most of all she could taste death in the chalky air rushing up her nose and into the back of her mouth.

God, help me find the door.

Hesitating for a moment, she reached her hand out to touch the wall, but she only waved at the air. With her lungs ready to burst, she lowered her face to the carpet and gulped a breath of relatively fresh air. She opened her eyes to get her bearings. A burning sting shot through her eyeballs. The air was a poisonous, murky soup. She kept creeping forward until her head hit the wall. She slid her hand along it, feeling relieved once she ran her hand up the molding of the doorjamb.

Is this the door to the hall or to the closet?

She leaned the top of her head against the door. Her stomach ached. Her arms cramped, her lungs felt seared, her head woozy. Fearing she would faint before she reached the hall, she straightened herself up and lunged frantically for the brass knob. She yanked her hand back, her skin stung by the heated brass. Wrapping her hand in the comforter, she tried again to open the door. It slipped beneath the smooth cloth. Forcing herself to stand, she wrapped the cloth around the knob, turned it, and swung the door open. An impenetrable wall of swirling smoke confronted her.

Is this my closet or the hall?

Reaching out both arms, she thrashed the air blindly. Not touching any clothes, she became convinced it was the hall.

Are the stairs to the right or the left? Why can't I remember?

She dropped to her knees. With her lungs on fire, she crawled out into the hall. Gasping short breaths, her arms buckled every time she leaned on them. Her legs felt like she was dragging two lead weights. The roar of the fire above her grew louder. When she reached the stairs, she planned on lying down and sliding headfirst to the bottom.

I just need to get to the first step.

Every movement brought more agony to her body. The

possibility she wouldn't see Paul and Vincent urged her on, even as every sinew of her body pleaded with her to just lay down, wrap herself in hot smoke, and let it take her away. It would only take a long silent moment.

The stairs have to be right here. I want to be with my family.

Putting one weary hand out, she expected to feel the first step leading to her salvation. Instead, she hit a wall.

What's this?

Running her hand across it, she felt the edges of a door.

It's the linen closet—at the far end of the hall. I went the wrong way. I'll never make it back to the stairs! Oh God, I don't want to die. Help me.

Her head filled with a fuzzy noise like a staticky radio, she started to faint.

Tears rolled down her cheeks.

Please save me.

In anguish, she dropped her head to the carpet and sobbed. Then a gentle surge of energy came over her. It felt as if she had been given a sip of ice-cold water. Thankful for the tiniest of miracles, she lifted her head and she shrieked for help into the thick night.

⬥⬥⬥

When the Mercedes skidded out of the last turn to their street, Paul saw flames licking up the side of their home from a top story window. His father floored the accelerator, rocketing the car up the road, then slammed on the brakes, sliding to a stop in front of their home.

Jerry Martin, their neighbor across the street, ran up to the car. "I've already called 911," he yelled as they scrambled out of the car. The smell of their burning home permeated the air. The fire popped and crackled as it ate through the top story.

"Where's Marcella?" Vincent shouted to Jerry.

"She must be inside," Jerry yelled, following them onto the front lawn. "The fire department will be here in a few minutes."

"If we don't do something now, she'll be dead in a couple of minutes," Vincent said, nearly screaming. "Look at those flames." Vincent lunged toward the front door.

Jerry hustled in front of him and blocked his way to the house. "Wait one more minute. They'll be here." Jerry put a consoling hand on Vincent's shoulder.

"Dad, we have to do something now!" Paul yelled, coming up behind his father. The noise of the engulfing flames was deafening.

Sirens sounded in the distance. Vincent stared at Jerry with a clenched jaw. He pushed his neighbor out of the way and ran to the house. Paul trailed behind his father.

Vincent unlocked the door. A wave of heat and black, toxic smoke blasted them as they stormed into the house. They both stopped at the foot of the stairs. A thick river of black smoke poured down from the second floor. They whipped out their handkerchiefs, covered their mouths, and started up the stairs.

The heat threatened to suffocate Paul as he followed his father. It pierced his clothes as if he didn't have anything on. The smoke clawed at his eyes, the hot air in his nostrils and lungs felt like he had swallowed a pincushion. With his handkerchief clasped to his mouth, Paul and Vincent found their way into the master bedroom.

"She's not here," Paul yelled, grabbing his father's arm.

"Check her closet," Vincent shouted. "I'll check mine."

Crouching low, Paul crept into his mother's walk-in closet. He crawled around in the pitch-black and was convinced she wasn't among the clothes and shoes. He met his father back in the main bath area.

"She couldn't have gone far. She has to be around here somewhere," Vincent said.

A faint cry came from the hall.

"That was Mom."

They ran back to the door, dropped to their knees, and peered down the hall. They couldn't see through the black smoke.

"I can't see anything," Vincent said.

"She must have turned the wrong way," Paul said in his father's ear. He began coughing and couldn't stop.

Vincent grabbed his shoulder. "You go back. Tell the rescue people where we are."

"No way. I want to stay with you," Paul protested, still choking.

"This is no time to argue." He pushed Paul out the door, toward the stairs.

Paul reluctantly crawled away.

Vincent watched his son disappear into the smoke. He then plunged blindly on all fours into the hall.

It didn't take long before he felt Marcella's lifeless body. Vincent cradled her in his arms and headed to the stairs. He didn't see any signs of life, but he stopped looking at her face to concentrate on where he was going. At the top of the stairs, he felt for the first step with his foot. For a second he turned his head and tried to penetrate the thick gloom flowing down the staircase from the third story.

The chair, he thought.

He couldn't think about it right now; he had to get Marcella to safety. He struggled carrying her down the stairs. He never realized how hard it was to carry a limp body. Once he was outside, the fresh air hit him as if he had dived into a bucket of ice water. He laid her gently on the grass.

A paramedic slapped an oxygen mask over her face. Another one opened Marcella's nightgown, began to attach electronic leads to her chest, and then listened to her heartbeat with a stethoscope.

"She's breathing."

The voice of a doctor at a local trauma center barked over the radio asking for readouts of her vitals from the paramedic's instruments.

Vincent lay on the lawn beside her, gasping for breath. Another paramedic rushed over and gave him an oxygen mask. Paul came beside him, a mask strapped to his face. They both lay side by side taking long pulls of cool, clean air. Vincent crept to her side, with the mask pressed against his face, and held her hand tightly while Paul worked his way to other side. Vincent bent over and kissed her forehead. "Whatever happens, I love you," he whispered.

Another paramedic came over, put his arm around Vincent, lifting him to his feet, and guided him out of the way. "You're a real hero, Mr. LaBont. You saved her life." The blond-haired man patted his back reassuringly.

Vincent found his son. "I want you to stay with your mother. Don't leave her. I'll meet you at the hospital."

"Aren't we going together? What are you going to do?" he asked with a raspy voice.

"Please, stay with your mother. I need to talk to the firemen and see what can be saved." He motioned toward the just arriving firemen running hoses and carrying ladders. He stared into Paul's eyes. "I'll come down to the hospital as soon as it's under control. Stay with her," he said sternly.

They both watched as the paramedics loaded Marcella onto a gurney and then slid her into the ambulance. Paul climbed in behind her and glanced back at his father standing on the lawn facing the house.

※※※

Paul watched as Vincent stretched the elastic straps of the oxygen mask over his head and slung the canvas straps of the metal

35

cylinder over his shoulder. *What's he doing?* His father glanced around at the firefighters who were busy laying their hoses. All of a sudden, he took off running for the front door of the house just as an attendant slammed the back door of the ambulance in Paul's face.

"No!" Paul yelled, but one of the paramedics put a hand on his shoulder and pulled him down into the seat as the ambulance, sirens blaring, moved away from the curb.

※※※

Vincent dashed for the front door, past two distracted firemen setting up their hoses, and took the stairs two at a time. He was determined to find Leonardo's chair before the house was flooded with water. The fire seemed hotter now. The smoke stung his eyes with a renewed vengeance. He breathed the cool oxygen heavily through his mask.

From the second-floor landing, he saw flames licking up the wall at the top of the stairs. Sweat rolled off his scalp, stinging his eyes. His heart skipped a beat when fiery debris crashed through the ceiling at the end of the hall where Marcella had lain a few minutes before.

He mounted the stairs cautiously, flames curling up the walls on both sides of him. The heat and noise increased in intensity. *The chair has to be okay. It can't be destroyed.* He felt like his whole body could flash into flames.

At the top of the stairs, he scanned the floor where his studio and priceless chair had resided—his heart sank. The third floor had been transformed into a naked darkened shell of itself—a massive skeleton with no body, no soul, and no chair. The walls were gutted, the books disintegrated into a heap of ashes. In places, the floor was burnt down to the joists, the furniture nothing but smoldering ruins.

Vincent balanced himself on the top step at the edge of the

landing. As he stood, too stunned to move, staring at the spot where his chair used to sit, he heard chopping on the roof, men yelling to each other. Then a thundering crash as a section from above caved in and smashed debris onto the floor a few feet in front of him. Smoke and fiery embers plumed up, stinging his eyes. He teetered backward, not wanting to be enveloped in the cloud of embers. He swung his arms to regain his balance. Losing his footing, he reached out and grabbed the flaming walls. Pain, like a thousand piercing needles, told him he'd made a grave error. It shot through his hands, streaking up his arms. He tried to move them but nothing worked, his heart beat so fast it felt like it was going to explode.

He screamed long and loud.

As consciousness slid away, he seesawed back and forth, losing his hold. He floated backward toward the sound of heavy footfalls and excited voices. For an instant, through the gaping hole in the roof, he glimpsed a bright star set in the inky sky. It sparkled brilliantly like a diamond on black velvet reminding him of a distant hope that was now beyond his reach. The tiny sparkle disappeared as if a curtain had been dragged over his eyes. Not a shred of light penetrated his darkness.

The rules of experience are all that is needed to discern the true from the false.

—Leonardo da Vinci, *Notebooks*

2

*F*or nearly two weeks, Paul exhausted himself shuttling back and forth between two hospitals. His father lay in the burn unit at the University of California, and his mother was on a ventilator at Mission Hospital in Mission Viejo. Paul lived among the antiseptic halls and the white-sheeted beds, slept in chairs, on hard cots set up in their rooms, and occasionally in a empty patient bed.

This morning he woke with a backache from sleeping slumped in a chair beside his mother's bed. She breathed rhythmically beside him, hooked to machines that never hesitated or hitched, only beeped and whirred. He sat up quickly when he remembered that his father's doctor wanted to meet him early this morning to go over his progress.

He brushed back a wisp of dark hair from his mother's forehead. She was doing well and would be breathing on her own in a day or so. He headed to the basement cafeteria and ate a breakfast of ham and eggs. After eating he raced to his father's car in the parking garage. The only remnants of his past life were the suit he had worn for the first few days and his father's Mercedes. Everything else had disappeared in the fire.

At the UC Irvine Medical Center, Vincent lay sleeping in a private room on the fifth floor, his hands and forearms bandaged to his elbows, his face expressionless. At times, when they wheeled new patients down the hall, the unmistakable stench of seared flesh nearly overcame him. During those moments, memories of his father's mad dash into the flaming home haunted him. He gripped the chrome railing of his father's bed and sat motionless amidst the beeping wake of the monitoring equipment until the disquieting image passed.

For a fortnight, his father had barely moved, except when a doctor coaxed a response from him; still he reacted with only a nod or a grimace.

This morning he lay perfectly still, his eyes glassy and unseeing. But Paul sensed he simmered silently, sorting through what his life would be like without the hands of an artist.

Dr. Sanders, in his crisp white coat, stethoscope slung around his neck, with his name stitched in blue cursive thread, stood at Vincent's bedside, reciting his findings as if he were going through a pre-flight checklist. The good doctor hit the highlights: Vincent's wounds were healing fine. The surgeries so far had been successful. He would recover most of his motor skills and tactile sense in his left hand. His right hand, though, would be more problematic.

Paul thought he saw his father's eyes twitch slightly.

The doctor continued. Vincent would have the use of his right hand, just not the dexterity he had before.

His painting hand, Paul thought.

Vincent turned his head and bored holes of anger through the doctor.

After Dr. Sanders left, Paul slumped in a chair beside the bed. For that one brief moment when the doctor had spoken, a sign of life had flashed across his father's eyes, but his face now resembled the listing hulk of a shipwreck, slanted to port, slowly sinking. Paul had wanted to be free of his father's orbit, but not because of some nearly fatal twist of events. Everything he knew, everything he had wished to become, and everything he was, he owed to his father. He had vainly thought this morning would bring some hope.

Why did you have to run back into the house? Why didn't I try to stop you?

But that single moment he could have done something had passed so quickly, he could never retrieve it. Paul slouched in the chair. He thought of praying. But he hadn't prayed since he was a kid, and that was something people did in moments of weakness. This was such a moment, but it wouldn't be fair to plead with God just when the chips were down—if God cared at all.

He looked at the figure lying helpless beside him. In a feeble attempt at fairness, Paul knew that his father himself had cracked the door open to his own destruction. No one had forced him to reenter the house. Life had exacted a pound of flesh from him for one foolish act. Was this some form of judgment?

Paul shook his head. He had no reason to believe God would hear any plea for help he could utter. Besides, what did it matter? The events of that night had unfolded so rapidly in front of him as he stood by helplessly. No one could undo the tragedy that had come upon his family. He pushed himself up from the chair and lightly squeezed his father's arm. Paul needed some time to recharge before he came back here again. He had to find some relief from the uncaring part of the world.

Later that day he drove to the secluded bluffs above Victoria Cove. A few days ago, he'd bought some jeans, a few shirts, a few pair of socks, new tennis shoes, and some underwear. Then he stopped at Chandler's Art Supply and purchased all new equipment: paints, brushes, a paint box, a couple of small canvases, a portable aluminum easel, a sketch pad, and pencils. He now lugged them to the deck above the crashing waves of the isolated cove.

Paul dropped his equipment to the ground and leaned over the iron railing on the observation deck built into the side of the hill. Below him the liquid crash of perfectly formed, tightly curled waves pounding the rocks felt like a strong dose of medicine to his soul.

He set up his easel on the cement deck and slowly ran his finger through the bristle of a new brush. He felt in someway fortunate. The flames had not consumed everything. He had his health, his future, and all the artistic inclinations he had accumulated from a lifetime of watching his parents. He possessed their legacy, but he would gladly give it all up to have them whole again. He needed to get back to work, to reestablish the momentum he'd lost over the last several weeks.

Putting his brush to virgin canvas had always given him a magical sense of certitude. It assured him that despite the fickleness of events, his life was meaningful. The fire could threaten to boil that confidence out of him, but he refused to let the rancid smoke and flame take away what truly mattered. He centered the canvas on the easel and began squeezing paints from tubes onto his palette. Methodically mixing the paste with his palette knife, Paul wondered about his father's rash behavior. He always seemed so measured, so calculating. He was probably the only man in Laguna Beach who still wore button-down shirts with his ties.

The chair was more important to him than Paul had imagined. He knew the story behind it, but his mother had always made a point when just the two of them were alone of scoffing at his father's story. "Who wouldn't like to paint like Leonardo da Vinci?" she would tell him. "Whatever you do, don't get involved in that nonsense." She'd warned him nearly every day when he was young not to go near it. He remembered sitting in it once and it made him feel funny. After that he'd refused to go near it. His father didn't like his reluctance, but never again pushed him to sit in it. He had decided early on he wanted his art to be his own. If he used a crutch, he'd never be free. But if his father found comfort from the rough-and-tumble artist's life by sitting in an ancient chair, what was the harm? Many artists turned to drugs and alcohol and other destructive lifestyles to ease their anxieties. It was a wonder what people could talk themselves into believing. Especially intelligent ones like his father.

Paul stood with the palette in his left hand, a new fine brush in his right, and studied the horizon before him. To the south stood an outcropping of rock, bathed in afternoon light. He'd seen it innumerable times, but today the dark, rugged cliff radiated a tangible strength. It had withstood the blasts of the Pacific Ocean for centuries. He loved painting landscapes and re-creating the expanse of nature in paint. He wanted to capture the color and line of its inner strength. He wondered why his father was so against him painting landscapes if it was what he loved to do.

He dipped the thin point of his bristles in a light shade of brown. While bringing the dusky, pointed brush close to the canvas, something stopped him from touching the fresh skin of linen. His ability to complete this most simple motion vanished from his hand, his arm, his mind, wherever it existed within him. He forced himself to touch the wet bristle to the canvas but every ounce of desire to paint had vanished. He couldn't even remember what he'd wanted to paint. Glancing up at the sandstone cliff he'd studied a moment before, he saw nothing but dirt, eroded by time, a cliff with jagged edges, scraggly ridges with scrawny shrubs stunted by the harsh salt air. How could this be? What had he just seen a minute ago?

He sat on the cold concrete deck and wrapped his arms around his legs. He looked at his easel and the palette of paint standing next to him. A chill seeped up his spine and spread through the muscles in his back. He never had suffered a moment's hesitation to put a brush to a canvas. Nothing in life he could imagine doing could give him greater pleasure than creating a work of art, and now that enthusiasm had vanished. Just like that.

What's happening to me?

Maybe fatigue had finally caught up with him. He slowly packed up and found his car. Once he rested, his desire to paint would return—it must.

A few days later, Paul perched himself beside his mother's bed in Mission Hospital. Not too long ago she had been on a ventilator, and now she was breathing so well that she had been transferred out of intensive care. In a few days, she'd be strong enough to be released.

Paul held his mother's hand while she slept. Touching her cheek with the back of his hand, he brushed his other one over her flowing black hair and smoothed it back. She would be okay. Soon she would be back to her old self.

He wanted to have a house ready by the time she was released. The insurance adjuster had given him a check to cover living expenses and enough to lease a place. The adjuster said rebuilding would take nine months to a year. The old site would have to go through extensive demolition before construction could begin. His mother's older sister had come from Texas to help with finding a house to live in while Vincent and Marcella were in the hospital. Lynette had already located several suitable houses for the family to rent. One of them came completely furnished.

"Paul," Marcella said opening her eyes. She gave him a wan smile.

"Mom. You're awake."

He bent over the hospital bed and kissed her on the cheek, which had a hint of red, but her skin was still ashen. Her black eyes, which normally sparkled with energy, were dull and tired looking, her lips blanched.

She held onto his hand tightly. "Paul, why did he do it?"

Paul leaned closer to the bed rail. "Do what Mom?"

"Your father. Why?" She held onto his hand tightly, as if she intended not to let go until he told her what she wanted to hear.

Paul took a deep breath, but was silent. He didn't want to talk about his father until she was home and well on her way to recovery.

"Lynette told me what happened. He was injured badly wasn't he?"

Paul patted her hand. "He was hurt, Mom, and he's in the hospital."

"Where is he?" she said weakly.

"UCI Burn Ward," Paul said, trying to sound casual, but it came out like a hammer hitting a piece of glass.

"Burn ward?" She raised her head from the pillow.

Paul placed his hand on her shoulder. "Mom, relax. He's doing better. Really he is."

"What ... what happened?"

"What's important right now is that you get your strength back." He stroked her forehead. "You're doing so well. I promise when you get out, I'll sit down with you and go through everything."

She looked at him with a stern look. "Paul, what happened?"

"He's getting better every day. I'm going there later to see him."

"He's dying, isn't he? That's why you and Lynette won't tell me anything." Her voice was tense. Paul could sense her fear. He leaned over and kissed her. He knew eventually he would have to tell her what happened, but as hard as it was for him to think about what had happened, it was even harder to talk about it.

"Lynette said he went back into the house after he rescued me. Is that what happened?"

Paul nodded.

"It was for that chair, wasn't it?" she said her voice rising.

"Please Mom, you're getting too worked up."

"Paul, it almost killed him."

He wanted to take control of the conversation, swing it around to a topic more suitable to his mood, like the weather, but there was no escaping her inquiries. When she got like this, she would never let go.

"Yes it did. He's lucky to be alive."

She turned her head toward the window.

"His hands are burned, and he'll probably never paint again," Paul said, glad that it was finally out.

"I knew this would happen some day. That's why I told you to stay away from that thing."

"Yeah, I know. But it's just a piece of wood, isn't it?"

She examined him with her look, the dark half-moons under her eyes were portentous as if she knew something she didn't want to tell me. "To your father it's more than a piece of wood. It's always been more than a piece of wood."

"Well, it's gone now."

"He didn't get it?"

He shook his head. "It disappeared in the fire."

Her eyes widened with surprise. "Good."

"So, why was Dad so fixated on that chair if it was just a piece of wood?"

"It doesn't matter now since it's destroyed. Thank goodness

you never went near it and you're father's still alive. That's all that matters." She gave him a weak smile. She needed to rest, so he kissed her good-bye and turned to leave. He was almost through the door when she called to him.

"Paul," her voice was weak, but steady. "If for some reason that chair does show up again, God forbid that it does, stay away from it."

He nodded. "It's history Mom. Nothing survived the fire except a couple of charred paintings."

Miserable mortals, open your eyes.

—Leonardo da Vinci, *Notebooks*

3

Vincent started his third week in the burn ward when Paul stopped by to visit. The room looked different to him, as if it had been redecorated, but the walls where still a blinding white, the side chairs still orange Naugahyde with dark wood frames, and the antiseptic smell as strong as ever.

"Hi, son." Vincent managed a pallid smile. He laid flat on his back with a sheet over his body up to his neck.

Paul knew that under the covers his father's hands had been attached to his thighs to foster skin growth. He wanted to wipe out of his mind the thought that his father's hands, like desecrated shrines, would never possess their power to create again. But his father's eyes looked clearer, his black hair combed straight back, and his face cleanly shaved. His appearance was a welcome change.

"Dad, you look good." Paul sat down next to his bed.

"I have some good news," Vincent said, his voice still weak.

"You've been asked to paint the Sistine Chapel on your back without using your hands?" Paul said, hoping his father's sense of humor had returned with his smile.

Vincent rolled his eyes. "I want to start my rehabilitation as soon as I can, but I need your help."

"That's great." He couldn't help wonder about his father's sudden change of heart, but now wasn't the time to question him. He relaxed in his chair.

"I need your help, Paul. I won't be able to get started without you."

"Sure, anything." *Even up to half my kingdom,* Paul thought. *Yeah, what's left of it.*

Vincent motioned with his head to the nightstand next to him. "Open the drawer."

Paul stared at the drawer. He pulled it opened slowly and peeked inside. On top of the Gideon Bible was a business card. Paul picked it up.

"Take it. I want you to go see him." His father's eyes were downright hopeful.

Paul studied the card. "Claude Harrison, private detective, Beverly Hills. What do we need a private detective for?"

"He was just here this morning. He's found the chair."

Paul wanted to laugh, but he didn't dare. He sat back down in his seat and briefly rubbed his forehead. "What do you mean he found the chair?"

"He knows where it's at," Vincent said, with a degree of animation Paul hadn't heard for a while.

"And?"

"I want you to retrieve it," his father said, lifting his head as far off his pillow as he could strain.

"The chair? You certain it wasn't destroyed?" Paul thought of his mother's face when he told her about Vincent going back into the fire to get the chair. What would she say if Paul were to bring it home?

"Hey, are you with me here?" Vincent said.

"Yeah, sure, Dad. But why should I go after it?"

"I will need the chair if I'm going to fully recover."

"Dad, get real. The doctors say it will be because you work hard."

"Of course. But I'll need every edge I can get."

"How do you know for certain it wasn't destroyed?" Paul asked skeptically.

"The insurance adjuster came last week. He told me about the proposed settlement without the chair. I asked him why, and he said they are still investigating its whereabouts. They think it might have been stolen before the fire started."

Paul nodded slowly. He had been naive in thinking this little secret could be kept away from his father for very long.

"So, was this Detective Harrison hired by the insurance company?" Paul asked, trying to figure out who worked for whom.

His father gently shook his head, "No, I hired him as soon as the adjuster left. Their investigators would never have found the chair. Harrison is a specialist."

"Dad, how did you hire a detective? You can't even use the phone."

Vincent's eyes darkened. "I had one of the nurses put a call into John Olson."

"Your attorney?" Paul asked.

"He took care of the details. Harrison is the best," his father said, smiling again.

Paul nodded slowly. "Well, where is it anyway?" Paul was now intrigued.

"Somewhere in France or Italy."

"Dad, I just can't traipse off to Europe and search every little antique store until I find it." He sat up straight and rubbed his chin. He couldn't be on some wild errand while his mother needed him here. What was his father thinking? Besides, what about his career? All of his paintings had been destroyed. And he'd promised Mr. Kraemer he'd have a whole set of landscapes for his show next month in San Francisco.

"Just talk to the detective. He'll answer all of your questions."

"Dad ... I don't know." It just didn't seem fair for his father to ask him to chase down a piece of furniture.

"Listen, I know my injuries have caused you and your mother a lot of anguish. If I have any chance of painting again like I used to, I have to have the chair. And Paul, I can't do it without you."

Paul sighed deeply. *I didn't think I'd ever hear those words come out his mouth.* Glancing down at the business card, he wondered what his mother would say when he told her he was going to retrieve a chair that had become the bane of the family. "Dad, I'm not sure about this."

"I am. I need you to do this for me. You're the only one I trust to do this." He fixed his big, gray eyes on Paul.

His father's hope had been rekindled. He felt his resistance melting. Maybe he could use this errand as a wedge to force more cooperation out of him. If there were any chance of recovering the chair for that reason alone, it would be worth a discussion with the private eye. "And if I'm able to bring it back, you'll work your butt off to get well."

His father gave him a pleading look. "Paul, do this for me. I promise I'll work harder than you've ever seen me."

Peering down at the card in his hand, he decided to give this Claude Harrison a call and set up an appointment.

"And whatever you do, don't say anything to your mother about this."

A man is at peace when he finds his destiny.

—Leonardo da Vinci, *Notebooks*

4

Mason, Harrison and Levine, Private Detective Agency, had a suite of offices over a fashionable boutique on Court Drive, two blocks west of Rodeo Drive. After seeing their offices, Paul decided he had read too many detective novels in high school. It wasn't the stuffy little place he imagined with gray filing cabinets, stacks of papers, scratched-up furniture, and a receptionist who chewed gum like a machine gun as she filed her nails. Instead he found a well-appointed waiting room with a signed Picasso lithograph hanging on the wall over the lobby chairs. He recognized it as *Olga in an Armchair*, a Cubist-style painting of a beautiful woman seated in an armchair, staring straight at him. Dark walnut furniture filled the room and a well-dressed receptionist smartly answered a busy phone.

She took his name and asked him to be seated. Mr. Harrison, she explained, was finishing a conference call and would be with him shortly.

Paul studied the Picasso with his arms crossed at eye level to

Olga's serious gaze. The intensity of her stare reminded him of his father's eyes moments before he ran back into the fire. For a second, Paul was transported back to the night his house burned down. He had just entered the back end of the ambulance with his mother when he turned to catch his father's look. The look burned in Paul's memory.

Why hadn't he jumped out of the ambulance and tackled him? He knew he was going to sprint into the flames. If it weren't for his father's obsession over that chair, he'd be at home working on his art, putting his life back together.

"Mr. LaBont."

Paul turned to see a pretty brunette smiling at him.

"Hi, I'm Cindy, Mr. Harrison's assistant. He can see you now."

She ushered Paul into a large corner office as grand as a senior partner's office at one of the larger law firms in town. It had a large teakwood desk and credenza with matching side chairs, a comfortable-looking white sofa, and a small table in one corner with four chairs pushed around it. Paintings dotted the walls and a bust of Picasso stood in the corner behind the desk. Paul was certain it was Picasso. Glancing around, he recognized another Picasso, a Davies, and a Leger hanging on the wall. The other pieces he didn't know.

The detective, a short, balding man with a sharp little nose, greeted him with a warm, firm handshake, and introduced himself as Claude Harrison. He wore an expensive navy blue suit, bright yellow tie, with a matching yellow handkerchief folded neatly in his coat pocket. Holding out his hands, he invited Paul to sit at the table in the corner. Slats of warm sunshine played across the room, and the secretary set down two cups of steaming coffee on the dark surface.

Paul sipped his coffee.

"I want to thank you for driving all the way out here this morning. I know it's a long drive."

Paul nodded appreciatively and relaxed.

Mr. Harrison had a disarming manner about him. He was no Sam Spade; he was as smooth as a piece of finely polished Italian marble. "When the insurance company claimed the chair was stolen and not destroyed in the fire, your father's attorney contacted me in the hopes that I might be able to locate it for him."

The small man opened a thick manila folder full of photos, copies of reports, and other documents, and took out a long typewritten report. "Over the years our agency has garnered a reputation for tracking down stolen art. We've become aware that there's an international distribution network for art that can't be sold through regular channels. Pilfered art never shows up at Sotheby's or Christie's. Such pieces usually end up in private collections and rarely see the light of day."

Paul ran his hand through his hair and pressed his lips together. It didn't surprise Paul that the man seemed to know what he was talking about. But lingering in the air like a bad odor they were both too polite to mention, was a question that had yet to be asked.

"My colleagues and I have tracked this distribution network for years. We can usually do in weeks what takes months or years for public agencies or those less familiar with the art world."

"That's impressive, but don't you think this whole investigation begs the question?"

"What question is that?" Harrison asked, folding his hands in front of him on the table. The diamonds on his pinkie ring glistened in the morning sunshine.

"If the chair was stolen," Paul said. "Why would a thief take just one antique chair in a house full of original art?"

Harrison gazed intently. "Because, technically it wasn't stolen, it was returned to its original owner."

Paul puzzled over his answer for a moment. "You mean an owner other than my father?"

Harrison nodded.

Paul sat up straight, his heart racing. "Then you know where the chair is?"

Harrison nodded again, but didn't smile. "Yes, I do."

Paul hadn't expected such an unequivocal statement from Harrison. He thought he'd say he had an idea where it was, or he thought he knew who possibly could have it.

"Have you turned your information over to the police?"

Harrison gave a faint smile and closed the folder. "Unfortunately, there's not much the police can do about it."

"Why not? It was stolen, wasn't it?"

"As I said, taken, not stolen. The chair has been returned to its original, and most likely, rightful owner."

"What do you mean?" Paul asked. "That chair's been in my family for nearly fifty years. Someone just can't steal it and say it's theirs."

"Did your father tell you where the chair came from?" Harrison said, with a serious look in his eyes.

"Vaguely," Paul said, knowing he had been given only the sketchiest details of how it came into his grandfather's possession.

"Before World War II," Harrison continued, "the chair belonged to a well-known collector in Europe, the Duke of Savoy. The Nazis stripped his castle clean, and the chair was one of the many confiscated treasures."

"You're saying it was stolen?" Paul asked. "My father assured me it was obtained legally."

The detective leaned forward as if he were going to confide a state secret. "Paul, our world today is different than it was after World War II. The fabric of society in Europe as we knew it was shredded into pieces. After the war, the occupying armies tried to trace the provenance of thousands of art works stolen by the Nazis. Where ownership was disputed or unverifiable, pieces were arbitrarily auctioned off by the allied armies."

Paul knew a little about all of this, but none of it mattered. "If my grandfather obtained it legally at one of these auctions, then it belongs, legally, to us, right?"

"In the United States, perhaps."

"What do you mean?" Paul said.

"It's been over sixty years since the war ended, and ownership of art work all over Europe is still in dispute. Jews and others are still recovering gold, artwork, furniture, insurance proceeds, and other property they owned before the war. Possession does not automatically mean ownership in the cases of stolen art or gold or insurance company proceeds. These cases are being litigated every day in Europe. Another complicating factor here is the Duke of Savoy."

"What do you mean?" Paul could feel the pinch of the briars.

"Savoy is an ancient principality in the Alps between France and Italy, ruled by the duke himself."

Paul leaned back in his chair, finally getting the picture. "So, I would have to go to court in Savoy to retrieve the chair."

"The principality is governed by Italian law, and I doubt that any European court would have much sympathy for an American in a case like this. Artworks are being returned every day to their prewar owners from all over the world."

Paul couldn't help giving out a little laugh. It was either that or get up and walk out. "Well, suing him won't work. What do you suggest we do? Steal it back?"

"That's certainly an option, but not a good one." His eyes twinkled for the first time. "I think your best course of action is to offer to buy it back. If you went there personally, it would be more powerful than working through an intermediary or broker. It would be much faster and more effective than any legal recourse you could pursue."

Paul rubbed his lower lip thoughtfully. He hadn't received the answers he expected. He thought that if Harrison had found the chair, it could be turned over to the police or their attorney. But getting it back now meant a personal visit and a financial transaction.

"If someone went to all this trouble to steal it," Paul asked, "why do you think he would sell it to me, just because I asked him to?"

Harrison sat back, his face relaxed for the first time. "I've dug up quite a bit of information about the Duke of Savoy. I know he's definitely in deep financial trouble. In the near future, he's going to have to sell a portion of his vast collection. Timing is everything, and you might just arrive at the right time."

"How do I get in touch with him? Do I just show up on the man's door step?"

"I have a contact, an art dealer in Milan, Giocomo Tosatti. He's discreet. He's sold numerous pieces to the duke, and he's the only one I know who can arrange a meeting with him. I suggest you stop in Milan first, meet with the art dealer, and then drive on to Savoy."

Paul had always wanted to go to Italy, but a trip to Savoy did not sound like a vacation as long as the prospect of his father's recovery was at stake. When he did visit Italy he wanted to see all the art treasures of Florence and Milan. But he didn't see any chance that he could think of anything else but the return of the chair. Yet strolling the streets and museums of those ancient cities was exactly the inspiration his creativity needed. When he returned, he'd be able to get the rhythm of his painting back and move on with his life. Paul nodded his head in agreement. He would go and meet with the Duke of Savoy, then he would immerse himself in some of the finest museums in the world.

Later that night, he stole into the little studio he and his mother shared and took a sketchpad and a few pencils. He went outside into the backyard and sat in a deck chair on the patio under the starry Laguna sky. He wanted to do something simple. Something he could complete quickly to jump-start his creativity. He tried to draw the luminous slice of the moon, but as soon as he touched pencil to paper, every urge to create evaporated. His pencil on his paper sat still; nothing moved; his mind went blank. He closed the sketchpad and laid it on the cement patio at his feet. He had heard about artists who lose their creative abilities, but he never thought it was something that could happen to him. Maybe he hadn't lost anything, but it was a normal reaction to his parents' condition. And once his father was up and around, he too would be back to normal.

But then the thought occurred to him. *The chair.* Why did his mother say it was more than a wooden thing? He'd only sat in it once or twice when his mother wasn't around, and it hadn't made him feel very good. Paul looked at his hands; he held them palms up. His were the hands of a gifted artist. He'd only sat in it to humor his father, and he'd never expected to gain any talent from its use. But now that it was gone, it was as if a lock had been placed on the talents. Could there be any connection?

Going to Italy and finding out about this chair could answer a lot of questions. He needed to do this for his father and for himself. He would travel to Italy, meet with the art dealer, then on to Savoy to parlay with the duke, retrieve the chair, and bring some healing to himself and his parents.

Tomorrow he would go the bank and retrieve his passport.

Truth alone was the daughter of time.

—Leonardo da Vinci, *Notebooks*

5

When Paul finally made it into his room at the Hotel Rosa, the sun dipped behind the Milan skyline, leaving arcs of red and orange streaking over the city. His room overlooked the *Piazza del Duomo* at the center of the ancient part of the city. Glancing out the window, he could see the massive *Duomo*. Narrow streets lined with ancient stone buildings broke off from the piazza like tentacles reaching for the nether parts of the city. But the cathedral, magnificent and huge, dominated the skyline like a marble house prickling the heavens with its multitudes of tapered towers. The church had a plain gray look as if bleached out by disuse and pollution.

The streets were empty and quiet, more subdued than any big city he'd ever been in before. He realized this was the first time in his life he had ventured away from home by himself not to paint. He'd worked so hard in college; he was determined to prove himself an artist, to develop his own style, to become his own person. He hated the thought of getting his art from someone else, even his father. He had focused so intently on his painting he hadn't even attended a party until his senior year, and then he had gone just to meet a girl. The party had turned into a waste of time, the pungent odor of beer, men and women packed shoulder to shoulder, music so loud the beat pulsed through the floor up his shoes. The flat monotone voice of the Smashing Pumpkins' singer drove his raspy voice right through Paul's head while he tried to carry on a conversation with Lisa. She had a nice smile, warm brown eyes, a pretty laugh, and a body that drove him to distraction; but an instinct told him he'd better not bring her home to meet his parents. He thought it odd that he would think that way about her as she tried to speak to him over the raucous, swaying, beer-swilling crowd. Her teeth were so straight, her smile model perfect, her makeup rosy on her high cheeks. He felt an attraction for her as he looked into her attentive brown eyes, and he knew she sensed it by the way she stared back.

But Paul couldn't get past the idea that his father would sift her like sand through the fine sieve of his own ambitions until whatever defects lying below her charming appearance were obvious to all. He didn't have any idea how to get past the fear anyone he brought home wouldn't be good enough.

He closed the curtains and lay down on the bed. Propping himself up on several pillows, he laced his fingers behind his head, closed his eyes, and fell asleep.

Paul stood in a dark room feeling lost. A bright, round, narrow shaft illuminated the center of the large room casting long shadows everywhere. He'd never been there before, but he felt as if there was something in the room that belonged to him. He couldn't see clearly into its dark fringes. The column of light cast a shadowy glow; dark hulks in small groups sat squat and quiet around its edges. The walls disappeared in the gloom.

A voice, a man's smooth voice, called his name from the light. He fixed his gaze on the opaque column of dull whiteness. He stepped closer. The light had a frosty glow; he could not see into its soft center.

"Paul, we've been waiting for you." Her voice was pleasant, not seductive, but inviting.

He paced three steps closer.

A hand, a creamy-skinned, delicate hand, beckoned him from out of the turbid shaft. He rested his hand in hers and she gently led him into the light. Blinking in its brightness, his vision cleared. Beside him stood a striking blonde-haired woman, about his age, her hair cascading in large curls down her back. She was dressed in diaphanous layers of white silk flowing to the floor. Her skin was snow white, her lips red and full, and when she smiled he felt calm, relaxed. He felt stunned by her beauty, entranced, like Dante seeing Beatrice for the first time.

"Paul, this is for you." She waved her hand toward the center, and in front of him sat his father's chair: Leonardo's Chair. He stared at it incredulously. What was it doing here?

She led him, holding his hand, toward the chair, until he stood in front of it.

"Touch it, Paul. It's yours." He bent forward and laid his hand on its arm. A warm sense of contentment came over him. He turned around and slowly sat down. He wondered if any place could be more peaceful.

Suddenly a deep ravenous craving wracked him. His thoughts began to swirl as if they were caught in a fast moving maelstrom, pulling him deeper and deeper. He clamped his eyes shut. A pit in his being opened and he could see straight down into the center of the rampaging vortex. He was nothing but darkness inside. A living darkness, as if it was another part of him he'd never met before.

He felt hot, then hotter, then so hot that he felt he would burst into flames. He opened his eyes and all around him flames leapt and danced. He tried to flee, but he couldn't move, the chair held him. The flames mounted higher, higher, all around him. The harder he struggled, the firmer the chair held him. He called to the woman for help.

"Don't fight it, Paul. Look into your darkness, it's your power."

He tried to scream, but there was no air in his lungs.

Paul awoke gasping for air. He dragged himself out of bed feeling the affects of jet lag, and opened the curtains. The sun filled the piazza down below. He shook his head. It was just a dream? After dressing, he found the continental breakfast downstairs. Over espresso and pastries, the *portiere* gave him directions to Via Brera. Setting off into what looked to be an overcast day, Paul skirted the *Piazza del Duomo* and found his way to the Via Manzoni, which was a busy traffic-choked street filled with large shops and gray medieval-looking buildings. Crossing Via Manzoni, he found Via Brera, a winding street that snaked through the ancient quarter of the city behind *La Scala*. The address that Mr. Harrison had given him, Via Brera 15, occupied an old *palàzzo*. The building, like most of the older structures in this part of town, looked cold and forbidding. Its facade was stained black and corroded by decades of pollution, but inside it proved to be an elegant haven for lovers of art.

Inside the massive front portal led into a garden. Paul went straight through to a set of worn marble stairs leading up to the front door of the shop. It was nearly eleven a.m. by the time he arrived, and the shop was empty except for a gentleman off to the right dusting some statues. Paul asked for Giocomo Tosatti, and the dark-complexioned man pointed silently to the back of the store. The place appeared more of a museum than an art gallery. Large tattered medieval tapestries hung on the wall to his right, on the other side statues of Roman gods and goddesses lined the stone wall. Beyond them hung large canvases of nineteenth-century romantic landscapes and mythological figures. In the middle of the long room two complete sets of medieval armor stood back to back.

Paul stopped to consider the exquisite armor.

"Buon giorno, Signor," said a gray haired man standing in the doorway holding a cup of espresso.

"Good morning," Paul replied, a little startled. He liked the friendly look in the man's eyes. "I'm looking for Giocomo Tosatti."

"Ah," the man said. His face was chubby and wrinkled with age, but he looked like a man who had aged gracefully, like the many pieces of artwork around him. His hair was short gray and curly and his face tanned with a strong chin and a Roman nose like one of the statues Paul had just passed. He wore an open-collar white shirt and gray wool sweater that was unbuttoned except for the last two buttons down by his ample belt buckle.

"Americano?"

"Yes ... yes, I am. Are you Giocomo?"

He nodded with a broad smile. "Sì. Please, follow." Giocomo turned and ambled slowly into another room filled with more paintings and furniture from periods Paul didn't recognize. The man walked carefully as if being diligent not to spill his coffee.

In the back of the set of rooms was a capacious office with a thick oriental carpet and hand-carved mahogany furniture. Giocomo motioned for him to sit on the sofa, and his host settled into a stuffed wing chair across from him. The walls were graced with pastoral paintings; men hunting, others astride horses in armor, and a large Lombardy landscape filled the wall behind the desk.

"Signór, what brings you to my humble shop?"

"You speak good English," Paul said.

"Ah … I have many customers from America. It a great country." Tosatti's smile was broad and inviting.

Paul began to relax. "We have a mutual friend: Mr. Clyde Harrison from California."

Tosatti pressed his thin lips together. He put his coffee cup down on the little table beside him. "Ah yes, Signóre Harrison. A fine man. Are you the young man he told me about?"

"Yes, I am."

Tosatti leaned forward toward Paul as if he was going to touch him. "I am sorry to hear about your father. I light a candle for him the day Signóre Harrison call. But why you come here? You should be home. Help father and mother, no?" His hands moved fluidly as he spoke.

"That's exactly why I came to see you," Paul said, crossing his legs and trying to relax. "My father would really like his chair back. Mr. Harrison told me you could help me."

Tosatti got up, took a portfolio off his desk, and took out a photograph. "Is this the chair?" He gave the photo to Paul.

Jacob Stein pulled up the collar of his wool winter coat against the chilling wind pushing its way up Via Brera. This was usual weather for early spring. It would be another week or so before the hot Italian sun came out in full force. He had followed Paul to the *palazzo* belonging to Giocomo Tosatti. He hadn't been surprised when Tosatti called last week to inform him the young LaBont planned to visit the art dealer soon. In fact they expected such a visit. What surprised them was that it had taken the LaBonts so long to come to Italy seeking their lost chair. He sauntered a few storefronts up from where LaBont had entered and gazed in the shop windows. This street had some of the best art galleries in all Milan; it was a shame he didn't have more time to look around. He might find something he especially wanted to own.

Stein crossed the street, dodging the brisk traffic, and leaned against the stone facade directly across the street from Via Brera 15, propping himself up with one foot against the wall. He pulled out the day's racing form and studied the races running at *Ippodromo delle Campennelle*. He wouldn't get to Rome anymore until their business with LaBont was finished. Stein knew Tosatti would instill a little fear in LaBont, but it should do nothing more than whet the young man's impetuous appetite to come to Savoy. The duke had counted on the older LaBont coming to Savoy after his chair, and it had sent a ripple of shock and disappointment through the stately aristocrat when the duke read in the *Times of London* that LaBont's hands had been severely burned in a fire. Their plans had ground suddenly to a halt, but Stein had seen the remarkable progress of the young LaBont. He was a painting prodigy. If he came to Italy, surely he could fit into their plans.

Stein marked the horses he had a hunch about while he kept one eye glued to the entrance of Tosatti's *palazzo*. Today should be uneventful; all he had to do was make certain LaBont reached Savoy safely.

⨯⨯⨯

"That's the chair," Paul said, fingering the photo. "Where did you get this?" He handed it back to Tosatti.

"Signór, how you paint?" Tosatti asked, holding his right hand up in the air with his thumb touching all of his fingers together.

"What kind of question is that?" Paul rammed his back straight. "You want me to explain all my technique and training? How I mix my colors—"

"Sì, everything. Explain now," Tosatti said, punctuating his words with an up-lifted palm in the air.

"What is this? I came to get information from you."

"Sì, Signór. You no explain your art. I no explain mine. From all over, people come to my little shop and show me photo and say get. They pass me envelope and I get. I no explain. They do not wish to know," he said, waving his hand in the air. "Capisce?"

Paul nodded his head slowly and leaned back into the plush sofa. "I understand."

"Now we understand each the other." He picked up his coffee cup and sipped the cold beverage as if it was a tradition to seal a mutual understanding with a drink no matter what it tasted like.

Paul sat back and took a deep breath. "I came here because Mr. Harrison said you could arrange a meeting with the Duke of Savoy."

Tosatti leveled an index finger at Paul. "What you know about the chair?"

Paul leaned forward, propping his elbows on his knees. This conversation seemed to be one-sided, and Paul didn't want that trend to continue. "What I know is that my grandfather legally purchased it," he said, pointing to the photo on the table in front of them. "It was illegally taken from my house and I want it back."

"I think you have hard head like Italiano."

The muscles in Paul's jaw began to tighten. "Listen, Mr. Tosatti, I didn't come here to ..." He held back a moment. "I was told you could help me."

Tosatti waved his hand in the air. "I help any way I can, Signore." He stuck his thumb in the air. "First, I tell you about chair. It has ancient tradition; much mystery surrounds it. Some say it has great powers. It has been in the duke's family since sixteen hundreds. Why you think it belong to you now?"

"Mr. Tosatti, people have been buying and selling art treasures for a long time. Just because a person owned it in the past doesn't mean they're the rightful owners forever. Things just don't work that way."

Tosatti didn't answer, only rubbed his chin as if he was giving Paul's comments careful consideration.

"I want you to arrange a meeting with the Duke of Savoy so that I can discuss getting back my father's chair," Paul said firmly.

"Signór, what are you to offer the duke?"

"I'm prepared to buy the chair back from him if necessary."

"And why he sell it to you?"

"Every piece of art in the world is for sale for the right price, don't you agree?"

Tosatti raised both of his bushy eyebrows as if the remark startled him. "Duke is most, how you say ... dedicated collector."

"Are you saying he probably won't sell it to me?"

"No Signór. I say that he never sell anything so far. But he not meet you before."

"Well, can you help me meet him or not?"

Tosatti shrugged and sighed deeply. "Sì, Signór. I help." He turned toward his desk and took up a large manila envelope. He turned back and handed it to Paul. "I tell you. Some people collect beautiful things because they like to have parties and show off what they have. Others because the art is important to them ... it's ... it's their ..."

"It's their life," Paul said, trying to finish Tosatti's belabored sentence.

"No ... religion."

Paul knew something about ardent art lovers. "So, he has a real passion for collecting."

"Ah ... passion. Sì, passion good word to describe him. You must impress upon him how important the chair is to your family. Sometimes money is not the only currency."

Paul squinted, appraising Tosatti's cryptic remark. "What do you mean?"

"Signór, if you must have the chair, then you must be open ..." he motioned with his hands as if trying to find the right word.

"Open to what?" Paul asked with an exasperated shrug. "I

need to be home in a week with the chair. You don't understand how ill my father is."

He rubbed his chin. He looked at Paul with his deep-set black eyes. They spoke of some hidden danger.

"Is the Duke of Savoy a vampire or something?"

Tosatti's polite smile vanished. "Danger come in many forms, Signór."

Paul wanted to swat the man across the face. He seemed to speak only in circles punctuated with hand signals. "So, what form of danger can I expect?"

Tosatti wrinkled his forehead as if he was trying to decide what to say. "Now not a good time to go."

"Why?"

Tosatti moved to the edge of his seat, almost falling off. He tugged on his ear as if he was considering his words. "Sì, Signór. Times are difficult now for Savoy, but I see that you must go. Just remember that desperate men can often seem most unreasonable." He punctuated his words with a chop of the air with his right hand.

Paul forced himself not to smirk to the man's face. Meeting the duke wouldn't be any more difficult than meeting some of his father's more difficult clients. He had envisioned, instead, a reasoned conversation with the Duke of Savoy followed by a mutually satisfying business transaction. That's the way it worked most of the time in the art world. He hoped that's the way it would work this week. And if the duke became unreasonable and demanded an exorbitant price, one Paul was not in a position to pay? He would just have to impress upon him the seriousness of the situation.

Tosatti leaned forward and lightly touched Paul's leg. He could smell the coffee on the old man's breath. "There are many traditions in our country hard to understand."

"You seem as superstitious as my father." A warm flush came over Paul's face. Was this some convoluted way of warning him off, discouraging him from going after what was his?

"Do not scoff at what you no understand, my young friend."

"Right!" Paul said, with a ring of sarcasm in his voice.

Giocomo's jaw dropped, the portly man abruptly stood. "I call the duke, tell him you are coming. Then I light a candle for you today at Mass." He stuck out his hand; Paul stood and shook it. His hazel eyes narrowed, the old man earnestly gazed at Paul, the unmistakably firm handshake was a message written in flesh.

So much more noble are the possessions of
the soul than those of the body ...

—Leonardo da Vinci, *Notebooks*

6

Vincent LaBont lay awake in his hospital bed staring out the window as the morning light slanted into his room. He had the nurse pull the blinds as soon as she came in this morning so he could see outside. His only view was of passing clouds, floating by in their carefree way. He lifted his head as if doing so he could see in the distance where Paul was now. He should be in Savoy by now or close to it. He dropped his head to the pillow in a rush of guilt. He wondered what kind of reception he would receive when he met the duke.

He remembered the inauspicious meeting many years ago with the handsome young man who had introduced himself as Frederick de la Cloy, Duke of Savoy. Vincent had a premonition the tall, regal looking man hadn't come all the way from Europe to his small studio by the beach only to have his portrait painted. He remembered the curious look in his eyes as he sat rigid, with a stately air of grace, in the chair Vincent had given him; his body still, but his deep brown eyes constantly roving the room as if he were searching for something specific. Vincent told him he'd look more stunning standing than sitting, but he rejected Vincent's idea and kept asking if he had a more antique looking chair, one from the High Renaissance, that might give the portrait a noble feel. When he asked about an antique chair, Vincent's heart thumped like a hammer on steel. He showed the chair to no one and talked about it even less. And he never kept it in the same room that he painted in, because he didn't need to, lest some paint splash on its wood and mar it. Rather he kept it at home in his study and used it each morning. He lounged in it as he filled his notebook with sketches.

Alarmed that the duke's mission may be to retrieve it, he bent himself diligently to quickly finishing his portrait.

The duke spent the better part of a week in Vincent's studio, and by the end of the sitting, had related the whole story of the antique chair he'd come to America looking for, while Vincent painted in silence. He never met the man's eyes as he related how the chair had resided in the Castle of Savoy for nearly five centuries, and how the Nazis had taken it, and then how his ancestors who had used the chair to further their art and had achieved great brilliance and then inexplicably died—by fire.

The duke, in his mellow but grave voice, stated that the incidents were too many and too profusely documented in his family history to be mere coincidences. Cold chills crept up Vincent's spine as the duke described the details of his ancestor's deaths. Names that now had slipped into the mists of Vincent's memory but whose agonies were etched forever in his mind.

He painted quickly, wanting the duke to leave with his portrait. But near the end of the sitting, as he put the finishing touches on the background, the tall, lean, princely looking man stood over the easel, staring into Vincent's face like a coal miner probing for a shaft of black truth in a mountain of cold rock. He smoothed out the dark colors of the background and tried to ignore him.

"If you know such a man who owns a chair like this, you should warn him to return it," the duke said in somber tones.

Vincent worked on in silence.

"If one were to use it there is no telling what could happen," the duke said. "His life would be in grave danger."

Vincent began to sweat, but he worked on, not letting his brush hesitate for a moment. As the duke left with his portrait, Vincent wished him success in finding his magic chair. The duke turned and gave him a frozen smile.

"I will find it," the tall aristocrat told Vincent, "if it takes my life-time." With that he turned and left.

Vincent shook for days after the man left. He wavered between believing the stories of tragic deaths and thinking the man's visit was a ruse, a devilish subterfuge, a wily method of scaring him into willingly giving up the chair. After all, the visitor had no legal claim to its ownership. Vincent never told Marcella about the true nature of the man's visit, and he made a point of never mentioning him again. Except for the portrait, Vincent made certain no record was kept of the duke's visit, but soon afterward he moved his studio home.

At that time, Vincent's work had just started reaching a wider audience. Making a living as a portrait artist wasn't easy, but now a steady stream of referrals were finding their way to his door. His income had become more secure. What part of his success he attributed to the chair and what part to his own skill, he wasn't certain. He had become convinced they were the same. His passion to succeed burned deeply, and if the chair stoked those fires, he would not dispense with it.

The night he saw his house in flames and his wife lying choking on the grass, the image of the duke standing over his easel shot through his mind. Was the fire, her near death, the destruction of his home all a coincidence? Running into the raging flames was a strong urge his sensible mind told him was foolhardy and stupid. But a deeper, darker part of him feared that if the chair burned into black ash so would his talent.

Standing at the top of the third-floor stairs in his burning house he didn't want to believe what he witnessed. The fire had eaten into everything he cherished, and his only response was a silent, angry frisson. As he lay in the hospital room, he tried to restrain sullen urges to cry, but there was no controlling the warm rivulets running down his face. He tried to shut off the tears by tensing all the muscles in his face, but it was no use.

Everything ... everything was lost.

Over the last few weeks the doctors explained to him that the skin grafts had started to take, but he might never recover feeling in several of his fingers. He tried wiggling his right hand: first his index finger, then his middle finger, then the third finger, and then his pinkie. They responded, even though the pain was sharp. He was thankful he could feel them. When he tried flexing his thumb—it didn't respond—at least he couldn't feel it. He wasn't even certain he had a thumb. Pain throbbed in the area where his thumb should be.

He had asked the nurses on several occasions how his right thumb was doing. The last one just looked at him with a flash of doubt in her eyes, like a sad puppy dog before the everything-is-going-to-be-all-right-smile broke out across her face. It seemed all nurses had that smile. He wondered if they held practice sessions in class.

I'll never hold a brush again.

It wouldn't be long before the gallery owners who had reserved space for his work or referred clients to him would start looking elsewhere. Art was a business, and the owners of the galleries and their customers would make business decisions that best suited them.

His slow progress convinced him that the only chance he had of recovering the use of his right hand, so he could work again, lay with his son and the chair.

If the way seems dark, then light a candle. If that doesn't work then light a hundred candles.

—Leonardo da Vinci, *Notebooks*

7

The meeting with Tosatti left Paul eager to leave for Savoy. He hustled through the morning sunshine to the Hotel Rosa, into the lobby elevator. The meeting with Tosatti had not only unsettled him, but also piqued his curiosity. Was that fat antique dealer trying to eke a commission out of him by scaring him into hiring the man as a go-between? Or was he truly concerned for Paul's safety? If men learned the polite art of damning with faint praise, Giocomo Tosatti appeared an expert. His cryptic comments sent chills down Paul's spine. After reflection, he realized the duke was probably no more of an eccentric art collector than Paul's father.

He flung items into his toiletry bag, threw a pair of pants into his suitcase, and zipped it shut. He checked out, stowed his suitcase in the back of his green Range Rover, and sped out of Milan up the straight four-lane *autostrada* toward the snow-capped Alps in the distance. He'd heard it said that one of the elements that made Italian art so distinctive was the quality of sunshine over Tuscany and Lombardy. The sky was the brightest cobalt blue Paul had ever seen, shot through with streaks of gold. The broad green meadows racing toward the foothills were one continuous carpet of grass flecked with yellow, purple, and orange flowers. The countryside was indeed stunning. He checked his watch. It was barely 10:30 a.m. He would be in Savoy by suppertime.

By late afternoon, the wide roadway narrowed and turned upward into the looming Alps. He switched on his headlights. After climbing for a solid hour, he reached what he thought was the summit, then the road cascaded down into a wide green valley. At the low point of the valley, the surface turned into an uneven, two-lane alpine road. Paul eased off the accelerator and drove warily. Fearing he might have missed a turn, he pulled over to check his map. He could reach the eastern edge of Savoy from the road he now traveled. He drove on through the late afternoon, looping up and down the serpentine road into the towering mountains.

Early evening in the Alps brought a visual thrill. Upon each turn of the rugged road came new vistas of craggy cliffs and green meadows with waving grass crawling up gradually curving slopes to the tree line. Old stone barns stood as silent sentinels in the meadows. He would love to stop, get out his sketchpad, and go to work, but he couldn't stop. Innocent beauty fled by his windows under ten-thousand-foot peaks.

He wondered what kind of reception he would receive upon his arrival. Maybe he should have considered more carefully what the duke would be like before he visited him. But time threatened to undo everything Paul had worked for if he waited even another day. His father, lying listless and languid in a California hospital bed, depended on Paul's successful and quick return. He was convinced the chair was nothing more than a placebo, but it didn't matter. The sooner he brought it home, the sooner he and his father could move on with their lives. Just thinking about his own stalled career galled him. He had to put off Kraemer's offer to exhibit his paintings for a few months, maybe even a year while he traipsed across the Alps. His only consolation was that once his father was on the solid road to recovery, Paul knew his own frightful case of artistic malaise would also disappear. The last thing the rational side of his mind wanted to do was attach any significant powers to that piece of carved wood. It was inert, insentient, and totally incapable of influencing his art or his life.

Darkness settled across the deep valleys, then hastily slid up the slopes until the blanket of night enveloped everything but the cones of his headlights. The Range Rover's beams sliced through the darkness, revealing craggy drops, and large boulders clinging to the mountainside above him. Paul realized he hadn't seen a trace of civilization for the last hour. The cold night air seeped into the car, so he switched on the heater. He rode deeper into the alpine darkness, accompanied only by shadows that seemed to play just beyond the reach of his headlights.

The road flattened and immediately immersed him in a dense bank of fog. He cut his pace to a crawl, his visibility no more than five or six feet. According to the directions Tosatti gave him, the border of Savoy was marked with only a sign greeting visitors, and he'd been warned if he drove too fast, he'd miss it. Shortly after the border marker, he needed to turn north until he reached the duke's castle, lodged atop a ridge overlooking the valley below.

He entered a flat mountain pass and his lights reflected off a white object ahead. He steered his car all the way onto the shoulder, gravel crunching under his tires, and brought the Range Rover to a stop in front of a triangular road marker bearing the universal symbol for no parking.

Why would someone have a no parking sign out here in the middle of nowhere?

Beyond it was a rectangular white metal sign announcing in

Italian his arrival in Savoy. Clicking on his high beams, he saw the crest of Savoy, a black eagle on a blood-red shield. Under the eagle were sentences written in Italian. He had a hard time keeping up with most Italian speakers, but he could translate if he had time. He rolled closer until it was directly in the path of his lights.

He killed the engine, stepped out of the car, and walked closer. A blanket of silence covered everything. The cold mountain air bit into his ears and face, and he plunged his hands into the pockets of his jeans. The aroma of pine mingled with fresh mountain air invigorated him. Trying to peer into the eerie darkness around him was useless. The fog and mist dampened his face and clothes, and he began to shiver. Even the stars were obscured. He slowly translated the Italian script at the bottom of the sign.

Welcome to the ancient Kingdom ...

Something moved on the hillside above him. He thought he might be imagining things. He tried to scan the mountain above him to his right. Sheathed in fog, he couldn't see five feet in front of his face. It was probably just a rabbit. Gazing back at the sign, he continued reading.

Welcome to the ancient Kingdom of Savoy. Founded in the year of our Lord 1035 by Humbert ...

Paul froze, then bent his head to listen. Something definitely moved. He heard a crunching sound as if someone had stepped on some gravelly rocks on the hillside above his head. It was impossible. No one could be on those sheer cliffs. It had to be an animal. As long as he stayed in the wash of his own lights, he'd be fine. Concentrating on the sign again, he continued to read.

Humbert the Whitehand, when he defeated Eudos of Champagne in ...

For a fleeting second, the ground shuddered under his feet. The vibration startled him; his heart raced wildly. Running back to the car, he yanked open the door. The ground shook violently again. He stumbled, almost falling to the ground, but steadied himself by grabbing onto the car door. A rending movement from above and beyond the passenger side of the car, as if the mountaintop had ripped apart, caused the door in his hand to shudder. Paul squinted into the darkness. What was going on up there? He heard a rolling, clattering rumble as if something huge but cloaked in fog hurtled toward him. He clambered into the driver's seat, cranked the engine, but it didn't catch.

Something crashed through trees, smashed rocks, and hurtled down the slope creating a deep-throated roar as it gouged a course toward him. The steering wheel shook in his hand as the rumble worked its way closer. Something hit the small gully of the shoulder with a vibrating thud; the car bounced from the impact.

He cranked the key and frantically pumped the gas pedal, but the engine only turned over with a whimper. Glancing out the passenger side window, he froze at the site of a huge boulder lurching toward him.

With his heart racing toward uncontrolled madness, he leapt out of the car to the rear. The rolling thunder slammed into the passenger side rear panel, crushing and tearing into it, pushing the car across the road as if it were cardboard. He'd only had time for two running steps before the rear bumper, shooting behind him, clipped the calf of his leg as it passed, sending him sprawling out of the path of the side-slipping crash.

With a violent, grinding shriek, followed by a shower of sparks, the melded mass scraped its way across the uneven surface of the road. Paul spun a couple of times along the ground, and then banged his knees and forehead on the cold pavement. Hurt ran through him like a hammer on flesh. Sprawled face down in the center of the narrow highway, wrapped in icy air, he shivered uncontrollably. The pungent taste of decades of auto residue shocked him as his lips wiped the greasy surface. He felt a trickle of liquid running from his nose.

A deafening sound of screeching metal and rock locked in a raging march into the darkness on the other side of the road assaulted his ears. He tried lifting his head to see the commotion when he felt a tingle on his hand. A frigid liquid rippled against his fingertips. He recognized an acrid smell, but couldn't place it. Wetness ran up his fingers, numbing his hands. His shirt-sleeve soaked up the liquid like a wick.

Gasoline!

The rock had ripped his gas tank open, and it purged its fuel along the ground in a stream of chemicals. He tried to move, but pain sliced through his side. A brief vision flashed through his mind of his father's hands burned like melted brown stubs.

The journey of car and boulder came to a crescendo with a shuddering collision against the far cliff. The tangled mass exploded into flames, lighting the area like it was day. Forcing himself to lift his head, he saw a river of fire ripping toward him, straight for his hand. Ignoring his aching body, he jerked his hand out of the pool of fluid and flipped his body over. The sheet of fire tore past him with just inches to spare in its race down the sluice of gas.

Paul lay prone on his back, staring up into the night sky. The strip of burning pavement a few feet to his right warmed him. At least he was alive and warm; for that, he was thankful. But his passport, clothes, plane tickets ... everything was gone. He could hear the crackle and pop of his car and all his belongings going up in flames. He felt sore all over, but he didn't think he had any broken bones. How would he get back to Milan? Maybe someone would see the flames and investigate. He had to get out of the roadway before a passing car ran over him. Too exhausted to move, he lay prone on the macadam.

Above the roar of the fire, he thought he heard a high-pitched whine moving toward him. He perked his ears to the unmistakable sound of a high-performance engine making its way up to the pass. The engine seemed to dance as the driver pushed the car through the gears. Paul tried to roll over, but it took all his energy to get on his side just as two quartz halogen headlights broke over the last ridge and entered the flat of the mountain pass. Paul froze in the brilliance of the headlights. Squinting into the brightness, he tried to move, but his body wouldn't respond. The car sped toward him, shifting into a higher gear, gathering speed. Paul was certain the driver could see the flames, but he wasn't sure he would see his body in the middle of the road. The car continued eating up ground by the second. Paul flopped onto his belly, wincing at the pain, and strained to crawl out of its path. A sliver of pain shot through his back and knees. He realized he couldn't move fast enough. He sat up on his knees and waved both hands in front of his face.

The driver downshifted, the headlights tilted down as the driver braked heavily. The car came to a stop about three feet from Paul's face, smoke filtering through the beams of lights. He put his head down on the pavement, and let out a deep sigh of relief.

A man jumped out of the car and ran over to him. *"Signore. Che è successo?"*

Paul lay face up on the pavement. *"Parla inglese?"*

"Sì." The man knelt down beside him. "What happened?" he asked in perfect English.

"I was attacked by a mountain." Paul nodded toward his burning car.

The man glanced over at it too. "Come, we must get you off the road. Can you walk?"

"I'm pretty sure I can. I don't think I broke anything." Paul lifted himself with the man's help. He led Paul to the passenger side of his Porsche Carrera. Once inside the sports car, the man drove around the patches of fire in the road and angled toward Paul's car.

"My friend, I don't think there is anything left of your car. We will leave it for now and get you to a doctor." The man took a handkerchief out of his pocket and handed it to Paul. "Your nose is bleeding."

Paul pressed it to his nose, and sank gratefully into the soft leather seats. The man pushed the Porsche smoothly through the gears and steamed down the road.

"You drive like you've been here before." Paul held the cloth to his nostrils.

"I work in Savoy, but I often holiday in Rome. I enjoy the horses. And you?"

"I was on my way to visit the Duke of Savoy when I stopped at the border to read that sign."

"My friend, didn't you see the warning?"

"You mean the one that said no parking?"

"That is a dangerous area. Rockslides happen all the time. That is why they put up the warning. Everyone knows that."

Paul rubbed the knot on his head. "If it's so dangerous, why do they put a sign there with all that historical information?" Looking over at the man, he noticed his thin features, black hair, and natty dress.

The man smiled. "This is Italy. Why do they paint ceilings with frescoes, build towns under volcanoes, and have cities with rivers for streets?"

Paul wanted to smile, but he couldn't. He was almost killed by a rampaging boulder, and his benefactor seemed so cavalier, as if it happened all the time.

The man spun his Porsche effortlessly through the curves. "That spot is special to the House of Savoy, so it is only natural that it should be marked as such. But everyone knows not to stop there."

"You know the Duke of Savoy?" Paul blotted his nose, which had finally stopped bleeding. The Porsche wound its way along the ridge of a mountain. Between wisps of clouds, Paul could see tiny sparkles of light dotting the valley below.

"I've worked for him for many years. His is the only home close by. Since you were on your way to visit him, I am taking you there. He will attend to your injuries."

"How convenient," Paul said, staring pensively out the windshield. Maybe he shouldn't have said anything to this man about his visit to the castle.

The man looked over at Paul, his eyebrows furrowed. "You are a guest of the duke?"

Paul thought it best not to show his hand. "Yes. Tell me, why is that mountain pass so special to the House of Savoy?"

The man downshifted, the engine's RPMs jumped as he rounded a sharp curve. "The story goes that Humbert the Whitehand, the first Duke of Savoy, defeated Eudos by imploring the mountains to fall on his enemy's army as they invaded Italy. But in truth, those mountains have been falling on people, as they fell on you tonight, since they cut that pass at the end of the first millennium. That is why they call it the Hill of Sorrows."

Paul massaged the growing knot on his forehead. "So this has happened many times before?"

The man nodded and gave a slight smile. "Si. But we only ask the rocks to keep out our enemies. It is not good when it happens to a guest. I know the duke will be displeased at your misfortune."

Paul was beginning to wonder about that. "I hear the duke is quite an art collector."

"He is one of the most prolific in the world. His collection has surpassed what his grandfather had before the Nazi's confiscated everything."

"His grandfather started their collection?" Paul asked, as he inspected his tattered jeans. Holes were ripped in both knees.

"No. The family has collected art for centuries. Before the Second World War, they had one of the best collections in Europe. It has taken Duke Frederick many years to restore the collection. Only last year he found his lost Rembrandts in New York. Or I should say his agent found them."

The man's voice faded as Paul became lost in his own thoughts. He dabbed at an abrasion on his forehead with the hand-kerchief and smoothed back his tousled hair. The warm air relaxed him, and his aching body unwound into the contoured seat. This wasn't the way he wanted to meet the duke, arriving all bloody in some strange man's car; with only the scraggly clothes on his back; no passport; no money; and no way of leaving when the time came.

That bright ribbon of flames bearing down on his right hand—his painting hand—flashed through his mind. Was the fire trying to destroy his creative powers, just like his father's had been? He rubbed the throbbing knot on his head. Some ice for his bruise and a hot shower would go a long way toward feeling human again. His mouth tasted like oil. His clothes smelled like gasoline. He just imagined what his bloody face looked like.

"Signór, excuse me, how rude of me. I haven't even asked your name."

Paul gazed glassy eyed at the driver. "I'm Paul LaBont, from California.

The man nodded appreciatively. "Paul LaBont. Ah, yes, the duke has mentioned you."

Paul squinted, looking him over carefully. His face seemed hauntingly familiar. "Have we met before?"

He turned to Paul, smiling with his thin straight lips. "Not directly, but I've heard of you," he said, stroking his mustache with his finger. "My name is Jacob Stein. It is a great pleasure to finally meet you."

Pure gold is recognized by testing.

—Leonardo da Vinci, *Notebooks*

8

Marcella LaBont woke up early to the melodic rhythm of waves crashing on soft sand. She sat up in bed, truly thankful to be alive. The images of dark smoke filling her bedroom, of choking so hard she couldn't breath, had stopped intruding into her dreams. The terror of her near death lingered, but it seemed to stand a few inches further away, giving her a little room to feel normal again.

Her life had never been shaken so deeply. Tragedy was a word she used to describe what happened to others less fortunate than herself. At times she struggled between keeping the benign view of the world fixed in her mind and being overwhelmed with the terror of the fire: One of her sipping an ice-cold lemonade on her dappled patio on a clear, cool afternoon, the breeze gently caressing her cheeks; the other of a tragic world that arbitrarily reached down and consumed her husband and almost destroyed her.

She opened the bedroom window; the blue sky and the

blue-green ocean like a crystal covering the earth, sent a shimmer of joy through her. She thanked God for her health. The smell of the fresh spring air, the song of the gulls and sea birds brought a moment of peace. Her joy, always a big part of her life, now came back like a lame prodigal returning from a long journey.

Today would be a much better day, but nothing could erase the deep crease of sorrow burned into her heart. As she put on her makeup and dressed to go see Vincent, she determined to face him with joy in her eyes. Vincent was perceptive about her moods, but since his accident he'd been in so much pain it was hard to speak to him unless it was just as the morphine wore off.

She put on a new dress. It was white silk with small, hand-painted red roses. Finished with her hair, she set the brush down on the dresser. She put on her earrings and then checked herself in the mirror. Her color had come back, and it radiated in her cheeks. If only everything else important in her life could be restored so quickly.

Marcella carried a Nordstrom's tote bag with three books on tape and some fresh cut flowers into the UC Irvine Medical Center burn ward. Stepping into Vincent's room, she greeted the nurse who was just leaving after giving him his medication. The room smelled of strong antiseptic and had a bright white hospital glow. When she came around the side of the bed and put down her bag, she could see that something was terribly wrong. She put her hand on his forehead. "Sweetheart, what's wrong?" She had never seen him cry.

He turned his head away from her. "Nothing. It's just my eyes. They're watering."

She pursed her lips, pulled some tissue from the box next to the bed and started to dab at his eye.

"Don't do that," he ordered sharply.

"I'm just trying to help."

He lay staring at the other side of the room. After a minute he turned and faced her. Deep circles of red rimmed his eyes.

She wiped the tears from his left eye, then with a new tissue she worked at his right one. "What's wrong?" she asked.

His burning red eyes glared at her. "I'm dying, Marcella. Everything I am is dying."

She put her hand to his cheek and rubbed it softly. "You're not—"

"You know I'll never paint again. You know it. The doctors know it. The nurses know it, and everyone only humors me."

She dropped the tissue in a wastebasket by the bed. "I don't know if you'll paint again, but we're all alive and we have each other. I'm thankful for that."

He didn't say anything.

"Paul is fine and I'm well and you're getting better."

"I'm not getting better, that's the point. I'm not. I have no feeling in my thumb and the pain is excruciating."

She stroked his forehead, trying to comfort him. "Honey, please relax. It doesn't do any good to get angry like this."

"You just don't care, do you?"

"I care very much," she said.

"If I don't paint again, how will we live?"

"We've got plenty of money in the bank. We'll be fine for years. We just won't do everything we used to."

"We don't have as much as you think."

"That's ridiculous. Last time I looked we had—"

"I gave it all to Paul," he said, turning his head away.

"What?" She put her arms akimbo. "You gave him all that money to take a one-week trip to Europe?"

"It's not just the trip."

"What then?" Surprise in her voice.

He didn't say anything.

"What did Paul need all that money for?"

"I've found the chair and he went to purchase it back. It's in Europe."

She felt the flush rising in her cheeks. Her heart begin to race. She didn't know what to say. Her last conversation with Paul about that stupid wooden thing was that it had been destroyed by the fire. "I though it was destroyed."

Vincent shook his head, no.

"You sent our son to Italy for that … that chair?"

Vincent meekly nodded. "It was our only hope of making it."

She let her anger come to the surface; she couldn't talk herself out of it anymore. "No, it isn't. I was prepared to go back to work, to do whatever it took to help us stay together."

Vincent let out a sigh. "What would you do? Paint?"

"You know how good I used to be."

"You do gift-shop art, Marcella. Come on. You know what it takes to be successful at the level we're used to."

She slowly shook her head and clenched her jaw. She caught her breath before saying anything. She tried to rationalize that it was just the bitterness of his injuries speaking, but deep down she knew better. "You don't think I could do anything without you, do you?"

"Marcella, that's not true. You know what I mean."

"I gave up my art to support you, and now that I think about it, it was a big mistake."

"Marcella …"

She didn't want to listen to him anymore. She'd heard him say things like this so often that she could say all of his lines herself. She had so much she wanted to say to him, but she worried that if she said it now it would set back his recovery. She took a deep breath. It was time to leave; she had things to do.

Marcella composed herself, and replaced the flowers in the

vase on the nightstand with the fresh one's she'd brought. She placed the books on tape neatly next to the vase.

"I have to go," she said.

Vincent's eyes glazed over as the morphine took effect. He didn't respond.

On the drive home, Marcella fumed. She was tired of him putting her art down. Instead of driving straight home, she stopped in downtown Laguna Beach at Rhonda's art gallery. She collected her equipment she had stored in the gallery's small studio and stopped and bought some fresh supplies. Within a couple of hours, it was all packed in her trunk.

At home, she moved her supplies into the vacant fourth bedroom since it was only furnished with a stuffed chair and a bookshelf. It had a south-facing window that brought in the afternoon sunlight and had a view of the coast. She covered the carpet with a tarp, and set a small table in the corner by the window that she would use as her workbench. Setting up a small folding table adjacent to her workbench, she laid out her brushes, several jars of clean water, charcoal sticks, masking fluid, razors, sponges, and her paint box. She arranged an Imperial-sized drawing board on her workbench and stretched a new sheet of 90-pound rough onto the board. She then trimmed it, sponged it with warm water, taped it down, and then pinned the corners with small tacks to ensure the paper laid flat. In the opposite corner, she set an easel she would use for making final touches on her landscapes. Since the newly stretched sheet would take a few hours to dry, she took her sketchpad, settled comfortably in the stuffed chair in the warm sunshine, and began to draw.

Fingering the pencil over a clean sheet of white paper, she remembered the day she set aside her pencils and paints. It was a day like today, bright and cheerful. She had been sitting and drawing when Vincent walked in and gazed over her shoulder. They had been married barely three years. He told her how superficial it was for her to be spending her time on such low forms of art. It hurt her deeply, and she had stored those feelings deep down where they couldn't be found.

She began to sketch, drawing a scene of the jagged coastline out her window. She had spent her whole adult life serving Vincent and Paul, and now the house was empty.

Her paintings would sell. She knew it. Building a bigger portfolio would take time, but she could do it. When Vincent came home from the hospital, she wanted her work on every wall in every room in the house. She would find a gallery owner to help her organize a show. Marcella would survive and thrive, and she would keep the family together. And Vincent would eat his words. If she had to sell watercolors to tourists that's what she'd do. And if a night out meant dinner at McDonald's, then so be it. But no one—no one—would stomp on her dreams anymore.

The artist ought first to exercise his hand by copying drawings from the hand of a good master.

—Leonardo da Vinci, *Notebooks*

9

_P_aul could barely keep his eyes open as Stein pulled off the road into a long gravel driveway. Coming around a sweeping curve in the drive, lights blazed from scores of windows in a mammoth stone castle set among tall pine trees. Four round, peaked towers, one on each corner, bathed in the glow of powerful floodlights, poked into the night sky like massive spears. Passing through an arched gateway, under which he imagined a drawbridge at one time kept the lord of the castle safe from his enemies, Stein wheeled the Porsche into a cobblestone courtyard. Paul sensed that time had bypassed this patch of the world. Peering at the cold, pinkish stone walls he wondered, _What kind of man wraps himself in the structures of his ancestors?_

He had traversed half the world to come here for a chair. A chair that not too long ago in his mind had a dubious efficacy, but now it seemed intertwined with his life like a tightly woven tapestry—the warp indistinguishable from the woof. If he could tell where one thread ended and another picked up, he might be able to unravel all these incidents. He couldn't help but wonder what he would find in this place. Was the duke simply a collector of unusual wealth and tastes, or did mysteries lurk in this medieval fortress?

Two great oak entry doors swung open and a shaft of warm yellowish light flooded the spot in the cobblestone driveway where Stein parked the Porsche. A short, rotund man hurried down the steps, opened the passenger-side door, and helped Paul out. Leaning on Stein and the short man's shoulder, Paul limped up the steps between his two helpers into an ornate lobby. The foyer led into a spacious hall with crystal chandeliers suspended from a high ceiling. The magnificent marble floor and columns gave the room a grandeur Paul had never seen. The soft glow of candlelight from tall silver candelabras, scattered throughout the room, produced a flickering light that ran shadows up the walls, glistened along the polished marble floor, and danced from column to column.

The room didn't have the worn-down medieval look he had observed in the ancient section of Milan, but it had a fresh face of one that had been meticulously maintained.

The short, rotund man introduced himself as Gerhard. He spoke with a heavy accent, but his English was clear and precise. He draped Paul's arm across his broad shoulder, and the two men almost carried Paul up the grand staircase to a bedroom on the second floor. Paul was not too tired to feel chagrined at his ragged appearance, as the impeccably dressed Gerhard, in a black dinner jacket and slacks, white shirt and bow tie, helped him out of his clothes. He dropped Paul's rags into a pile and helped him into a silk robe. He left Paul lying on the bed while he ran a hot bath then disappeared to inform the duke a doctor was required.

Paul winced as he lowered his bruised body into the hot water, but soon he lay relaxing in a luxurious Jacuzzi tub surrounded by pale-blue marble walls. A tapestry of a knight in full armor sitting on a charger hung on the far wall. He felt embarrassed that he didn't come into the duke's palace ready to do business, but instead he had to be carried in, limping, tattered, and torn. Not a good way to start a negotiation session.

Gerhard reappeared and helped him out of the tub like a doting grandfather. Paul found a fresh pair of silk pajamas laid out on the king-size bed. The doctor would be here within the hour. Paul didn't think he needed one, but Gerhard continued to fuss over him as if he were royalty. Having someone hold his pajama tops, while he slipped his arms into the sleeves, turn down his covers, and hand him a glass of water, at first made him feel awkward. But after he was propped in bed supported by a pile of puffy pillows, he knew it was something he could get used to. While he lay back, letting his body melt into the bed, Gerhard brought a cold compress and laid it gently on the throbbing lump on his forehead.

The doctor arrived, his hair and clothes rumpled as if awakened from a sound sleep, carrying his black bag. He introduced himself with a courteous handshake, then examined Paul carefully. After cleaning and dressing the scrapes on Paul's knees, back, hands and face, he said in his thick accent how fortunate he was that he wasn't killed. The most serious injury he could find was a sprained wrist and ankle. He told Paul the bump on his forehead was turning shades of purple, but it wasn't serious and would heal in a week or so, and he would be sore for at least that long. The doctor promised to check in on him in a few days. He left a bottle of Vicodin for his pain. Gerhard immediately offered him two and a full glass of water.

After swallowing the pills Paul lay still, holding an ice pack to his head. He closed his eyes and shut out the world, but the memory of the thundering rock smashing his car, of it exploding into flames, and the fire screaming across the road toward his gasoline-soaked hand, would not recede into the past.

Was there some kind of connection between his arrival in Savoy and his accident?

Despite what Giovanni Tosatti had told him, the duke so far was a most gracious host. Thoughts of the mess he left behind in California dissolved into a groggy mist as the medication started to work.

Gerhard recited the menu for the evening while he plumped up Paul's pillows and smoothed down the crimson comforter. Paul shook his head and mumbled how tired he was as the painkillers jumped his system. His eyelids fluttered uncontrollably as Gerhard stood over him and announced a visitor. When the servant lifted the ice pack from his head Paul thought he saw a tall, imposing man standing before him in a white dinner jacket, but his face wouldn't come into focus. The towering figure receded into a shadow as drowsiness overtook him.

Paul stood in an archway peering into a large room. A faint glow emanated from the far interior. The furnishings were only vague outlines against the darkness. Strolling through the room, he had the feeling he'd been there before. He had, but he didn't know when. When he saw a column of light, opalescent and opaque, in the center the room, he knew what was shrouded inside. His legs began to move forward of their own volition. His arms swung at his sides, his reluctance tempered by his curiosity. At the edge of the pillar, he could feel the heat from the light. It felt good.

"Paul, we're here waiting," she said. The same voice had called to him before.

A hand stretched through the wall of light, and he put his

hand in hers. Her grasp was soft and warm, the hold firm. He passed through the wispy barrier and stood beside her. Her blonde hair in lustrous curls cascaded around her face, down her shoulders. Her lips were red, her snow-white skin shone in the light; when she smiled she had little dimples on her cheeks. He followed her gaze.

The chair stood in the center of the light, luminous and bright as if it had been polished a thousand times. She guided him to it. He touched its warm surface.

"This is for you," she said.

He didn't want to sit in it, but he did. Why? He didn't know. He sat, feeling its strength. The air grew hotter, then flames mounted high around him in colorful licks, a raging fire. Someone put a hand on his shoulder. He tried to turn to see the face, but he couldn't move.

"The flames are good, Paul," the voice from behind him said. It was a deep voice, an aged voice, but strong. The hand stayed on his shoulder but the man was now at his side, now in front of him. The man's face, equine in shape, was withered, unsmiling, with shadows settled into the creases of the wrinkled flesh. His eyes were like pieces of coal that glowed hotter than the fire around them.

"The flames are good, Paul," he said like a chant that purled up into the billowing fire. But when Paul looked down at his hands resting on the arms of the chair they had melted and his bones lay bare and white, gleaming on the burnished wood.

He awoke, sweating. He sat up in bed, his heart pounding from the dream. He pulled his hands nearly to his nose and examined them. It was just a dream. But that face—the wretched black pock-marked face—was etched in his mind. Outside his bedroom window he heard a vibrant concerto of birds telling him he was back in the real world now and everything was okay. The bright morning sunshine filtered in. A polite but insistent knock interrupted the songfest. He called for the visitor to enter.

Gerhard, dressed in a light blue waistcoat and matching slacks, stepped a few paces into the room with subdued civility, and announced that breakfast was served.

Several outfits were arranged on the two wing chairs opposite his bed. Paul was impressed. In the bathroom, a shaving kit was laid out on the marble countertop. He shaved slowly, a surge of pain rippling through his back. Paul dressed gingerly in a pair of dark wool slacks, a white Egyptian cotton dress shirt with the Savoy crest—a black eagle on a blood-red shield—on the left breast pocket, and a pair of black Italian loafers. He was surprised, but pleased, that everything fit. Checking himself in the mirror, he nodded his approval. He was ready to meet his host.

With his painful limp, he thought it would take him all morning to traverse the long hall, carpeted in a deep blue oriental pattern. The walls were paneled in rich dark wood with crystal sconce lamps staggered on each side. His head still hurt, but the throbbing had diminished. He couldn't put out of his mind the dreams he'd had now two nights in a row. What did they mean? Maybe nothing. It was probably just his anxiety over his father's condition.

Gerhard waited for him at the top of the stairs, and offered him a wooden cane.

"I thought you might benefit from this, Signore," he said.

Paul put his hand on the carved mother-of-pearl grip and rested his weight on the oak staff.

"Thank you. This will help."

He steadied himself by gripping the oak banister with his other hand. At the bottom of the stairs, Gerhard led him into the great room, then steered him left into a small dining room.

Three people stood at the far end of the square room. Paul

recognized Stein, and with him stood a tall aristocrat and a most beautiful young woman. He knew he'd never met her before, but she looked familiar somehow. They gathered around a silver setting of coffee laid out on a burnished rosewood buffet. Gerhard led Paul to the statuesque man in the middle.

"Signore LaBont, may I present His Excellency, the sixteenth Duke of Savoy, Frederick de lá Cloy." Gerhard gave a slight bow and stepped back.

"Signore LaBont, welcome to Savoy," Frederick said with a deep voice and the broad smile of a man in control. He extended his large, puffy hand and they shook warmly. "I am so sorry about your accident last night," he said in English, with a noticeable but elegant Italian accent.

Paul liked Frederick's firm grip. He studied his host as they shook hands. The man stood well over six feet, probably six-four, with a deep tan, and oval face. His receding hairline with his high forehead gave him an intelligent look. His thick, wavy black hair was combed straight back, with distinguishing hints of gray on his short side burns. He wore a navy blazer, powder blue shirt, and cream-colored pants.

"I appreciate your kindness and your hospitality," Paul said. The man had such an elegant way about him.

Frederick nodded slightly, flashed an acknowledging smile, and then turned to his right. "And this is my daughter, Lady Isabella."

She offered her hand. It was white and delicate with a soft grip. Her smile made Paul forget the pain in his legs. He stood stunned, his gaze fixed on her face. He'd seen her before, he was sure of it. The creamy-white skin, the delicate hold on his hand, the full red lips.

"A pleasure to meet you," she said with a look of interest that seemed more genuine than a Picasso original.

Paul held her hand, continuing to shake it. Her wavy strawberry blonde hair flowed gently around the white skin of her face and neck, cascading down her shoulders, her soft green eyes were polished emeralds. His dreams, he'd seen her in his dreams. He had to be imaging this.

"Excuse me," he said letting her hand go. She wore a navy blue suit with flowing pants, and a low-cut, white-silk blouse.

She dropped her hand to her side. "I've heard so much about your father's work. I am so sorry he couldn't come with you." Her gold necklace glinted in the morning light.

He couldn't help but notice the little dimple on each cheek when she smiled. It was the same woman, of that he was certain. "I'm sure he would be here if he could. I suppose you've heard about his accident."

"Yes. I'm so sorry," Frederick said.

"How is your father doing?" Isabella asked in her contralto voice.

"Not well."

"That is grievous news for you and for us who appreciate his work," Frederick said with solicitude.

Gerhard pulled out a chair for Isabella to be seated. She took her place on her father's right. Frederick motioned for Paul to sit next to him, directly across from Isabella.

Stein sat to her right. Every time Paul glanced at Isabella, the thin, wiry man gave Paul a penetrating look with his steel gray eyes.

Breakfast started with a cup of steaming cappuccino, a plate of pastries, which Gerhard served with silver tongs from a hand-worked silver platter. Then he served a plate of fruit.

"Has Gerhard taken good care of you?" Frederick asked.

"Yes, thank you." Paul speared a piece of cantaloupe with his fork. He glanced up at Isabella and caught her staring at him. She quickly lowered her eyes.

"I took the liberty of having Jacob make arrangements for your car," Frederick said. "I have a friend in the American Consulate in Turin, and I spoke to him this morning. He said he would work on replacing your passport, but he will need to speak to you personally."

"Thank you. You're thoughtful," Paul said.

"I went back to your car after I left you here last night," Stein added. "The fire department had arrived and doused the flame. There wasn't much left, except for the rental company's decal on the back bumper. I contacted them and they made arrangements to have it towed and replaced."

Paul gave him a nod of thanks. "That's some mountain pass you have there."

Frederick laughed loudly, Stein joined in and Isabella gave him a bright smile.

"You at least have a sense of humor," Frederick said. "Mont-Cenis has a long history for our family. It is where Humbert the Whitehanded, the founder of the House of Savoy, defeated Eudos of Champagne."

"You would think it would run out of rocks to throw around after so many centuries," Paul said, not wanting to spoil the convivial spirit, but trying to dig a little deeper into its history.

"Exactly what we have thought for many years," Frederick said, "but the geologists tell us that the harsh winters and the composition of the soil in this area constantly causes shifting and disruption in these mountain peaks. It is a natural phenomenon."

The explanation seemed plausible. Yet, he distinctly remembered hearing someone walking around the hillside. His host seemed too polite for such Machiavellian actions. As he sipped his coffee, he saw again the stream of fire angling across the darkened road raging toward him, as if it purposely had hunted him down. He shook off the thought.

"The doctor informed me of the extent of your injuries. You are welcome to stay, if it helps you to heal," Frederick said, waving his hand in the air.

"I appreciate your generosity." Paul said. Tosatti's warning not to stay in Savoy still rung in his ears, but the man's hospitality and old-world charm enchanted him.

"We would love for you to stay for a while and see the sights," Isabella said. "There is so much to see."

Paul pursed his lips. "I hadn't made plans to stay."

"If you must get back to Milan," Stein said. "I put myself at your disposal."

"I am certain," Frederick added, "he will get you there quickly and safely. Whatever your pleasure is, please let me know. As for your clothes, Gerhard will see to everything you need."

He thought about Frederick's offer as he sipped his cappuccino. What would a day or two matter? He wanted to spend a few days in museums of Milan before heading home, but staying a few days wouldn't put too much of a crimp in his plans. He glanced up at Isabella.

I would like to paint her portrait.

This was the first time he'd been truly motivated to take up his brush for some weeks.

"The gardens are marvelous this time of the year, Signore LaBont," she said.

"You can call me Paul," he said, and then finished his pastry.

She smiled. "Have you ever seen the Alps in the spring, Paul?" The light from the window behind her turned her hair a shimmering blonde.

"Have you ever seen the Pacific Ocean on a summer's day?"

"Yes, I have."

Paul raised his eyebrows, a tad chagrined. "You've been to California?"

"Stanford, Class of '97." Her smile turned into a smirk, as if pulling out her credentials was a bit of fun.

Paul rested his forearms on the table. He tilted his head slightly to the side as he spoke. "No, I have never seen the Alps in spring."

She smiled and flipped her hair off her shoulder. "I would be glad to show you around."

His bruises wouldn't heal for a few more days. The idea of staying awhile grew on him. Besides, the chair wasn't going anywhere. More time here meant more of an opportunity to accomplish his mission. And having a Stanford-educated princess as a docent in a private mountain museum wasn't a bad way to convalesce. But speaking to Frederick was his priority, and it would be easier if he did it right away. Paul didn't think he could relax until they'd talked.

"It sounds like a great idea," he said to Isabella. Shifting his gaze to Frederick, "But first I must discuss some business with your father."

"Please," Frederick said, in his most avuncular manner, "in Italy time is not money. I am told you are a great art connoisseur. There is so much to see in Savoy. When you are feeling better, then we will talk. In the meanwhile, let Isabella show you around. If you will excuse me, I have some pressing matters to attend to." Frederick pushed his chair back and rose, as did Stein. The two left the room.

A silence fell over the breakfast table. His mind flooded with questions. How could he have dreamed of a woman he'd never met?

She pushed her chair back and stood up. "I know you have many questions, and there's a lot to see and enjoy. Would you like to get started?"

He folded the linen napkin, put it on the table, and pushed his chair back. She came around the table and weaved her arm under his as he stood, and they walked out into the great room.

"As long as we move slowly, I'll be okay," he said, resting his weight on his cane.

"I shall start by giving you a little history of the House of Savoy and how my great-grandfather rebuilt the castle after World War I," she said with the self-assurance of one who had told the story many times.

"Please, lead on." They slowly walked together and stopped in the middle of the gleaming marble floor.

With her free hand, Isabella pointed straight up. They both craned their necks to look up at the soaring ceilings. "This is the great room where we begin our story."

As he gazed up at the marvelous frescos, he couldn't help but fear she intended to lead him into the room with the chair and force him to sit in it. Would he burn like he had in his dream? He shook off those thoughts. She was far too pretty, too polite, and too cultured for such a ridiculous scheme. Besides, the chair was powerless, wasn't it?

Wisdom ... is the only true riches of the mind.

—Leonardo da Vinci, *Notebooks*

10

Stein followed the duke out of the dining room, and into the corridor leading to a staircase. They ascended two flights together. At the landing Stein grabbed the duke's arm, pulling him into a corner.

"I feel uneasy about taking our time with LaBont. We need to get on with our project," Stein said urgently but with a low voice.

The duke pulled his arm out of Stein's grasp, and smoothed the wrinkles from his coat sleeve. "You're overreacting. He has just arrived. If we push him too fast it could scare him."

"We've already wasted a couple of weeks waiting for LaBont to arrive. We can't wait anymore. Did you forget that unless we have a masterpiece to sell in the next month, you're going to lose control of your own castle? You have financial obligations that must be met."

The duke stood erect and pursed his lips. "None of that has slipped my mind. But we can only take one step at a time."

"Tosatti will be here in a few days to check on our progress and we'll have nothing to show him. He's already getting itchy about the money he's fronted you."

The duke sighed, and put his hands on Stein's powerful shoulder. "I know the urgency, my friend."

Stein pushed the duke's hand away. "This is no time for cold feet."

"You saw what that mountain did to LaBont's car, and what it almost did to him." He stared unblinking at Stein. "We must proceed carefully."

"Isabella wants to use the chair. There's no reason to keep her from it."

"You have no daughter, have you?"

"If she were my daughter, I would take her by the hand and lead her to the chair—and show her how to use it. Every great achievement entails an element of risk."

"How profound," the duke replied. "We agreed that when LaBont came to Savoy to retrieve his chair, we'd persuade him to complete our plan. That's what we shall do. I will not have Isabella's life jeopardized under any circumstances. Is that clear?" The duke notched his head up a degree.

"You are giving into your superstitious tendencies, Frederick. This is your moment to get what you want. Don't be stupid."

The duke clenched his jaw. Before he could respond, Stein stomped up the stairs and disappeared. There was much in this little operation that gave him pause, and working with Stein was turning out to be one of its more unpleasant elements. He could tolerate Stein's mocking attitude toward him for the period of time the two had to work together, but the man's willingness to let Isabella so easily slip into a role that could destroy her infuriated him. He was not certain what destructive powers the chair still possessed and that bothered him even more deeply. For some time he had entertained the possibility the chair had lost its destructive curse, especially since LaBont had used it for nearly forty years without any "accident." But the fact that the senior LaBont had nearly died in a disfiguring accident rekindled all of his fears about the chair. And the mountain slide that nearly killed young LaBont only caused Frederick even more concern. There were too many accidents, too much history that he'd uncovered about those who had used the chair to take these incidents as merely coincidental. No, his attempts to use its powers must be measured, despite the pressures around him.

But what shook him even deeper than any of these fears was the trepidation that there was nothing he could do to stop Isabella from tapping into the chair's mysterious powers. He'd known of her ambitions to paint like the masters that decorated the walls and ceilings of the castle ever since she was a child. But even if he forbade her to go near it, she had as much disdain for the testimonies of their ancestors as Stein did. He knew she couldn't hold out very long under the temptation of its power. He had to continue to search for a remedy for the chair's curse and in the meantime persuade LaBont to taste its power, to see with his own eyes if the curse had been lifted.

Later that morning, the duke strode across the marble floor of the great room to greet two guests. He would have to work hard to be pleasant with these men. Ando Giamatti, director of Banco National's trust department, had called yesterday and insisted on today's meeting. The duke didn't expect his personal visit was social. He'd successfully put the banker off in the past, but Giamatti was adamant this meeting take place. In Italy news about every aspect of life traveled slowly, except about money. Only a few days ago the duke had inquired at a bank in Milan about a personal loan using some of the castle's paintings as collateral, a feinting maneuver to forestall his creditors. He couldn't tap the family trust fund any longer, and a small six-figure loan seemed like such simple business. He never imagined such a small sum would reach Giamatti's radar, but then here he was in the duke's home.

The duke greeted them as if he had invited them himself. Giamatti introduced his tall, wiry associate as Carlo Poma, managing director of the bank's legal staff. The duke shook his hand and tried to evade the man's sharp gaze without seeming obvious. He ushered both of them—dressed in dark Armani suits, their ties smartly knotted—into a small book-lined library off the great room. He offered them drinks, but they declined. A fire crackled in the stone fireplace. After closing the doors, the duke seated himself on a sofa across from them. They were separated by a polished rosewood coffee table centered on a lush Oriental carpet, only a few feet in terms of distance, but in coldness, an unbridgeable gulf.

"To what do I owe this visit?" the duke said at his amiable best. He sat back and crossed his legs.

"It has come to our attention," Giamatti began, "that you've inquired about selling some of the trust's assets."

"Not quite. I am merely arranging some bridge financing with some of the castle's paintings as collateral," the duke said confidently.

"Signore Giamatti asked me to this meeting," Poma said, "to remind you of the articles governing the family trust."

"I'm aware of how the trust works," the duke replied.

"Evidently not, Frederick," Giamatti said, leaning forward. "As the trustee and legal owner of the castle and all its furnishings, we are to be consulted before an encumbrance is placed on any of the trust's property. Considering the current financial condition of the trust, I cannot allow you to encumber any of the castle's assets. Everything purchased with trust money is under the trust's control."

"You put me in an awkward position, signors," the duke said calmly. "My understanding is that I have full latitude to administer the affairs of Savoy."

"In light of your current financial condition, it's incumbent upon us as fiduciaries to take a more active role," Poma said.

The duke sighed and uncrossed his legs. "Is the loan the only reason you came all this way?"

Giamatti sat forward. "There is a more pressing matter. One we have discussed with you many times over the last several years."

"You speak of the balance in the trust fund," the duke said dryly.

"Rather the lack thereof," replied Poma, emphasizing his point with his hands.

"I've assured you repeatedly, Ando, I'm working on that," the duke said.

"And what good are your assurances at this point?" Giamatti said. "The trust has reached the point that it can no longer support the upkeep of the castle and its amazing collection, no less pay your annual stipend."

"Ando, please," the duke said, sitting forward on the edge of the cushion. "I will have a long-term solution to the financial ..."

Giamatti put his hand up to stop the discussion. "Frederick, you've been working on your so-called 'remedy' far too long. There is no longer a tomorrow."

The duke sank back into the sofa. "I sense you have come with a proposal."

Giamatti glanced at Poma who cleared his throat before speaking. "Prince Cassini, of the Turin branch of the Savoys ..."

"I'm familiar with who the prince is," the duke said, mildly irritated.

"Of course. Forgive me," Poma said. "The prince has offered to replenish the trust fund to self-sustaining levels, if ..."

"If what?"

"If he and his heirs are named beneficiaries and allowed to operate the castle."

The duke pursed his lips and took a deep breath.

"He has proposed a detailed plan to the board of trustees to make the castle's collection self-sustaining within three years," Poma said.

"Why was I not summoned to such a meeting?" the duke asked.

"The matter required urgency and the prince asked for an exclusive opportunity," Poma said.

The duke sat up and jabbed his finger in the air. "If I can remind *you* of the articles governing the trust, that is an illegal action."

"It's not without precedent under the circumstances," Poma said, forcefully. "We were within our rights to investigate every viable alternative to the financial solvency of the trust."

Giamatti frowned and studied his hands for a moment, then looked at the duke. "Frederick, I've warned you over the years to be careful how you spend. You've done a marvelous job with the collection, but you developed no sources of revenue as the prince has done with his holdings."

"So, Cassini wants to turn Savoy into a tourist stop with a gift shop selling cheap postcards and an espresso bar in the courtyard," he gestured toward the door. "The man just wants to see me homeless."

"That is not the case," Poma said.

"He would grant you and your heirs the Victor Emanuel palace in Turin," Giamatti added, speaking softly.

"What? And I should become a museum curator?" the duke said.

"Your choices are limited unless you have other abilities to earn a living," Poma said, his look as sharp as his words.

"I have a plan."

"Frederick, it's time to deal in reality. We can afford no more promises and fantasies. In three weeks you must make a decision or we will be forced to make one for you. I'm sorry." Giamatti took a packet of papers from his jacket pocket and laid them on the polished table. "Here are the details of the plan. The income you could expect, and the duties you would assume along with other particulars. The stipend is not what you're used to, but it is livable. It's the best we could do."

The duke studied the folded papers on the table then abruptly stood. "Thank you for stopping by, signors. I will give your recommendations serious consideration."

The two bankers stood and exchanged curt handshakes with the duke and left him standing alone. He took the documents off the table with a sweep of his hand and tapped them against his palm. Time was ebbing, but not completely gone. Unfolding the papers, he glanced at them. Prince Cassini had no scruples about throwing open the doors of the castle to the great unwashed to let them trample through these corridors just for a few measly lire. *Savoy will never become a museum.* He crushed the documents into a large ball, crossed the room to the fireplace, tossed them over the top of the wrought-iron screen, and watched the red-blue flame turn them to ash. The lost da Vinci must be completed soon.

My works are the issue of pure and simple experience, who is the one true mistress.

—Leonardo da Vinci, *Notebooks*

11

Slumping over the coffee maker a little before seven a.m., Marcella slowly scooped another tablespoon of French roast into its basket. Lynette slid into the kitchen with a smile to match the morning sunshine.

"Since when did you start drinking coffee?" she asked, in her slight Texas accent. She stood, hands in her jeans pockets, beside Marcella.

"Since I started working twelve-hour days," Marcella said, flicking the coffee maker on and coasting over to the oak table. She slumped into a chair. Marcella wrapped her burgundy silk robe tightly around her and patted down her hair, which she hadn't felt like brushing. Lynette not only looked perky, but her hair was combed and her makeup already done. Her wavy dark hair, red blush high on her cheeks reminded Marcella of what she used to look like when she had more time to take care of herself.

Lynette took two mugs from the cabinet and placed them

next to the rumbling coffee maker, then eased into a chair across from her sister. The morning light flooded the warm breakfast nook through a large window.

"Don't you think you're pushing yourself too hard?" Lynette asked. "I mean, all you've done since I've been here is paint."

Marcella propped both elbows on the table and rested her head on her hands and stared at her.

"Okay, okay. If this is something you really think you've got to do ..." Lynette leaned forward and put her hands on Marcella's forearms. "Just be careful. Those horrid dark circles under your eyes have come back these last few days."

Marcella poked the puffy sacks around her eyes. "I know, but I have to have this piece done by this afternoon when Rhonda and her friend come over. Rhonda begged me to have at least a couple of seascapes to go with my landscapes, and I can have the second one done by noon if I get to work."

"Is starting your career at this stage in your life really necessary? I mean, do you really think Vincent won't be able to paint again?"

"Whether Vincent makes a full recovery or not, my painting is important to me."

Lynette raised her palms toward her sister like a pair of stop signs. "I just want to make certain you know what you're doing."

Marcella had thought about painting again for such a long time, and now when her resolve had finally translated into action she didn't need someone feeding her own self-doubts. She pushed her chair back and pulled herself up, poured two cups of coffee, and brought them back to the table.

"Thanks," Lynette said.

Marcella spooned some nondairy creamer into her cup, and stirred the hot liquid languidly. "I've known what I wanted for a long time."

"It always amazed me that you stopped painting," Lynette said, then let out a short laugh. "I remember when you decided to do that Monet thing. Everyone thought you were nuts."

She lowered her cup to the table. "You were convinced I had lost it."

Lynette sighed, and rolled her eyes. "I couldn't believe you wanted to paint ten pictures of the same mountain just because some dead artist painted a church—"

"The Ruen Cathedral," Marcella said.

Lynette looked at her sister with a furrowed brow. "He painted The Ruen Cathedral twenty times."

"Twenty-six."

"I remember you explaining to Mom and Dad that you wanted to experiment with light, and ..."

"But you were certain I was crazy, weren't you?"

"I was a sophomore in high school, and you were in junior high. Everything your little sister does is stupid," Lynette said with a measure of hesitation in her voice.

"Sometimes, I *was* pretty annoying."

Lynette leaned forward, letting out a sigh as if she was working hard inside to dredge up something. "I've wanted to tell you this for a long time. After I saw all those paintings of the Sierra on the front porch that day, I was breathless. I felt bad about giving you such a hard time. They were all done so well. They were all the same, yet I could see the differences between them. I listened to you explain them to Dad. I ...," she lowered her voice. "I was a little envious."

"Envious! You! The 4.0 student, the class valedictorian, the homecoming queen. Come on, you were so much better than me. You had more boyfriends—"

"Marcella, please. As I stood behind you that day and listened, I knew what you had was special. Not only did you have a gift, but also you had the drive to pursue it. I was ... I was proud of you."

Marcella took her sister's hands and held them tight. "Did you really think that?"

Lynette's cheeks reddened. "I've always thought you would paint something great, something fantastic."

"But I never wanted to be famous," Marcella protested as she brushed a tangle of hair out of her face.

"But don't you see? I knew that. Mom and Dad knew that. All you wanted to do was create. You didn't care if it was perfect, you just loved it. I think that's why everything you did came out so beautiful." A serious glare crossed her face, and she lowered her voice. "You must really love Vincent to have given up so much."

"I still do." Marcella thought for a moment. "I never thought of it in terms of what I gave up. To support such a talented artist like Vincent and to teach my son to paint were gifts I wanted to give."

"Well, then, this time to paint is a gift to you," Lynette said, standing up. "I guess that's why I've come all the way from the great state of Texas, to help my little sister."

Marcella felt a lump in her throat. She'd always dreamed that someday she'd have the time to pursue her passion, and that someday had arrived with the least likely booster. She stood and embraced her sister in a silent hug, one she sensed bridged the gap of all those years of misunderstanding.

"I'm sorry for all those mean things I said to you growing up," Lynette said.

Marcella held her sister tightly. "I'm sorry for being such a brat."

They were both silent for a moment.

"I'll rustle up some breakfast. Why don't you go get ready to work? I'll tidy the place up for your guests," Lynette said, letting her sister go. She scooted over to the stove to start cooking.

After eating, dressed in her work clothes of faded Levis, an old denim shirt, and tennis shoes, Marcella made her way to the small studio in the back bedroom. Her half-finished seascape lay on the workbench. Working off a set of photographs she had taken when she and Paul had vacationed in Cabo San Lucas, she picked a stretch of deserted beach to paint that had particularly excited her.

Every time she walked that lonely stretch of sand during her stay she felt startled by the blueness of the sky. The brisk westerly winds pushed the cumulus clouds over the horizon like herds of animals on a bright veldt of air. They were a canopy to her thoughts. The crystal-clear water stood in transparent pools among the rocks, off shore the water transmuted into different hues of blue-green. The white trackless sand created a timeless sense, as though the elements had worked in concert for eons just so that she could bask in its beauty for a few silent moments.

These unadulterated colors didn't pose questions as much as offer bright variegated answers. If she could capture the essences of these colors on canvas she was convinced the viewer would be thrilled with her work the way she was thrilled with what she saw. Leaning over her workbench, she felt an unsettling fear that she didn't have the skill in her hands to bring forth what she saw in her mind. Yesterday she had laid down a light blue wash, then using the wet into wet technique applied viridian into the sea until it turned the shade of blue-green she'd seen. The colors had dried into a soft and wispy look, as if the Pacific Ocean air soughed across her painted paper. Now that all the paint had dried, she could use her fine sable brushes to fill in the details of the clouds, the rocks, and sea turtles lying in the sunshine. She kept at it until what she saw in the eye of her mind came to life on her board. Nearly finished, she took a break and let it dry, then placed the painting on her easel by the window. Under direct sunlight from the window, she worked with her finest sable brush at the delicate final touches. Stepping back with her paintbox in one hand, and her brush in the other, she admired her work. The color was nice, but not perfect, not exactly the way she had envisioned it. But it would do.

Glancing at her watch, it was nearly noon. She took another peek at the seascape. In the midst of her deep satisfaction she wished Vincent were here to share her joy, the way she had shared his. But for now, she would have to harbor her pleasure alone. If she had to feed herself on her own sense of accomplishment, she could do that. But she treasured a tiny ray of wishful thinking that it would not always be so.

Padding down the hall to the kitchen she heard Lynette washing the dishes. She had prepared a fresh spinach salad for both of them, which was laid out on the table. She decided to sit down and eat now, figuring she had enough time to eat lunch, freshen up, change her clothes and do a little primping before her guests arrived. She didn't want to look frumpy and covered with paint. Not with Rhonda coming over.

Before their salads were half eaten, someone knocked vigorously at the door.

Lynette gave her a look of surprise, then jumped up to answer it. Marcella worked on finishing her salad. She heard Rhonda's distinctive, high-pitched voice in the living room. Marcella shoved the food into her mouth with her finger and bolted from the table. If she could make the bedroom before Rhonda greeted her, then she wouldn't come out until she was ready.

Before Marcella could reach the hall Rhonda appeared in the doorway.

"Marcella, darling. You look so ... so positively rustic." Rhonda glided across the floor, her stiletto heels clicking on the ceramic tile. She rested her hand on her shoulder. "I can see you've been a busy bee. Sorry we're so early, but Scott has to be in L.A. by three. You know that drive takes hours."

Marcella rubbed her hands together, trying to purge the paint from her skin. "Scott who?"

"Scott Bezcotta, the gallery owner from L.A.," Rhonda said, placing her long index finger on her cheek and smiling like someone who had just let out a deep, dark secret.

"*That* Scott?" Of course Marcella knew of Scott Bezcotta. He might come to her house to see Vincent, but not her.

"I told you I'd help you, honey." She smiled mischievously.

"He's one of the largest gallery owners in L.A."

Rhonda put her hands on her hips and stood like a statue in her purple pantsuit, red hair, and dangling gold earrings. "I think that's where your work belongs. Come on, now's not the time to dawdle." She gripped Marcella by the arm and led her toward the living room, clicking as she went. "He's dying to meet you."

"But, Rhonda, let me go clean up at least—"

Rhonda swished a long white hand in the air, a gold ring on each finger. "P-l-e-a-s-e," she said dragging out the word. "Scott loves the dung-in-the-stables look. He's a real hoot."

Marcella tried to protest, but soon realized it was fruitless. Her home had turned into Rhonda's show. The woman had a need to orchestrate everything, but she did it with panache.

"Scott, here's the LaBont you've never heard of," Rhonda said, nearly dragging Marcella into the living room.

Scott Bezcotta, a dapper man in a tan double-breasted suit wasn't overly handsome, but he had a sincere presence to him that intrigued Marcella. His intelligent, soft brown eyes made him easy to approach. His sandy brown hair was parted on the side, with short sideburns. His face was long, with a strong chin. He offered his hand.

"Marcella, so glad to meet you. Rhonda has been singing your praises nonstop."

As they shook, something about his manner told her she could relax; he was here to help.

This might be okay.

Marcella had met so many gallery owners over the years but always on behalf of her famous husband. But now this man shaking her hand was here to cast a critical eye over her little babies, to examine her craft like a doctor giving her a physical; it felt a little invasive. Her stomach felt queasy. She wasn't certain how she would hold up if he didn't like her work.

"Listen, honey, Scott doesn't have a lot of time," Rhonda said. "He has to meet with a client who wants to spend, spend, spend ... so where are your little darlings?"

"Oh, yes." They followed her down the hall. Once in the back room, she ushered them in and took a seat on a small chair in the far corner. She had already arranged the finished paintings along the wall across from the window. The light hitting the colors on her canvases gave them a shimmering effect. The one she had just completed was propped on the easel drying. She crossed her legs and put a finger to her lips. Lynette came in, stood beside her, laying her hand on Marcella's shoulder.

Scott looked over the first one carefully, and nodded. He turned his head to one side then the other, as if to look at it from different angles, then moved to the next one and nodded again without saying anything.

The man's silence was irritating. Marcella fidgeted. It was going on longer than it needed to. He should just come out and say something. But she had seen a sophistication in those soft brown eyes of his, a sense that he had spent a considerable amount of time around artists and knew the fickleness of their temperaments. If he didn't like them he wouldn't say anything. Rather, he would be polite and nod, give a slight bow of appreciation, shake her hand warmly, tell her how much her work reminded him of John Sell Cotman or Jean Dubuffet, and then she would never hear from him again.

She watched as he slowly stepped sideways down the line of paintings inspecting them like a master in a slave market. At the last one he stopped and bent over, nearly putting his face to the colored surface.

He probably hates the colors and thinks my brushwork is unrefined. This is ridiculous. I should have never listened to Rhonda.

Standing up, he pulled his coat jacket down, smoothed down his tie, and tucked it back under his coat. Turning to Marcella with an intent look on his face, he asked, "Are there any more?"

She shook her head. Why? So he could embarrass her thoroughly?

"I'm impressed. These six are ready to go, if you want to sell them." He pointed to the ones along the wall.

The room was silent. Marcella didn't think she understood him. "You like them?"

Scott looked at Rhonda as if they were finishing a conversation.

"She's such a dear, isn't she?" Rhonda said, standing in the corner by the door with her arms folded under her breasts. "I mean, what do I know? Go ahead—you tell her."

Scott hesitated as if he was looking for just the right words. He leaned forward and spoke with a soothing voice. "Marcella, you have an exquisite touch. Your brushwork is sophisticated; your use of washes is unique. I think your overall technique is superior to many painters today. My patrons know the value of fine art and they'll pay top dollar for your work."

Marcella wanted to cry, but instead she put her fist to her mouth to stifle anything that might come out.

He gave her a quizzical look. "Did I say something to offend you?"

She still couldn't talk.

"I think, actually, she's happy," Lynette said, in her slight Texas drawl. "Why don't you take and sell them?" She patted Marcella's shoulder.

Scott gave Marcella a sympathetic glance. "I'm sorry but I have to run. It's been a pleasure meeting you." He held out his hand, and she stood to shake it. "So, you'll let me show your work at my next exhibit?"

She nodded her head but didn't say a word.

"Good, I'll send someone around to pick these up," he said, looking her in the eyes. He enfolded their joined hands with his other one. "I will take care of everything for you," he said. "You just paint."

"Thank you," she said.

"You'll be coming up for the show, won't you?" Scott said, his brown eyes warm with encouragement.

"Of course," Marcella said.

Scott left, followed by Rhonda, and after a few minutes Lynette left too, leaving Marcella alone.

Plopping back down into the seat, she took a deep breath. She quivered inside, but not from fear. That had been the most nerve-wracking yet satisfying meeting she'd ever had with a gallery owner. She liked him; he made her feel accepted; part of the club she'd always wanted to join. She knew all along she could paint, and a sense of vindication grew within her. Why had she ever listened to Vincent? He'd done nothing but ridicule her work, and he was always so obsessed with classical painting, and that stupid chair of his. Her work was every bit as important as his.

When Vincent came home, she intended to have a talk with him about her work. But right now she wanted to bask in this glow of accomplishment, and for the moment bury the creeping fear about Vincent's reaction to her new career.

Though I may not ... be able to quote other authors,
I shall rely on that which is much greater
and more worthy—on experience.

—Leonardo da Vinci, *Notebooks*

12

Craning his neck to scan the high ceiling of the great room, Paul became lost studying the pageantry of colorful figures swirling above his head. The center of the fresco was dominated by a majestic figure in flowing robes descending out of the clouds through a brilliant blue sky. At his feet a man, who had just fallen off his horse, lay flat on his back writhing in pain with an anguished look of fear on his face. Other panels radiated out from the center in a cornucopia of color and action. Paul struggled to take in the breadth of the scenes as they unfolded over his head.

"My ancestor Umberto Godvico painted this ceiling in 1563," Isabella said.

"Incredible!" Paul said, straining to take it all in. The room was long, probably a hundred feet, and at least sixty feet wide. "This is as big as the Sistine Chapel," Paul said.

"Bigger," Isabella said with the self-assurance of an experienced tour guide. "The Sistine Chapel, which took Michelangelo four years to paint, is 5,880 square feet. This room is 6,543 square feet.

Umberto used the same fresco technique as Michelangelo, but he finished this work in three years."

"Umberto Godvico. I've never heard of him," Paul said, studying the panels of the ceiling.

"He died young, and this is his only extant piece." She pointed to the center panel with the angelic figure coming down out of heaven. "He chose as his theme the conversion of the world, starting with Saul of Tarsus. That large figure in the center is Jesus Christ, and the man lying on the ground is the Apostle Paul."

"Yes, I see," Paul said, letting his eyes wonder over the panels. The one next to St. Paul was of the twelve disciples in the Upper Room, when told by Jesus to go into the whole world and preach the Gospel. In each direction he looked, Paul saw the disciples going out in the city streets of the world converting the heathen. He couldn't stop himself from studying each section of painting.

"There is much more." She took him by the arm and led him across the marble floor through a set of double mahogany doors leading into the grand banquet room.

The polished dark wooden table down the middle was long enough to seat a hundred people. Silver candelabras were placed every few feet, and silver chandeliers hung from the ceiling. But it was the fresco on the far wall that caught his attention.

Isabella guided him around the table until they stood in front of the painting that had caught his eye. The mural took up the length of the wall.

"The original is in the Galleria dell' Accademia, in Venice. Veronese painted it for the Doge of Venice. My ancestor re-created it, in its entirety, and exact in every detail to the original. It's called, *Christ in the House of Levi.*"

Paul swiped his hand through his hair. "I've never seen the original, but it can't be much better than this. This ... this is astonishing. Who painted this one?"

"Ecco Godvico in 1609," Isabella said. Putting her hands behind her back like a docent, she approached the muraled wall. "Christ is in the middle of the loggia seated at the banquet table with Levi next to him. Veronese set Christ in contemporary Venice, with the rich and famous of the day seated with him, but also clowns, misfits, and others the local Holy Inquisitors objected to. They accused the painter of impiety for positioning sinners so close to Christ, so he had to redo portions of the work at his own expense." She turned to Paul and gave him a serious look. "My ancestor reproduced it as Veronese had intended." She motioned toward the far corner of the painting. "Sinners are seated with Christ. And they are the better for it." She fixed her green eyes on him; the light made them sparkle. "Don't you think?"

He couldn't say if the poor were better off seated closer to Christ than farther away. What did proximity to Christ have to do with being rich or poor or blessed or not blessed? This seemed like such an arcane question. He'd forgotten how beholden the Renaissance painters were to religious themes. He'd only seen their works in books, which were mere shadows compared to the originals. "Why were the Inquisitors so adamant about the poor not being close to Christ?" He asked hoping it wasn't a stupid question.

She pivoted on the balls of her feet in military precision and gave him an odd smile. "I forgot, you're from California. These paintings must seem foreign to you."

He shrugged. "I've never had an opportunity to study Renaissance art up close."

"Of course." She turned to the wall. "The story is that Jesus came to the Jews as a poor carpenter, but he displayed all the power and signs that he was the Messiah promised to the world since the days of Adam and Eve. In those days religious men did not have anything to do with the common sinners like beggars, prostitutes, and tax gatherers. But Jesus counted many of these kind," she pointed to the poorly dressed men and women at the end of table, "as his converts. This infuriated the religious men of the age, who thought Jesus should favor *them*."

"And the Holy Inquisitors wanted to uphold that tradition of only showing the favor of God to those who needed it least?"

She gave him quick glance. "The religious men of the time didn't really understand the power of the Christian myth to appeal to the social outcasts."

Paul rested his weight on the pearl handle of the cane. He looked again at the mural on the wall. The banquet table on the wall seemed as long as the actual one behind him. The skyline of Renaissance Venice was in the background behind three monumental arches. Paul stepped closer to examine it. The faces, the architectural detail, the variety of expressions were so realistic. The brushwork was deft and precise. Paul knew Veronese to be one of the last *maestros* of High Renaissance craftsmanship. But this painting was perfect. The vibrant colors shimmered. The artist had skillfully used the whole spectrum, but avoided the solid colors for half-shades—light blues, sea greens, lemon yellows, rose, and violet—creating flowerbeds of tone. The beautiful craftsmanship made his heart race. It was beyond compare. Veronese himself, by some miracle, had been transported to this isolated castle sequestered in the Alps. But how? "This piece is like looking at the original."

"Yes, it is," Isabella said. "Veronese's intentions are clear in that he wanted to depict man's basic instinct for closeness to God. It was a recurring theme in Renaissance art."

He perused the figures on the wall once again. He'd been looking at the painting solely as an artistic achievement, but it was now evident that as important as that was, it was the religious significance of the painting that compelled Isabella's attention. He looked at the long table again with Jesus in the middle. The crowd of well-dressed nobles on one side of Jesus and the beggars and prostitutes on the other were both accepted by him as equals. Closeness to God. That certainly was one of the aims of the religious art of Renaissance times. "Is such a thing really possible?"

She stopped and turned slowly toward him. She looked at him with such a sublime expression as if she'd been asked the perfect question. "Every culture has its tradition of God. This," she motioned toward the wall, "depicts our tradition. Jesus is said to be the Son of God, so he brings us God's message, which in our country is found in the rituals of the Holy Catholic Church. But to answer your question directly, I think our rituals only allow us a proximity to God, not an actual intimacy, as experienced by the men in the painting who were said to have actually dined with Jesus."

She turned and promenaded down the length of the painting. Paul followed behind her, limping. All of the paintings he'd seen so far depicted the religious yearnings of the times. People seemed more concerned about such things back then. He'd always been so busy with his work, he just hadn't give much thought to religious things. Following behind Isabella, he noticed she was a nice work of art herself: her long blonde hair, the color of sunshine, played down her back. He couldn't help but notice her slim figure in her tailored pantsuit.

"Your family's very talented."

"Thank you. Please, let me show you more." She stopped and let him catch up and hooked her arm in his and strolled at his limping pace out of the dinning room into a long hall that served as a gallery. Isabella explained that the castle was built in a rectangle. The corridors they now traversed were originally designed to connect the towers in each of the four corners. The rooms off to their left once held the various services and functions the castle's occupants needed to survive: smithy shops, barracks for troops, stables, granaries, food storage. The castle had gone through many remodels, with the most recent one right after World War I by her grandfather. The halls, where they now walked, had been completely gutted and made into galleries for his burgeoning collection. The stone walls were paneled, and new marble covered the ancient floors.

They entered another section of the long corridor, which had been transformed into a long portrait gallery. The walls had rich walnut paneling and delicately carved crown molding.

"This is the family portrait gallery," Isabella said, with a flourish of her hand toward the long row of portraits. She stopped at the first portrait, which looked old.

"This is the first Duke of Savoy and founder of the house, Humbert the Whitehanded. He received our ancestral lands from the Holy Roman emperor Conrad II in 1035."

Paul studied the dark portrait. The technique was ancient, two dimensional, bereft of later advances in perspective and chiaroscuro, the use of light and shadow. But the nobility and fierce countenance of the man shone through as he stood in front of a dark drape with his left hand in a white glove on the hilt of his sword; the other resting by his side. Isabella moved along the line of portraits, showing him ancestor after ancestor, gradually unfolding the pageantry of the House of Savoy. The men were conquerors, warriors, king makers, and had built a family heritage through war and conquest in an age that had slipped beneath the sea of time. But within these walls they lived in memories as vivid as the bright mural on the dining room wall.

She explained the history of the House of Savoy. There were many branches of the family, from Spain, Germany, Italy, and Austria. The Godvico branch, which she had descended from, was from Tuscany and had been the artists of the clan. Their works resided solely in this castle.

Paul agreed with that assessment as he listened patiently. The early portraits were flat and somewhat crude, as the artists were merely practicing the level of craft popular at the time. But the portraits done by the Godvicos starting in the late Renaissance were outstanding. He had rarely seen such brilliance. They reminded him of ones his father had done over the years. The brushstrokes, the use of color and perspective, and the classical poses had a vague similarity.

Paul stopped in front of the last portrait. It was of a young man that looked familiar, not only the face, but there was a glimmer of recognition in the artist's work. He had seen it before.

"Who's this?" Paul asked. It was the portrait of a man, sitting regal and erect, wearing the ducal sash of the House of Savoy.

"That's my father."

"I thought he looked familiar. Who painted him?" Paul bent forward to read the signature. He froze, not believing what he saw.

"Do you recognize the signature?" she asked.

"This can't be." He slowly shook his head.

"Your father did that more than twenty years ago."

Paul straightened up. *Dad never mentioned he met the duke.*

"I didn't know that the duke and my father had ever met."

"They were both young. It probably wasn't a meeting your father remembers. He's done so many portraits since then."

"But how can this be?" Paul said, not wanting to move until she explained everything.

She tugged on his arm. "I'm sure my father will explain it to you. Come. There's so much more." Isabella guided him through room after room and he saw some of the most amazing pieces. Some were originals, others copies, but all were astounding examples of high Renaissance art. They all carried religious themes, which was common for the time. Paul had a sense that Savoy was more than a house full of collected works. Certainly there was a prodigious collection of the masters, but the heart and soul of the work he saw were reproductions: perfect reproductions. Ones done with such skill and craftsmanship, even the masters themselves would have trouble telling them apart from their own work. What was going on here?

Once they finished with the galleries in the north wing they entered the northwest tower on their way to the galleries in the west wing. Paul stopped near the center of the round tower, which must have been forty feet wide. A spiral marble staircase wound up into the air, all the way to the top. It stopped at a massive wooden door.

He gazed up the stairwell. "Are there more galleries up in the towers?"

"Not this one." She said leading him to the door into the west wing of the castle.

He didn't move, but continued to study the stairway. It had no visible supports and no balustrade along the edges. It had definitely been built during the Renaissance or before. It was an architectural marvel. It didn't look like it would even hold its own weight.

"This a magnificent stairwell."

She glanced up at it. "Completely unsupported. There is one transverse beam almost to the top that supports the walls, not the stairs. Many think Leonardo himself designed it."

Paul rested his injured foot on the bottom step just to take the weight off his ankle, so he could take a closer look up the winding stairwell. He had no intention of climbing it.

"Please, my father would be upset if anyone went up there."

He took his foot off the step. "May I ask why?"

"He stores his most cherished religious artifacts up there."

"Religious artifacts? You mean like the Holy Grail?"

"Possibly," she said, not smiling for the first time today. She turned and led him out the wooden door into the west wing.

Limping quickly to catch up. "Isabella, I'm sorry. I didn't mean to make light of your father's collections. I'm just trying to find out what you mean by religious artifacts."

She turned around abruptly. Her hair swished around her. Her pleasing smile returned, as she brushed strands of hair off her shoulders. "I know. It's hard to take all this in. I'm so used to it. But yes, it would be exactly like the Holy Grail, if such a thing existed. Or like the crown of thorns, or the shroud of Turin, or pieces of the cross of Jesus, or whatever has any spiritual powers at all."

"The duke collects those things?"

"He does so, very seriously."

"And what does he do with them up in that tower?"

She didn't smile. "My father is a religious man."

He could smell her perfume as he inched closer to her.

"I'm sure he'll discuss it with you, if you ask."

He nodded. "I didn't mean to put you through an inquisition."

"It's okay," she shrugged. "Shall we continue?" She moved ahead of him at a brisk pace.

Paul followed her into the west hall. The ceilings were arched with Doric columns along the inside wall in a cloistered walk facing the courtyard. Large casement windows between the columns let in streams of mountain sunshine. It was a brilliant day outside, and the light played along the walls and on the inside of the spacious galleries as if it belonged among the ancient artifacts.

Paul had a hard time concentrating as they walked among the displays of armor and weapons used by her ancestors to subdue their enemies and protect their lands. Why hadn't his father told him that he had met the duke and had painted his portrait? He wondered what else his father hadn't told him.

Isabella tugged on his arm. "Are you coming?"

"Of course," he said, smiling to hide his quandary. This was an imminently successful family, politically, economically, militarily, and in the arts. The Godvicos were not just artists—they were masters.

Why hasn't anyone heard of them? Where have they been hiding? Why doesn't any of their work hang in the Louvre?

Isabella seemed to sense that he wasn't absorbing much of what she had to say. "Maybe this is too much all at once," she said, in her soft lilting voice. "Let's take a break in the garden, and then I'll show you the chapel." She escorted him outside through a set of French double doors into the sunshine.

The fresh mountain air was comfortably warm. A circular cobblestone driveway divided the carefully manicured courtyard. The gardens and walks on either side were interspersed with green lawns. They walked arm and arm along a pebble path, the soft crunching beneath their feet echoed against the walls, chirping robins and wrens serenaded them from the trees arching over the path.

Paul winced in pain.

"I'm sorry. I forgot all about your injury. Let's stop for a while." She guided him to a stone bench along the path. Once he was seated he could see the peaks of the Alps over the north crenellated wall. Several were still covered in snow, their little white nightcaps on their pointed tips.

The galleries left Paul feeling confused. He could not doubt what he saw with his own eyes. The castle of Savoy was filled with the richest treasures of art, but most were the work of copyists. Men who used their consummate skill not to create, but to recreate. Why?

"Your family is talented. But I don't remember hearing anything about their work."

"All of my ancestors' work is in this castle," she said.

"I don't understand how they can be this accomplished and not have had a wider acceptance."

Isabella gazed toward the chapel. "Maybe if you learn more about my family you will understand."

"What is it I need to understand?" he asked. Paul had seen enough to know that the ability of the family artists accelerated to a higher plateau around the time of the Renaissance.

"Come, it's better you see for yourself." She helped him stand and led him along the gravel path that turned into a wide lane paved with white stones. It meandered across a grassy rise to the entrance doors of the Savoy Chapel.

Paul hesitated at the heavy cast bronze doors to take in the sculptured work. The entrance bay was flanked by two columns on each side capped with a Baroque pediment made from polychrome marble. How a building of such beauty could exist in such an isolated part of the world was a marvel to him. The bronze doors were well over fifteen feet tall and divided into panels depicting scenes from the lives of the kings of Israel. The detail packed into the five panels on each door was exquisite.

"These are a wonder, aren't they?" she said, as if she'd just seen them herself for the first time. "You can pass these doors a thousand times and still see new things in each of the scenes."

"These look like they should be in a museum somewhere," he said, running his fingers over one of the reliefs.

"The originals are in the baptistery of the Florence Cathedral. That one is my favorite," she said pointing at a bottom panel. "It's called the *Meeting of Solomon and the Queen of Sheba.*"

"And these were done by one of your ancestors?" he said standing on the small step leading into the chapel. Nothing seemed beyond the ability of her ancestors.

"Antonio Godvico. He studied under Lorenzo Ghiberti in Florence before he came back here and designed these doors. Wait until you see what he did inside." She pushed the door open and pulled him into the dark chamber.

Isabella dipped her index finger in a bronze water dish and crossed herself and then genuflected facing the altar. The chapel was dark except for a stream of radiant light diffused through a small window high over the altar. Paul could see the area above the altar was decorated, but he was too far away and the light too dim to see clearly.

He squinted into the darkness, straining to see. Beyond the communion railing three red-carpeted steps led up to the altar covered with a white linen cloth. A golden cross in the middle and three golden candlesticks on each side were its only adornment.

Paul followed Isabella as she moved in measured steps across the marble floor as if in a processional. She stopped in front of the small cross on a pedestal at the top of the steps, her hands clasped in front of her in a pose of prayer. Paul thought she was praying with her eyes lifted up toward heaven, until he hobbled up beside her and followed the track of her gaze into the dim light of the high arch over the altar.

The light bore down in thin, bronzed beams onto the wall behind the altar. About twenty feet or so above them, across the whole width of the wall, was painted a string of life-sized figures. If Paul hadn't already seen the most convincing reproductions already this morning, he would have been convinced Leonardo da Vinci himself had come to Savoy to paint *The Last Supper* on the chapel wall. The twelve disciples, reclining in groups of three, were animatedly discussing Jesus' declaration of treason against him. The depth of the room behind the disciples was so accurate the chapel looked another thirty feet longer. It was a masterful use of perspective by the artist. The carefully crafted expressions of the disciples that Leonardo had scripted were as clear and lucid on their lifelike faces as if they were standing across from Paul in flesh and blood: expressions of fear, of doubt, of protestation, and of love. The reactions of the apostles were haunting. Truly this was Leonardo's finest work, but the picture he viewed had been painted by a copyist. How could this be? The coloring was vibrant and realistic; the wall was obviously a better canvas than the original in the refractory of the church of Santa Maria delle Grazie in Milan. The tempura adhered here, unlike the peeling and flaking original that had been restored at least seven times since Leonardo's day.

"It's amazing isn't it?" Isabella said, as if in a trance.

Paul noticed her look. Her face was radiant and expectant as if she anticipated something happening as she studied the mural. "Your ancestors had an affinity for Leonardo's works?"

"Like Leonardo, Antonio believed he could bring out the emotional intention of the characters—what they were actually feeling at that moment when Jesus announced that someone would betray him. Can't you see the shock on Peter's face, and the disputing of Thomas, and the wicked reaction of Judas as he dips his bread in the broth? How could they not know his treachery? Yet, Jesus is so calm, so full of peace. I always want to cry when I look at this." She continued to keep her eyes fixed upon the figures seated at table.

As far as Paul was concerned her ancestors had one-upped Leonardo. The expressions on the characters' faces were real, palpable, they could speak their lines. The intensity of the emotions drained out of the scene as if the Last Supper were taking place before him. Paul didn't know if it was the brilliance of da Vinci or the genius of the copyist, Antonio Godvico, speaking to him from across the centuries. He could sense the remonstration of Peter, and the quandary and dismay of the other disciples as they tried to determine who among them would betray Jesus.

He wanted to ask her what else Antonio had painted but watching the expression on her face he could see she didn't want to speak. He didn't want to spoil this moment for her, but couldn't help himself. "This painting makes you sad?"

She nodded. "He was so misunderstood."

Paul looked up at the expansive painting stretched across the width of the chapel.

"Yes, I think Jesus probably was misunderstood."

"No, I mean Judas."

"Judas?"

"Yes. He wasn't trying to betray Jesus. He was trying to talk him out of getting killed. He thought that if he turned Jesus in to the Romans they wouldn't kill him, but would keep him from getting killed by the Jews."

Paul glanced up at the placid face of Jesus, with his eyes half shut, one hand facing down, the other up in resignation to the unfolding events that swirled around him. He knew that Judas would betray him, yet he remained calm.

"Are you saying that Judas didn't want Jesus to die?"

"Precisely. Jesus came to set up his kingdom on Earth—and would have if it weren't for the religious men of his time and the wicked Romans."

Paul pursed his lips, thinking about what she'd said. She seemed as sad for Judas as she was for what happened to Jesus. According to what he remembered, things didn't end too well for Jesus, and most people considered Judas a traitor. Paul didn't know what to think.

He studied the painting in the waning light. Judas was half-turned toward Jesus and from what Paul could see of him his face had an evil scowl. His profile was so lifelike he seemed to breathe. Yes, there. He did take a breath, even blink his eye. Paul shook his head. He'd been staring at too many paintings. He looked again and Judas slowly, but as certain as the sun rises, turned his head to Paul with an ugly sneer, a shot of fiery hate.

Paul jumped back, his heart thumping, stung by a crystal clear moment of recognition: it was the same black-creased face from his dream. Had he seen the face of Judas in his dreams?

"What's wrong?" Isabella asked.

He steadied himself with his cane, but he refused to gaze up at the wall.

"Paul, you look like you've seen a ghost," Isabella said. "Are you all right?"

He turned his back to the altar, "I think I've seen enough for today." His leg throbbed and he didn't want to look at any more paintings. Everything in Savoy looked a little too real, too perfect, too familiar. Even the paintings were infused with a life of their own.

It is better to imitate the antique
than the modern work.

–Leonardo da Vinci, *Notebooks*

13

---

*S*tein didn't mind living in the shadows. His whole life had consisted of living behind the scenes, until not being noticed became his strength. His livelihood depended on his ability to move around unaccounted for, dropping in and out of the lives around him as the need required. But he never wanted to leave anyone with the impression he was a mere shade or that his opinion didn't matter. So, in order to protect the most important cog in his plan, he had spent nearly the whole morning skulking behind sculptures, ducking in doorways, while shadowing Isabella and Paul as they strolled through the galleries.

If he wasn't mistaken, and he didn't think he was, the two had become chummy in their short time together. Stein had enough experience with women to know that when a man was first attracted to a beautiful woman, the rush of adrenaline could be addicting. Paul definitely had that I'm-interested look in his soft brown eyes. He would follow Isabella around the castle forever if Stein didn't step up and orchestrate things.

The midafternoon sun slanted lower through the south gallery windows as Stein strode purposefully through the halls on his way to Isabella's studio in the top of the southwest tower. Paul had already retired to his room to rest his leg, and everyone else in the castle was relaxing for the afternoon *pisolino*. Nearly everyone observed the Italian tradition of a nap between one and four p.m., except for Isabella and Stein. Isabella had changed her habits while away at school in America, and Stein always considered it a waste of time to sleep during the day.

Stein needed to impress on Isabella the urgency of moving forward with their agreement. Her father's financial situation was in shambles. Stein scoffed at the idea of spending so much money to keep this mausoleum to ancient art alive. If it were his, he'd turn everything into cold cash and hit the racetracks of the world—one at a time. But the duke's problems had become Stein's opportunity. He briskly mounted the spiral staircase leading up to Isabella's studio.

She sat at her easel, her back to the door, her hair almost down to the small of her back.

"Isabella, it's time to talk," Stein said, pushing the door closed behind him.

She swiveled on her stool, her hair swirled around her. "About?"

"I have convinced the duke to meet with Paul this afternoon."

"You've convinced!" she said with an air of disdain. "You're always thinking how good you are at getting people to do the things you want."

"Come, come. Now isn't the time for bickering. Your father wanted to wait, let him roam around the grounds, and then speak to him. I think that's unwise."

"Because you sense he's attracted to me." She turned back to her work.

Stein moved closer to her. "Because we are on the verge of what we've worked for. And I abhor distractions."

"No, there isn't time for that, is there? But there's always time to paint," she said over her shoulder, half ignoring him.

Stein edged closer to her. "What is time for, if not for painting? We've been planning the homecoming of the chair for years, and it's been back for a couple of weeks, and now someone is already pounding on the door wanting it."

"Father won't give it to him until he paints the da Vinci."

Stein rubbed his closely shaven chin. "Yes. That is the plan. But I'm more concerned about you. Now is *your* time." Stein stepped behind her, looking over her shoulder.

"You know about my father's superstitions," she said, continuing her work on the canvas in front of her. "I don't want to upset him. Once he's certain it's safe for me to use it, I will."

"Yes, of course." He moved to her side so he could examine the drawing she worked on. "But you and I both think this curse thing is nonsense. So what would be the harm of you using it first?"

She glanced up at him. He could read the disdain in her eyes. She was so independent; convincing her would be difficult, but not impossible.

"I think we need to let my father's plan work. LaBont will use it first. The curse, if there is one, will rest on him," she said.

"I realize that. But Signóre Tosatti will be bringing the materials he's been collecting to help with your work. He will want some results for the lire he has invested in this project. Besides, you have always wanted to paint like your ancestors. The chair is your legacy as much as your father's."

She sighed deeply, flipped her hair off her shoulder, and continued painting as if he didn't exist.

He hated when she ignored him. She had picked up too many

bad habits while she was in America. He calmed himself. "I thought this is what you wanted," he said, watching her work. "Isn't it your dream to be a great artist? Isn't that why you came home from California?"

She continued in silence.

"Isabella, you will have everything you've ever dreamed of," he said, almost whispering.

She jerked around to face him. "All I've ever wanted is to be recognized for how hard I've worked to become a serious artist."

"And so you shall. You shall. You could be one of the greatest of all time, just like the maestro himself," he said, quietly. "If you were to use the chair, and become skilled enough to paint the da Vinci, you could escape this monastery and live in Florence, like you've always wanted to. I would set you up in the finest studio and you could make us all wealthy. Even da Vinci would glow with envy at the studio of Isabella—and it all begins with a visit to the chair."

She smiled wanly and then with a look of resignation in her eyes, she said. "Paul will find the chair soon. You'll have what you want."

"But what about what you want?"

She continued to work on her painting. "I'll use it in my own time."

"What about my offer?" Stein asked, waiting silently for her response.

"The studio in Florence and the use of the chair?" She filled in the deep lines around the eye sockets of the woman she was depicting.

He nodded. "Your father has decided that the chair goes to the one who paints the da Vinci for him. Why should it be LaBont, especially since you don't hold to your father's superstitions?"

She put her brushes down and slowly turned to him as if she

was giving serious consideration to his proposal. She gave him a hard stare for a long moment. "I will think about it."

"Yes, you do that." The knot in his stomach eased. He could smell the thrill of the race, the clang of the opening bell, the clunk of the gates as they snapped open, the thunder of the hoofs down the turf track. He could see the sweat beading up on the gleaming coats of the thoroughbreds as they flew by his seat in a gaggle of horseflesh as colorfully clad jockeys strapped their mounts all the way to the finish.

She would bite. He was certain of that. And when she did, he would have more than enough to pay his debts, and still play every track he'd ever dreamed of. He patted Isabella on the shoulder and left her tower-top studio with the gleeful feeling his longshot bet would finally pay off—big. Bigger than any daily double, bigger than any trifecta, bigger than any pick-six.

Later that afternoon Frederick stepped purposefully up the spiral staircase inside the northwest tower. The afternoon sunlight in narrow shafts of yellowish light filtered in through the small slits in the tower windows. At the top of the stairs he pushed open the rough-timbered wooden door. The round tower was vacant except for a series of glass display cases on metal legs lining the stone walls. He approached one on the farthest side from the door and lifted the covering glass, propping it gently against the wall. Carefully he lifted a red leather-bound volume, its cover worn from use, its metal clasp flecked with rust, but clamped tightly shut. For the last five years he's planned carefully for the return of the chair. He'd searched every major library in Europe for shreds of information on the mysterious power of the chair and how it might be solved. He'd hunted for a ritual that would counteract its negative forces without disturbing its artistic goodness. He'd gone to great lengths to purchase certain holy artifacts that were said to have mystical powers, and since the chair had come home to Savoy he had put his sacred articles in close proximity to the chair in hopes they would drive out whatever evil still possessed it. But when he read in the *Times of London* that LaBont had run back into the flaming home to retrieve his belongings and had been horribly burned so that he could never paint again, Frederick had become despondent. Was there no freedom from this curse? He feared he had brought it home only to release its plague of death on the House of Savoy.

His one hope lay in this ancient volume a bookseller in Madrid had sold him. When he had first seen this book of ancient rituals, he had determined this would be his best hope. He'd paid handsomely for it, money he could ill-afford spending, but he had to own it.

As he carried the heavy volume down the stairs and turned in the hall toward the Chapel of Savoy, he wanted to spend the evening reciting the prayers in the book. He had to find a way to rid the chair of its power of death before his beloved Isabella became a victim of its scourge.

The sun was low in the window and not as bright when Paul woke later that afternoon. Slowly rising, he stretched his arms and legs. The pain resumed, but not with the same intensity. The rest had helped. He found his freshly pressed shirt hanging in the closet.

He had not wanted to sleep, but his leg throbbed so badly he had come back to his room, taken two Vicodin, and laid down. Despite his turmoil, he drifted off tp sleep. He still could not get out of his mind that horrid face staring down at him from the painting above the altar. How could he see faces in his dreams of people he'd never met before? He'd always believed that dreams had more to say about his own life than the future or about anyone else's. But it was hard to explain away first see-ing Isabella in his dream and then Judas. And when Judas' ugly face turned in the painting, he was in his dream again. It was one of the ugliest faces he'd ever seen.

Was he hallucinating? Knowing he wasn't given to delusions, the dreaded reality set in that Savoy was probably spooked. He laughed to himself and sat down on the edge of the bed. All he had to do now was figure out what "spooked" meant, then he could decide what do about it.

But his job wasn't to solve or fix whatever was going on here at Savoy. His mission was to retrieve the chair and get home. He had to work to keep that idea fixed in his mind because so many other images wanted to crowd into his thoughts—particularly ones of Isabella. If there was a reason to stay in Savoy longer than he'd anticipated, she was it. He rose and finished dressing.

Gerhard had left a sheet of paper on the desk with the American Embassy's phone number and the name of the man Paul needed to speak to about his passport. He called and made arrangements to have his passport replaced. It would take about a week.

Paul smiled at the turn of events. He wasn't exactly forced to stay here. He could wait out the week slogging through the museums of Milan and Florence, but it wasn't likely he would get to see such an impressive private collection as the duke's. Besides, docents like Isabella were rare. He would love to see her work. He could tell she took art seriously. Just like everyone in his family. They had more in common than they thought pos-sible.

Maybe, after all, these dreams were telling him something about himself: he was anxious about coming here to Savoy. Anyone would feel a little queasy about coming to such a strange place. He put his quandary about his dreams aside. As soon as he left this place with his father's chair he would give them more thought, but for now he had a transaction to negotiate with the duke.

He finished dressing and left the room. At the bottom of the stairs he found Gerhard, who escorted him into the dining room. He offered him a light meal of salad, soup, and pasta. Paul ate ravenously. It wasn't long before Isabella showed up.

"How are you feeling?" she said, sliding into a chair next to him.

"Much better, thanks." He dabbed his mouth with his linen napkin and placed it beside his plate.

"Are you ready to continue your tour?"

"I was thinking I'd like to see some of your paintings." He pushed back his chair and stood.

"And what makes you think I paint?" she said with a mischievous grin.

"Just a wild guess."

"As you requested, we'll start with my studio." She led him through a door into a large sitting area.

"This south wing takes us over the drive you came in through. In these galleries," she waved her hand at the rooms they passed, "we keep all the works by our eighteenth and nineteenth century artists." The hall was long and the floor tiled with white-polished marble like the others, but the exterior walls were left unpanelled and had the texture of smooth, red limestone. Large arched windows broke up the wall that faced the interior court. She led him up four flights of stairs, and down another long hall to the southwest corner of the castle.

As they walked along the long corridor, Paul's thoughts went back to the paintings he'd seen earlier done by her ancestors, the Godvicos. "Men who can paint like your ancestors would not live long in this castle before the world would come to them."

"Antonio died on his way to Paris to paint a portrait of King Henry IV of France. He was thirty-one."

"I'm sorry." Paul felt stupid for pushing his inquiry. How unfortunate for one so talented to die such an untimely death—and what could have been if he had only lived longer, as long as Leonardo or Michelangelo or Caravaggio?

The two entered the southwest tower from the fourth-floor hall. The round wall of the tower jutted into the square lines where the halls of the west and south walls came together. She opened a wide oak door and ushered him into her studio.

The round and spacious room had a vaulted ceiling. Light flooded in through three large pointed arch windows looking out over the forests into the green valley below. Her oversized easel dominated the middle of the room. On it lay the half-finished work of a magnificent still life. The ornate chair that had sat in his father's studio his whole life was not in the room. Paul put his hands behind his back and inspected it closely.

She quickly came up beside him and tugged at his arm. "I'd like to show you my finished ones first," she said, and guided him over to the interior wall away from the windows. Five oversized paintings leaned against the reddish limestone wall. Paul recognized their Baroque influences.

It was obvious she had a distinct command over certain aspects of her craft—her human figures were well proportioned and realistic. Her still life scenes showed excellent use of color. The proportions were acceptable, but in the larger scheme of what she was trying to accomplish, in the composition itself, each piece seemed defective. He couldn't put his finger on it, but that she didn't paint like Caravaggio or Rembrandt wasn't a criticism. She was a good, competent craftsman. But the works as narrative pieces on a par with the men she was trying to imitate just didn't hold up.

Trying to identify what was lacking in each piece reminded Paul of a college exam. The first one—with two horsemen facing each other standing in the foreground, with the land sloping off into the hilly distance—her use of perspective was oddly off. Not that Paul thought he could do any better, but the vanishing point seemed misplaced, unlike the da Vinci in the Savoy Chapel. The second one—of a couple sitting in the living room of their country manor—was beautifully colored, but the use of chiaroscuro, the gradations of light and dark, was wrong. The light came from the opposite direction of the highlights it rendered on the faces, distorting the images. Yet the detail of the faces showed that she had mastered drawing the human body. All of her work was well done at a certain level, but not up to the standard of what he had seen throughout the castle.

As he concentrated on the last canvas a thought gripped him.

She's not happy with being a good painter. She wants to paint like her ancestors and the Old Masters. That must be why they brought the chair back to Savoy. Not just because it belonged here, but because she intended to use it.

He tightened his jaw and pursed his lips as he thought of his father. It hurt to think that Isabella would build her future on his father's misfortune.

"Is there something wrong?" she asked, eyeing him from a few feet away.

He couldn't bring himself to talk about his misgivings. That was something he needed to take up with her father. "No, not really. I was just thinking how excellent a painter you are."

"Thank you. You're the only one around here who thinks that." She seated herself at the far end of the line of paintings, slumping in the chair. "I've worked so hard, but I can't seem to get it right."

"Get what right?" He continued to study the last painting.

She waved her hand at the paintings. "You know what I mean. You see what's wrong. I can tell by the look on your face."

"It's that whole expectation thing."

"The expectation of perfection is the way I like to think of it." She took a deep breath, sat up straight, and composed herself as if she had momentarily slipped into a mood she knew wasn't dignified. "I think I nailed it on this one," she said, pointing to the one on the easel.

Paul moved in front of the easel. The light cascading in through the tall, arched windows made viewing it easy. He perched himself on the edge of a wooden stool, studying the scene before him carefully. It was a large, linen canvas on which she had traced the central figures in the foreground and the scenery of the background. He could see that she had moved the horizon several times, and the vanishing point in this looked accurate. She was no prodigy; she had invested study and effort. This one appeared to be her best, but since the color wasn't on, Paul would have to see how she finished the light, and from what direction she would have it flow into the painting. The background hills and foliage needed more detail, but that would come. He thought of taking up a pencil and helping her out, but he sensed she didn't want that.

"This looks like your best piece."

She came up beside him. "You think so?"

"So far, you've gotten the perspective right."

She put a hand on his shoulder. "Thanks."

She smelled like lilies. "I need to know something," Paul asked.

She pulled her hand off his shoulder, as if sensing his serious tone.

"What's the story behind the chair?"

She didn't say anything.

He turned away from the picture toward her. "You know why I've come here, don't you?"

She glanced down a moment at her shoes. She nodded. "I'm sorry about your father. After all those years he'd used it and nothing happened, no one thought …"

"Then you understand why I've come?"

She looked up at him, her green eyes threatening to burn him with their intensity. "It's only natural you'd want to do anything to help your father. But I'm not certain what we can do to help."

"I've come to ask your father about buying back the chair." He watched her face carefully for her reaction.

She took a few steps back as if in shock. "That is a difficult request."

"It would help my father recover. Why is that so hard to understand?"

She crossed her arms over her chest. "Have you spoken to Father about this?"

"You heard him this morning. He wanted me to have a look around first. What's all this secrecy about? Do you know the story behind the chair?"

"Most of it," she said.

"I've come a long way. I'd like to hear it all," Paul said, studying her face to see if he could determine if she couldn't talk about it or wouldn't.

She hesitated, a look of quandary in her eyes. "It is a long and difficult story."

"Does the chair have special powers or not?"

She stood with her arms crossed and her weight resting on her left foot, staring at her paintings stacked along the wall. "Is that all you want to know?"

Paul raised his eyebrows. Before he could open his mouth to respond, the wide-arched door opened and Stein, with a liquid stride, entered the room. He glared at Isabella, and then gave Paul one of those saccharin smiles, phony to the bone.

"Sorry to disturb you both, but the Duke of Savoy will see you now," he said, motioning with his hand to Paul.

Paul sat rigid on the stool, biting his lip. He couldn't believe the man's timing. Isabella gave Paul a knowing glance as if to say there were no secrets between these stone walls. Then her face relaxed and she smiled, locking her eyes on him. At first he wondered if she was smiling because that was expected of her when others were around, a polite, enchanting, *Mona Lisa* smile, but then it became clear. It was a message in its purest form: It was time for him to hear the answers he came for—whether he liked what he heard or not.

To create the appearance of life
is more important than life itself.
The works of God are never better appreciated
than by other creators!

—Anonymous hand on a page of
Leonardo's *Notebooks*

14

*I*n the three days since Marcella's meeting with Scott Bezcotta, she had worked to have everything perfect for Vincent's homecoming. Yet, she still had time for a significant amount of painting.

The clouds over Laguna Beach were uncharacteristically low and gray as she drove him home from the hospital. Vincent hunched laconically and motionless in the passenger seat beside her. She thought her husband's arrival home would be a celebration, but instead it was as dark as the afternoon sky. Tiny drops fell out of the mist and intermittently pecked at her windshield. Stopping at the guard station outside her exclusive Monarch Bay development, she smiled at the man in uniform, he nodded, smiled back, and hit the button for the gate. As the wrought iron gates, with their swirled M in the center of each one, swung slowly open, rain began slanting down in heavy sheets. She pressed the accelerator and slid through the gates.

Vincent leaned his head against his window, staring blankly into the gloom. She eyed him furtively as she waited for the garage door to finish opening. She had thought about having a cake, a special dinner, and even a few friends; but his mood for the past week had been uncommunicative, and she feared a party turning ugly. His face had paled during his hospital stay, and he hadn't shaved in a few days, leaving his face stippled. His normally bright-black eyes had lost their bristling luster for life and had taken on a brooding darkness. Vincent had always kept his hair short and neatly combed back, as if he was always ready to have his photo taken, but now it had grown longer and looked disheveled.

She pulled the car into the garage, cut the engine, and then hurried around to the other side to open his door. His hands were lightly bandaged, and he hugged them closely to his chest as if he were guarding them against any more calamities.

Inside the house Lynette greeted them with an inviting smile. A paper banner hung over the fireplace in the living room welcoming him home. Marcella steered him into the large room with its plush contemporary furniture, but he didn't pay any attention to the decorations. With his arms crossed in front of him like two swords, he only grunted as he looked around.

Marcella swallowed and felt the muscles in her back tighten. She tried chatting with him about the house and the progress of the settlement with the insurance company and how good he looked. But after thirty minutes she realized, she was talking to a dead man; she relented and fell into a clammy silence.

Lynette had lit the gas logs in the fireplace to make the place feel cozy, but in Marcella's heart a coldness sifted down into places it had never touched before.

Sitting across from Vincent, who slouched on the sofa with his eyes closed and head back, she wondered how long it would take him to regain his vibrancy. The antiseptic hospital smell still clung to him.

It was nearly noon and Lynette came into the room carrying a platter of roast beef sandwiches. They ate in silence. Vincent resisted any help from Lynette. He negotiated eating by grasping a sandwich between both hands as if they were paws.

After lunch he perked up, and Marcella gave him a tour of the house. But his few comments were terse and sharp. At the door to the back bedroom, which Marcella had carefully closed before leaving for the hospital, Vincent hesitated and glared at the door. She had walked by it hoping he'd follow her. Using both of his bandaged hands he slowly turned the knob and pushed the door open with his foot. A work in-progress lay on her easel, and eight other completed watercolors stood propped against the wall. She was glad Scott had arranged to have the ones for the show picked up yesterday. He was so considerate.

She could feel little beads of sweat rising on her forehead and under her arms as he scrutinized the contents of the room. She was glad she thought better of her impulse to hang her work throughout the house. But this moment had the same awkward silence as the time she showed her seventh-grade art teacher her first landscape of the early light coming off the Sierra behind her home.

Vincent didn't make a single comment—only his upper lip twitched as he stood in front of one of her finished landscapes. Abruptly turning, he disappeared into his room and closed the door.

She stood at the door of her studio, alone. She had been so busy getting ready for Vincent's homecoming that she hadn't decided when she would sit down and talk to him about her painting. She knew he wouldn't be pleased, but she had steeled herself not to back down, no matter how dark his mood became.

But it wasn't in her to be cruel. Just sitting with him in the car on the way home she sensed his deep disappointment at the turn of events in his life. She wondered if she should have moved her studio back to Rhonda's. Marcella shrugged. When would he accept her new life? Shuffling into her studio she slumped into the stuffed chair in the corner.

A few days later, on the Saturday of her show, Marcella was busy dressing when Paul came to mind. She hadn't heard from him in almost a week. This wasn't the time to stew on what she had learned about the real reason for his trip to Italy, neither did she want to worry about him, but that was like asking her to not scratch an itch. He had promised to check in every few days, and he hadn't called since the first day he arrived in Milan.

Slipping into a stylish black dress, she wished she had some of her jewelry—especially the silver bracelet Vincent had bought her—but like everything else that was gone. She grabbed her black clutch purse, and before leaving the dressing room she checked herself in the full-length mirror. She looked nice. The dress showed off her slim figure, and the blush on her cheeks gave her a bright look, one that hid the sadness that threatened to swallow her. She practiced smiling—tonight she would need an engaging smile and quick laugh even if she didn't feel like them.

Marcella checked her watch; it was almost one o'clock. She'd planned to drive to L.A. to meet with Scott. The show was a private reception for some of his best clients, with only three other artists. Since she was the last addition, he warned that her pieces wouldn't be in the spotlight. He asked if she could show up by four to meet the other artists. She hated this drive into L.A., but she wouldn't have to do it that often. And besides, Scott was a bright spot in her life right now, a friend who seemed to understand not only what she wanted to do with her art but also the pressures she was under. He had taken care of all the details for the show; she truly hadn't had to lift a finger.

Vincent had barely talked since he came home. He lay in bed all day, ate his food, and watched TV. A visiting nurse came and changed his bandages and checked on his progress. Lynette helped around the house with the cooking, so Marcella settled into a routine with her painting and attending to Vincent that started to feel comfortable.

Coming out of the dressing area into the bedroom, she thought about telling Vincent where she was going this afternoon, but she feared she'd just be talking to a wall.

Vincent lay on the bed, his back toward her, with the covers pulled up over his shoulders.

"Honey, I'll be back in a couple of hours," she said to the back of his head. She walked around to his side of the bed and stroked his forehead. His eyes were open but unseeing.

Poor guy, I wish there was something I could do to help you.

She ran her fingers through his hair and felt torn. Maybe her place right now was by his side until he recovered. What if he came out of his stupor and wanted her and she was not here? She laughed to herself. He hadn't even tried to touch her since he'd been home. His desire would come back—it had to. Sex had always been a participatory sport for both of them since the first day they were married. But now they were both on the sidelines, which bothered Marcella.

Vincent, please get better. She wanted to feel close to him again, to feel his love for her, to feel loved by him, and to love him back. She took a deep breath and sighed. He would be okay here with Lynette. She stroked his cheek gently and left the room to start her new life as an artist.

First draw from drawings by good masters done
from works of art and from nature.

—Leonardo da Vinci, *Notebooks*

15

*S*tein showed Paul to the foot of the marble staircase lead-ing to Frederick's study in the northwest tower, then left him. Fragments of late afternoon sunshine, in shafts of faded yellow, fil-tered through narrow windows no more than slits in the stone walls. The air smelled cold and dusty and his footfalls echoed as he mounted the steps.

Winding up the stairs, his mind settled on Isabella. He'd never imagined meeting a woman as interesting and as beautiful as her; but for one who lived in such idyllic surroundings, she seemed under incredible pressure. The family expectations alone—to match the quality of the art that hung on the castle walls—would be enough to create doubts in any aspiring artist. While Paul wouldn't mind helping her master her technique, he didn't know if she would accept his input. What she struggled with was old ground to him. His father had drilled him in the use of light and darkness and the different theories of perspective ever since he could hold a brush and he felt he could use them competently. But he had sensed in Isabella an insatiable desire to achieve; he didn't think she would be happy with a mere competence. He hoped her desire to live up to her family's expectations wasn't tied to some ulterior motive, some grand scheme. If she intended to add to the reproductions that were scattered throughout the castle, he didn't see her having a happy future.

The stairs emptied into the middle of Frederick's study, which took up the whole top floor. It was the same dimensions as Isabella's studio, but furnished differently. Hers had a Spartan artisan look, his was elegantly opulent. Dark mahogany bookshelves lined the curved walls. The bookshelves were at least halfway up the twenty-foot walls. Thick Persian carpets covered the marble floor, and in front of his massive mahogany desk lay a white square rug with the crest of Savoy, the black eagle on a blood-red shield, embroidered on it. Two French provincial side chairs in red and black upholstery sat on either side of the carpet.

He located Frederick on the other side of the room, perched on the top of a rolling ladder, perusing an old leather volume.

Paul cleared his throat.

"Ah, Signore LaBont, thank you for coming up to see me. I understand you've been busy." He clambered down the ladder as if he'd done it a hundred times before.

"It's been a long day," Paul said, "but not too busy to talk."

Frederick wore a white shirt with a red pullover cardigan sweater with his family crest emblazoned over his heart. A pair of reading glasses rested halfway down his long elegant nose. "Please sit down and make yourself comfortable." He motioned toward a pair of overstuffed chairs under one of the arched windows facing the dense forest below.

Paul sank into the soft leather with Frederick across from him. Light cascaded in muted shafts through the high window.

"Now, tell me about your tour. Have you found it interesting?"

Paul considered him closely. "I enjoyed what I saw. Your daughter's a lovely lady, as well as a fine artist."

"I'm glad you think so." He laid down his book—which had an ancient leather binding—on the walnut table between them.

Paul steeled himself. "One of the first things she showed me was the gallery of the Dukes of Savoy."

"Ah, and you saw a most intriguing portrait, no doubt." He steepled his hands in front of him as he sat comfortably, crossing his long legs. "A portrait painted by your father, correct?"

Paul nodded. "Would you care to fill me in?"

"Gladly." He stood up and crossed over to other side of the spacious room and took up a carved onyx box from his desk. Back at his chair he opened it and offered a cigarette to his guest.

"No thanks," Paul said, shaking his head.

He placed the box on the table between them, and with his slender fingers he took one out, put it in his mouth, and lit it. Taking a deep drag, then exhaling languidly toward the ceiling, he sat back and crossed his legs. "It's a long story, but since you've come all the way from California, I suppose you want to hear it all."

"If you don't mind," he smiled.

Smoke curled upward as the duke spoke. "You know that the chair was created by Leonardo da Vinci, but do you know why?"

"I have no idea."

"Da Vinci was obsessed with the possibility of perfection. As an artist, he wanted to create lifelike pictures that resembled nature—this was his passion. He believed he could capture the emotion, the feeling, the deep intent of the subject he sought to paint. He instilled his work with a life of its own. This was Leonardo's dream."

"Like the faces on *The Last Supper?*"

"Precisely," he nodded, "an emotional effect. An aspect of life that reflects back to the viewer the actual intent of the subject."

Paul rubbed his chin and thought about the face of Judas. "Did he accomplish his intent?" he asked.

"Somewhat. But near the end of his life he had only scratched the surface of what he thought he should have accomplished."

"Because of his obsession with perfection?"

He paused, taking another drag. "In his old age he realized he had squandered his talents by his lack of productivity. So during his last years in Amboise, France, he set about to create a means to pass on his prodigious gift."

"That's why the chair came into existence?" Paul asked.

"The manner in which he created it, we are not certain."

"So you believe in its power?" Paul asked.

"Most assuredly, I do." He flicked an ash into an ashtray beside him.

"Intriguing. But what you haven't told me is why there is a portrait of you painted by my father over twenty years ago hanging on your wall."

He put the cigarette to his mouth and the end glowed red as he inhaled. The smoke streamed out as he spoke. "The chair has been in my family's possession for more than five centuries, until the Nazis stole it during the war. I've worked for over thirty years to restore the collection stripped by them, and the chair was one of the prize pieces of the collection. Under the guise of having my portrait painted, I went to see your father to confirm a rumor he possessed it. I informed him that my family had owned it for the last five centuries. But he claimed he knew nothing of it."

"And that was that?"

"Not exactly. I also told him the chair possessed a curse and that whoever used it was in grave danger for their life."

"I don't understand," Paul said leaning forward. "Were you threatening him?"

"No, of course not, my friend." Frederick pushed himself out of the chair and stood. "Bear with me one moment and I will show you what I meant." He disappeared into the shadows on the other side of the room. Paul heard him sliding the ladder on the marble floor, it squeaked under his weight as he mounted it.

The duke reappeared with an ancient leather-bound folio in his hand and slid back into his chair. He laid the volume down on the table in front of them. He carefully unfastened the buckle of the leather strap and slowly opened it.

"This is a history of my family since they came into possession of the chair," he said, leafing through the book. "As much as the chair is a blessing, it has one dangerous aspect to it. You saw some of the art my ancestors were able to create. Each of them that used the chair was on his way to a brilliant career when his life was tragically cut short."

"All the users died prematurely?"

"Yes," he said, raising both eyebrows.

"So, the accident I had coming up here wasn't necessarily an accident?"

"It was most tragic and unforeseen," he said, stubbing out his cigarette. "Your father is the oldest user of the chair in the records. No one who had used it continuously, and had finished projects while possessing it, has lived past the age of thirty-five. We considered that your father's good fortune was because he followed the advice I gave him—or that the curse may have passed."

"When you visited him, you told him about its little quirk?"

"Most assuredly. I was concerned that he was jeopardizing himself and his family. You see, I have studied carefully its history, and I found one common denominator in all the deaths. My ancestors worked here in the castle where they stayed close to the chair, and nothing evil happened. But when they came to the attention of a distant patron and were summoned to court to do a portrait or to decorate a king's rooms ..."

"They died because of a horrific accident, usually by fire."

The duke nodded. "Most unfortunate, but true. So, you see the danger."

"And this is documented." Paul pointed toward the book.

"In meticulous detail." He held open the leather-bound folio. "In the middle of the nineteenth century my predecessor stopped anyone from actually sitting in the chair, and that's when the accidents stopped, but the quality of the art also declined." He placed the open book on the table between them.

Paul looked over the ancient manuscript. "When did they first discover the chair's unusual side effects?" He asked, tapping his finger on a page of the hand-copied text.

"The entries go back to 1545, and the first one is by Bartolomeo da Vinci himself. He is the half-brother of Leonardo, and the only one in his family that truly admired the great artist. It was to Bartolomeo that Leonardo bequeathed the chair. The maestro's brother was so heartsick over his death that he became determined to outwit nature. He went to Vinci, married a young woman similar in appearance and temperament to Caterina, Leonardo's mother, and openly prayed for a son. When a boy arrived in answer to his prayers, he wanted to name him Leonardo, but his brothers prevailed upon him to name the boy after his father. Pierino da Vinci's talent was immediately noticed. By the age of ten he was sent to study with Bandinello and later with the sculptor Tribolo. The story goes that Pierino amazed his masters and his fellow pupils. He traveled to Rome, taking the chair with him. On his way back from Rome in 1545, while staying in Pisa, he died in a house fire. He was only twenty-three."

"And the chair?"

"Pierino left it in Rome, at the home of Cardinal Tourimi. After his death, Bartolomeo retrieved the chair and some of his son's drawings."

"And all this is verifiable, and not just some old wives fable?"

"Two of Pierino's sculptures survived. One, *Water God,* is in the Louvre, and the other, *Samson and a Philistine,* is in the Palazzo Vecchio in Florence. He was a magnificent talent and would have surpassed both Leonardo and Michelangelo, if he had lived." The duke turned a leaf in the folio and perused a page, then gently closed the book.

"What happened to the chair after that?"

"Bartolomeo became despondent and sold the chair and several of Leonardo's notebooks to Louise, the duchess of Savoy. And that is how it came into our possession in the year 1546."

"But Pierino's premature death didn't stop the Duchess of Savoy from sending her sons to a flaming death?"

Frederick furrowed his brows. "How were they to know then what we know today? Bartolomeo was grief stricken over his son's death and blamed the chair for all manner of sorcery. The duchess wasn't a superstitious woman, and she wasn't about to let an invention of the great maestro slip through her hands."

"So she brought it here to Savoy in order to build a dynasty?"

The duke closed the leather cover. "Some who used it lived longer than others, but they all perished. But by that time my great-great-grandfather stopped anyone from using the chair. He had built the family trust fund sufficiently that he no longer needed to sell art to support the castle. So, he became a collector."

Paul bolted upright in his chair. "So, your ancestors used their talents to support the castle?"

"Many people make a living by their art—even you."

"I haven't seen one original work since I've been here. They were all copyists."

"You could call them that. Each was an expert at duplicating the works of a particular artist."

"Whatever brought in the most money?"

"You could say that. But they also took other commissions."

"I'm sure, but the big money would be in copying the masters. Maybe even finding a lost work or two of one of the other old masters." Paul laced his fingers together in front of his mouth and waited for Frederick's reaction.

Unsmiling, he shifted in his chair. "I'm sure some of that went on."

"So, once your ancestors' trust fund was well-stocked they became collectors because they didn't need to kill off their sons anymore." Paul sat up straight.

"Signore LaBont, you are making my family sound mercenary."

"Weren't they?" he said.

"Everyone has to find a way to secure their way of life," he said, with a flustered look. "Once our ancestral lands were plundered—"

"Your family took up the time honored trade of forging the old masters to support their lifestyle."

"Having never been in our position, Signore, it may be best for you not to wake sleeping lions."

Paul studied his host's face, thoughtfully. "You're right. That is ancient history and none of my business."

Frederick nodded once, and raised a black eyebrow.

Paul took a deep breath then let out a thoughtful sigh. "But why bring the chair back here now? I'm sure your trust fund's intact. Why make it available to your daughter?" Paul asked.

"I know of Isabella's ambitions," he said, "but it is not my desire for her to taste its powers. Do you think I would put my own daughter in such jeopardy?"

"I just assumed that was why you brought it home." Paul felt his face flush.

He sighed, gazed down for a moment then looked at Paul. "We brought it back because this is the safest place for it. As I have said, no one using the chair regularly has lived past thirty-five, and most died much younger, except for your father. This is not a future I wish for my daughter."

"But then you must have known bringing it back here to Savoy would put my father in great danger?" Paul asked. Asking the question made Paul even angrier thinking about the duke's callous disregard for his father's safety. He took a deep breath and calmed himself. It would not serve his purpose to lose his temper here.

"The chair always belonged here in Savoy. I warned him about its curse. He was a fool to let anyone else besides himself sit in it." He said, fixing his black eyes on Paul. "Wasn't he?"

Paul let his eyes wander over to the bookshelves.

"You know as well as I do, he was. And it is a miracle you have not suffered the same fate as he."

Paul turned back to Frederick. "So, let me see if I have this straight. If a man uses this chair and becomes an accomplished painter and lives in close proximity to the chair, everything's fine. But the moment he leaves, even if it's just to go on vacation, he gets zapped—by what, we don't know."

"I think you understand," the duke said, arching an eyebrow.

Paul pursed his lips. "So the chair is a curse as well as a blessing."

"Exactly, in the same amount that it gives, it ultimately takes."

"But why?" Paul asked.

"I think Leonardo was a proud man, and that pride and arrogance drove him away from God."

"You think that's a shortcoming in a man?"

"Yes, I do," he said. "To have such gifts, talents, and abilities and not to acknowledge him as the Creator of all things is the height of arrogance. When one as amazing as Leonardo sets up an idol to his own greatness in his heart and worships it, well … you can see the destruction that has brought into the world."

Paul tapped his finger on his chin. "So, the chair is not good."

"The chair is nothing more than the golden calf the children of Israel built in the wilderness."

"You mean an idol?" Paul said, surprised by his comment.

The duke nodded slowly. "It allows men to worship at the altar of Leonardo's greatness. It is not good, my friend."

Paul saw again in his mind that line of fire ripping toward him on the road. It wanted to destroy him in the darkness and leave him maimed and useless—just like his father. And if everything Frederick told him was true, he had to take the chair home to his father. "My father is lying in a hospital bed, with his career and health destroyed because of this chair. I think it was a mistake for you to bring it back here."

"I understand your position," Frederick said, his eyes softening, as if he was truly concerned. "In light of your father's long life, the results of bringing it to Savoy were totally unforeseen."

"I think the best remedy for my father's condition is if you sell the chair back to me. Once my father is well, we can discuss where the chair should be permanently," Paul said.

The duke's look of solicitude vanished. His eyes took on a grave look of concern. "That is not possible, Signore. That is not at all possible. The chair must remain here."

"But if you understand what it's done to my father then you owe it to him to let me take it back to California," Paul said, leaning forward in his chair. "It's the only right thing to do."

Frederick studied him for a long moment. "You may have a point. What do you have in mind?"

"I'm prepared to purchase it from you."

"Signore," he spread his hands, "how do we put a price on such an item?"

"Exactly. How can we put a price on my father's life?"

Frederick pensively touched his top lip with his fingertip. "I have a plan that might interest you, which could solve both of our problems."

Paul sat back, "Oh?"

"I could not even begin to put a price on it that would compensate the family estate fairly—at least one that your father could afford."

Paul laced his fingers together, listening.

"What I propose is that you furnish one last painting for the family collection. This painting would complete our collection of all da Vinci's works." He sat up straight, a serious expression on his large face.

"A da Vinci! You want me to paint a da Vinci?"

A smile rippled across his mouth. "Of course."

Paul sighed, almost laughing. "I can't paint a da Vinci."

"You certainly can. I would make the chair available to you. In a matter of weeks you will be a master, like your father."

Paul shook his head. "No, no, that wouldn't work. I need you to set a price for the chair. Then I can decide if—"

"Signore, I have given you my price. My only price. One da Vinci to hang on the walls of my ancestral castle, to complete our collection. It is an easy task. One you are up to. In a matter of weeks you will be home in California with the chair, and your father and yourself will be safe." Frederick stopped abruptly, settled back, waiting.

"And if I don't paint your da Vinci then my father's doom—and maybe mine too—is sealed," Paul said, staring intently at the duke. "Either way, I'm a hostage to this so-called curse of fire."

The duke pursed his lips, as if considering Paul's statement.

After a few moments, he said, "It seems you are in a difficult place. You may stay for a few days until you are healed, and during that time you can think about my offer, but time is of the essence. I can not hold out this offer to you past Wednesday." He leveled his dark eyes at Paul. "After that, I must ask you to leave the castle as I will then have pressing business to attend to."

The boulder thundering down the hillside toward him; the fire burning across the road; the taste of blood in his mouth; the last thing Paul wanted was another brush with death. But if he agreed to the duke's terms, he would be doing something he never wanted to do: use that blasted chair. But if he didn't agree, according to the duke, he and his father were burnt toast.

"Do you have any questions?" the duke asked, with a firm voice.

"My father needs help now. Can't I just pay you for the chair?"

"Please, Signore LaBont. It's important you understand my terms. If you paint the portrait I have asked for then you are free to leave Savoy with the chair, Leonardo's Chair. It will be your family's forever."

Paul shook his head not wanting to let out an incredulous sigh. "You want me to do something I can't do, and my father's dying."

The duke slapped the arms of his chair, "Signore, you underestimate the power you have available to you. Painting one da Vinci is a small thing. Did you not see the *Last Supper* in the chapel? You can paint like that. Then the chair will be yours in perpetuity."

"This is an impossible request. I can't stay in Savoy. I need to get back to California."

The duke stood. The afternoon light had waned and twilight swept into the room lengthening the shadows. "You have until Wednesday to decide."

Paul followed his host down the staircase. As he dressed for dinner, he thought about the absurdity of the duke's request. He had absolutely no intention of painting a da Vinci. But the sharp truth sunk in as he knotted his tie: The fire on the road was no accident, but some sort of fated ritual that had played out across the last five centuries on those who have been closest to enjoying the talents of Leonardo. He realized for the first time he was in as much danger as his father lying hurt and inconsolable in his hospital bed. Leaving Savoy empty handed wasn't an option if he valued his ability to have a productive artistic life—or a life at all. If the duke was correct and he left the castle on Wednesday, there was no certainty he would survive the mountain this time. But paint a da Vinci?

Those who are in love with practice
without knowledge are like a sailor who gets
into a ship without rudder or compass.

—Leonardo da Vinci, *Notebooks*

16

When Marcella arrived at Scott's gallery in Brentwood on San Vincente Boulevard, two men in T-shirts and jeans were setting up long tables and laying white table clothes over them for the caterers. Marcella snooped around. She had been in many galleries over the years but had never seen her work hanging on a gallery wall.

Wandering around the large main room, she trembled. Nathan Bailey was showing eight pieces that she knew would attract a lot of attention, and Thomas Rhodes had a series of still lifes. Harper Jones had several nature scenes. Marcella had always admired Harper Jones' ability to capture the beauty of nature on canvas. Scott had works by some of the best artists in the area here today, and she wondered if she were even in the same league with these guys. She peeked around a wall and saw her blue-green seascapes hanging in the entrance to the east gallery. Scott's designer had placed lights along the top of the partition, and three of her watercolors sparkled under the glare just ten feet from Jones and

Rhodes. Her face flushed; her hands shook.

I wish Paul and Vincent were here.

She felt a twinge of guilt that she was going by herself. Why couldn't Vincent be on her arm, escorting her through the gallery? But for the first time she had the sense that even without him she would do well. She couldn't take her eyes off her paintings. Her doubts kept telling her they were someone else's. She checked the signature in the bottom right-hand corner just to make certain they were hers. Beside each painting was posted the credit and price. She gasped at what Scott was asking.

A smooth voice from behind her said. "Nice aren't they?"

She spun around at the compliment to find a beaming Scott Bezcotta.

"Scott, you scared me."

"My apologies." He looked sharp in a taupe colored double-breasted suit with a matching paisley tie and an off-white shirt. A black silk handkerchief was carefully folded in the breast pocket of his jacket. His short, brown wavy hair was combed straight back and glistened in the afternoon sunshine. "We have some time before the show. Can I buy you a latté?"

She nodded, and they walked up San Vincente to a Starbucks. He ordered two Latté Grandes, and they sat at a small round rose-wood table in the back.

"You have quite a lineup of painters tonight. I can't believe you're showing mine with them," she said, holding her latte with both hands.

He stirred the foam on the top of his drink. "You don't know how good your work is, do you?"

"I'm just feeling a little nervous."

"My patrons are discriminating." He lowered his penetrating brown eyes at her. "I wouldn't waste their time by showing your paintings if I didn't think you were good. You are going places."

He patted her hand.

"And where is it you think I'm going?" she asked.

"I think you can be as popular as Harper Jones or Nathan Bailey."

"You said as popular, not as good."

"Those two are synonymous in my mind."

Marcella started to relax. "That's nice you feel that way."

He took a sip of his latte. "It's not just me. I've had others in the industry look at your work these past few days—people I admire—and they feel the same way."

She didn't know what to say. Why didn't Vincent ever tell her this? She looked up at Scott with her most confident gaze. "Do you think they'll sell for the prices you're asking?"

"You've been in this business for a lot of years, Marcella. If this was anyone but yourself you wouldn't flinch at those prices."

She nodded. He was right. It was amazing what people paid for good art. It was just hard for her to put herself in that category.

He squeezed her hand again and let his warm palm linger on hers. "Listen, I know you're going through a tough time with Vincent's injuries and all. If there's anything I can do, please don't hesitate to call me—anytime."

"You've already been a big help. I mean getting me in your show."

"You deserve this. So when my guests come tonight, you hold your head up high and act like this is just another day's work and if they don't buy today, the prices will be higher next time."

Marcella laughed. This would be fun. Scott took her arm and escorted her back to the gallery. As the other artists arrived, he introduced Marcella and made certain she felt comfortable with them. Nathan Bailey said some nice things about her work and sent his best wishes to Vincent. Harper Jones spent a considerable amount of time with her talking about his craft and where he liked to paint. She told him how much she had enjoyed his work over the years. He responded by inviting her to visit his studio in Malibu. Marcella was thrilled.

Thomas Rhodes came in late and was cool toward her at first, but after a while he warmed up.

By the time guests started arriving around four, she felt like she had been an artist all her life. Every single one of her pieces sold by closing time, around eight o'clock. Each of the other artists gave her a hug before they left. Scott walked her to her car.

"You did very well tonight," he said opening her car door for her.

She pushed a strand of hair out of her face. "Beyond what I expected."

"But not beyond what I expected," he said leaning on the open door beside her.

"So you've told me." She stood between the open door and the driver's seat.

"Will I see you again?"

"Of course. I'd like you to look through my other paintings and give me an idea of what will sell."

"I'd be happy to. I'll be in Laguna Beach early next week. Can I come by and see what you've completed?"

"Oh no, that wouldn't work." She put her hand on his arm.

"Well then, bring your work down to Rhonda's. We can meet there. You can't lose your momentum." He inched closer to her. "Maybe we can have lunch together. You look like you need someone to talk to."

"A friend," she said, putting her hand on the car door.

"A good friend," he said. "Who believes in you." He inched closer to her.

She put out her hand to shake his, but instead he wrapped his arms around her and gave her a hug. With his arms wrapped around her, she wanted to cry; his arms felt safe and strong. He kissed her on the cheek. She jerked her head away and stared at him. He dropped his arms from around her.

"I'm sorry, I didn't mean to startle you. I'm just so happy for you."

She could feel blood warming her face. She put her hand to the hot skin of her cheeks. She knew she must be turning deep shades of red.

"I didn't mean to embarrass you." He gave her a look of genuine concern.

"Thank you for all of your help." She climbed in and closed her car door.

Driving home, she felt elated at tonight's sales. Things would be okay financially for her and Vincent for a long time.

She hoped Vincent would be up when she arrived home. She wanted to tell him everything. She would be delicate, but she couldn't hide her excitement. If some of Vincent's worries were about money, she had solved them. Things didn't seem as difficult as Vincent had made them out to be. There were a lot of people who enjoyed watercolor landscapes, and they paid nicely for them. Not as much as Vincent's portraits, but they didn't take a couple of weeks to finish either. She had never had so much fun in all her life, and the comments from her peers were food for a part of her that had been starved for a long time.

As much as she wanted to share her excitement with Vincent, she doubted if he would be up to hearing about her success. At least Lynette would be there to share her joy. Someday Vincent would accept her work. He would have to.

She didn't know how to thank Rhonda for introducing her to Scott. She felt comfortable around him; she trusted him. He was truly helping her, and not simply trying to take advantage of her. His kiss shocked her at first, but as she considered it she realized it was as he said—he was just happy for her. He believed in her. She could feel it—just the way he talked about her to the other artists and to his customers. She didn't want to ruin any friendship they were building.

Her head spun. Tonight was a dream come true. She hoped that what she saw in Scott's eyes was nothing more than a desire for a good friendship. That was one thing Marcella was clear about in her mind: the line of fidelity was etched deep in her heart. She had no intention of crossing it—ever.

It was shortly after 9:30 p.m. when she pulled into her garage in Monarch Bay. She found Lynette sitting on the sofa in the den staring at a blank TV with a look of anguish on her face.

Marcella plopped down on the cushion next to her and put her hand on her shoulder. "What's wrong? Did something happen to Vincent?"

She shook her head. Marcella could tell she had been crying.

"What's happened?" she asked again, stroking her sister's back to try to comfort her. "Are you okay?"

"I'm better now. Just give me a minute." Lynette took a deep breath, trying to compose herself. "I didn't know how to stop him."

"Lynette, what are you talking about? Did Vincent hurt you?"

"I'm fine. It's your work," she said, almost starting to cry again.

"What do you mean my work? Lynette, please, what happened?"

She let out a deep sigh and leaned back into the sofa. "About an hour after you left, Vincent came out of the bedroom, looking for you. I told him you weren't here. He got angry and wanted to know where you were. So, finally I just told him. He flew into a rage and walked around the house, through every room, as if he were looking for you, ending up in your studio. I didn't follow him in there, but I could hear the noise." She stopped to take a breath.

"What noise?" Marcella asked.

"At the time … I didn't know what he was doing. It was an awful noise, but I didn't dare go in there." She crossed her arms and shook visibly.

Marcella clenched her jaw, and her face tightened. She feared to see for herself, but she felt compelled. What had Vincent done? She stole down the hall to her studio. The room was dark, and she reached in and put her hand on the light switch. Expecting the worse, she flicked the light on. Her workspace looked like it had been assaulted by a madman.

The paintings she had left propped against the wall had been torn to tiny pieces. They had all been ripped into shreds too small to recognize. She picked up a piece of yellow watercolor paper and examined it closely. It had teeth marks on it. He must have held her paintings between his bandaged hands and then torn the paper apart with his teeth like a frenzied animal. The one on the easel had also had been ripped into shreds, the easel tipped over and smashed. Her paint box had been dumped over and paint tubes ground into the carpet. Red, yellow, green footprints were smeared all over the room. Her pallet was pulverized and fragments kicked into the corner. The spare papers she had stretched that had been neatly stacked in one corner were trashed. Paint was splattered on the walls; even her brushes had been broken. Not even the little stool Marcella used in front of her easel had been spared—it had been trampled into an unrecognizable form. There was nothing worth salvaging.

She turned the lights off and stood in the darkness with her hands over her face. Lynette must have been horribly frightened at the violent noise she heard. Marcella could feel Vincent's rage permeating the room like the residue of his cologne. She fell to her knees in the midst of the debris.

The past few hours with Scott, her life had taken on the tone of one of her watercolors: light blue washes with yellowish sunshine playing across sunbaked beaches—innocent beauty frolicking with childhood dreams. But now a darkness descended across the face of her life—dreary with a threatening gloom large enough to swallow her. An urge burgeoned within her, like a volcanic pressure pushing to vent its red-hot magma. Among this riot of colored fragments lay her fondest wish, now hopelessly tattered, that someday Vincent would acknowledge her talent. But instead he had chosen to crush her in a place more vulnerable than Achilles' own heel. Her anger flashed in scenes of vengeance, bright pictures done in gaudy oils of crimsons, cadmium yellows, viridians, and cobalt blues. Anything she did would be a justified reaction; no one would blame her for going mad with rage—not even herself.

But it would take all her energy, of that she was certain, and her dream would vanish like a flickering ember doused in buckets of water. She held her hands tightly to her face and clenched her eyes shut to keep any more images of destruction from invading her mind. In the midst of this sea of damnation, she was determined not to let it drown her.

"Are you all right?" Lynette said, coming up behind her in the darkness. She put her hands on her sister's shoulders.

Marcella started shaking, and then took deep breaths to calm herself. "I … I'm going to be fine."

"I think he must be going insane, Marcella." She sank down behind Marcella and hugged her sister.

They both knelt motionless in the midst of the darkened chaos.

"Would you do me a favor?" Marcella asked. "Would you go in my room and get me a few things? I'm going to sleep in Paul's room for a while."

"Good idea."

Before Lynette could leave, the phone jangled, sending a chill through Marcella. "I'd better get it before it wakes Vincent," she said.

They could hear the phone ringing but it was buried under debris. They both rummaged around the room.

"I found it," Lynette said, answering the phone.

After a greeting, she handed the phone to Marcella. "It's for you. It's Paul."

Among all the studies of natural causes and reasons,
light chiefly delights the beholder.

—Leonardo da Vinci, *Notebooks*

17

A little before seven o'clock the next morning, Paul sat on the edge of his bed holding the receiver to his ear. *She's taking an awfully long time to come to the phone. I hope I didn't wake her up.*

"Mom, you there?"

"Paul. I was beginning to worry about you."

"You sound like you're upset. Is everything all right?"

"I'm okay ..."

He heard a tremble in her voice. "How's Dad doing?"

"Not too good, I'm afraid."

"Is it his hands?"

"I think it's his head," she said, sounding exhausted.

"Is he depressed?" he asked, trying to keep the conversation moving. It sounded like she was having a hard time talking.

"You could say that. I don't know what the problem is ... when are you coming home?"

"I'm not sure." He felt guilty for not being specific. Her voice sounded so down, as if the whole world was resting on her shoulders. "Mom, tell me what's going on."

She told Paul about her show and the great response she had.

"That's wonderful. You should be floating on air," he said, having even more difficulty understanding her sour mood.

"Then when I came home, I found your father had trashed my studio."

"What?" he asked, bolting up from the bed.

"He tore up every one of my watercolors into tiny shreds. My photo collection, my paints, everything is destroyed," she said, her voice cracking.

He sighed. He wanted to kick himself for being in Italy when he should be home with her. His mother had worked hard, and now this. He feared for her. Would she drop over the edge like his father had? She sounded like she wanted to give up.

"Listen, why don't you lay low for a while? Don't paint anymore at home. Can you get your old studio back from Rhonda?"

"I don't think she's rented it out," she said slowly.

"Good. I'm doing everything possible to wrap things up here as fast as I can."

"Where are you now?"

"In Savoy."

"Paul, your father told me the real reason you went to Italy."

He knew he should have told her before now. "I'm sorry, Mom. I should have been up front with you."

"I don't blame you. I know your father put you up to it."

"I know, but—"

"Now's not the time to discuss this. I just need you home to help me. I'm afraid of what your father might do next."

"How can he do anything worse?" Paul asked, trying to plumb her concern.

"I don't know. I don't think anyone knows. But his mood gets darker every day."

"Mom, he thinks this chair will help him, so I'm doing my best to find a way to come home with it." Paul sat on the corner of the bed.

"If that thing will help him through all this, then bring it home." Her voice started to sound stronger, as if just talking gave her some hope.

"What do you think his reaction would be if I come home without it?"

There was silence on the other end of the line.

"Mom?"

"I don't know what he would do. I just think it would be better if you had the chair. Is the duke willing to sell it?"

Paul took a deep breath. He couldn't bear to tell her the details of the duke's proposition. "In a way, yes."

"Can we afford what he wants?" Her voice sounded subdued, tired.

In some ways it would be cheap. Just complete a painting. All he needed was to put in his time. "I think we can afford it. But we're still negotiating."

"Paul ... you know how much money we have. Do your best to come home with the chair." Her voice now was pleading. He wanted to drop the phone, run through the castle, grab the chair, and race home. But life just wasn't that simple.

She asked Paul for a number she could reach him at. He gave her the duke's number and address that was on the notepad Gerhard gave him.

"Please, honey, come home as soon as you can," she said, shamelessly pleading.

"I will." Paul said. He dropped the phone in the cradle and then slumped onto the bed. He had to find the chair and get it home to California, quickly.

In his cramped office above the castle's living quarters, Stein wore a headset with the voice muted on his end, listening in on LaBont's conversation with his mother. As he feared, LaBont hadn't taken the duke's offer seriously. Even if the duke could talk him into painting the da Vinci, LaBont was going to be a source of trouble. If LaBont was convinced of the chair's worth, he would have jumped at the chance to own it. And that was the part of the duke's plan that rankled him: giving the chair away. When the duke first suggested that strategy, Stein thought he was kidding. But not the duke. He intended to follow through with his part of the bargain. But if the forgery worked once, it would work again and again. No, he needed to come up with an alternative to letting LaBont prance out of the castle with the priceless art object, and he would start with Isabella.

As the conversation between mother and son ended, Stein clicked off the dial tone on the base of the phone and tossed the headphones onto his cluttered desk. He needed to watch LaBont closely. He would demand that the duke get an agreement from LaBont to provide the painting or leave the castle. But whether LaBont stayed or left, he intended to continue to prod Isabella to get on with her ambitions instead of spending so much time in her studio entertaining LaBont.

His sparsely furnished office was a small square of white walls. Except for three bookshelves against the far wall crammed full of art books from almost every era, Stein had made no effort to decorate his office. He yanked open the top drawer of his worn wooden desk and rifled through it until he found a small plastic device with two short stainless steel prods. He checked the battery by giving the trigger a pull. Blue sparks arced across the steel prods. He hadn't had occasion to use it for a long time, but he wanted to have it fully charged in case he needed it. He plugged it into a charger behind his desk.

He then pulled open a bottom drawer and took out his nine-millimeter Beretta, slapped in a clip, slid a round into the chamber, set the safety, and tucked it into his belt in the small of his back. He donned his sport coat before leaving his office, and strode down the hall. He wanted to check on the readiness of the workshop he'd set up in the castle's old dungeon. Tosatti would arrive soon with the materials, and the project needed to get underway. Whether Isabella or LaBont did the painting didn't matter to him. It just had to be completed on schedule. He planned to see to it that from now on, everything ran smoothly.

The painter ... must remain solitary, and particularly, when intent on his studies.

—Leonardo da Vinci, *Notebooks*

18

*P*aul gazed out the window at the lush mountainside and wondered why his father would do such a thing to his mother's art. She didn't deserve to be treated like that. His mother's dry and tired voice frightened him. What if she just gave up and left? He realized if he didn't do something soon he wouldn't have much of a home to go back to.

The duke had been clear that he didn't plan on relinquishing the chair unless Paul agreed to compete a painting. Not just any painting but a da Vinci. It didn't take any great leaps of logic to understand what the duke intended to do with a fake da Vinci. It was anyone's guess how much an original da Vinci would be worth: fifty, sixty, eighty, a hundred million dollars. No one could say until such a painting were authenticated and auctioned.

He assumed the chair was in the castle somewhere. What if he were to find it, stuff it in his car, and hightail it back to Milan? How hard could it be to abscond with it? If he were going to come up with some kind of plan, he'd at least have to know where it was and what he was up against.

He glanced at his watch. It was a quarter past seven on Sunday morning and Isabella had invited him to attend church with her family. They celebrated mass in the Savoy Chapel much as they'd done for the past five hundred years. He had a couple of hours before he needed to meet her.

Opening the door, he skulked downstairs, through the great room, and snaked his way through passages until he came to the hall of family portraits. Paul had never stolen anything in his life; he'd never had a reason to. But the defeated timbre of his mother's voice rattled him: that was reason enough to do something.

Once in the northwest tower at the base of the stairs, he gazed up at the spiral staircase leading to the room with the duke's special collection. Isabella had said her father housed his religious artifacts up there. Good chance the chair was stored up there. It wouldn't do any harm to take a look. He quietly moved up the spiraling stairs. He'd just act lost if someone stopped him. Shafts of dim light sifted through the window slits, casting a pall on the stairwell. The steps wound around, leading him farther into shadows until he disappeared into the darkness. The stairwell was constructed exactly like the ones leading to Isabella's studio and the duke's study, which came out on a small landing at the top. Reaching the last step, he stretched his hand out and felt the rough oak planks of the door. He found the knob in the middle of the door, but it wouldn't budge. Locked.

He quickly found his way into the long hall of the west wing. A colonnade to his right supported a cloistered walkway that at one time had been open to the courtyard, but was now sealed off by a row of windows a few feet behind the Doric columns. The entire west wing lay in the fallow darkness of morning shadow. He remembered walking along this corridor yesterday with Isabella.

He'd seen a stairway at its far end. Isabella had told him there were galleries in the floors above, so it seemed like a good place to start searching. Unless it was conspicuously placed in one of the galleries, he wondered if he'd ever find it.

As he neared the end of the hall, he saw a figure move out of the intersecting passageway, crossing in front of him. He ducked behind a pillar, then peeked out. Maybe it was his imagination. He hurried down the last stretch of hall to where the two wings met. He froze a step inside the south wing. A tall, lanky man stood facing an open closet door. The man fumbled with something in front of shiny metal panels. It was Stein, he was certain. Paul stepped back to disappear into the shadow. A few more feet and he would be behind one of the columns. He glided back noiselessly until his heel tapped the pillar, like a slap of water against the shore. But it seemed to echo through the halls. Paul froze, holding his breath.

Stein pivoted, cocked his ear, and peered right at Paul. He didn't dare move, but he knew Stein couldn't see him in the shadow unless he moved closer. His pulse beat loudly in his ears; he was certain Stein could hear him.

The man strode forward and stopped. He reached into his jacket and pulled out a black metal object. It was a gun. Stein had a gun. Paul fought to hold his breath.

Why would the man carry a gun in the castle?

Holding the pistol in front of him about waist high, he stepped forward. The pain bit Paul's lungs, but he refused to let out even a sigh.

Stein hesitated and scanned the shadow. Suddenly the metal walls slid open behind him with a soft whir. It was a small elevator. Backing up one step at a time, he never took his eyes off where Paul had hit the pillar. The man lowered the gun, backed into the elevator, and the doors soughed closed. Paul expelled his breath and gasped but was too frightened to move.

The doors suddenly glided open again and Stein stepped out and froze as if expecting to catch someone moving. He glared into the darkness toward Paul for a long moment, then grabbed the handle to the closet door, and pulled it behind him.

Paul was too tense to move, but he had to get back to his room. After waiting long enough to make certain the elevator was on its way, Paul ran back up the west hall the way he'd come. An elevator hidden in a closet. Stein packing a weapon. A locked door at the top of the stairs. He'd found a lot in forty-five minutes of exploration, but not what he was looking for.

Back in his room, he lay down on his bed to catch his breath. Stein must be the muscle behind the duke's whole scheme. Paul wondered what role Stein had in stealing the chair from his family. Just thinking about the whole mess his family was in made him angry; the chair belonged in California with his father. It couldn't be considering stealing to take what rightfully belonged to his family. He shook his head in quiet dismay. All of this tragedy just so the duke could fake a painting.

In the middle of his thoughts, he was disturbed by a knock at the door. He opened it to find Isabella, radiant in a long lavender dress, her hair up in a French braid, wearing pearl earrings and a matching double strand of pearls around her neck.

"Are you ready?" she asked, sizing up what he was wearing. "The men usually wear coats and ties."

"Oh, yes, church. Give me a few minutes." He closed the door. After quickly shaving and brushing his hair, he found a dark blue Italian suit and several shirts and ties in his closet. Paul was amazed that everything fit so well. Gerhard was a real pro.

Five minutes later he opened the bedroom door wearing his suit and a matching blue and red Italian silk tie. He found Isabella waiting in the hall.

"You look dashing," she said.

"You look ... incredible." He took her arm and they headed toward the chapel.

"I want to apologize to you for being snippy yesterday," she said, holding his arm tightly.

"This whole situation is kind of awkward. Don't worry about it."

"My father told me you might stay with us for a while," she said, looking over at him with a curious smile.

"I'm thinking about it." From the tone in her voice, his staying on to paint a da Vinci for the duke seemed more like a lark than what he saw it as, a most audacious forgery. Or was it that she didn't have a clue why he had been asked to stay? But extending his time in Savoy certainly had collateral benefits he'd never considered, and the main one was tightly twined in his arm at this very moment. She certainly was worth getting to know, and along that path of discovery he hoped to find out why she was in his dreams. Was her appearance a sign of some sort? He'd never been much for supernatural moments because, quite frankly, he wasn't sure such a state beyond what he could see and touch even existed.

They walked through the garden up the steps of the chapel and into the darkened church. Paul had never been to a Catholic mass before. The sweeping vaulted architecture of the stone church—and the light that streamed down in narrow rivers from a small window high over the altar to illuminate the painting behind it—made Paul feel a sense of reverence he'd never felt before. They seated themselves in the front left-hand pew. The duke sat farther down the row. He nodded to Paul as he settled next to Isabella who sat between them. The small chapel was nearly full. He recognized some of the household help as they came in, but other faces he hadn't seen before.

The service was rich in a tradition and language Paul didn't understand. He did recognize that the service was being recited in

Latin. He was under the impression priests used the vernacular to say mass, but evidently not here in the ancient Savoy Chapel.

Paul had a hard time keeping up with the homily, which the priest gave in Italian. He picked up some of it, but the man spoke too quickly for Paul's basic knowledge of the language.

As he strained to listen to the priest, a round shaft of light from above caught his attention. The shaft moved in a slow march, as if marking the progress of the service, across the faces of the disciples in *The Last Supper* that towered over the altar. Paul saw the stunned reactions in the expressions of Jesus' followers as they asked among themselves who was to betray him. Finally the light touched the serene flesh-colored face of Jesus—his expression resolute, his gaze firm.

Jesus' confident smile was so real. It spoke to Paul like thunder in paint, as if it was not possible for a mere mortal, no matter how devious, to hinder his mission. Paul was somewhat familiar with the life of Jesus, but before this moment had only given him passing thought. But the artist's ability to capture that very moment in time when he sat with his disciples the night before he died, the moment so much history revolved around, was a marvel indeed. But what, Paul wondered, was so important that Jesus was willing to die for? From his time in Sunday school, Paul was aware of the jealousy of the Sadducees and the Pharisees that surrounded the death of Jesus. The kindest, most loving man to walk the face of the earth, was going to be betrayed, treated like a common criminal, hung between thieves, his life ignominiously stripped from him. But he showed no sign of agitation. Paul didn't dare look at the ugly face of Judas to the right of Jesus.

Golden light glinted on the bridge of Jesus' nose. His eyes blazed at Paul in a moment of certainty—*he was ready to die for what he believed in.*

"Paul, are you ready to go?" Isabella shook his arm gently.

The mass had ended while Paul was lost in his reflections. Paul glimpsed back up at *The Last Supper.* The shaft of light had moved on and the painting lay shrouded in darkness above the altar.

It was just a painting. He didn't understand why all of a sudden he was so taken by the life of Jesus.

"We have to go first before everyone else can leave. It's a tradition," she whispered in his ear.

The duke stood and cleared his throat. Paul gathered his thoughts, rose, and exited the pew. He hesitated a moment to let Isabella and the duke out. They both faced the altar, genuflected, then turned and reverently marched up the aisle to the church entrance. Paul followed as they proceeded, arm in arm. Paul had never been exposed to so much stiff formality. This was no beach culture of flip-flops, shorts, and brief pithy sermons couched in bite-sized, easy-to-understand chunks. This was the ancient Gospel wrapped in Latin. The ritual and ceremony held little meaning to him, but the piercing eyes of Jesus had found Paul in the crowd, singled him out, as if he had waited all those centuries behind the altar for him to show up.

Paul didn't understand the rituals he'd just observed, but he sensed his host and hostess had a deep respect for what had taken place, as if the traditions didn't bind them simply to their past, but to a true sense of themselves. He had a new admiration for Isabella and her father as they briefly paused in the vestibule to let the priest bless them, then the procession unfolded into the golden Italian sunshine that was shot through with deep shades of golden blue. Wasn't this life they had here in Savoy worth preserving? If painting a da Vinci would help them maintain this quaint and elegant life, how could that hurt? Maybe helping the duke was the best way, the true way, the only way to help his father.

Without perspective nothing can be done well or properly in the matter of painting or drawing.

—Leonardo da Vinci, *Notebooks*

19

*L*ater that afternoon, Stein worked his way up the stairs to the duke's study. Frederick hunched over his desk, poured over an ancient book. Stein seated himself in front of the desk and cleared his throat.

"Has LaBont made a decision?" Stein asked.

Frederick sat back in his leather chair and took off his glasses. "I gave him until Wednesday."

Stein slid forward in his chair. "Wednesday! Tosatti will be here with supplies to start the project tomorrow. LaBont needs to decide today or leave the castle."

"You become quite ugly when you're angry." Frederick said not smiling.

Stein felt like exploding, but he held back. "Your house of cards is ready to fold over your aristocratic head, and you act like you're on a picnic."

"This is no picnic, I guarantee you." Frederick reached for his cigarette box, he took one out, lit it, inhaled, then leaned back. "I was very clear with him about the terms of the proposition. If I was too forceful I believe I would have lost him. I know he will bite. Soon this will all be over," he waved his hand, a swirl of smoke following, "and everything will be back to normal. You'll see."

Stein sighed and shook his head. "There's too much riding on the shoulders of this young man to be cavalier about what decision he'll make. We need to have a backup in case LaBont gets cold feet."

Frederick frowned. "Our best contingency is to be patient."

"Did you show him the Book of Fire?" Stein asked.

The duke nodded. "He will come around, believe me. He does not want to leave Savoy without the chair."

"I overheard him telling his mother he may come home without it. If he leaves here without helping us, he'll have figured out what our plan is. I'm sure of it," Stein said.

Frederick stroked his chin. "You need to relax, Jacob. I saw the fear in his eyes when I showed him the history of our ancestors."

"I don't know how you can be so calm. If he figures out our plans, he could jeopardize everything."

"He will take up my offer, believe me." Frederick smiled. "It's only a matter of time, Jacob, before we'll have the da Vinci."

"I just hope your confidence doesn't get us four bare walls in a slum when we get run out of this place. Isabella could paint the da Vinci in a heartbeat and you know it."

Frederick sat up, forearms on his desk. "You read what happened to Vincent LaBont. The curse is as real as the air we breathe. Can't you understand that?"

"What I understand is you've let yourself be dominated by your superstitions. That could have been nothing more than a coincidence. The papers even reported it started with an electrical fire. I told you what happened with the lamp I was looking at. But let's just say that you're right about this curse. If she uses it, it stays with her and she'll be safe. She has nothing to fear."

The duke's nostrils flared and he sat forward. "She has everything to lose, and I forbid her to use it," he slapped his desk with his fist.

Stein sat back and took a deep breath before continuing. "We're taking too big of a risk to have an outsider paint the da Vinci. You underestimate her. This is what she wants."

"I won't change my mind on this. We'll only address this again if LaBont gets cold feet." Frederick put his glasses back on and stared at Stein as if to punctuate his determination.

Stein stood. "We'll see then, on Wednesday."

Frederick nodded once then leaned over his book and continued reading as if he'd never been interrupted.

Stein stomped out, practically running down the stairs. It was insane to get so close to their goals and have its success or failure rest on whether one kid from California decided to cooperate or not. Stein had the suspicion LaBont didn't believe Frederick would give him the chair once he painted the da Vinci. Or he feared using it. And why not? After the duke went through the history of those who'd used it, it would be hard not to fear being burned to death. And then what happened to his father must be weighing on his mind. Stein shook his head; Frederick's whole plan seemed built on supposition and probability from the very beginning. In the back of Stein's brain a simpler, more achievable plan had percolated for sometime, and now it was time to implement it for Frederick's own good, for Isabella's good, for everyone's good.

⚔⚔

Early the next morning, as the sun crested the far peaks of the valley overlooking Savoy, Isabella, dressed in Jodhpur boots, riding britches, and a long-sleeve white turtleneck, stood in the third-floor gallery in front of Leonardo's chair. She'd agreed to meet

Stein here before her morning ride. The chair sat in the center of a round dais surrounded by a purple velvet rope hung from chrome stands, and it was illuminated by a single recessed lamp in the ceiling that showered it in a shadowless circle of light. She stood behind the velvet barrier in the darkness and studied the large wooden piece of furniture. She lifted her chin as she observed the highly polished chair glinting with an innocent luster, as if it had no consciousness of the pain it had supposedly caused her ancestors. How could it? It was only a chair. And that's what bothered her about the mystique surrounding the chair. How could all of those men who used the chair die as a result? She just didn't believe it possessed the power to kill that her father attributed to it. Accidents were an everyday occurrence back then as well as now. It didn't make sense to blame the chair and its amazing gift for the misfortune that befell people all the time. The coincidences were striking, but that's exactly what they were—coincidences. But that it possessed a power to bestow a special gift to paint like the maestro himself was something she doubted less and less as she grew older and learned just how difficult it was to paint like da Vinci.

She'd known its story since she was a little girl growing up in these halls. It was always told in the same tone her nanny used when reading Snow White and other fairy tales: the lilting voice of a socially acceptable prevarication, a doomed damsel saved by Prince Charming. Such things didn't happen in real life.

But the fact that her ancestors were highly gifted painters was indisputable. The evidence confronted her every time she traversed the length of the great room, or went to mass, or heard her father talk about art. He longed to restore the glory of the House of Savoy, and he talked about his plans at dinner the way other men discussed sports or politics. These conversations had driven her to scurry off to her room and put a pencil to paper. She'd wanted nothing more than to draw with the authority and convincing reality that she'd observed in the paintings around her. Regardless of how hard she worked, everything she drew had only the glimmer of greatness, not the aura of accomplishment she saw displayed every day. The desire to paint burned so deeply within her she became convinced that her life would be hopelessly unfulfilled if she could not perform like the ancient Godvicos.

But these desires couldn't entirely explain what she was doing here in the halls of Savoy at this time in her life. She could have stayed in California. Her years at Stanford had opened doors into the business world. She'd interned two summers in one of the largest advertising agencies in San Francisco and had accumulated an impressive portfolio. They'd offered her a job after graduation. Her work was superior to the other artists coming out of school and assured her of significant commercial success. And San Francisco was a heady city. A city built up from the ground just a mere hundred and fifty years ago. It was all wood and glass and steel coated with the varnish of a newfound wealth. Isabella could smell the newness every time she walked up Market Street. It was a city with no traditions, no history to speak of, and no cultural ruling class. Anything was possible in such a place. She could make herself a grand life, if she could be happy drawing tennis shoes, milk cartons, cows, and whatever else American business needed. The harder she worked, the more she felt her art becoming a product, a commodity of exchange in the marketplace of images used to impress people to buy. No one admired her work for its beauty alone. She knew she'd lose herself if she stayed in California.

She'd come home once and for all to separate fact from fable, and she stood before this wooden relic with only one intention: to find out if this ancient piece of wood could give her what she wanted. But to step over this velvet cordon, if fable were fact, would be irrevocable.

"Isabella, are you ready?" Stein said, coming up beside her. Before she could respond, he disappeared into the darkness toward a control panel against the far wall. He slipped a key into an alarm panel and turned it one-quarter turn, until a red light blinked green.

Back beside her, Stein handed Isabella a small, round barrel key. "This will get you past the alarm."

Isabella tightened her jaw and scrutinized the chair. Its size was intimidating, larger than what she thought was needed by anyone to simply rest in its seat. Neither did it look comfortable, but like a hard slab of wood bent to a specific purpose, as if its intent was not to give leisure.

He waved his hand toward the dais. "This is what you've wanted, isn't it?"

"I always thought if I worked hard enough, I would not need to trust in something so arcane," she said in a forlorn voice, not taking her eyes off it.

"Do you fear greatness?"

She exhaled with a smirk. "If I feared such things, I would not have come back to Savoy."

He unhooked one of the velvet cords and let it drop to the floor. "Then step forward and fulfill your destiny."

She stared at the fallen rope. Something was missing from her work, that fire, that spark that would propel her over the borderlands of potential into the realm of her ancestors. Was it worth the rumored risk to see if this chair could kindle in her what she wanted most? It was so hard to measure accurately the consequences of using it: what part of its history was embellished myth she would never know. But she would never know the measure of its truth if she didn't at least try it.

"You know your father's financial condition. You alone can help so that all this"—he raised his hands in the air—"will not disappear."

"How touching. If you and my father hadn't spent so much time at the racetrack maybe we wouldn't be in this position."

Stein shrugged. "But *you* would never get closer to what you've always wanted."

"You know so little about what I really want."

"Maybe so." He swished his hand toward the chair in an exaggerated arc. "But without this you will never know what you can accomplish."

"And once I've finished your work?"

"You will have the finest studio in Florence, as I promised."

"And the chair?"

"It will go where you go."

She glared at the walnut piece of furniture and smiled. "You've worked this out with all the parties concerned?"

"Your father is not in the best bargaining position. His horse-racing habit has run all his resources dry."

She looked him over dryly. "I'm sure you didn't have anything to do with that."

"Isabella, now's not the time for bickering. The wolves are at the gate. You must act." He took her hand and led her across the velvet barrier to the foot of Leonardo's chair.

※※※

Later that morning Stein led Isabella down a cobblestone corridor deep under the castle. The dark stone halls, lit only by naked, low-watt bulbs strung along the ceiling, sloped downward. Stein took a sharp right into a long corridor that led past a set of iron double doors into a spacious, well-lit stone room.

"Ah, Signór, so good to see you again." Giocomo Tosatti, in a green sweater and a white silk shirt, stood in front of a large easel. Stein warmly shook Tosatti's hand.

Isabella looked around the room, which smelled strongly of varnish and linseed oil. The room, with stone walls and floors, at one time had been the castle storeroom for perishables. A workbench lined the wall to her right. A large corkboard was attached to the wall. On the board were tacked up a photo enlargement of Leonardo's *The Portrait of a Musician* and one of Leonardo's self-portrait drawings. Isabella knew that the original drawing hung in the Louvre. Next to the drawing was an enlargement of *St. Jerome in the Desert*. Expensive light fixtures gave the room the same feel as natural light coming over her left shoulder.

"You are pleased, si?" Tosatti asked, looking at Isabella. He swept his hand through the room as if to emphasize all of his preparations.

"You can work here in privacy," Stein said.

"I forgot about these old cellars," Isabella said, looking around the room. The only sign of its former use as a storeroom was a small pile of lead pipe stacked in a far corner. She marveled at its transformation into a studio.

Tosatti looked at her admiringly. "We are ready, signorína."

She nodded and gave the portly man her full attention.

The art dealer explained that the canvas on the easel dated back to an eighteenth-century artist whose work had been poorly restored and thus was worthless. His workmen had removed all but some of the background paint, and it would be a perfect example of one of da Vinci's portraits transferred later from the original wood panels to canvas.

Tosatti had chosen Leonardo's self-portrait for her to paint because of its rumored existence as a work done by the maestro but subsequently lost. The one he wanted Isabella to paint would have the same features of both the men in *The Portrait of the Musician* and Leonardo's self-portrait drawing. He noted that the paintings and drawing were photos of the originals and not copies.

With photos, the details of his brushstrokes and shading could be studied closely. He went point by point and showed the marks or fingerprints of Leonardo's hand upon the three works on display. The structures of the ears in *St. Jerome* and in the self-portrait were strikingly similar. The eyes of *The Portrait* and the drawing had the same depth and brilliance. The declivity under the lower lip and the rugged strength of the chin were similar to the chin of *St. Jerome*.

Tosatti pointed out the fine line-drawn features of the forehead, nose, upper lip, and mouth along with the soft hair curling down the shoulders. He went over all the peculiarities of the Leonardo's masterful use of shading and shape that could be clearly seen in Leonardo's self-portrait. The unique feature of the Louvre drawing was Leonardo's clean-shaven face. So, the self-portrait would likewise be clean-shaven.

Tosatti took Isabella gently by the arm and escorted her closer to the photo of the self-portrait. He explained that the drawing was probably done sometime before 1505 and most likely showed Leonardo's most developed technique. Depending on the results she achieved, he planned to date her finished portrait during his stay in Florence in the late 1490s. So, while the painting did not need to be exactly like the self-portrait drawing, it needed to show Leonardo's distinctive traits of shape and shading.

He suggested she start by doing a set of sketches, to make certain she mastered the shading. He pointed to the dark areas of the eye. "The photos are so exact that you can see how Leonardo drew in the deep, shaded areas under the eye socket and in the mastoid passages. I have spent years scouring Florence, Milan, and Venice for Renaissance-era pigments and I have accumulated an impressive amount of drawing instruments you will need to complete the work." He took her left hand in his. "You have beautiful long fingers and you are left handed, just like the maestro."

Isabella blushed. She continued to study the photos hanging on the wall, then settled onto a stool and began to sketch on a large pad.

Stein took Tosatti aside while Isabella worked and motioned him toward the hall, then closed the door behind him so they were alone.

"How's the search for materials progressing?"

"We have found almost all the pigments we need to finish our project. They are being prepared in the studio in Florence as we speak. I have chosen the perfect place," Tosatti said.

"Good," Stein said.

"I thought LaBont was going to paint the portrait for us?" Tosatti asked, concern in his voice.

"The duke has been unable to persuade him and we can't lose any more time. She's part of my plan to persuade him," Stein said softly, not wanting his voice to echo in the stone corridor.

"This is an unusual turn of events. Do you think she can produce the same quality as LaBont?" he said nodding to the closed door.

"Of course not, but the American has no stomach for our proposition, so I must pull out all the tricks. By Wednesday, I'll have LaBont down here drawing, you'll see," Stein said.

"But what if he leaves? He knows our plans," Tosatti said, his eyes large and inquisitive.

"He wants the chair too badly to leave without it. He is not someone to worry about. As soon as he's completed the painting," Stein said with a crooked smile, "he will have a most unfortunate accident."

"You must be careful how you do this," Tosatti said. "Nothing must draw attention to what we're doing."

"Accidents happen in these mountains all the time and no one thinks twice about them." Stein smoothed down the lapel of his coat and put his hand on the door knob. "If LaBont starts the sketches on Wednesday, he will be ready to start working with oils in less than two weeks. When you come back, bring the pigments."

"Si. When I return, I expect to see magnificent progress." Tosatti held Stein's gaze.

"Soon we'll be fabulously wealthy." Stein smiled for the first time that morning.

"When the painting is finished, *then* we will all be rich, very rich," Tosatti said with a wry smile on his wrinkled face.

If the Lord—who is light of all things—vouchsafe
to enlighten me, I will treat of Light.

—Leonardo da Vinci, *Notebooks*

20

----

*E*arly on Monday morning, Marcella greeted Lynette in the kitchen. Over a cup of coffee Lynette broke the news that it was time for her to leave and go back to her family in Texas. She needed to be home by the end of the week. Marcella had been lucky to have her here for the last six weeks, and she realized it wasn't fair to ask her to stay any longer. They discussed some of Marcella's options such as hiring a visiting nurse, a live-in, and other possibilities to help with the work around the house so she could keep up her work while Vincent recovered.

Later that morning, Marcella drove to Rhonda's downtown gallery. Marcella knew that renting a studio from Rhonda Gillespi would include giving her squatter's rights to her personal life. Rhonda pried more as a hobby than a penchant for gossip. So, when Marcella approached her friend about renting the studio she'd given up a scant three weeks ago, she did so warily.

As Rhonda casually showed her around the bare room Marcella was already well acquainted with, she expertly dove into

Marcella's personal space like Sigmund Freud on a mission. Marcella kept her resolve to only give out what was pertinent to the business transaction at hand. If she cracked for even a moment, and revealed how Vincent had destroyed her work, she feared her anger would overwhelm the good feelings that had come out of the show at Bezcota's Gallery.

It had become obvious to Marcella that Vincent had submerged himself in rage, and he was bent on plunging her into his misery. Marcella didn't want to lose the tenuous hold she maintained over her feelings or her newfound productive creativity. Above all else, she feared being sucked into Vincent's turmoil, of experiencing his paralysis of spirit, of letting go inside with her grief and never gaining back any semblance of control.

She needed to talk to someone, but not to Rhonda.

After Marcella sealed her rental agreement, she drove to Shannon's Art Supply on the south end of town and bought all new equipment, brushes, and paints. She spent the whole morning setting up her studio and unpacking the few things she had been able to salvage from the rubble of her studio at home.

Sitting in a folding chair in one corner of the studio, she ran a finger over one of the beach photos she had rescued. She remembered taking the picture of the pristine sand along the Baja Mexico coast several years ago. It was the first vacation she had taken in years and she had taken it alone. Vincent had refused to leave home because he was working on an important commission, but he had not left Laguna for years. So Marcella had no choice but to go alone if she wanted a vacation.

The frayed photo was bent at a corner and folded down over a patch of sky, and another ragged crease bisected the scene diagonally into two. The memories it evoked were powerful. She could still feel the sandy softness between her toes from her strolls along the beach, and the salty scent of the blue-green water on the warm wind. The sensation of the afternoon heat beating on her bare shoulders came back with a rush. The beauty of one particular moment along that Mexican beach had brought stillness to her soul—it was an instant of clarity she had never forgotten.

Standing under the canopy of golden sunshine, staring into the azure breakers crashing onto the creamy sand, she realized everything in nature had a purpose. Why she had never seen this simple truth before surprised her. The afternoon sunshine beating on her skin was cooled by the light breeze from off the ocean. Even though it felt hot on her bare shoulders, it didn't burn her skin. The seas were the right temperature for the fish to spawn and feed humanity, and the sand was an effective terminus for its waves. It might slosh over its boundaries at given times, but the water always retreated from the land.

The fresh air, caressing her skin and swirling around her for her to breathe, was offered to her freely, as much as she wanted. Every part of nature had a place and a function. Even the tiniest part of nature could find happiness by simply fulfilling its created purpose. Seagulls scavenged relentlessly for food, crabs ran along the beach and burrowed into the sand when they needed a warm place to hide, and clouds scudded through the sky—each performing a given task. That was the way God created the world to work. It was a wonder, at times unfathomable, but nevertheless true. So why did she feel broken and out of sync in the face of such symmetry? As if her place in the whole universal order was in doubt.

If whatever purpose she was here to fulfill ran undone, would there be some cataclysmic consequences in the cycle of human beings? *Would anyone notice?*

That thought—would anyone notice?—rattled her. She didn't know why now it settled so dismally on her soul. She had never questioned her place in the cosmic order as a mother and a wife, but she couldn't deny that a deeper aspiration lurked below the surface of her everyday existence. She carried it about in her heart and soul, and no amount of domestic duties or mundane chores or disappointments or even the deep joy of motherhood could still its relentless pulse.

She knew she carried around a purpose she willingly ignored— a seed, once planted, begged to be watered. She had suppressed her dreams far too long. She wanted to paint, to bring to life what she saw, to memorialize the moment in vivid colors. Her desires couldn't be wrong, but she had believed too long that they were. It was as if the lights went on for the first time and all the furniture of her life, arranged in the rooms of her soul, was in the wrong place.

Why hadn't she seen that before? What was so wrong with being a mother, a wife, and an artist? Why did they even have to be listed in that order? Weren't these the talents God himself had breathed into her life, like he had whispered life into the wind? She could not deny that his power was in the floating clouds, and the face of the daisy, and the thunder of a horse's hooves. Then why wasn't he in the quiet longings of her heart?

Her whole married life, she had thrived on creating a peaceful environment that was totally out of balance. She had sought harmony over genuineness. And what had created harmony for others had only caused a nerve-wracking dissonance within. But she had always thought not painting was the right thing to do. Wasn't she a better person for making such a loving sacrifice? She had always believed it was what God wanted her to do—her moral duty. Now the creeping guilt of regret and uncertainty seeped into her soul. The price of peace had been paid with a currency that was irreplaceable, the golden threads of her own dreams.

But wasn't a happy marriage worth it?

And for the most part she had been happy. Vincent's many successes, Paul's growth into a handsome and competent young man were irreplaceable mementos in her scrapbook of happy memories. But what about the love between Vincent and her, why had she always thought it would endure forever? She had never before questioned her feelings for Vincent, even though he had always been an unlikely combination of taskmaster and tender lover. She never doubted for a moment, even during the most intense arguments, that he loved her.

She realized that some of her unhappiness lay in her quietude. She should have spoken up and made Vincent listen.

But would it have mattered? Would it have changed anything?

She didn't know. She probably would never know. Now, it was time to get to work. Standing up, she snapped the photo into a clamp nailed to the wall over her worktable. She rested her arms on her hips and stared at the empty watercolor paper on the flat surface before her. Was it too late? Had her dreams disappeared in the debris of Vincent's rage?

She sponged some warm water onto the Medium Not paper she preferred using. Its surface had the right amount of texture for delicate details, but would still take the washes that typified her work. She flipped it over and bathed the reverse side in warm water. Laying it watermark side up, she used her exacto knife to cut four lengths of gumstrips. Moistening the tape, she glued down the paper to her board, and smoothed the paper, leaching out the air bubbles and wrinkles. She tacked down the corners, and then went on to arranging the rest of her materials, since the board wouldn't be dry for a couple of hours.

Right before lunch Scott showed up at the door of her small studio as she tied on her smock.

He politely asked her to lunch. She hesitated for a moment. Scott looked handsome dressed in casual tan slacks and light tan print shirt. His thick brown hair was slicked back and his round face had the most charming, warm smile. His chestnut eyes were clear and trusting. Why not? Lunch with an interesting man might do her a world of good.

He drove her in his white convertible Jaguar to the Cliffside Restaurant on Pacific Coast Highway in South Laguna. They were seated at a table for two in a secluded corner by the large window overlooking the breakers crashing onto the rocks below. She enjoyed the quiet, relaxed ambience. She resolved not to cry on this good-looking man's shoulder, although she was desperate for a sympathetic person to listen to her.

"I was surprised to see you working out of Rhonda's," Scott said, spreading the linen napkin in his lap. He laid his hands on the peach-colored tablecloth and gently fiddled with his fork.

Marcella knew that would come up eventually. The last thing she wanted to do was tell him that her husband, the great portrait painter Vincent LaBont, had gone completely whacko. But she felt that if she didn't tell someone, she would go berserk. She worked to keep from frowning. "I need to be more productive, and her space was open for me to take right away."

Scott smiled. "Of course. After last Saturday's show you should be hard at it." He buttered a piece of bread. "Not only did the guests like you, but Nathan and Harper had some nice things to say about your work."

She could feel the reddening heat rising to her cheeks. "They were kind."

"They can be when they want to, but like most accomplished artists they're also keen critics. They weren't just blowing smoke in your face; they truly liked your work. They think you're a fresh new talent with a distinctive style."

She knew the generous comments should have made her glow, but all she could do was stare at the piece of brown bread she carefully buttered. *A fresh talent at forty-eight years old.* She wanted to cry, but instead she took a deep breath to hold off the tears. This was all happening so fast she didn't know what to say.

The waitress arrived just in time to save her from embarrassing herself. Marcella studied the menu and selected a Caesar salad and raspberry iced tea. Scott chose a salmon salad with a Diet Coke.

After the waitress left Scott leaned toward her. "I wanted to talk to you about your plans."

"What plans?"

"For your painting."

She smoothed the cloth napkin in her lap. She tried to sort out in her mind her plans before she saw her studio torn to shreds and her plans afterward. The two couldn't seem to disconnect. They ran together in a juggernaut of pain. She wanted to go home.

"I don't think you understand."

"Understand what?"

"The buzz you created the other night."

She raised her eyebrow a notch.

"You were terrific. Not only did Nathan and Harper go gaga over you, but that prig Thomas Lloyd even admitted to me you were a talent to be reckoned with."

Marcella could feel herself blushing. "They were all so nice. I felt flattered."

"You'd better be more than flattered."

Marcella pressed her lips together. She wasn't sure what he meant.

The wrinkles on his forehead disappeared, and he took a deep breath. "I received several interested calls this morning inquiring about the availability of your work."

Marcella rested her elbow on the table and put her forefinger across her mouth thoughtfully. Her mind wondered to the broken pile of finished landscapes that lay strewn across the floor of the small studio at home. Months of work lay shattered in useless oblivion. A tiny fraction of her heart lay among the wreckage, trampled by his uncontrolled resentment. It hurt to think about it.

"I would like to arrange a private showing next weekend for a few of my select patrons."

"Ah … I don't think that will work, Scott."

"Why is that?"

"I just need more time to finish some pieces. I don't have much to show right now."

"Nonsense, I saw all the finished work you had at your house. You only sold a fraction of what you had."

She shook her head and rolled her eyes. "No, you don't understand. None of that is my best. Let me take some time and put on a good show for you." Her jaw muscles tightened.

Scott fixed his eyes on his long-stemmed water glass, and slowly twirled it, lost in thought. He looked up at her with his penetrating brown eyes, as if he knew.

He was too sharp for her to slip this lie past him. She wanted to scream that the best she'd ever done lay in tattered fragments at home, that it would take time to make her heart whole again so she could paint with fearless strokes of golds and blues, but she didn't say a word. She only returned his quizzical look, with what she hoped was a disarming smile. "I will have what you want in a month."

Scott's intense gaze softened into a forced smile. "Why do I feel here you're holding something back from me?"

The waitress came by and carefully placed the Caesar salad in front of Marcella, and Scott's salmon salad in front of him. They both ate quietly.

"Did you not like the way I handled the show?" Scott said.

"Why would you ask that?"

"The only thing I can think is that you don't want me to represent you for all of your work."

She looked up at him, leaving her fork in midair. "Why do you say that?"

"Because I saw a lot of nice paintings in your back bedroom."

She let her fork finish its course to her mouth, and chewed slowly. Just thinking about what Vincent did sent a shaft of pain piercing her inside like a nail driven home into the soft flesh of her feelings.

He reached over with his right hand and placed it on hers. His hand was warm and comforting. She hadn't felt touched in a kind way for so long.

"Marcella," he said, gazing at her with his soft chestnut eyes. "If I did something to offend you I apologize. I understand if you don't want me to represent you exclusively."

She let out a deep sigh and gave him a limp smile. The muscles in the small of her back tightened. "I wouldn't think of working with another gallery. Please don't think that."

"If there's anything I can do for you please—"

"I don't know what anyone can do for me but to try and understand," she said, placing her fork in her salad.

"You need to let me in if I'm to understand."

She pushed herself back from the table and tossed her napkin over the salad. "Everything is just too ... I just need some time to work through some difficulties at home, and then everything will be just fine."

Scott was silent, and let go of her hand.

Rising from her seat, she refused to return Scott's gaze. "Would you mind taking me back to the gallery? I have a lot of work to do."

Without a word Scott laid some bills on the table and escorted her out of the restaurant. They drove silently back to the gallery in his Jaguar.

"I'm sorry about lunch. You've been kind to me," she said, as they tooled up Pacific Coast Highway through the afternoon traffic.

"There's nothing to apologize for."

"Yes, there is."

He glanced over at her. "Like what?"

"I don't have any paintings to sell right now."

"What about that roomful of work I saw last week?"

"It's all gone."

"Gone?"

She put her hand up to her mouth as if to measure what she should say. "Just leave it there ... please."

He gave a sigh. "Marcella, if you sold them already, I understand."

"Nothing's been sold. They ... they were all destroyed."

"Destroyed?" He slowed his Jaguar and gave her a look of incredulity. She hoped he could read in her eyes that she didn't want to say any more, not now. But it did feel good to finally get at least a smidgen of the truth out.

"There isn't anything I can do about it, so let's just drop it. I will have eight to ten good pieces in a month."

Scott sped up and steered his Jag behind Rhonda's gallery and slipped it into a parking stall. He killed the engine, and then looked over at her. "I understand things are tough for you at home, and you don't have to tell me anything. But painting will be good for you right now."

Marcella felt relieved. She knew she had been cryptic in her comments to Scott, but he seemed to get the picture. He was right. She needed to paint like some people needed therapy. She marveled that this man could be so understanding and sympathetic. She patted his shoulder and let her arm fall to the console between the seats.

He took her hand up and squeezed it. "Whatever I can do to help."

"You've helped me immensely already." She leaned over and gave him a kiss on the cheek. It was a warm friendly kiss, and nothing more.

Back in her studio, she slumped down into a chair. She knew she had slighted Scott and unsettled him. If she had stayed any longer in that restaurant letting him hold her hands she didn't know what she would have done. His hand felt so warm and comforting. She wanted to take it up in hers, and hold it tight and wring some kind of security out of it.

A faint knock at her door disturbed her reflection. Opening it, Scott stood in the door with a sheepish look on his face.

"I just didn't want to leave the way I did."

Marcella motioned for him to come in, and closed the door behind him. They both stood in the middle of her cramped studio, studying one another.

"I'm sorry about lunch," she said.

Scott shook his head. "Did Vincent destroy your paintings?"

She felt a trickle run down her cheeks. She nodded.

He put his arms around her, "Marcella, I'm so sorry."

It wasn't that she didn't want to hug him; she feared it would feel good. Now that she felt his strong arms around her, she didn't want him to let her go. All day she'd felt like she'd fallen, and now Scott had caught her, made her feel safe, and in his arms everything would be all right. She wrapped her arms around him, and held him tight. She didn't ever want to let him go.

The painter paints himself.

—Leonardo da Vinci, *Notebooks*

21

*M*onday and Tuesday Paul worked beside Isabella. Much to his surprise, she took suggestions from him willingly. Isabella arrived in her studio at midmorning and they worked together through lunchtime. When Paul took a break to eat, Isabella continued working. She seemed to have a new energy, a revived passion. Paul used the late afternoons to work his way through the galleries in his interminable search. Time ticked down rapidly to the moment when he would be forced to give the duke a decision. He couldn't use that chair. He couldn't get out of his mind what had happened to his father, his hands burned nearly to stubs. And what would become of his art as a passion if he were to succumb to the chair's power? His art was his own, not another's; even if he could paint like da Vinci, he didn't think it would bring him the satisfaction he had from doing the simplest seascape of the crashing waves of one of Laguna's coves. Besides, he'd never felt a need to be perfect, to be the greatest, to live at the top of the artistic world. Even if he never became famous for the simple landscapes he enjoyed painting, would it be enough that his work was original? He'd always felt it would. Fame alone was not a benchmark of the value of his originality, neither was wealth. But would all that change if he sat in the seat of the great maestro? It would have to; it would be impossible to maintain his own originality while drinking from the well of another. No, he could not use the chair if he was to be himself.

Besides, what audacity to think anyone could paint as well as Leonardo to the point that the world's experts could be fooled. A da Vinci coming onto the marketplace would receive incredible scrutiny. But then he couldn't deny the quality of the works in the castle. These could fool anyone. Something had empowered the Godvicos to paint with such masterful technique. If it were not for the chair, then how did he explain the artistic legacy that had been passed down in such an exacting manner to so many in the House of Savoy?

On Tuesday before dinner they rode horses up the trails that crisscrossed the mountains around the castle. She never mentioned the chair he'd come to find, and he never told her about her father's proposition. Yet he figured she must know about the plan. During the evening meal no one said a word. Stein spent the whole time eyeing him suspiciously. It was eerie. Did Stein know Paul was the one in the shadows the other day?

In the last few days, he had developed a healthy dislike for being in the man's presence. The feeling seemed mutual. Whatever the duke was planning, Paul was certain Stein was the one who was making it happen. He had noticed Stein taking Isabella aside after the meals and whispering to her like she was a child. He had even thought he'd caught a glimpse of someone shadowing him as he was walked through the galleries.

He and Isabella returned to her studio and worked until she couldn't hold a pencil or a brush. Paul had misjudged her work ethic. When it came to art, she was no *prima donna*. She worked hard at her craft, and he saw marked improvement in her chiaroscuro and her use of perspective. Paul had never watched a left-handed painter work; it gave her painting a distinctive brush-stroke.

Despite the pleasantness of spending so much time with her, it was hard for Paul to erase the uneasy feeling that a hidden agenda was unfolding around him. He didn't want any part of it, especially becoming involved in forging an old master. Stealing the chair from Savoy would be far more favorable than getting involved in a fraudulent scheme to deceive the art world.

He'd already made arrangements with the airline to ship the chair before he left California. He only had to get it to the airport. The one glitch in his plan was that the chair was nowhere to be found. He'd worked his way through the north, east, and south galleries. The only section he hadn't covered was the top floors of the west wing. Although all the galleries were open, there were so many closets, storage rooms, and locked doors, he became convinced he might have walked right past the chair and not even known it. And where did that elevator lead? There were probably many parts of the castle he didn't have access to. Tomorrow was Wednesday. He'd have to give the duke his decision and he'd be forced to leave the castle.

He would make his move tonight. He and Isabella worked late in her studio and then sat around a roaring fire for about an hour talking. Once in bed, he set his alarm for two in the morning. When it went off, he rose quietly and dressed. He found a flashlight in the bottom drawer of the desk and he took it with him as he made his way downstairs. The halls had small night-lights every few feet and enough moonlight sifted in through the windows for him to make out his way. He made the foot of the stairs leading to the west-wing galleries with little trouble. The first room was dark and still; halfway through it something metal groaned. He froze in his tracks. After a minute he panned the room with his flashlight. Ancient suits of armor stood against the far wall. When his stomach stopped churning, he traversed several more galleries, scanning the rooms methodically with his flashlight. They were filled with early Baroque paintings, sculptures, and glass cases filled with pottery, jewelry, and an eclectic mix of artifacts from sixteenth-century Europe. But no chair. He wished he had time to stop and gaze at the displays, but he kept working his way through the rooms.

He rehearsed in his mind what he intended to do once he found the chair. Taking it out of the castle would be difficult, but not impossible. His new rental car was sitting in the duke's garage waiting. The chair would fit easily inside the large SUV, then he'd drive like mad to Milan. Paul moved through the last of the second-floor galleries and traversed the stairs to the third floor. He went through room after room until he came upon one filled with interesting ancient weapons. He couldn't help but stoop over one case and gawk at a huge sword. He played his light on the ancient metal blade.

"Have you found what you're looking for?" came a voice from behind him.

Paul spun around, his heart racing. He dropped his flashlight. Stein stood behind him by the wall. He flicked on the lights and Paul blinked in the brightness. With a few quick strides the lanky Stein came right up to him.

"The collection is truly eclectic and extensive," Paul said, trying to calm himself.

"Up a little early, aren't we? I take it you're looking for furniture. Any particular time period?" he asked with a sinister voice.

"Nothing special, really. You have so much to look at." He motioned back at the sword under the glass.

Stein stepped closer and stared at Paul with hard, dark eyes. "I've noticed you've gone through every gallery."

"Is that something you keep track of?"

"Among other things," Stein said with a low, raspy voice as he edged a little closer. "Especially guests who sneak around in the dead of night."

"I had a hard time sleeping. What else do you do around here besides shadow guests?"

Stein edged closer until Paul could smell the alcohol of his cheap cologne. "I clean up messes and solve problems." Stein rested his arm on the glass case behind Paul, blocking his way to the left.

Paul could see the closeness of Stein's shave, the meticulous trim of his graying sideburns, and the slight yellowing of his teeth. "You knew when you took the chair from my house someone would die, didn't you?"

"You'd be much better off if you didn't ask any more questions," he said with a serious voice.

"You not only knew it would happen," he said, looking at Stein who was just an inch or so taller, "you wanted it to happen."

Stein pursed his lips, his jaw muscles rippled. "What happened to your parents will happen to you if you're not careful. If I were you, I'd take up the duke's invitation to help the House of Savoy. You're fortunate to be asked."

Paul took a deep breath to settle himself. "Are you threatening me?"

"Why would I do that?" he said, raising his eyebrows.

"If I find out that you had anything to do with hurting my parents—"

"You'll what?" Stein said, jabbing his index finger into Paul's chest.

Paul brushed the man's hand aside. "I'm a guest of the duke, touring his collection. Do you have a problem with that?" he asked sharply, shoving Stein's arm off the glass that blocked his way to the left. "Maybe I should take up your behavior with my host."

Stein jerked his chin back, dropped his arm, and sniffed the air. "It's almost three o'clock in the morning. Don't you think you should be getting your beauty sleep?"

Paul cast a look briefly at the dark doorway in the distance and then left the room. The man had staked out this room of all the rooms in the castle. The chair must be close. Stein followed him all the way back to his room. He didn't put it past the man to stand guard outside his door for the rest of the night. Paul crawled into bed. He was running out of time. He'd have to give the duke his decision later on today. One thing he knew for certain: He had no intention of painting a da Vinci for them. He would have to come up with another plan.

※※※

Later that morning, as Isabella sat on a small stool in her cellar studio, Stein came in and quietly peered over her shoulder. Her long hair was pulled back in a ponytail. In the space of two days her progress had been amazing, beyond what even she had expected. Her new sense of control in her hand, her ability to see objects with a new-found visual acuity, and the skill to paint what she saw was what she'd always missed in her craft. Stein went over to the wall and she watched out of the corner of her eye as he studied the two large pencil renditions of Leonardo's self-portrait she had taped up. She continued to work, not wanting to see his reaction. Her technique had improved remarkably through each successive iteration, and given time it would be perfect. She heard him circle around behind her so he could look over her shoulder at her current drawing.

"This is good." But his voice tailed off as if he left more unsaid.

"But what?" She said, not moving her head. If she just had a few more weeks. If she worked at it day and night, there was no telling how far she could improve.

"If it doesn't fool me, then it's not going to get by an expert. We need LaBont."

She didn't say anything but continued to draw.

"Isabella—"

"Not now," she said.

He skirted around the side of the easel so she could see him.

"We have to talk."

"Can't you see I'm concentrating?" she said, knitting her eyebrows, but otherwise ignoring him.

"We need your help with LaBont."

She held her pencil steady over the large pad, then set it down on the small worktable by her easel. "You think this is easy, don't you? That you can come down here and disturb me anytime you want, like I'm some kind of machine."

"Did you hear me?" he said determined not to be ignored. "You need to encourage Paul to use the chair."

"You don't think I can do this do you?" She laid down her pencil.

He gestured toward the drawings on the wall. "We need his help. You know that."

"Tosatti thinks I can do it," she said with an exasperated tone.

"We need to be realistic. If we had a couple of months, you could do it, but time is short. We need to make quicker progress."

She picked up her pencil and continued her work.

"Listen to me," he said, grabbing her arm.

She glared at his hand on her bicep, and then looked up at him with a frown. "Get your hand off me," she said slowly.

He dropped his hand. "Take him to the chair and encourage him to sit in it."

She sat back and studied her drawing. "It's good, don't you think?"

"We need everything in place within two weeks to start painting. We have one shot at this and we have to get it right the first time." He leaned over her easel as he spoke.

"LaBont won't do it; I can see it in his eyes," she said, wiping the lead point with a cloth. "All I need is another couple of weeks."

"In time, I know you'll be as good as anyone, but right now time is one thing we don't have. We need LaBont to complete the da Vinci so we don't find ourselves out on the street. If he doesn't paint this portrait for us, you won't have a studio in Florence. It's as simple as that. Don't underestimate your abilities to persuade, Isabella," he said in his dry, cool voice.

She dropped her pencil on the easel and glared at him with her deep green eyes. "So you just wanted to use me as bait to catch a bigger fish?"

Stein stood up straight and brushed back his dark hair. "Isabella. It was important for you to believe in what the chair can do. Now we need you—your father needs you—to convince LaBont to help us. You will be as good as anyone who ever painted, but not before the castle is lost."

She clenched her jaw and stared at the drawing. It was good, but she knew he was right. Given time, she could be very good; but events were moving too swiftly for her to have the luxury of progressing at steady pace.

"Isabella, he trusts you," Stein said in his soft, mellow voice.

She picked her pencil back up and continued to work. "When will the pigments be here?"

"Soon. That's why we need to be ready."

"And when do you plan to move to Florence?" she asked, not looking at him.

"As soon as the painting's completed. Tosatti has arranged everything."

She didn't say anything.

"We need to stop this game, Isabella. You know what you want, and if you expect my help, you need to get LaBont to cooperate. Once he's a part of it, there's no turning back."

She fixed her green eyes on him. "For anyone?"

Stein stood still and wiped his forehead with his palm. "Especially for LaBont."

She rose and faced him. Though smaller, she knew she could stand up to him if she needed to. "I agreed to help you with *one* da Vinci. Then you agreed to help me. I'll follow through with my commitment; you'd better remember yours."

Stein smiled and seemed to relax. "I'll come through. But as they always say, 'ladies first.'"

She turned away from him and sat back down in front of her sketchpad. She heard the door close behind him as he left the studio. It bothered her that LaBont had become part of their plan. When she returned from California six months ago, she came with the impression that she would be the one who would carry on the artistic legacy of Savoy. She knew of her father's superstitions, but she thought his financial condition would lower his resistance to her using the chair. And when she heard of her father's plan that whoever painted the da Vinci would possess the chair, her ambition only soared. In her father's eyes it would be a fair trade that would give the family such overwhelming financial security the chair would be a moot point—to everyone but her. But when she heard, from her father's own mouth, that LaBont would be enticed to the castle to paint the da Vinci, she felt like she'd been disinherited. She had tried every argument she could think of to convince him to leave the chair in Savoy, to let her drink of its gift, to let her paint the da Vinci. Despite her father's convincing argument, particularly his use of the Book of Fire, she didn't believe any of his nonsense about the curse. The accidents were explainable, like Vincent LaBont deciding to run back into the fire. It wasn't reasonable to think of the chair devouring those who used its remarkable gift.

But that the chair could impart Leonardo's gift of observation, his hand control, his ability to see nature better than any of his contemporaries, was something she could no longer dispute. She could feel it coursing through her as she worked, and she liked what she saw coming to life on the pages of her sketchbook in front of her. The last thing she wanted was to let the chair, and its wonderful gift, pass from her sight.

She was growing fond of Paul, and she felt sad that she had to convince him to do something that he didn't appear to want to do, but her father's situation was critical. She could not stand by and allow the castle and its treasures to fall out of her family's control. She could not live with herself if she had an opportunity to help him and did nothing. But she felt equally sad for herself at the prospect the chair would leave Savoy forever. She knew her father would hold true to his promise and give it to Paul to take home to his ailing father. As she worked on the sketch of the aged figure, forming the head of full hair with swift, arcing lines, she decided she had to come up with a way to get LaBont to paint for Savoy, and also to keep the chair within her reach. She never wanted to lose this feeling of accomplishment. She only wanted to get better, to master the techniques and skills of the preeminent maestro, and to be counted among the greatest ever to have painted.

By midmorning in Isabella's studio, Paul tried not to let his troubling encounter with Stein intrude with his work. He watched over her shoulder, helping her perfect a line and shadow, pointing out where a highlight on a face worked best until she spun and gently cocked her head, then wrinkled her nose. Paul understood her meaning.

For the rest of the afternoon, sitting and watching her work from a distance brought back memories of his time with his parents. Watching his father paint and listening to his mother talk about art were all behind him now. As much as he enjoyed helping Isabella, all that he cherished was unraveling in California. And he felt certain what he wanted was in the gallery Stein blocked him from entering earlier this morning.

"Is there something wrong?" Isabella asked, a look of concern on her face.

"No, no." He shook his head. "Just thinking of things."

"They must be troubling things," she said with a sympathetic look. "Maybe you should pick up a brush and do something you enjoy."

"Good idea." He picked out a few brushes from a table. It seemed like ages since he'd wanted to paint. He felt a little jittery as he ambled to an easel holding a new canvas. He arranged the easel so he faced Isabella, dressed in blue jeans and a short-sleeved silk blouse, lost in her work.

He let the brush dangle in midair, centimeters from the smooth, clean surface. His stomach muscles tightened. He didn't know if that was normal anxiety or another wicked reaction. Touching the soft tip of the brush to the new canvas made Paul wince. He didn't think he could paint, but he intended to force himself. He leaned to his right and studied her face intently absorbed in her work. With the roundness of her cheeks, her soft chin, and deep green eyes, she would be as beautiful to paint as she was to study.

Moving his hands over the canvas, his stomach muscles

tightened in excruciating pain almost forcing him to vomit. He dropped his brush and doubled over, nearly knocking the canvas off the easel.

"Are you all right?" asked Isabella, rushing over.

He straightened, and took a deep breath. Nodding, he brushed back his hair and smoothed his shirt. She smelled like magnolias. She massaged his back, sending warm waves through him. He closed his eyes until he could breathe without any pain in his stomach.

"I must be coming down with something."

"Poor dear." She took his hand and led him to a leather chair near the door. "Why don't you rest for a while. We'll cut out early if you're still not feeling well. Oh, by the way, Father told me to tell you he needs to speak with you tonight after dinner."

The da Vinci. The duke expected his decision. The only way he figured he'd be allowed to stay was if he told the duke he had accepted his terms. Then they would have to show him the chair, and he would have the time he needed to finish the painting. And after he made his decision to paint for the duke, Stein wouldn't guard the chair every night since he would be expected to use it. Eventually he could find a way to smuggle it out without arousing Stein's suspicions. That man scared him; he didn't know what the pistol-packing guy would do once he found out he couldn't paint the da Vinci they wanted. It wasn't a meticulous plan, but it was the best he could come up with at the moment. He would have to make it work.

From his seat, he admired Isabella's remarkable progress. Isabella was blossoming like a rose in spring. She would soon outstrip him while his talent lay bound up inside him. He swallowed hard. He wasn't naive. He knew he could bring her along, but not this fast. But how could she suddenly begin to master the techniques that had troubled her for most of her painting life? The thought came to him that she must be using his father's chair. At first he wanted to laugh, but around here one didn't laugh at absurdities. But if Isabella was using it, and it was helping her progress in a way that years of training hadn't been able to, then he had completely misunderstood what the chair could do. Could it have some spiritual powers he'd never heard of? How could a piece of polished wood, no matter how beautiful, have an effect on one's ability to paint? A bigger question, one he'd put off thinking about for the last several weeks, was why, after the chair disappeared, did his talent seem to dry up?

It was time he determined once and for all what this wooden beast had to do with his painting.

"Isabella, are you ready to break for supper?"

She set down her brush and rubbed her hands on her apron. "Are you feeling better? I could use a swim, how about you?"

"You never finished showing me around the castle."

She frowned. "I'm sorry, I've been so busy."

He rose, and held out his hand. She took it and sighed. "All right. I did promise. But first I want to clean up and change."

In the early evening, as the day cooled and the brilliant blue sky turned magenta laced with rose and the clouds thinned into stacks of orangish wafers marching toward the horizon, Paul and Isabella strolled arm in arm along the top of the west wall toward the northwest tower. In the waning light, he looked out over the crenellated parapet across the undulating pine-covered hills down into the valley. Part of him wanted his time here to go on forever, but lingering thoughts of his father, depressed and bedridden, and his mother having to endure his anger, rankled him. And what about his own art? It lay fallow and dormant within him. This place was the closest thing to paradise he'd ever imagined. But if he spent the rest of his life here and could only watch others paint or admire the works of the dead on the expansive walls of the castle, he would be the most miserable man in the world.

"Is there something wrong, Paul?" she asked in a comforting voice.

"Yes, there is." He had a thousand questions for her, and he didn't know where to start.

She stopped and looked at him. He realized he'd never used that forceful tone of voice with her before.

"Have I done something to offend you?"

"Isabella, this is the most amazing place I've ever been, but there are so many things I don't understand."

"Such as?

"Do you believe that Leonardo's chair has power to impart his gift?"

She pursed her lips and stood still as if she was thinking, her head slanted barely to the right. "I do," she said softly, with the firmness of a bride assenting to her matrimonial promise.

He swallowed the urge to smile. Isabella didn't strike him as superstitious, but rather as a serious woman, but now this. "Do you believe there is a curse attached to its use?"

"You've been talking to my father, haven't you?"

"He seems pretty convinced. He even showed me an ancient history of the family."

"We call it the Book of Fire."

"It had the history of all those that have died by fire after using the chair."

She took his arm again and continued to stroll. "That book has never been authenticated. It's more myth than fact."

"But the deaths of all those men. They were so young. And what about my father's burns, and what about the mountain nearly falling on me on my drive up here?"

"Paul, what about all the traffic accidents that happen every day in Los Angeles? Could you say, by producing a history of all the people who died in head-on collisions, that there was a curse attached to driving? Accidents happen every day. In my ancestors' case, a significant amount of men and woman died young. It was part of the risk of living during those times. I'm very sorry about what happened to your father, but if he hadn't run back inside the house, he wouldn't have been burned, would he?"

Paul had to agree about his father. It had been his decision to plunge into their burning house to try to save the chair. "But head-on collisions don't usually happen to successive generations of a family."

"Paul, most auto accidents are caused by carelessness: Someone drinking too much, or falling asleep at the wheel, or just not watching what they're doing. We know what causes them, so we can avoid drinking or falling asleep or whatever, but in my ancestors' times they didn't understand cause and effect. That doesn't mean they didn't try to understand events around them. When they couldn't explain a house fire or an illness or a premature death they always looked to the supernatural. It was a very superstitious age." She seated herself on a bench, with her back to the wall.

Paul stood in front of her. It made sense what she was saying. It relieved him to think these incidents were more coincidental than part of some grand scheme. Even his near death on the road to Savoy could be explained. It had happened many times before. "Okay, so let's get back to the gift. Have you been using the chair to improve your painting?"

"Would that offend you if I had?"

"It bothers me that so much of what I see in the castle is the work of copyists, and I never wanted my art to stoop so low."

"Low. Are you telling me that the rendition of *The Last Supper* in the Savoy chapel is 'low?'" she said, her voice dripping with disbelief.

"Of course not." *The Last Supper* was the most amazing painting he'd ever seen. Even done by a copyist it was a sheer masterpiece.

"I know that it spoke to you," she said, one hand on her knee, the other resting on the stone bench. "I could see it on your face." She looked at him as if she knew what he was thinking.

He couldn't deny that the painting had spoken to him. He couldn't deny that ugly face of Judas had turned and looked at him. He couldn't deny he'd been affected by the characterizations in paint upon the wall. But it was curious she had used the word "spoke" to him as if it was an experience she also had. He didn't think she meant "spoke" in the sense of an artistic epiphany. "Has the painting spoken to you?"

"Every time I look at it, I'm reminded of the meaning of the power of the chair."

"No, I mean have any of the characters *spoken* to you?"

She raised her thin eyebrows. "You mean words?"

"Yeah, words."

She hesitated for a long moment. "Sometimes."

"And do the characters' faces move?"

"Quite often," she said less hesitantly but softly.

"Which ones move?"

"One," she said. Isabella turned her face and looked away into the darkening sky. A hardness came over her looks as if she didn't want to talk anymore about it, then she turned abruptly back to him, a glare in her eyes. "You think I'm crazy don't you?"

"Not necessarily. I'm just trying to understand what's going on here. I see paintings moving, speaking to me, chairs that are alive. Can you just tell me what's going on here?"

She motioned to him to sit down beside her. The air grew chilly but Paul didn't care. He would stay out here if he were in the middle of a blizzard to get the answers he needed.

"I suppose my father has told you his story about the chair, its gift and its curse."

Paul sat down next to her on the cold stone bench. "He told me that the chair was nothing more than Leonardo's giant ego trip and that no one using the chair had lived past middle age, except for my father."

She nodded as if she'd heard that story before. "That's one view."

"You mean there are different stories surrounding the chair?"

"Leonardo had so much to accomplish and resented the fact that he had to die with so much undone. That's when he decided to give the world his gift of art. He created his chair as a way of blessing mankind. He would never sabotage his gift by attaching a curse to it."

"What about all these deaths and maimings?"

"Paul, we've already been over that," she said, with the most sincere expression.

"Yes, just accidents."

"That could have been prevented. We don't know the facts surrounding each and every death, but we know what happened with your father. He didn't have to run into the fire. It was his choice."

He nodded in agreement. "But how does *The Last Supper* remind you of Leonardo's chair?"

"There have been men and women who were singularly gifted throughout history. They have blessed mankind with their gifts."

"Like Leonardo?"

"Exactly. And Jesus was another one of them."

"But wasn't he different? I mean didn't he claim to be God?"

"Jesus never said he was God. Others enamored with his gifts put that label on him. And only one of his disciples tried to put a stop to those who wanted to kill him."

"Who? Peter?"

"No. Judas."

"But I thought he betrayed Jesus?"

"That's the way the story's been retold to protect those who make a religion out of worshiping him as God. But Judas, like Leonardo, wanted those special gifts now, on earth, so all mankind could benefit. For that he was called a traitor. Think how much suffering could have been alleviated if Jesus' gift of healing had been enjoyed by all the world, and not just a few who saw him live."

Paul stared at her in shock. She expressed herself so confidently and cogently. He had never heard this before, but it sounded so reasonable. Could it be true? "So the face that talks to you from the painting is Judas?"

"Yes, and that's why Leonardo painted him as the most handsome, comely man in the group. Even more handsome than Jesus himself." She folded her hands in her lap.

He slowly shook his head when she said Judas. As he looked into her green eyes, he realized—in one those moments of clarity people are blessed with so few times in their lives—that she saw movements among the painted beings under the proscenium arch of the altar, but not the ones he saw. To him Judas was an ugly urchin straight out of the hell. *What gives here?*

"What's wrong, Paul?"

"You've just given me a lot to think about." He could see in his mind's eye the ugly rutted face of Judas glaring at him.

"Come on. Let me show you something that will help you understand." She stood and took his hand and led him toward the southwest tower, down to the third floor, through a series of arched doorways into a long hall.

"These are the third-floor galleries where my father keeps all his collections of ancient armor and weapons."

Paul followed her through a series of marble-floored rooms.

They passed glass cases filled with swords, knives, and shields into a room filled with suits of armor. The hollow metal statues lined the walls and in the center stood a half dozen lit glass cases. Isabella stopped at the first case.

Paul, beside her, peered into the glass. The rectangular enclosure was about five feet long, and on a bed of red velvet lay a magnificent sword. It was the same one he'd been looking at earlier today when Stein accosted him.

"This is the sword of Constantine, the first Christian Emperor of the Holy Roman Empire."

It had an intricate gold-plated hilt with meticulous scrollwork along the worn steel blade. From the size of it, the emperor had to have been a strong man to wield it.

"This is incredible. How did your father find this?"

She brushed her hair back over her ears. "All these pieces in this room have been in the family for a couple of centuries. There is more." She sauntered over to a large oblong case. It must have been six or seven feet long with a thick bedding of black velvet. On top of it lay a massive sword. Its hilt was heavy and ornate with horizontal grooves etched into the grip. The beaten steel blade was uneven and tiny chunks of metal were missing in places, but it looked like it was still sharp enough to whisk someone's head off.

"What is this? Hercules' sword?" Paul asked.

"Tradition says it's Goliath's."

"Goliath?"

"My ancestors were astute collectors. About ten years ago my father hired experts from the British Museum to verify the provenance of all the weapons in this room."

Paul gaped at the sword that glinted from under the sharp light. "It's in remarkable condition."

"All of the artifacts in this room are in good condition for their age," she said leading him around to case after case. Isabella finally took him by the arm. "Come on, we've seen enough of these for now."

Paul followed her into another room. The furniture, arranged in period groupings around the room, glistened under the recessed lights that illuminated the bright upholstery and carved polished wood. Paul wanted to examine each display, but his eyes scanned the room for one piece.

"What you're looking for is over there," she said, pointing to the center of the room.

The chair, with its dark walnut sheen and elaborate carvings, sat in the center of the exhibits on a two-foot tall marble dais, splashed in light from three small spotlights above it. A set of burgundy velvet ropes attached to chrome posts surrounded it. Paul hustled over to the ropes, which cordoned off a circle twenty feet in circumference. A sign attached to each post said in Italian, "Do not approach past ropes. Dais is alarmed."

"So, your father really doesn't want anyone near it," Paul said.

"His superstitions run deep," she said, lightly touching the velvet rope with her index finger.

She put her hand on his shoulder. "You have to be willing to take some risks if you want to achieve greatness," she said. She fished a barrel key out of her pocket. She went over to a panel on the far wall and disarmed the alarm with a quarter turn. A tiny light turned from red to green. She returned to Paul's side.

"Won't your father know you've turned it off?"

She shook her head. "The castle doesn't have a central monitoring system yet. It's only a local alarm." She unhooked the rope, mounted the dais, and sat on the chair facing Paul. She looked like a queen on her throne. Her white skin and strawberry-blonde hair shimmered under the light.

She lowered her head and eyed him with a beckoning grin. "Paul, are you afraid of greatness?" she said in a low voice.

Of course he wasn't afraid of being an accomplished, skilled artist. But he did have a modicum of apprehension. He'd seen the fruitful and unfruitful results of those that had used it. Using it was against everything he believed about his art. He would become a copyist. It would somehow overwrite his personality the way you could copy over a file on a hard drive. Yes, he wanted greatness. Didn't all artists deep down want recognition for their artistic expression? But at what cost? Would he have to sacrifice his individuality, his unique passions, his way of seeing the world that only he could see and express? It just seemed like too much to give up for the measure of greatness he would get in return.

She motioned with her hand for him to come closer; her green eyes glinted. "There is nothing to fear."

But what he feared most was that this ancient creation was the real root of his own accomplishment. Was everything he worked to learn and master only another man's legacy? Was not having the chair around the real reason he'd lost his ability to paint?

"Come here," she said, with a firm voice. "There's nothing to be afraid of." She held out a confident hand. Her smile captivated him. Speckles of light danced in her hair as if she were charged with an electrical current. Her neck—long, slim, white, and soft looking—reminded him of a ripe peach. Her pouty red lips dared him to kiss her. Paul wanted more than anything to take her hand, pull her to him, and wrap his arms around her.

He stepped forward, then hesitated at the velvet barrier. The thought shot through him to run; to run faster and farther than he'd ever run from anything before, to not stop until he was home in California. He turned to leave, and took several steps away from her.

"Paul, this is for you," she said. It was the same voice from his dreams. "You can have everything you've ever wanted and more."

At the door leading out of the chamber, he stopped. If he left now he would never know for sure what power was contained in the polished wood. And if it didn't have any of the bite of fire that the duke said it did, what could be the harm of it? He turned slowly and moved toward her. Her outstretched hand beckoned him.

Something collapsed inside, a wall of resistance tumbled down. He crossed the rope, mounted the dais, and put his hand into her warm palm. A rush coursed through him like the surge of excitement the first time he'd drawn a perfect face. She drew him to her, and he could smell her fresh magnolia perfume. He bent over and kissed her soft lips. A tingle dropped down his spine into his legs. Every ounce of reserve, of effort to say no to what he feared might harm him, vanished. Everything felt so good, so right. He wanted Isabella, and he wanted a taste of whatever Leonardo's chair had to offer.

Nature has beneficially provided that throughout the world you may find something to imitate.

—Leonardo da Vinci, *Notebooks*

22

Vincent stared out the living room picture window into the gray sky marshaling off the coast. A bank of fog, like a hastening veil, rose off the Pacific Ocean in dense columns. It rolled over his home, smothering his view in an opaque sea of mist.

He had surveyed this landscape too often, on too many days, and nothing had changed—nothing, he feared, would ever change. He was still maimed, unable to paint, although a tiny range of motion had returned to his left hand so that he could flex his pinkie and ring finger. The skin over the back of his wrist and forearm had grown back, and new pinkish skin crept toward his fingers. The fingers on his right hand lacked any significant dexterity. They were insensitive to anything except the driving pain every time he tried to flex his fingers. But every time he tried to grasp an object an excruciating jab of pain shot up his arm. He would never again be able to make a fine line or a gentle curve.

The dense bank of fog broke up in wispy patches. He could see the waves whipping across the choppy face of the dun-colored sea. It had been two months since his accident. At least that's what everyone was calling it—a tragic, unfortunate accident. The truth gnawed at him. As soon as the red-hot embers bit into the soft flesh of his palms and fingers, he knew it was not just a bit of bad luck. The warnings he had received thundered through his mind like a runaway locomotive.

Standing at the window of his living room, he wondered if his irrational behavior of shredding Marcella's watercolors to pieces was part of the curse too. He had never wanted to hurt her. It wasn't that he didn't like her work when he saw it in the back bedroom—actually he did. But when he picked up one of her brushes and laid it in his palm and tried to grasp it—pain shot through him like a .44 slug to the heart—a giant sense of unfairness washed over him that Marcella could enjoy what had been stripped from him. It triggered an uncontrollable rage inside him. He never thought he was capable of such anger. He wanted to tell Marcella how sorry he was, but now she wouldn't even come close to him.

And if she did listen, what would he tell her? That he didn't mean to destroy her beautiful paintings; it just happened, like a toddler who couldn't help screaming every time he felt a hunger pang?

How had his life gotten so out of control? He was like a man caught in the midst of a raging forest fire, a fire he himself had set. Was there any stopping this downward slide? He didn't want to answer that question, but he had to. He didn't want to hurt Marcella or Paul any more than he already had. He had to do something. Maybe he should just end it all. He had enough Vicodin in the other room to make it easy. He just wouldn't wake up. Easy solutions sounded so rational, so simple. Just thinking about not waking up to the pain in his hands, to any remorse in his heart, to any anguish on Marcella's face, to any more kindly doctors assuring him of something that would never come to pass, gave him a moment of peace. He turned away from the window and ambled over to the large half-circle sofa in the middle of the living room. For the first time in a long time, things seemed so reasonable. He slouched down onto the sofa and wrapped his terrycloth robe tighter around him.

He wanted to talk to Marcella one more time, and see if he could explain to her what he was going through. He wanted to apologize for what he had done to her paintings. When she came out of her room, she would have to walk pass the sofa. He intended to sit there until she did.

Holding his hands up in front of his face, he grimaced. He hung his head sheepishly, and placed his wrapped hands on his face. Soon all of this would be over.

Hence O! painter, beware lest lust of gain should supplant in you the dignity of art.

—Leonardo da Vinci, *Notebooks*

23

---

*I*sabella sat upright in the chair like a queen on her throne. Paul stood before her, transfixed by the gaze of her emerald eyes. Her smile took on a dark seriousness as if she were plotting to take over the world.

"I've waited a long time for his chair to come home," she said, her wavy hair cascading down the sides of her face.

"Is this the reason you came back from California?"

She nodded as if he were one of her subjects. "I believe it's my destiny to enjoy the maestro's genius, and I want you to enjoy it with me."

He couldn't turn from her gaze. How could he feel so attracted to someone who had caused his family such pain? "It would have been better for my parents if the chair had stayed in California."

"It would have been better for everyone if it had never left Savoy in the first place. Some things cannot be avoided. And neither of us can turn our backs on our destiny." She tried to pull him closer. Paul let her hand go. Her eyes pulsed with a raw intensity, her cheeks flushed. "Deep down we both want the same thing, don't we?"

Her skin appeared whiter, almost like cream, and her hair covered her shoulders like a royal mantle. She sat regally, one hand resting on the massive arm; flashing across her face, a familiar glare reminded him of his father's unrelenting determination.

"Your art has suffered much," she said in a soft but authoritative voice, with the lilt of a prophet, "and now you need to discover the truth for yourself." She rose, stepped aside, inviting him with a wave of her hand to take a seat.

He breathed deeply. He had come to Savoy solely with the intention of gaining the chair for his father. But he couldn't deny one solid truth—his talent lay blocked inside him. Was his journey to Savoy really to discover for himself the true power of the chair?

Paul stepped forward and lowered himself into the seat, resting his head against the straight wooden back. He felt the light touch of the carved surfaces of the intaglio work through his thin cotton shirt. Warmth suffused his body, a blush rose on his face. For a brief moment, in a surge of thoughts from a dark corner of his mind, he knew what it felt like to be a king on his throne. Then the liquid images washed out of his consciousness like a wave retreating from a sandy beach.

He'd sat here before, but never with the stakes so high. He had never come to it seeking something he had lost. But besides a spreading ribbon of heat inside, which could have been caused by a slight case of anxiety, he didn't feel any different. This intricately carved piece of wood had no vitality of its own, just a mythical tradition fueled by man's insatiable desire to be touched by the soul of genius.

He felt her take his hand and pull him up and away from the

chair. The heat inside had gelled into a ball of burning. He glanced back at the chair as she led him to the door. The light glinting off its walnut patina seemed less brilliant, as if it had sent a charge through him, and now lay spent and silent in the center of the room. Hand in hand, they darted through the tangle of halls and stairways until they reached her studio.

In her studio, Isabella placed Paul in front of the canvas with the preliminary marks he had made earlier. The waning sunset, like dying embers from a roaring fire, gave a soft light to the studio from the high windows. She pulled a wooden stool up to his easel and seated herself. The light caught her face and hair in its last rays, gleaming on the highlights of her cheeks and lips and down her porcelain neck.

"Paint," she said, not so much a command as an invitation.

He picked up his brush and approached the canvas warily, with a halting movement. His last touch of a brush to this surface had paid him back with a sledgehammer to his stomach. That was an experience he didn't want to repeat. He dabbed lightly at the canvas. He let the soft sable bristles kiss the surface of the cloth. Nothing bit him from within.

He glanced at her, and she urged him on with a look. He poised his brush over the tiny line he had laid down earlier in the day, then created an elegant curve to capture the perfect line of her jaw. He joined another line to her delicate chin. As he depicted more of her face, a ripple of joy coursed through him, followed by a solitary twitch of a stomach muscle. He jerked the brush from the canvas.

"It's all right. Keep going," she said in a soothing tone.

He studied her, then back at the canvas. He wiped beads of sweat off his forehead with the back of his hand. His stomach felt fine—the twitch was nothing. Hesitantly, he poked at the surface again, picking up the line. Nothing chewed at his insides. A smile broke out on his face. There was nothing he could do to contain his joy.

His hand flowed freely over the canvas for the first time in months. He studied her face, the length and roundness of her cheeks, the soft chin and deep green eyes.

She's as beautiful to paint as she is to watch.

His artwork came easily, as it always had before he'd stumbled into that blank time in his life. It was pure elation working close to his art again; to have his mind focused on the portrait in front of him, giving it life.

He somehow had fallen into a time warp of some sort, where a person lived out his dreams in the shadow of the real world. Recreating the beauty around him was the apex of art. And laying down the lineaments that brought Isabella to life created a connection to something greater than the figure on the flat canvas. A deeper feeling arose that he couldn't deny. He wanted to move beside her, take her in his arms, and kiss her. Instead he poured the intensity of his feelings into sketching her face, and then he quickly filled his palette and brushed his passion on in reds, blues, and flesh tones with golden freckles. Breathing hard, as if he'd been exercising, he strove to capture the life that glistened in her eyes like a drop of morning dew upon the petal of a rose.

His gift had come back to him like a raging torrent, as if it had always lurked just below the surface. He felt an exhilaration from within—he was better than he'd ever been, better than anyone before him.

Paul laughed. *I'm not better than Dad, or the great masters. Where did that idea come from?*

He doubted he would ever approach the greatness his father had attained. But he knew his father had paid a price for the mastery of his craft. Paul had watched as his father had become obsessed with his art.

But I can be better than all of them. He shook off that thought. He would never allow his talent to go to his head. His father had made art his god. Paul would never make that mistake.

He continued filling in her face with deft strokes of flesh tones as he began to lose the natural light. He had always scoffed at the supposed power attributed to the chair, but he couldn't deny that something wonderful had just happened to him. Those few minutes of sitting in it seemed to have restored his gift as if a missing jewel had been returned to its setting. He could paint with a delicateness and realism he'd seen his father practice over the years. His brushstrokes were smooth and effortless, as if he'd never been away from his work. He felt that raw sense of mastery within, and he could focus it to the bristle points of his brush.

How could he feel this way so suddenly? He didn't care. He just didn't want the inspiration to leave him anytime soon; it had been gone far too long.

Isabella came up behind him and put her arms around his neck. He could smell her closeness. He dropped his brush on the palette, turned, stood, and held her tightly around the waist, looking into her inviting eyes. Closing his eyes, he kissed her, and it felt like liquid sunshine coursing through his veins.

Paul lay in bed listening to the sound of the crickets drifting in his bedroom window as the luminous dial on his clock moved closer to midnight. Unable to sleep, he let the events of the last few days rumble through his mind. By Wednesday evening when the duke summoned him to his study, his decision to stay and paint the da Vinci had come so easy, effortlessly, and without the undue concerns that had previously bothered him. The duke appeared delighted.

Every afternoon for the past two days, he and Isabella had taken turns sitting in the grasp of the ancient chair and letting its power seep into their being. Yesterday he had borrowed the key to the alarm from her, ostensibly for a one-time occasion, and had not given it back. She hadn't asked for it either. It lay on the night-stand next to him. He tossed and turned, hankering to lounge in the grasp of the ancient *maestro's* chair one more time.

Dressing quickly, he grabbed the key and headed toward the third-floor gallery. Outside in the courtyard, the darkness of the Alps was unlike any he'd seen before. The crisp air, scuttling off the faces of the sheer mountains surrounding the castle, sent a chill deep into his bones. The stars shone with brightness unrivaled by anything his imagination could conjure. In California they merely twinkled in the distance, here they radiated as if the night sky were a carpet of diamonds sprinkled with patches of dark coals.

Stealing along the stone path toward the gallery in the north wing, he gripped the small barrel key in his hand. He stopped in the doorway leading into the gallery with the chair. A circle of ambient light from the recessed fixture in the ceiling illuminated the chair. The rich walnut finish glimmered, making it appear brooding and dark, guarded by the carved lion heads in the arms. He found it hard to believe the chair could contain anything evil despite the duke's misgivings. How could something so wonderful be anything but good? Isabella had been right after all.

He turned off the alarm, jumped the rope barrier, and ensconced himself in the chair. He thought about how his portrait of Isabella had turned out. She was ecstatic and had urged him to do one of her posing on her horse. For his next project, he wanted to do something grand, something large and epic. Something like Leonardo's *Last Supper,* only bolder.

Why suddenly did he feel challenged to tackle such large projects? He had never been enamored with the classical approach to painting and had only practiced it to please his father. But now it seemed logical, right, full of purpose, the highest use of his talents.

His change of heart didn't really seem that odd when he thought about it. He had always admired his father's work and the work of the great masters. He just didn't like it being shoved down his throat. Maybe coming here to Savoy, and experiencing the power of classical art, had wrenched the rebellion out of him. Work beckoned him now more than sleep, more than eating, and at times, even more than Isabella.

He mulled over how this simple wooden chair could have such an effect on his soul. It had to be nothing more than the pure power of suggestion.

But I have become so good these last few days. If I keep at it, I could be as good as Dad, if not better.

He pushed himself off the chair and wound his way through the darkened halls to Isabella's studio. The chilly night air swept in the half-open windows. He turned on several lamps and rubbed his hands together for warmth. Pushing the large windows closed, which pivoted vertically, he turned on a space heater. He donned a smock, then chose one of the canvases from the stack against the wall. It was six feet by four feet. He would do one of Isabella that would sweep her off her feet.

He studied the huge canvas on his easel. It seemed to take up half the room. Wanting to draw something beautiful, captivating, awe inspiring, he pondered different subjects. *Isabella on her Arabian. Why not?*

He found his sketchpad and began working. He wanted the light to come from an angle on the side, as Raphael would do. The sharp peaks of the Alps would be in the background, with the broad green valley under her horse's feet. The perspective would be perfect. Isabella would ride majestically through the valley in the full bloom of spring, as queen of her realm.

He drew furiously but accurately, only stopping to sharpen his pencil as he sketched different angles of the horse and the exact turn of Isabella's head. After an hour of frenzied work, he moved in front of the gigantic canvas. With a new set of brushes, he composed the outline of his painting. He labored into the morning, oblivious of the time; the starlight dimmed and the first flicker of dawn glimmered through the windows. Finally exhaustion overcame him. He lay down on the Persian carpet by the door, pulled a blanket over him and dropped into a sound sleep.

Light cascaded down the castle walls into the tall windows of the studio like a waterfall. It beat the morning's warmth into his eyes. He blinked several times and felt the chill of the floor. Sitting up he wiped the sleep out of his eyes; his back aching from cold muscles twisted into knots.

The door to the studio swung open and Isabella, fresh and bright, wearing black pants and a green top, bounced into the room.

"I figured you must be here. I stopped by your room and you weren't there. I wanted—" When she spied the canvas in the middle of the room she walked toward it with her mouth open. "Paul, this is amazing. You did this in one night?"

He propped himself up on one arm, brushed his scraggly hair into place, and looked at his previous night's work. "I ran out of gas a few hours ago or I would have started painting."

"I can't believe this. It's … it's so well done, so—"

"Perfect."

"Yes." She continued to gaze.

He clambered to his feet and stretched his muscles. He joined her for a moment in admiring his work, marveling at what he had accomplished. It was better than he had thought he could do. When he focused and put his mind to it, he could be as great as any painter working today.

He wandered over to the window and watched the morning unfold below. He unlatched the pane and pushed it open. The air, crisp and invigorating, washed across his face. Yes, he had created the beginnings of a masterpiece. All he needed to do was put flesh on the bones he'd outlined.

She came over and put an arm around his waist. She smelled like freshly picked magnolias. "You have come back with a vengeance. You truly are great." She kissed him on the cheek. The morning light danced in her eyes.

He smiled at her, and then studied the shrubs and trees in the valley below. Yes, he was good. Very good. And he knew, as assuredly as the sun waltzed across the sky, he was destined to be as accomplished as the maestro himself.

The forms of bodies could not be understood in detail but for shadow.

—Leonardo da Vinci, *Notebooks*

24

Marcella wouldn't allow the gloomy morning to dampen her spirits as she dressed hurriedly for her breakfast meeting with Scott. She wanted to get out of the house before Vincent woke up. She didn't want to get caught in the tailwind of one of his tantrums.

Sitting at her small vanity, she stroked on her eyeliner. She kept telling herself that this morning's meeting was nothing more than a planning session for her next show. But then another thought nudged its way into her mind. However reluctantly she entertained the idea, it pitched its tent in a corner of her thoughts. Images of Scott's warm, accepting smile brought a measure of solace to the wave of trouble that threatened to swallow her.

Her mind returned of its own accord to the dark vision of her work ripped into viscious shreds. Vincent had not only mutilated her watercolors, but also her affection for him. The thought of him touching her repulsed her.

Scott was everything Vincent wasn't: kind, supportive, communicative, helpful, and the list could go on. Every time he touched her hand, all the tension inside her that had built to a pleading crescendo, unwound. Time with him was quiet, calming, and reassuring.

Eventually she would have to confront Vincent, but right now she was too angry. *Of course she loved him* she told herself often. She feared she said that to herself in the same way she would tell a dying person they would be just fine.

She lightly dabbed blush on the apples of her cheeks. But why did she have to keep telling herself that she loved Vincent? After twenty-five years of marriage, did she have to convince herself of how she should feel? It made her miserable thinking that what had been a deep love between them had transformed into a sympathetic tolerance.

If we could only get back to what we had before.

What a foolish thought. Their relationship had worked because of her willingness to compromise, but there was no going back to that tired formula. Their quiet arrangement had disappeared in the wind-whipped flames that consumed their home. And she doubted if he would ever find a way to accept her for who she was. Even if his hands healed, he would still be the same stubborn Vincent.

Looking into the mirror, she saw herself as a young student in downtown San Francisco at the Harrington Art Gallery. The first time she saw Vincent was from behind and he was explaining his paintings to a customer. He sounded so sure of himself, his voice full of energy, she had to stay and see what he looked like. When he turned around and saw his square jaw and warm eyes, she knew she had to meet him. She had fallen hard for him over the next few months. He brought her roses so red she would blush. He made eyes at her over dinner, and made her feel like a queen. Then her smashed and mangled artwork came to mind in an unedited panorama. He must have known what he was doing; from the first moment she met him, he always knew what he was doing. But what he didn't know was that when he smashed her lovely watercolors, her heart went dry for him. His rage had pushed her over the edge into a different place of willingness to let another man's eager look please her. She had never wanted to think like this, but she found herself wanting more than anything to feel Scott's warm touch on her arm.

She felt a twinge of guilt, like a little terrier yapping at her feet. But she convinced herself she didn't really have a choice. Dressed in black slacks and a white silk blouse, she steamed out of her bedroom with an old Beetles song, "Hey Jude," running through her mind. Suddenly, she had a lightness to her that she hadn't felt in a while. Work enthralled her. Paul would probably be home any day now. And this morning she and Scott were going to plan her first private showing.

Exiting the hall into the spacious living room she froze when she spotted Vincent slumped on the sofa, his head hung low, his white-bandaged hands on top of his head.

She remained rigid, unmoving. His dark hair was mussed, and his print terrycloth robe she had bought him for the hospital was cinched tightly around his waist. He sat motionless. She heard what she thought were soft moans. Not wanting to disturb him, she tiptoed quietly to the door and into the kitchen.

"Marcella."

Turning slowly, she looked back at him. "Good morning," she said, hesitating at the edge of the kitchen.

He sat on the other side of the round sectional that took up the whole corner of the living room. The white, deeply upholstered sofa faced the picture window. She pushed her hair behind her ear, and crossed her arms over her chest.

"Marcella." He smiled wanly.

She studied his face for signs of anger. She saw a murky turbulence.

"Are you feeling better?" she asked.

He raised his eyebrows and gave out a shallow sigh. "Can I talk to you?"

She glanced at her watch. "I have a few minutes." She moved tentatively to the sofa and took a seat on the far side, across from him, clutching her small purse in front of her like a shield.

"I know you're mad at me, and I deserve it."

She stared, unsmiling. She didn't know how to take Vincent's attempt at transparency. Was this some new tactic he had cooked up?

"I'm sorry about what happened the other day ... about your paintings."

"Uh-huh." The muscles in the back of her neck and shoulders tightened.

"Marcella, please." He laid his hands on his lap.

"Are you asking me to forgive you?" She scraped around in the back of her mind for a good reason why she should.

"I'm asking you to try and understand what's happened to me."

"What about what I'm going through?"

"That's what I want to talk about. I know—"

"No Vincent, you don't have a clue how you're hurting me." She tried to take deep breaths and pace herself.

He shook his head slowly. "I know I've been ..."

"You've been an enemy to me, that's what you've been." She didn't mean to say it, but it was the truth. His halfhearted attempt at an apology irritated her.

He hung his head.

She had never seen him look like such a whipped man. "Vincent, I'm sorry I said that."

"No, you're right. You don't understand. I wasn't mad at you, I was mad at myself."

She leaned forward, resting her elbows on her knees.

"I tried picking up a brush, and the pain was so bad I couldn't hold it."

She sighed deeply. He had made it so hard for her to feel sorry for him.

"It was just too much for me to take. It's so unfair."

She wanted to comfort him, but the words wouldn't come. He raised his eyes to meet hers. His facial expression told her a head of steam was building inside him. He rubbed his bandaged paws through his hair, which stuck up at odd angles on his head. The corners of his mouth sagged, as he seemed to struggle for the right words.

"You don't know what it's like not to be able to do something you love, something you've done all your life."

Her back stiffened. But she did know. She knew exactly how it felt to have something she loved stripped from her. Their whole marriage he had taken steps to squelch her desire to do what she loved. It didn't surprise her that he couldn't see the hypocrisy of his self-absorbed grief. She let out a sigh, pursed her lips tight lest anything hurtful come out.

She wanted to comfort him, but she felt comfortless; she wanted to cry for him, but she needed to cry for herself.

"You just don't care, do you?" he said, his pitch rising.

"Vincent, please. I care very much. It's just that—"

"You don't care, or you would understand *these*." He raised his bandaged hands as if they were proof of his anguish.

"Vincent, I'm sorry for your pain, for what's happened to you, but I can't make it better. You want something from me I'm not able to give you."

"All I want is a little sympathy."

"You have my sympathy; I'm just not certain you have my heart anymore." The moment she said it, she knew how right it sounded.

A defeated look washed through his deep black eyes, and his face seemed more lined than ever. "You hate me because I can't paint?"

"It has nothing to do with your painting. All I've ever wanted is for you to love me for who I am. Can't you understand that?"

"If only Paul would bring home the chair, things might be different."

He looked so pathetic, so unable to hear her. "I wish you would get well without taking it out on me."

He looked at her with a dull, glassy gaze. "I can't go on like this," he said, raising his hands, like two white scoops. "I won't go on with these." A pallor came over his face as if something had broken inside, fatally.

For the first time she realized that he could not claw his way out of this pit he had fallen into. But none of this was her doing. Vincent had run into the fire for that chair, but he had also run into the fire to save her; Vincent had created the myth about that ridiculous chair. She had tried to talk him into getting rid of that thing a long time ago. If he had, none of this would have happened. Vincent was responsible for his own life, wasn't he? She couldn't watch over him every minute.

She glanced at her watch. Scott was expecting her at Las Losos by the beach for breakfast any minute now.

What was she feeling? Anger, yes. Pity for his suffering, yes. But love? Would anyone blame her if she didn't? She closed her eyes, and thoughts of their life together raced through her mind. Then she saw her studio, wrecked as if thugs had trashed it.

She stood up and brushed the wrinkles out of her slacks.

"Vincent, I have to go." Scott, her career, her new life, were all waiting for her, and she was behind schedule.

Vincent's face stayed buried in his hands.

Slinging her purse over her shoulder, she strode confidently out of the living room—without looking back—into the kitchen, through the small laundry room, and into the garage. She climbed into her Lexus and rummaged through her purse for her keys.

What does he expect me to do for him?

She keyed the ignition and raced the motor.

Why should I love him after all the things he's done to me?

Hitting the button for the garage door opener, she put the shifter into reverse. Light swiftly filtered into the garage as the door rose.

He ruined all of my paintings. He degraded me.

When the door finished opening, the garage fell silent, except for the soft purr of the Lexus motor. She bit her lip, then let her foot off the brake, the car rolled out into the pale sunlight.

I can't save him.

Wispy clouds of fog let shafts of bright sunshine through, like a sieve, dappling the driveway and the car. She hit the brakes hard at the bottom of the drive where the cement turned into the gutter.

It was Vincent who saved me.

He had put his life on the line, risking everything, to save her from the fire. The paramedic even called him a hero. Somewhere in the vague shadows in her mind, she remembered him coming to her through the smoke when no one else could find her. He put his strong arms around her, scooping her up when she had lost all hope. Why didn't she believe that God had answered her brief, desperate prayer? He didn't send an angel, a fireman, a neighbor— he sent Vincent. She felt what it was like to be carried by another, when she had no strength to walk.

Vincent carried me.

That's what she needed right now, more than anything, was strong arms around her.

She could go to Scott, and he would hold her.

But Vincent had saved her. And maybe it was time for her to carry him.

She slammed the gearshift into drive and hit the gas making the car lunge into the garage, then she jammed on the breaks and it slid to a stop. Clambering out, a palpable chill raced across her heart. She didn't know what to do about his depression. Should she call the doctor? He would only prescribe more drugs. She doubted that he would see a psychiatrist, but she could insist. He needed help now, something to shoot for again.

Returning to the living room, she shuddered when he wasn't sitting on the sofa. Racing into his bedroom, she found him slouched on the edge of the bed, holding a pile of pills perched on his bandaged right hand. He had unwrapped his left hand so he could open the bottle. The bandages lay in a pile at his feet next to the empty prescription bottle.

She sat down beside him, and took the pills out of his hand. She put them back in the bottle. Then she wrapped her arms around him, drinking in his clean scent of soap and shaving cream. She could feel the pain in his shivering muscles.

"It's all right. I'm here. We'll get through this together. I'm not going anywhere."

She didn't want to move from his side. He needed her touch, her love, more than anything else right now. And if all she could do for him was hold him, then she would. If she had left, she knew he would have swallowed those pills. But she couldn't watch him every second. That would be impossible. But she could collect all the drugs, medical supplies, anything that could be swallowed, even the aspirin, and lock them away.

And then she would call Paul. As much as she thought he was on some kind of wild goose chase, if he was able to bring back that stupid chair, it would give Vincent a real boost. Even if things never returned to the way they were before, at least they could back off the edge of the precipice they were all dangling over. Tomorrow she would bring some of her things from Rhonda's and set up a small studio in her room. Vincent would have to learn to cope with her painting. But she didn't dare leave him alone right now.

Please, Paul, hurry home.

The art of perspective is of such a nature as
to make what is flat appear in relief.

—Leonardo da Vinci, *Notebooks*

25

---

*P*aul finished the painting of Isabella on her Arabian. On Thursday afternoon she brought her father to view it. He stood five or six feet back from the canvas, contemplating it in quiet awe, then he turned to Paul. "I had heard about your craft, but this is beyond what I expected."

"Thank you," he said, as he watched the duke study the painting. Isabella, between the two men, took Paul's hand and held it tight. She shot him an affectionate smile.

Warmth permeated his body.

"Have you done this kind of work before?" the duke asked, still fixated on the huge canvas.

"This is the first time I've attempted such a grand scale. I felt inspired after seeing your collection."

The duke rubbed his chin thoughtfully. "This is every bit as good as anything in our gallery." He wagged a finger at the painting. "Even the Van Eycks, the Gainsboroughs, or the Rembrandts."

Paul nodded. The sense of what he had accomplished grew in

his mind. But why should he be surprised at the quality of the art he produced? At first, he'd been reluctant to compare himself so favorably to the old masters, but the duke was a serious art collector; he knew good art when he saw it. Paul held his head high as they all gazed upon the large canvas.

"I would be honored if you would allow me to hang this in the east gallery with the other masters."

"Of course." Paul could not keep himself from smiling. *It belongs in the hall of the famous.*

"Your use of light is familiar. Who did you have in mind when you painted this?"

"I studied the rendition of *The Last Supper* you have above the altar in the chapel. Leonardo's intention to have the light come from the rear through the three arches allowed him the greatest use of perspective. I wanted a similar effect, so I had the light from an early morning sunrise coming over the mountains. Having it backlight the horse gives the kind of luminescent effect Leonardo achieved in his work."

"It is one of the finest uses of chiaroscuro I have ever seen."

Paul felt his face flush. He knew he'd captured the horse's raw energy as he strode vigorously over the landscape, his muscled limbs rippling under his glistening black coat. And with the penetrating look in Isabella's green eyes, the horse and rider appeared raised and detached from the canvas, as if the beast threatened to jump off into the room.

"Isabella's features are so exact. You've captured her emotional intensity better than anyone I've ever seen."

Paul knew that by any measure it was a complete artistic achievement. "I would like to *give* you this piece as token of my appreciation for your hospitality."

As the duke turned to Paul, his jaw dropped. "That is not possible. This is worth more than a hundred stays here."

Paul held up his hand. "Please, I insist."

The duke paused as if considering how to respond. "It will be a welcome addition to our collection."

Paul nodded in appreciation.

He turned to leave then hesitated. "Your stay here seems to have given you great inspiration. I'm certain your next project will be even more amazing." The duke's dark eyes fell on his daughter. "Isabella, may I speak to you a moment outside?"

She followed her father out the door with a swirl of her long hair and her swish of her black velvet gown.

Alone, in the stillness of the stone studio, with his brushes and his thoughts, Paul mused over the events of the last week. His artistic ability had returned with a torrid outburst of creative energy. He'd worked almost around the clock over the last few days to finish the painting, and now fatigue tugged at his body. His legs and arms were weak and rubbery. He slumped into one of the leather chairs against the wall.

Gazing up at his finished canvas, he knew that if he never painted another piece, this one would stand out from his other work. He had made his mark. He never thought he would reach a specific day when he sensed his arrival as an artist. That type of confidence usually came over a period of time as a painter proved his skills and his body of work demonstrated consistent greatness. At this moment, he felt he could accomplish whatever artistic goals he set for himself.

Move over, Vincent LaBont. Paul boy is coming through.

He wanted to sit back and enjoy what he had created, but an undeniable restlessness rattled him. He couldn't sit still.

Why can't I just lie back and enjoy this for a while?

He felt like he'd drunk a whole pot of coffee. He stood and paced over to the large open window overlooking the forest meadow below. He breathed deeply of the chilly late afternoon air, his mind flooded with new ideas for painting projects. Landscapes, still lifes, another portrait, a scene from the gospel of John all flitted through his thoughts like a slide projector displaying a montage on the walls of his mind. If he concentrated on one, it would come alive. Its size, subject, composition, and colors all laid out for him, as if he were pulling already completed plans from an archive.

Maybe this frenetic surge of creativity stemmed from not painting for the last two months. He wondered why he felt suddenly drawn to these types of projects. But then, he'd never been around such a large and varied collection as the duke's. He paced thoughtfully in front of the tall window. The light outside faded into a washed-out paleness falling away toward twilight. His body dragged, but his mind raced like a pack of greyhounds chasing a chimera.

Tomorrow he would start working on the da Vinci. Then—

"What are you doing?" Isabella asked, standing just inside the door, a tone of curiosity in her voice.

He stopped midstride. "I'm thinking."

"Whatever it is, it must be good." She moved closer to him.

He smiled. "I was mulling over some ideas for new projects. Is everything okay? I mean, with you and your father."

She nodded. "I need to show you where you can work on the painting you promised to do for my father."

"Yes," he said, grabbing a cloth and wiping his hands. "Let's get on with it." His most difficult work was yet to come.

The diminution of objects as they recede
from the eye is known as Diminishing Perspective.

—Leonardo da Vinci, *Notebooks*

26

*I*n the still darkness of the early morning the duke led Father Domenici through the west-wing galleries to Leonardo's chair sitting on its illuminated dais. Light glinted off the polished patina of its dark walnut as the two men stood side by side behind the velvet cordon.

"This must be performed with great care, Father."

"I hope you understand there is much risk in using these holy prayers. Whatever gives this chair its powers for art may disappear with its evil."

"I've read every detail of the rite. I'm convinced if it is done correctly we will have great success."

Father Domenici nodded and took out an embroidered stole from a pocket in his cassock. He kissed the cross stitched into the middle, placed it around his neck, then stepped forward. He motioned for the duke to come beside him. The tall aristocrat came up beside the priest and opened the thick, red-leather volume to a cloth marker, and held it open for the father to read the ornate Latin script. He made the sign of the cross and put his finger under the first word on the top of the verso side of the page and started reading the long prayer, his voice rising and falling until settling into a steady rhythm. Sweat beaded up on the duke's forehead as he held the heavy book. He knew the ceremony would take nearly a half hour to read, but it would be worth the suffering of standing motionless for so long to have the fiery forces extinguished forever. He had studied the church's solemn adjuration and was convinced of its singular power. It was a seldom-used ritual with a long history of effectiveness dating back many centuries. The duke felt certain of this morning's success. By the time Father Domenici was finished all that would be left under the chair's walnut surface would be the exquisite, purified power of the maestro. It would be potent but harmless. And he would sleep easier knowing his daughter would be safe and the castle and its collection would forever be under the guardianship of his heirs. He took a deep breath and smiled as the good father continued his solemn recitation.

Down the elevator into the cold cellar studio, among the drawings that hung in wicked testament to the duke's plan, Paul sat in front of his easel, handling a pencil, pondering. He was almost finished with a final sketch of Leonardo's lost self-portrait—a brilliant drawing—a task worthy of a maestro. It had barely taken him a week and a day. Yes, he could do it. Energy throbbed through him as he focused on the drawing of *St. Jerome*, studying the swirls around the ears, under the eyes, and across the flat surfaces of the cheeks. His hand worked with meticulous detail as he drew in feverish strokes. Finishing the drawing he hung it on the wall next to the photographic reproduction of the *St. Jerome*. His technique was superb. To his trained eye, his drawing was indistinguishable from the photos of Leonardo's paintings. He could do this, he was certain. Tomorrow the pigments would arrive and he could begin by preparing the canvas.

Isabella swished into the room behind him. He could smell her perfume as she placed her hand on his shoulder. "You've been working very hard. I though we should do something very special tonight."

"What did you have in mind?" he asked, continuing to work.

"There's an opera in Turin. It's just an hour's drive. We will be home before midnight."

Paul thought about the rock falling on him in the road, and the stream of fire striking at him like an angry cobra. "I think I'd better stay here. I have a lot to do."

She sighed. "An evening off would do you good. You will be refreshed and ready to start with the pigments tomorrow."

"I need to finish my drawings tonight so I can get an early start."

She was silent a moment. "I already bought the tickets."

Paul turned and caught an eager glint in her eye. "Do you think it's safe?"

"You can't get my father's story out of your mind, can you?"

"You didn't almost get burned up on the road like I did."

She moved close and rested her hand on his shoulder. "The Opera National de Paris is performing. You've never seen anything like it. It will be a good opportunity to witness the emptiness of the myth yourself."

"Does your father know we'd be leaving the castle?"

She smiled mischievously. "Does he need to know everything we do?"

Paul gazed at her while thinking of his burning car and lying sprawled in the middle of the road.

She pulled on his arm. "Why are you acting so afraid?"

"Will we be traveling over that same mountain pass I came

through before?"

"Of course—that's the only way out."

He stared at her, wondering if Isabella would put herself knowingly in the way of danger?

"Paul?" She stepped closer, her perfume smelled like roses and fresh air. "Is something wrong?"

He smiled. "I was just thinking about something I'd really like to do."

He laid down his pencil and gently pulled her to him. Her sweet perfume lifted his weariness. He closed his eyes as her warm lips met his. They were soft and smooth. Paul realized this should be one of the most exciting instants in his life. But painting projects ran through his mind like a herd of wild ponies over a windswept prairie—unstoppable, uncontrollable—trodding his passion into vague clouds of dust.

He put his hands on her thin, small waist, but pulled his lips away.

She smiled. Through her red lips showed straight, white teeth. She searched his eyes with a questioning gaze, as if to ask why he stopped.

Paul held her close and studied her face: The little wrinkle of her nose when she smiled enchanted him, and the intelligent glint in her eyes invited him in. He had wanted her in his arms since he'd first met her, and now she was so close he could see the pale freckles on her porcelain skin, reminding him of tiny dewdrops the color of honey. He leaned forward and kissed her intently, her warm breath mingling with his. He kissed her longingly but gently until the tenderness of her embrace washed over him like a strong ocean current, pulling him away from every other thought, every reason why not. He knew what he felt for her was lasting, and that he wanted to be with her as deeply as he wanted to paint, which until this moment was the brightest passion he'd ever known. He had only dreamed he could feel this way about a woman, and now holding her so tight he could feel every ripple of her body, he never wanted to let her go.

※※

Paul and Isabella departed Savoy for Turin shortly after lunch. The rounded softness of the clouds floating over the calm mountains belied the turmoil Paul worked to hide behind a pleasant smile.

With Gerhard at the wheel, they calmly traversed the Mount-Cenis pass. With Isabella beside him in the back seat, Paul gripped her hand when he spotted a scorched rock and blackened patch of dirt on the shoulder of the road. The large boulder had been removed. Once out of the pass, Isabella shot him a confident smile. Paul nodded and loosened his grip on her hand.

"I'm glad you're finally relaxing. This will be so much fun," she said, her eyes sparkling as she spoke.

"Your father and you have very different views on Leonardo's chair. How did that happen?"

Isabella wore a gorgeous navy pant suit, and her blonde hair framed her lovely face, cascading down her shoulders. "When I was a teenager a friend and I were running along the top of the north wall, and she jokingly stood in one of the crenulations and acted like she was going to jump."

"Did she?" Paul asked.

"She tottered back and forth, and I thought she was kidding, which till this day I'm convinced she was."

"What happened?"

"She fell."

Paul put his arm around her, "That must have been horrible."

"I thought her parents would be angry at me, that we were playing on the walls and we shouldn't have been."

"They weren't?"

"Oh, they were angry, but that soon wore off and they were blaming an old family curse. Evidently, Eva's grandfather committed suicide. They were convinced that God didn't forgive suicide and that punishment for his sin had been passed down to Eva."

"Rather superstitious, don't you think?"

"Exactly. And that's when I began to question my father's story about Leonardo's chair and all those fiery deaths. I think in our country it's impossible to separate myth from reality, and quite frankly, no one wants to. So when it came time to attend the university, I knew that unless I moved away I'd never have the freedom to discover the truth for myself. That's why I decided to attend Stanford," she said.

"You learned about the chair at Stanford?"

She smiled at him, "In a way. I learned about history stripped of superstitions and myths. Accidents were part of life in Medieval and Renaissance Europe. Men were famous for creating myths to explain what their limited knowledge couldn't comprehend. Accidents were part of daily life back then, and dying from the simplest disease or injury was an everyday occurrence. House fires were a common part of life in Medieval Europe. I think the myth of the fire grew up around the chair because it was one way of comprehending their experience and the chair's mysterious powers."

Paul gazed out the window at the Alps as they streamed by on the road outside. "So you're saying that the deaths by fire probably did happen, but they were all coincidences."

"Accidents that could be explained if one knew the details."

"Like my father's decision to run back into the fire."

"Or your decision to stop at a point in the road known for falling rocks."

Paul nodded. Of course it all made sense to him. Isabella was right that the two incidents that he knew of, his father running into their burning house and his near fatal accident on the mountain pass, could both be explained. If he had lived in a time when the connection between cause and effect were vaguely understood, if at all, it wouldn't take too many experiences like those he had witnessed until he started putting some otherworldly meaning to them. So during the time the House of Savoy used the chair, the superstitions must have grown year by year as the incidents occurred one after the other.

"I think you were very brave to set out on your own and question everything your father taught you."

"My father cannot separate the traditions that have no basis in facts from his passions that need no facts."

"You seem to share his passion for religion?"

She sighed. "Religion is another thing my father and I don't agree on either, but I just don't discuss it with him."

Paul shook his head. "Wait a minute, I've seen you in church. You seem as devout as he is."

"Devotion means different things to different people. In California I learned that religion comes in every color. One thing I love about Americans is that they are fearless at throwing off any form of the past. They are always inventing their own future. But one thing I disliked about Americans is that they have no regard for the past, as if it didn't exist. They are so brash, they think they can do anything they want any way they want. But I came to the conclusion there can be no meaningful future without a healthy reverence for one's history. That doesn't mean we should be slaves to it, but respect for it helps us to understand it. There is power in our traditions if you separate them from myth."

"What kind of power?"

"Good power, the kind you can use to live a better life, and to use what God has given us to enjoy."

"You mean like the power of Leonardo's chair?" he asked looking at her.

"And the power of the rituals in our religion. My father thinks they bring him closer to God by pleasing him in some way. If he performs the rituals regularly he's at peace with God. It assuages his guilt."

"But you don't believe that?"

"Of course not. Think about it. If God was truly all-powerful and created us, how is any ritual going to make him happy? What would make him most happy is that we used the powers he'd created in us as humans. He wants us to enjoy the power of his gifts. My father wastes so much of his time worrying over his guilt. It's so much part of our culture, he can't escape it."

"But then why do you go to church? You seem to enjoy it so much."

"I believe there's a God, but I think he's very misunderstood. I think the painting of *The Last Supper* plumbs some of those misunderstandings. When Leonardo finished it, it was at that moment he decided to follow in Jesus' footsteps and leave a legacy for mankind, but one they could use."

"You mean the face of Judas?"

"And Jesus. The myth surrounding him is that because he was a wonder worker, healing the sick and the blind, the jealous religious zealots of his day put him to death, and that his death was all part of God's plan."

"But that is the story."

"Paul, of course it isn't. That story is part myth and part truth. When you separate the two, you will begin to understand the power that Leonardo left to us and the power that Leonardo alluded to in his painting."

Paul turned and quickly scanned the countryside as it swished past. The details of the story of Jesus came quickly to his mind from his time in Sunday school. He turned back to her, "What part of the Jesus story is myth?"

"He came to bless mankind by teaching peace and healing. But before he could bestow his gift of healing on others, the zealots of the day, who were afraid what would happen to their power if such a man were allowed to live, crucified him. But Jesus' early death wasn't in his plans. Can you imagine what the world would be like today if Jesus had been able to rule the kingdoms of the earth? That's all the Judas wanted, but the religious men of the day portrayed him as a traitor to cover up his real mission."

"So Judas didn't betray Jesus?"

"Not at all. He thought that if he got the Romans involved they would keep him from the jealous men who wanted to kill him."

"He was trying to save Jesus from death?"

"So he could rule the world."

"It would be a different place if he had become king."

She leaned her head on his shoulder. "Paul, Leonardo realized the truth as he painted *The Last Supper* and he decided he would find a way to pass along his gifts. Leonardo narrates all this in the Madrid Codex of his notebooks, along with sketches of the chair. The notebook was found in the University of Madrid library in the late '60s. My father has a copy of it. Leonardo never intended it to possess evil powers, but as something God wanted us to enjoy. That's why the rituals of the church remind me of what could have been and what can be if we are brave enough to take advantage of the opportunities that are before us."

He could smell the distinctive orange scent of her shampoo and feel the softness of her cheek upon his shoulder. There were many gifts given to man, painting was only one of them, the beauty of nature that spun by outside his window another, but nothing seemed to compare to Isabella. He was simply amazed at her explanations, and for the first time in his life, the supernatural elements of world that swirled in his mind in vague images, coalesced into a workable whole. The earth is man's play yard, and nothing is taboo if it's for the greater good of man.

By two o'clock they were in Turin and Gerhard pulled into the downtown parking lot of the Pinacoteca Museum. It was an amazing museum filled with classical and baroque paintings Paul had only seen photos of. They had worked their way through only half the galleries before four o'clock. Isabella and Paul were standing at the curb when Gerhard, punctual to the minute, slid the black Mercedes sedan to a stop in front of them. He dropped her off at the Hotel Brusca where Isabella disappeared into the salon, and then Gerhard drove Paul to the American Consulate where he picked up his new passport.

At quarter past six, Paul came downstairs dressed in a navy blue, three-button suit and matching tie. He sat at a table in the bar where a waiter brought two glasses and bottle of Merlot. Paul sipped his wine, then tapped his watch. He hoped she remembered their dinner reservations at seven.

"Have you been waiting long?" a voice behind Paul said.

Paul rose and turned to see an Isabella he'd never seen before. Her strawberry blonde hair was wrapped in a French braid on her head, and a lock of curled hair hung delicately at each temple. She wore a lavender strapless gown that made her white shoulders look like mounds of cream. Every time she moved, the sequined dress shimmered, accenting the outline of her beautiful curves.

"You look like you've seen a ghost," she said to Paul.

"No, an angel," he said.

She twined her arm in his and he escorted her to the entrance where Gerhard waited with the Mercedes.

They ate dinner at the exclusive Giannino Restaurant and dined on course after course served by tuxedo-clad waiters in white gloves. The spacious dining room seemed like a meeting place for the well dressed and the gorgeous people of Turin.

"I'm glad to see you enjoying yourself," she said to Paul. "Wait until you see the opera. There is nothing like a Verdi opera in Italy."

When Gerhard pulled the Mercedes up to the entrance to the Teatro degli Aricomboldi, doormen dressed in white tails and top hats opened the car doors and warmly greeted them. The Aricomboldi was a beautiful traditional opera theater, and from their third-row orchestra seats Paul could see the makeup caked on the singers' faces. They performed Verdi's *La Traviata*. He understood only a smattering of the lyrics. He was able to follow the story by reading the libretto.

Isabella was right. There was nothing like opera in Italy.

After the opera they went back to the Hotel Brusca for a nightcap, and Isabella and Paul went to the lounges where a three-piece combo played. The music was slow and romantic and there were a few couples on the dance floor. Paul took her hand and led her to the center of the parquet floor. He held her as if holding a rare diamond, one hand in the small of her back.

"Today was magical," he said, looking into her eyes. "I've never enjoyed myself so much."

She smiled with an arched brow. "Have you been living in a monastery?"

"Maybe so." He swirled her around in a gentle arc. "I didn't know until today what I was missing."

"And what exactly is that?"

He put his cheek to hers. "This."

"When did you realize you felt this way?" she whispered in his ear.

"Today when we kissed. It just seemed that everything inside us matches each other."

She pulled away and looked at him, her eyes wide with interest but not saying anything. She then rested her head on his shoulder and snuggled her forehead under his chin. It fit perfectly.

It was well after midnight when Isabella and Paul snuggled in the back seat of the Mercedes sedan on their way home to Savoy. The road was busy, cars and trucks swooshed by on the other side, their headlights glaring. She laid her head on his shoulder and shut her eyes. They left the *autostrada* and rose into the Alps behind a line of two other cars. His mind wandered to home in California. Soon he would be home, and he couldn't imagine Isabella not going with him.

He dozed on and off as they drove to the sound of Gerhard humming a tune. Paul's head lolled back, propped up on the headrest.

"What's that idiot doing?" Gerhard yelled.

Paul and Isabella woke with a start. They were ascending a narrow pass and a small pickup truck was passing a slow-moving van in front of them. The two were side by side near the top when, in the opposite lane, a tanker truck broke over the summit, headlights and running lights blazing, picking up speed as it headed downhill— head on to the pickup. Gerhard slowed so the pickup could fall back behind the van and let the tanker by. Instead, the driver sped up to pass the van. The two trucks were only car lengths away from each other. The tanker blared its horn and slammed on its brakes. The sound of screeching brakes tore through the night air. The pickup overtook the van, swerved into the right lane in front of the van.

Paul sighed in relief.

But the tanker's brakes continue to squeal, rubber screaming, the round chrome trailer full of liquid jackknifed and slipped sideways toward the line of three cars. Paul could see the horrified face of the truck driver, fixed in the headlights of the van in front of them, as he frantically yanked the steering wheel trying to regain control. The pickup hit the tank broadside, shearing the top of the pickup's cab, decapitating the two occupants. The roof of the pickup impaled the tank. The tanker continued sliding toward them, his brakes locked, liquid gushing all over the road.

Isabella screamed and buried her face in Paul's shoulder.

Paul swore. "Get over. Get over," he yelled. "Go around it." Gerhard veered to the right—scraping the Mercedes against the rock face of the mountainside—and skidded to a stop while the punctured truck still bore down on them.

"Back up, back up," Paul shouted frantically.

Before Gerhard could throw the gearshift into reverse, the van plowed into the tanker in a shower of sparks. An angry orange fireball shot out, lighting up the night sky, hurtling toward the receding Mercedes. The force shattered its windshield into tiny bits. Isabella screamed and they all ducked as the granules of glass and the force of hot air shot into the car. Paul held her tighter. The heat inside became unbearable. Gerhard tromped on the gas shooting the car back down the mountain. A river of fire followed them.

Paul pushed Isabella down on the floor then scanned the road behind him. A car was coming up the hill. He yelled to Gerhard, who slammed on the brakes. Paul jumped out, threw open the back door just as a stream of flames reached the front tires, popping them with a bang and a hiss. All three of them scrambled up a rock face to a ledge high enough to assure their safety and watched as the flames rolled under the car and engulfed it. Paul held Isabella close to him and she buried her face in his chest as he watched the bloody conflagration in the narrow file of the mountain pass.

The acquisition of glory is a much greater thing than the glory itself.

—Leonardo da Vinci, *Notebooks*

27

*B*efore dawn the next morning, Stein knocked at Isabella's door until she answered it.

She came to the door wrapped in her burgundy robe, her eyes blurry with sleep. He pushed his way inside and closed the door behind her. She turned away from him and slumped into a pink and white Louis IV striped chair in the sitting area of her large bedroom. An intricately carved, four-poster, canopied bed with maroon velvet curtains occupied the center of the room. "What's so important to wake me so early?" she said.

"The studio in Florence I promised you is ready."

She rubbed her eyes and then looked at him wearily. "You didn't come in here just to tell me that, did you?"

He sat in the matching chair across from her. "As soon as LaBont is finished with the da Vinci, we're moving the operation to Florence."

She pushed her hair off her face and patted it down.

"You'll need to be packed and ready to go. The day he finishes we leave, and I'm taking the chair with us," Stein said. He coolly walked over and stood in front of her.

She sat up. "Paul's been promised the chair."

"You would sign your own death warrant by letting him take it. Everyone in the castle knows what happened last night. That was no fluke accident, Isabella. You need to think about your future. What you've planned for." He spoke in soft, subdued tones, meant to convince. "This is no time to give sway to mere sentiment."

"You're sure singing a different song this morning."

"Even you, the skeptic, must be convinced that some wicked power exists in the chair."

"If that's true, then taking the chair and leaving him here would mean certain death for him," she said rubbing her forehead.

"And death for *you* if he takes it." Stein knew that if he spoke reasonably to her what was best for her would eventually sink in. "By rights, by the long history of your family, that chair and its gift belong to you."

She bit her lip, thinking.

"You are in a difficult situation, I understand. He's a very handsome and persuasive man." He stood and walked slowly in front of her. "Letting the chair out of your grasp is the most shortsighted thing you can do. You know how quickly your art has come along. The moment he finishes the painting, you and me, the painting and the chair will be whisked off to Florence. There you will be able to work undisturbed on your art until you perfect your gift. It's your destiny, Isabella, your right."

"Did my father agree to this?" She slumped further in her chair, not looking at him.

"Your father will get his money and save his collection. That's all he wants. What we're deciding here is what's critical to your future."

She smoothed back her hair thoughtfully. "What if Paul decided to come with me to Florence?"

"You know that's not possible," Stein said, standing erect. "He would never keep our secret."

"People do the most amazing things for love."

He sighed. "Isabella, you can't let this opportunity for greatness slip by. Love will always come again, but this moment will only be here once, then it will be gone," he said snapping his fingers, "like that."

She finally looked up at him. "If Paul decides not to come to Florence with us, I will not go without him."

"Isabella, be reasonable."

"I am. I won't go without him."

Stein stood abruptly and looked down at her. He wanted to grab her by her arm and shake her until she stopped being difficult, but that wouldn't get him anywhere. No, he would have to convince her of her own best interests. He'd orchestrated everything so far, and they were within days of reaching their goals.

"Your future depends on LaBont finishing the painting quickly. If I were you I'd keep my distance from him for a while. He starts working with the oils tomorrow. He should be done in less than two weeks if he's not distracted. Then we'll move everything to Florence where you can continue your painting uninterrupted." Stein stomped to the door. He didn't intend to discuss the matter with her any longer.

"What about Paul?" she said as he reached the door.

He didn't turn, but spoke to her over his shoulder, "I promise you as long as he's painting, I won't harm him." He couldn't think of one reason, other than this impressionable girl's infatuation, why LaBont should go with them to Florence. He would only create problems Stein didn't want to have to spend the effort solving. By the time he grasped the cold brass of the door handle and harshly turned it, he had already decided where he would place the bullet in LaBont's handsome head—slightly above his right ear. And he knew exactly who he would set up to take blame for killing the arrogant American. As soon as LaBont finished the da Vinci, his knowledge of their plan would die with him.

Early on Sunday morning Paul took a call from his mother. She had a frantic, almost hysterical, pitch to her voice.

"Paul, it's been over a week since I talked to you. When are you coming home?"

"Mom." He could hear her voice shaking. "What's happened?"

"I'm afraid to take my eyes off your father. I know he'll do something to hurt himself."

"Have you talked to his doctor?"

She sighed. "Honey, that's not going to do much good. He's convinced that everything is lost unless you come home with that stupid chair. Have you talked with the duke?"

"Yes. But there have been some complications I don't want to get into," Paul said, not wanting to discuss his agreement to paint a da Vinci.

"So, when can you bring it home?"

Paul thought a moment but didn't say anything.

"I caught him with a full bottle of pain pills in his hand. He was ready to take them all. This is serious, Paul. I'm afraid for him."

Paul rubbed the frown on his forehead and took a deep breath. "Okay, Mom. I'll call you in a week. I'm pretty sure I can wrap things up by then."

After hanging up Paul lay on his bed thinking about what she must be going through. She was always the unflappable one in the family, but this morning she sounded as if the pressure were unbearable. Just saying the word suicide had the ring of death to it. If he didn't wrap things up quickly here, and bring home that chair, his father's blood would be on his hands. And that was something that he didn't think he could recover from.

He was too tired to attend church that morning and too disturbed over last night's incident on the road. When the pigments arrived later today, he intended to begin work immediately and get the portrait done.

By Sunday afternoon the pigments arrived, and down in the cellar studio Paul began preparing the canvas for Leonardo's self-portrait. It would be difficult working with these ancient pigments, but Tosatti spent the rest of the day and well into the evening showing him how to mix them until Paul felt comfortable. They needed great care in their handling, and Tosatti repeatedly emphasized how difficult it had been to find and how expensive it had been to acquire them and how irreplaceable they were. He focused all of his attention on his work. There would be no mistakes. He would complete the painting and be done with Savoy and on his way home to California and a new life.

As he listened to the man explain the materials and their use, he couldn't image spending the rest of his life doing anything else but painting. He loved his craft. But then the accident on the road last night came to mind. As they stood on the windy ledge, waiting for a car to come from the castle to collect them, he hadn't dared to ask Isabella if the explosion of the gasoline tanker was just another one of those explainable mishaps. She hadn't stopped shaking until they drove into the long driveway of Savoy. He wanted to ask her if she thought the truck exploding into flames was just one of those random events that took place every day on the highways of Italy, or did she, like he, have the creeping feeling that somehow this horrific and fatal scene was linked by some symbiotic spirit to Leonardo's chair. As a result of his time in Isabella's studio, enjoying the heady abilities of Leonardo's gift, an appreciation for her view had settled over him—it didn't seem logical that something that could grant the benevolent blessing of unusual talent could also bequeath malevolence like some petty

god on a midnight rampage. But after last night he knew this blessing mixed with malevolence was exactly how the universe was
arranged. The rules of the chair's use were clearly spelled out. They
had been handed down through successive generations, their
requirements written in the blood of her ancestors. And it was
now obvious to him that he disregarded them at the peril of his
life.

Call belief in the chair's power superstition, call it a warped
notion of the universal order, call it a delusion based on wishful
thinking—he had tried all of these, but the one thing he could not
call it was fickle. The chair's gifts and the chair's demands were consistent. Use it and prosper; be away from it and die. That death came
shrouded in the cloak of accidental events was inconsequential to
him. It came with thunder, it came with fire, it came with a total disregard for the simple motives that had driven him to sit in its velvet
seat. He was convinced that if he flirted with its sacred law, death
would find him at the moment of its own choosing and mete out its
full measure of wrath. He had crossed a Rubicon of sorts. There was
no giving back what had been taken, no saying he was sorry—he
hadn't meant to enjoy the fruits of its power. Once taken, once
tasted, he was forever mastered by its blessing. In that cold stone cellar, as he worked beside Tosatti in laying out the tins of ancient pigments and the old Italian rambled on about the alchemy of mixing
them to create the colors da Vinci favored most, Paul realized in a
despairing silence, that he had always been his father's son, but in
the last few days, despite his gravest efforts to the contrary, and his
unrelenting fears of it ever happening, he had become his father.
And there was nothing he could do to change it.

An irascible Frederick tromped down the hall of the living
quarters on his way to an early Sunday-morning mass. He stopped
in front of Isabella's door. He had heard about the incident on the

road when one of the house staff woke him to tell him a car was on its way to pick up the three travelers on their way back from Turin. As he sat up in bed, his blood ran cold thinking of everything he'd worked for the last few years—to return his beloved castle to solvency, to rejuvenate the splendor of Savoy, and to have his daughter near to him pursuing her passion—all seemed in equal jeopardy. And most of the agitation he was now feeling was because of the arrogance of his beautiful daughter. If she had just heeded his advice and stayed away from that wooden monster. Yes, that's what it seemed to him now, a monster that had invaded his peaceful home. He had known it would be too much of a temptation for her to resist its allure.

Standing in front of her wooden bedroom door, he wanted to beat on it and barge in and shake some sense into her skeptical head, but he doubted the efficacy of such an approach. First he must go to church and pray and calm himself, and seek some semblance of peace. He knew he was far too agitated to carry on a civilized conversation with anyone but God. Maybe last night was a sign of God's displeasure, not with Isabella, but with himself that he had toyed with the ineffable powers of fate and fame and had thought they could not harm him. It was obvious to him now that he had wasted his time with those useless incantations. Or were the powers he had sought to control simply too entrenched, too settled in their path of cause and effect to be changed by anything he could do? He studied the deep grain in soft patterns on the dark oak of Isabella's door as if they had some cryptic message he was destined to read, then turned in disgust and headed down the stairs to the Savoy Chapel. He had looked for hidden secrets far too long and had found nothing. He had spent his whole life in reverence of everything ancient—from art to the rituals of the mass that he deeply believed God himself had ordained for man's benefit. But now he began to wonder. He did not doubt the existence of God, like some weak-minded child who squawked uncontrollably when the heavens were silent to his requests, but rather he looked within himself. Maybe he had been asking for the right things in the wrong way? Maybe there was a penance he could perform to expiate his ignorance? Maybe God merely waited for him to figure out the right rituals to perform? Yes, these were distinct possibilities, and when he sat in the beauty of the Chapel of Savoy, and listened again to the rite of the ancient Mass recited for the innumerable time, God would bless him with a moment of illumination and it would become clear to him what he must do.

Isabella didn't eat with them at the evening meal, and it was a cold affair with the duke asking probing questions about their accident. The duke's face looked deeply troubled with a heavy frown and a glint of anger in his eyes. Paul knew he was disturbed over the accident that almost cost him and Isabella their lives, but also he knew the duke's deepest concern was for his daughter. Stein didn't say a word.

Paul spent twelve to fourteen hours a day for the next week working in the dungeon studio, and by the next Saturday had the outline of the head of the portrait and most of the background completed. He worked quietly by himself, but felt a tremor of concern that Isabella had disappeared the whole week. Had her father put pressure on her to stay away from him? He didn't doubt it. He couldn't think of leaving Savoy without her and wanted to speak to her about his plans. Surely, after the episode on the road, she wouldn't think of staying here alone once he left with the chair.

At dinner on Saturday night he made a point of informing the duke he would join them the next morning for mass.

On Palm Sunday morning Paul, Isabella, and the duke stood in their pew holding palm fronds commemorating Jesus' triumphal entry into Jerusalem.

He leaned toward her and whispered. "Where have you been?"

She shrugged then leaned close and whispered: "Meet me at the stables at four."

They both turned back to the service. The chapel seemed on fire from the scores of candles in brass candelabra staggered up the steps leading to the altar. The choir in the loft behind them sang a hymn in Latin, in soft, reverent tones, their voices melding together into a single paean of praise. The hymn, almost a chant, reverberated off the walls, echoing in the vaulted ceiling, doubling its intensity by the time it reached Paul's ears. The processional, at a dirge-like pace, filed down the center aisle led by an altar boy holding a brass cross above his head. Behind him, the priest, in a white chasuble, carried a smoking censor dangling on a chain and waved it back and forth until aromatic smoke filled the chapel. Three acolytes clad in black-and-white robes followed behind carrying tall candles in brass holders. The last one pulled a wooden donkey that rolled along behind him, the wheels squeaking as they scraped along the stone floor.

Isabella and her father knelt and recited passages from their missals with the rest of the congregation. The singing, the ceremony, the incense, overwhelmed Paul. He felt out of place—not because the chants and hymns were in Latin and the homily in Italian, but because while everyone around seemed to understand the significance of what they were doing, he could think of nothing but his painting.

The congregation sat on hard oak benches while the priest spoke from a carved wooden pulpit. Paul's eye caught a slim ray of light glancing off the faces in *The Last Supper* behind the altar. The expressions of the apostles, as they reacted to the betrayal of Judas, seemed more lifelike than he remembered from the last time. The apostle Peter swung back in shock, his mouth open, trying to figure out if Jesus had accused him. John attempted to repose on Jesus' breast, Andrew and James pleaded their innocence, while Jesus held the piece of bread over the cup, and stared across the altar right at Paul. A looping shadow stretched across the right half of the painting. Jesus' eyes stared hard at Paul, piercing the veil of his flesh, driving deep into his mind.

One of you will betray me.

Paul felt naked down to the marrow in his bones. He felt Jesus staring at him as if it were he who was to betray him. Why would this holy man single him out? He was only an artist. He hadn't done or said anything against him. So why was he pointedly gazing at him? Those dark eyes of his seemed to penetrate every ambition, every dream, every drop of love or hate he'd ever felt. The eyes kept digging through the veneer of his life, to things he dared not talk about—his selfishness in wanting all the artistic talents of da Vinci for himself—his arrogance regarding the greatness of his painting of Isabella on her mare. Paul cringed. He felt as if he's stolen something, as Judas had stolen the gifts of money given to the Master.

The painted figure on the wall, with his eyes fixed squarely on Paul sitting erect in the stiff wooden pew, passed the wine-soaked sop of bread across time and the altar to him.

Paul squeezed his eyes shut. But the image of Jesus' face came to life in his mind in vivid color. The pure black eyes fixed on him. His red lips mouthed words Paul had heard before.

One of you will betray me.

The robe-clad figure held a wine-soaked piece of bread in his outstretched hand. Paul didn't know why, but he saw himself reaching out his hand to take it.

He turned away from the painting toward the end of the pew where Jacob Stein sat, and for one brief moment Paul thought he saw the deeply lined, ugly face with a hooked nose, the face of his dream and the one in the painting. He blinked and Stein turned and flashed his depraved smile. Paul wanted to rise and leave, but he didn't dare, fearing he would offend Isabella. Instead he distracted himself by following the priest through the ceremony of the benediction. Searching eyes seemed to be probing him at every turn. Was he just imagining all this?

Fixing his attention on the priest, Paul didn't understand how a painting could have such sway over his thoughts. Was this the affect da Vinci strove to create in his paintings by reproducing the "intentions of the souls" of those he painted? Had the artist who had painted this work found some way to re-create the effect of the artistic brilliance of da Vinci? Or was the painting's message truly speaking to him in some spiritual link across time and circumstances, scrutinizing his motives and ambitions as if his very being had become an open book. How could this be?

Paul stared at the vaulted ceiling, trying to regain his composure. He hadn't betrayed anyone, particularly God. He had come to Savoy to help his father, and that's what he intended to do. Certainly, he had legitimate reasons to feel good about his talent—that didn't make him a traitor like Judas.

And since when did feeling proud about his accomplishments cross over into misdeeds? God wouldn't judge him for using his talents to their fullest.

He sighed. Paul shook his head slowly: whatever that morsel of bread soaked in wine handed to Judas represented, he felt certain it had not been offered to him. It was not a sin to live his dreams, to let the swelling tide of da Vinci's greatness carry him and Isabella to the highest levels of achievement. As they stood for the final prayer and he escorted her out of the service into the warmth of the afternoon sunshine, his self-assurance slipped.

The piercing recollection of those searching black eyes haunted him. They had stared straight at him, and the words the serene red lips had mouthed were unmistakable.

We know very well that errors are better recognized in the works of others than in our own.

—Leonardo da Vinci, *Notebooks*

28

---

*L*ater that afternoon he and Isabella met at the stables and rode up into the mountains and picnicked by a small lake. They settled under the shade of a tall pine tree and ate a light dinner of chicken and fruit while their horses nibbled at the tall grass in the sunshine.

"Where have you been all week?" he asked.

She looked out on the meadow; the afternoon sun glinted on her blonde hair. "My father thought it better that I gave you time to concentrate on your work."

"He seemed upset all week."

She nodded. "He was quite angry about what happened on the road. But he'll get over it. Do you think your father will be okay?" she asked.

Paul lay on the grass beside her facing the sky. "It sounds like he's turning suicidal."

"That's awful," she said. Sitting up, she put a hand on his shoulder.

Paul propped himself up on one elbow and looked at her. "But if it weren't for his accident, I wouldn't be here."

"Do you regret that you've come?" She looked at him attentively, her eyebrows arched.

"I regret I came so reluctantly."

"It's like we've known each other forever," she said smiling.

"Have you ever thought of going back to California?"

She pulled at a blade of grass. "Is that an invitation?"

"Definitely."

She faced him. "I would like to come to California."

"I have to get home in the next week, and I need to take the chair. I want you to come with me."

"It sounds so simple," she said facing him. "But after what happened the other day, I'm not certain Father will let you just leave with the chair."

"It's mine as soon as the da Vinci's completed, that's our agreement. And when I leave, I don't intend to ask his or Stein's permission." He sat up next to her and looked into her eyes. He held her hand softly. "Isabella, I love you and want you to be with me."

The afternoon sunshine glinted off her hair. "I feel the same for you, but I have some obligations that just can't be ignored."

"This is the twenty-first century. You don't have to do anything you don't want to."

"Look who's talking," she said, with a serious stare.

Paul smiled. "Touché."

She leaned her head on his shoulder. "I want to leave here too, but I need to go to Florence. Why don't you come with me? We can be together in one of the most beautiful cities in the world."

He stroked her hair. "I can't, Isabella. The chair belongs with my father."

"Why?"

"It just does," he said pensively.

"Savoy is nearly bankrupt. My father's a good man, but he has a severe gambling habit. He has gotten deeply into debt to men he should have nothing to do with."

"Why doesn't he just sell some of the paintings or artifacts? The collection is immensely valuable."

"That is not so easy. My ancestors put everything, the castle, the collections, even the furniture, in a trust. Nothing can be sold, ever. If the castle cannot meet its expenses, it will become a museum," she said sadly.

Paul slowly nodded. "Ah, so the da Vinci I'm painting will eventually be sold with the proceeds going to replenish the family trust fund, then everyone will live happily ever after." He thumped his fist on the ground beside him.

"I knew you'd figure that out," Isabella sighed. "That's why Stein must take it to Florence. It can't be found in the castle or it would become part of the trust's property. My father thinks it will sell for about fifty or sixty million dollars, but it could be more. There's plenty there for all of us. Why don't you come to Florence with me?"

"I can't believe your father's involving you in such a risky scheme."

"I don't think my father has much choice. He needs—" she sat up, and brushed her hair off her shoulder.

"Everyone has choices, Isabella," he said, his voice rising.

She looked at him, her mouth taut, her eyes flashing with anger. "Paul …"

He gently put his hand on her shoulder. "What?"

"You're almost finished with the painting, aren't you?" She spoke, gazing out into the empty meadow. "Tosatti is coming at the end of the week to view the progress you've made on the painting." She turned to him, with a look a disappointment in her eyes. "As soon as you're finished, we're moving to Florence."

"We?" he said, his voice shocked.

"Stein will take the painting to Florence. I would like you to come with me." She studied the green grass at her feet as she spoke.

"And you're going too?"

She looked up at him with her searching green eyes and nodded. A worry line creased her brow.

"Isabella, I won't leave unless you come with me," he said, wrapping his arm around her shoulders. "Come with me, and we'll have together what money could never buy."

She looked at him, her eyes gleaming with a hint of fear he'd never seen in her before.

"Isabella, when I take the chair, everything will change for you. Please come with me."

Her voice trembling, she said: "For your own sake, don't finish the painting."

"Why's that?"

"I'm afraid of what Stein will do. The moment you're finished, Stein intends to take the chair with the painting to Florence. Before you even realize it, the chair will be gone."

"Ah, and leave me here to fend for myself. Is that why you've been avoiding me all week?"

She plucked a few blades of grass and tossed them into the breeze. "I don't think he intends to leave you alive." She looked up at him with a serious gaze.

"Now you know why I could never go with you to Florence. As long as he's involved with you and your father, we can never be together."

She pursed her lips and nodded slowly as if she were seriously considering his words. "I know you're right about Stein. We could never be together with him around. But if I leave here with you, Paul, I can never come back."

"You will be home, with me. We'll have all the time in the world for one another and our work."

She looked at him sheepishly. "We'll share everything?"

"Everything," he said.

She didn't say anything.

"If it's money you're worried about, once we're in California and established, we will make more than enough money to help your father. You can send him whatever he needs. Besides, he'll have the da Vinci to do with as he pleases."

"For your own sake," she looked up at him, "don't finish it."

He sighed deeply.

"It's the only way you can escape with your life." She put her index finger to her top lip. "I'm afraid for you Paul."

He sat up beside her and held her close. "Then we must leave together as soon as we can."

She plucked a few blades of grass and tossed them into the breeze. She turned toward him with a somber look. "The best time for us to leave would be during Tenebrae."

"What's that?"

"It means darkness. It's a traditional celebration of the three hours of darkness the covered the earth when Christ died on the cross. It's celebrated in the Savoy Chapel just after midnight Thursday, early Good Friday morning."

"Why is that the best time?"

"Everyone in the castle, including Jacob, will be in the service. You will be able to slip out unnoticed and it will be hours before anyone notices the chair is missing. He thinks you'll be done by then, so he's arranged with Tossatti to come pick up the painting and the supplies."

"Tossatti's coming?" Paul asked.

"Not till later that morning—six or seven—by that time we'll be on our way to America."

She laid her head on his shoulder. They stayed snuggled in each other's arms until the light began to wane, then they headed back to the castle. Paul went off to the makeshift studio Stein had set up in the dungeons. He worked late into the night and made excellent progress on the portrait. On Monday, the duke came in to admire his work. He told Paul when the da Vinci was completed and dried it would hang with the others. During that afternoon's *pisolino*, Paul called the airline and confirmed his flight home out of Malpensa. He also made a reservation for Isabella. He made the flight for Friday morning, which would give him enough time to drive to the airport, drop off the chair at their airfreight department, and for both of them to make their plane. The clerk assured Paul the chair would be packed and shipped for him. If he were able to get it to them before seven in the morning, it would make his scheduled flight at nine o'clock.

The week passed quickly and Paul tried to stay focused on his painting. He didn't see Isabella at all. The house buzzed with preparations for Easter. Paul made certain his car started. He hadn't driven it since the rental company had replaced his destroyed one weeks ago. He was thankful Stein had made those arrangements for him. The storage compartment of the Range Rover was large enough to carry the chair once he put the back seat down.

He didn't want to seem conspicuous, so he didn't pack anything, and since all his clothes were gifts, he felt he should just leave them.

When Paul woke early Maundy Thursday of Easter week, it was a beautiful spring day that begged him to walk in its sunshine. Just before leaving his room, he scribbled a note on a square of paper to Isabella asking her to meet him. He folded it, and slipped it into his pocket. He moved swiftly down the carpeted hall, and stopped at Isabella's door. The hall was empty, so he slipped the paper under her door and hustled down the stairs.

He ventured out beyond the castle walls. Gravel crunched under his feet and echoed in the quietness of the mountainside as he strode down the path to the twin red barns that lay on a flat spit of land. The grooms were busy with the horses in their stalls, and he took up a position at the first corner of the barn and waited.

Soon he heard the crunching of boots on the gravel, and when Isabella turned the corner, he clutched her arm and pulled her to himself. "Why have you been avoiding me?"

Isabella's face and perfume hit him at the same time. She looked ravishing, dressed in tan riding britches, knee-high black leather boots, and a tight silk blouse.

"You told me we needed to be careful about being seen together these last few days."

"You're being a little too careful." He kissed her passionately, pinning her against the wall.

She came up for air. "You know we're leaving tonight. We'll have plenty of time for this later."

"Do you think anyone suspects?"

She pressed her body against his. "I don't think so. Stein wanted me to have my things in the basement studio by today. I did that last night. Do you have the tickets?"

"I have everything. We just need to get the chair and go."

"I'll tell my father around lunchtime that you're not feeling well, so that you will not be missed for dinner or for the service. As soon as the service is over we'll all go into the great room for a short reception. I'll excuse myself and meet you at the car, and we'll be off."

"Head for the garage as soon as you can. I'll be waiting."

"You'll need to get my suitcase out of the dungeon studio. If anything goes wrong, I'll meet you down there."

He kissed her again and held her tight. Soon enough they'd be together in California and could spend all of their time together.

Just before midnight, while a crowd filed into the chapel, Paul watched from a window on the third floor. He hadn't gone near the chair for the past week because he knew Stein would be watching him.

He chose this vantage point so he could see the people who entered the church. He wanted to make certain Stein was among them, but it was too dark to see faces.

Isabella had done such a great job of describing his sickness that Gerhard had even brought a tray of food to his room.

But Stein concerned him more. Did he buy Isabella's story? He saw the deacons close the outer doors, and the courtyard fell silent under the canopy of another gorgeous alpine night. Paul made his way through the armory into the anteroom of the exhibit hall that housed the chair. He checked his jeans pockets one more time for the barrel key. His plan was simple. He would snatch the chair, lug it downstairs, squeeze it into the Range Rover, and race to Milan. It would not be easy getting it to the garage—that thing was heavy—but he had traversed the path he would take several times during the week, and he was confident it wouldn't be any problem.

Stepping into the main exhibit hall, even though all the lights were out, he could tell something was amiss. The light in the center of the room that illuminated the chair was out, as were all the lights in the castle. He breathed easier. It had to be in front of him, resting in the darkness. He crept closer to the burgundy rope circling the chair and peered into the darkness. Flicking on his flashlight, his mouth dropped.

It was gone.

Every object we see will appear larger at midnight than at midday, and larger in the morning than at midday.

—Leonardo da Vinci, *Notebooks*

29

---

*F*rederick de la Cloy, Duke of Savoy, stood erect in his pew as the singing of the Lauds began. The chapel glowed in a hazy reflected light from the Tenebrae Hearse, a triangular, black-iron candelabrum placed prominently in the center of the altar. It held fifteen candles, seven on each steeply angled side, crowned with one large white taper.

As Frederick wrapped his arm around Isabella's shoulder, he noticed Stein slip into the end of the family pew just as the echoes of the first psalm rang through the chapel. He couldn't stop looking at the innocent face of his daughter. As the congregation sat, Frederick was so distracted he missed reciting one of the responsive readings.

Isabella glanced at him, asking with her eyes if he was okay.

He quickly found his place in his missal and followed along. Staring at the words on the page, he felt a chill thinking about the fire on the road. He had been so convinced that he could restrain her from going near the chair, but its allure was too powerful, deceitful. He had underestimated her ambition and Stein's deviousness.

He had not only duped himself but consigned his daughter to a horrific fate. He glanced again at her. Her lips moved so elegantly as she spoke the responses, the candlelight from the altar glimmering in her diamond earring. Tiny flickering flames reflecting in her exquisite green eyes made his heart heavy. He could not let her suffer the same fate as the elder LaBont, and that of the House of Savoy's ancestors.

Since her trip to Turin, he knew the only viable course of action would be to destroy the chair and let its power disappear with it. But his financial predicament and his arrangement with Stein precluded any rashness. Leonardo's self-portrait was nearly complete and it would be a masterpiece. His greatest fear was that once the portrait was finished, LaBont was promised the chair. Isabella was doomed unless he did something drastic to save her.

Father Domenici continued to read the nine Psalms of Matins and the five Psalms of Lauds. Each of the Tenebrae candles would be extinguished after a psalm was completed—then darkness. As the service progressed into darkness, he would plead with Almighty God to spare her life. What a fitting night to ask for such a thing.

Out of the corner of his eye, Frederick saw movement at the end of the pew. Turning, he could barely make out the silhouette of Stein heading toward the back of the church. As soon as Isabella was done with the painting, he would destroy that infernal chair, and rid his life of that leach Stein. A thousand Hail Marys and five hundred Acts of Contrition on his knees on the hard stone chapel floor would not wash away the remorse he felt at bringing that pariah into his family. It would be a great relief when he took the chair into the riding ring, doused it with gasoline, and destroyed it and its wicked power. He would baptize that wooden god with fire and strew its ashes to the winds and let them settle into the mountain meadows in an unmourned solitude. Then Isabella would be safe. Tonight he would pray that God would give him just a few more weeks of grace.

Paul paced the pitch-dark chamber in front of the empty dais. *Where could that blasted chair be?*

He had spent all morning with Isabella, and she hadn't said anything about her father or Stein moving it. If Stein had taken it, it could be anywhere in the castle. It would take a week to search every gallery, every storage closet.

Paul stopped in his tracks. It had to have been the duke who took it. After their episode on the road coming home from Turin, he had been strangely quiet, as if he had no further explanation for what had taken place. He most likely took it because he didn't know what to do about it. The one room everyone in the castle was prohibited from going into was the duke's private chamber in the northwest tower that Isabella said contained his religious relics. It had to be there.

He glanced at the luminous dial on his watch. It was twenty past midnight. He had to get moving if he intended to have everything ready by the time he met Isabella after tonight's service. Making his way through the dark galleries, he found his way to the bottom of the stairway leading up the northwest tower. His heart beat against his chest. It would be a challenge bringing that chair down the winding staircase, but he had to do it.

He slipped up the stairs, reaching the wooden door at the top. He assumed it would be locked, but when he leaned against the rough planks, it yawned slowly open with a grating squeak. A cold blast of air struck him in the face. He panned the area with his flashlight.

The spacious round room resembled the duke's study and

Isabella's studio. He played his thin beam across the smooth floor to the center of the room where the chair stood, facing the door as if it were waiting for him.

This is too easy. I can be out of here in no time.

He turned off the flashlight and stuck it in his back pocket. Standing in front of the chair, he placed a hand firmly on each arm.

Careful now, this baby's delicate. He lifted the heavy piece of furniture off the ground.

Just then, the lights flicked on. Holding the chair, he jerked his head around to see Stein standing at the door. He pointed a pistol at Paul.

"I knew you couldn't keep your hands off it," Stein said. He moved quickly across the room and held his gun level with Paul's head. "Put it down."

He dropped the chair the few inches to the stone floor.

Stein grabbed Paul's collar and yanked him away from the chair. "You thought you could just waltz out of here, didn't you?"

"Hey, take it easy."

"Not until I'm finished," he said with a menacing voice.

"This chair belongs to my father, and I'm leaving—"

"Shut up," he said. "You've been a real pain. You're going home the hard way. Put your hands behind your back. *Now.*"

Paul complied slowly and felt the clamp of a handcuff cut off the circulation in his left wrist. Instinctively, he yanked his right arm free, and kicked backward with his foot, hoping to hit Stein's kneecap.

Stein dodged away, and held onto Paul's cuffed hand. "Don't fight me, punk." He slammed the butt of his pistol on Paul's head.

The blow knocked him to his knees on the hard stone. Paul moaned while Stein clamped his other wrist and yanked him to his feet.

"You'd better cooperate, or you'll wish you had." Stein holstered his gun, and drew out his Tazer from his jacket pocket and shoved it into Paul's neck. "Walk."

Stein forced him down the stairs, to the elevator. Once the doors slid open in the cellar, he shoved Paul down the well-lit corridor, pushing him along the hall past the stone studio. Paul felt the cold pinch of the Tazer probes digging into his neck. *Where's he taking me?* A row of iron doors loomed on the right, which looked like ancient dungeons to Paul as they rounded a bend in the long, slanted corridor.

Stein pushed him past several doors and yanked on his shirt in front of the last one. *No one will ever find me down here!* The last black-iron door, in a row of a dozen, gaped open. Stein roughly shoved him into it. The tiny cell had no windows, no furnishings, just four stone walls, an uneven stone floor, and a low ceiling. Frigid air filled the small space. Paul could barely stand without hitting the ceiling.

Oh God, how am I going to get out of this?

"Welcome to your new home." Stein jammed the Tazer into Paul's neck and a jolt surged through his body. He shrieked in agony as a streak of pain flashed down his spine, and he slumped to the floor. He lost feeling in his legs and arms and the last thing he remembered was the shock of the coldness against his cheek, as if he had lain his head on an ice cube.

After slamming the metal door, Stein found a set of keys on a hook outside in the hall. He twisted the key in the ancient lock. Back up the corridor, he flipped off the corridor lights, leaving the cells in an impenetrable darkness.

He strode up the hall into the cellar studio. Paul's drawings were taped to the wall and the nearly completed da Vinci on the easel. One area, approximately a few square inches in the center of da Vinci's forehead, was left unfinished. The off-white of the canvas prep showed through surrounded by the exacting brush-work in flesh tones. It was obvious to Stein, LaBont had left this unfinished on purpose. Had Isabella tipped him off? He didn't doubt it, but after tonight the punk LaBont would be no more and Isabella would be free of distractions. He plugged his Tazer into a wall socket above a workbench. If he needed it later, he wanted it at full charge.

At a washbasin, he splashed water on his face, patted down his hair so he looked neat, and dried his hands and face with a towel. He straightened the collar of his shirt, and smoothed his mustache.

He glanced at his watch. It was a quarter to one. Lauds would be over soon and then the family would have a brief gathering in the great room before retiring. He still had a lot of preparations before Tosatti arrived in about four hours. Once he was done with the duke and LaBont, he and Isabella would be safely on their way to Florence. He hurried out of the room, switching off the light.

Paul lay on his belly with his hands behind him peering into a darkness he'd never experienced before. He wondered if whatever it was that Stein used on him had caused him to go blind. The back of his head throbbed. His neck stung as if he'd been bitten by a dog.

He lay on the cold floor shivering. No sound, no light pene-trated the room. The blood pulsing in his ears sounded like a rush-ing wind. He calmed himself by focusing on his breathing. He rolled on his side and forced himself to sit up, his back propped against the wall, his hands behind him. It was uncomfortable sit-ting on the hard stones in the eerie blackness. He waited for his eyes to adjust to the cold darkness, but they didn't.

Rolling his legs under him, he pulled himself onto his knees. Struggling to his feet, he lurched forward and bumped into a wall. Keeping his right shoulder to the wall, he followed it around until he felt the iron door. Turning his back to the door, he tried to grab a handle or anything that he could use to pull at it, but there was nothing to grip. No window, one locked door, solid rock all around him, there was no way out. He stumbled back to the far wall and slumped onto his knees. Would Isabella think to look down here once he didn't meet her at the car like they'd planned? He didn't think so. He didn't think anyone would find him before Stein returned with murder on his mind.

Peering into nothing, he realized this was what hell would be like. Not suffering and fire, just isolation, completely cut off from everyone and everything he loved, with no hope of ever seeing a ray of sunshine again. In some measurable way, he'd brought this on himself. If he hadn't tried to steal the chair, and if he hadn't been so determined to have Isabella, he wouldn't be in this dark hole. The room was a shade of black he didn't know existed. He closed his eyes to ward off the darkness.

When he opened them a few moments later a fragmentary ray of light caught his attention. He rocked back against the wall. Had the curse of the flame found him down here? But looking more carefully, from the other side of the cell, he saw two brilliant specks. He squinted to focus as they floated toward him. They were vaguely familiar, a set of eyes, the same penetrating eyes of Jesus that had stared down at him from da Vinci's *The Last Supper.*

He shook his head to ward off the hallucination. But the piercing gaze was unmistakable. They were the same eyes from the painting, and they were in front of him. He wasn't imagining this apparition.

They gazed into Paul the way they had last Sunday. They weren't looking at him, but *into* him. Had the painted eyes of Jesus been trying to tell him something all these weeks? The two piercing lights now watched him from only a hand's breadth away. The chapel wall had been transported to his cell, and he saw Jesus again sitting at the table with his disciples. Paul felt a part of the scene. He sat at the table with Jesus, and looked him in the eyes. The Master dipped his bread into the cup.

He who dips his sop with me, will betray me.

He heard the words clearly in his mind as if they had been spoken directly to him. Peter reeled backward in his denial. The other disciples cringed with anguish and fear with contorted expressions. These men were devoted to Jesus and were genuinely shocked with the idea that one of them would betray him. Just then Judas, his face rutted with dark lines, dipped his slug of bread into the bowl of wine. Turning, he stared at Paul while he brought the soggy morsel to his mouth. The ugly man with the hooked nose didn't say a word, but Paul could read his look like a news-paper headlines: Judas didn't love Jesus, but the power of Jesus: his healing miracles; his ability to know what other men were think-ing; his sway over people. Judas didn't want to serve mankind, but to rule over them. He ate the bread the way he would devour mankind if he had the power of Jesus.

What thou doest, do quickly.

Judas wiped his mouth on his sleeve, sneered at Paul and turned and headed to the door leading out of the Upper Room. Jesus fixed his eyes on Paul as if to ask a question. *Are you not going with him?* Paul looked to the far end of the Upper Room where Judas had stopped at the door. He motioned to Paul with a nod of his head to follow him.

Go with him? Yes, to the chief priests to tell them where Jesus could be found and easily arrested. Judas knew Jesus was suicidal. *What a waste of talent,* Judas was saying with his leering grin, *to sac-rifice yourself for others.* He would put a stop to the Prophet's insan-ity and make a little money on the side. It never hurt to have too much silver and gold.

For one tantalizing moment, he wanted to stand up and run

with the betrayer. He was as evil as the wicked Judas and he felt as ugly inside.

Paul looked up and Jesus gazed at him with his penetrating dark eyes. They were filled with anguish and pain as if the burden of the whole world weighed on his mind, but yet he radiated a deep peace. He knew that dying by crucifixion would be unutterably painful, worse than a thousand deaths, but he was willing to lay down his life, to fulfill his divine mission, to sacrifice himself ... for Paul.

Jesus held out his hand as if he were offering him something.

More than anything Paul wanted to be free from what drove him inside, from the compulsions that dominated his life, that had brought him so low, and from that curse of fire that dogged him.

Paul didn't know if such a thing was possible, but he held out his hand to a man he could not see, but that must be there.

Frederick held his daughter tightly, as Father Domenici read the last psalm. When the father finished, he nodded to the altar boy by the Tenebrae Hearse. The final candle puffed into a vapor of smoke and the chapel fell into a profound darkness.

Murmurs ran through the parishioners in the chapel, but Frederick held his tongue. He didn't know what went through the minds of the others sitting in the thick night. But to Frederick the deepness of the moment was sacred. This veil of blackness that sundered him from everyone else was a finger of guilt pointing straight at him.

He had tried to harness the chair's prodigious gifts for his own gain and he let its hurtful power of pride touch his daughter. Frederick lifted up his eyes. The darkness that reached to the apex of the vaulted ceiling reflected in the tiniest degree the gloom that wrapped his soul.

A beating of open palms, raucously thumping on wood,

echoed through the vacuous space of the chapel. The deacons beat on the doors and the altar to signify the earth's contortions after Jesus gave up his spirit. The agony, the suffering was over. The crucified one's plunge into the human bleakness had freed all men from their slavery to their own despair. But Frederick was not free from Stein, not free from the bankers, not free from his gambling, and his daughter was doomed to the curse of fire. He was sorry he'd gotten himself into this quagmire, and he would find a way out. There was nothing more to wait for. If he was to save his daughter, he must end the curse of the chair now. As soon as this service ended and his guests were gone, he would burn that evil chair into black ashes.

Frederick would not allow it to exist one more minute in his home.

If the eye is required to look at an object placed too near to it, it cannot judge of it well …

—Leonardo da Vinci, *Notebooks*

30

*S*tein crossed the courtyard just as the service in the chapel ended. He avoided the great room and took another route to the duke's study. Quietly, he made his way up the winding staircase. Sitting behind the duke's massive desk, Stein donned his gloves, then switched on a desk lamp and the computer. While waiting for it to boot up, he searched the drawers for the duke's pistol. Finding his Walther PPK in the bottom drawer under a pile of documents, he checked the clip. It was full. He flicked on the safety. He liked the feel of the compact blue-metal weapon as it slid easily into his jacket pocket. He also took a pair of the duke's leather gloves. He would leave them beside LaBont's body with the freshly discharged Walther. The evidence would be insurmountable. Turning to the computer, he tapped away on the keyboard. Stein had carefully culled the duke's own words and sentiments over the years, and no one would doubt he wrote this letter.

Dear Gerhard Tamboni:

You have served me faithfully for many years, and so I ask as your final act of kindness to me please deliver this letter to Ando Giamatti at Banco National in Turin. Ando, you rabid dog, you have stripped the last bit of flesh off the carcass of the de la Cloys and fed it to your whore Cassini. I spit on you. I cannot live to see you prostitute the castle of Savoy in the name of culture. Your plans to rob me of my dignity have left me with no alternative. Without Savoy, I am dead. Tonight, I will solve my own problems; tomorrow you will have yours. I take with me into the next world the American leach Paul LaBont. He is like your own son in that he would steal from the great treasure house that is Savoy. When I blow out his brains, I will think of what you deserve. May you rot in the deepest circle of hell with your benefactor, Judas. Give Gerhard, who has served me faithfully, a few lire to ease his way into a new life. Maybe you could give him the thirty silver coins Cassini has paid you to turn against me. It is the least you can do, since you can do no more to destroy me.

Frederick de la Cloy, the last Duke of Savoy

He printed it out, but left it in the printer. It wouldn't have the duke's fingerprints, but no one could say the duke hadn't typed it. Stein rearranged everything exactly as he found it, turned off the lamp, and left the study. Slipping down the north hall on his way to the tower, he couldn't help but smile. That note should make the greased-down hair of that worthless servant stand on end. Stein wished he could see that stuffed shirt's face when he read it. Gerhard had despised him for the last time. Pompous fool. Stein hurried out of the study; he still had a lot to do.

By now, the duke must have seen the light Stein had left on in the northwest tower and he should be up there inspecting the chair. Glancing at his watch, he grinned. Everything was on schedule. He and Isabella would be ready to leave when Tosatti arrived in a few hours. And tomorrow the duke's faithful servant would have a big mess to clean up before he delivered the mail.

Frederick and Isabella proceeded out of the Savoy Chapel after the service ended. He planned on escorting her into the great room where Gerhard had laid out refreshments and cakes for their guests, when a sliver of light by the fountain caught his attention. He jerked around. The windows in the northwest tower blazed with light.

"Stein!" he murmured. *He must be in the tower.*

"What did you say, Papa?" Isabella asked.

"Oh, just something important I need to attend to. Isabella dear, do you mind greeting our guests for me? I'll be back soon."

She kissed him on the cheek, and he watched as she disappeared into the crowd filing into the great room. Frederick then headed to the garage where he found a liter container of gasoline and a box of blue-tipped matches. He ran up the staircase two steps at a time. At the top and out of breath, he forced the door with his shoulder and stepped across the room. He stopped and faced the chair, its red upholstered seat shining at him like a mocking grin. He dragged it toward the open window then swung the casement window out, letting in gulps of chilled air. Once the seat was engulfed in flames, he would kick it into the night. Looking out the window, he could barely make out the large pile of rocks at the bottom of the eighty-foot tower. It would be broken in pieces and gone forever. Back inside, he doused the upholstered seat until the liquid ran over the side, splashed onto the stone floor and lay in a pool beneath it.

"What are you doing?" Stein said, dashing toward him.

"Don't come near me," Frederick said, not looking up as he continued to pour the liquid on the tall back of the chair.

"You foolish old man, put that down." Stein stepped briskly to within a few feet of the duke's side.

"Foolish is right!" Frederick flung the empty jug at Stein and took the box of matches out of his pocket.

"Don't! I'm warning you," Stein shouted, holding up his hands in front of his face.

"Get back." He stood up straight, took a match out of the box, and held it to the striker.

Stein lunged forward, grabbed the back of the chair, and dragged it away from the window.

Isabella stopped at the front steps leading into the great room, turned and watched her father walk swiftly across the lawn toward the garages. She pushed her hands into the pockets of her leather jacket.

Oh no! That's where Paul's waiting. What's going on?

Lifting her skirt, she ran across the courtyard just as her father left the garage with a container. She wondered why he needed gasoline at one o'clock in the morning. Something must have gone wrong. She watched him go back into the castle's west wing.

In the garage she went over to Paul's Range Rover. Her suitcase was in the back, but not the chair. He should be here by now. Was he hurt? Her first instinct told her to follow her father, but if he was in some kind of trouble, especially with Stein, she wouldn't be much help. Stein! That's what her father had mumbled. Stein must have stopped Paul from taking the chair. She needed to find Paul. She needed his help. The cellar studio. If something went wrong they had agreed to meet down there.

When she arrived in the stone studio everything looked normal, except drops of water were in the sink and she had not used it for the past several days. Then she saw a plastic object plugged into the wall above the workbench. She unplugged it and held it in her hand.

She read the label. *So, this is Stein's Tazer. Why is it down here?*

She pushed the button and it arced with a snapping sound. She jerked her head back, and dropped the Tazer. She quickly picked it up, keeping her finger away from the trigger.

Looking around the room, she noted everything seemed in order. She went out into the hall and looked both ways. To the left, it led back to the elevator. To the right, the hall disappeared into darkness. Standing perfectly still, she thought she heard something, like someone had shouted. She found a light switch and flicked it on. The long stone hallway lit up. She had heard a voice cry out.

The old dungeons! Someone's in the old dungeons. Paul!

She shoved the Tazer into her jacket pocket and ran down the hall until she reached the series of iron doors. She stopped at the first one and banged on it, calling his name. Finally at the last one, Paul called back. Frantic, she found the keys on the wall, unlocked the old door, swung it open, and rushed in.

"Are you okay?" she asked, kneeling down and hugging him.

"Thank God, you found me. We have to get out of here before Stein comes back. He wants to kill me."

"I'm concerned for my father too. Something's going on in the castle," she said as she helped him to his feet. Once outside they ran up the hall.

"What are we going to do about those handcuffs?" she asked.

"There are some tools in the studio."

Inside the stone studio, she led him to the workbench.

"Get that drill."

She scrambled to pick it up.

"Find a bit that will fit in the lock of the handcuff, and use it to drill out the locks."

Frantically she rummaged through a box of bits and checked several before she found the right one. Fitting the bit into the collete, she tightened it down. Paul squatted and propped his hands on her painting stool. The drill whirred; he could feel the bit piercing the lock. One cuff dropped off. She quickly drilled through the next one until it dropped off and the metal clattered on the floor. Paul stood stretching his arms in front of him, and rubbed his wrists.

"My father's up in the tower. I think he's in trouble."

"That's where I left the chair. Stein'll do to your father what he did to me," Paul said searching the room.

"I think we should call the police," she said, clutching his arm.

"Stein will be long gone long before they get here. Besides ..." he looked over at the pile of lead pipes. He picked up one of the short lengths. "I'd like to find him myself. Let's go."

They ran through the halls to the foot of the northwest tower. They bounded up the stairs and Paul ran through the open door, Isabella right behind him.

Stein pushed the duke toward the window, away from the chair, raised his gun and brought it down on the duke's skull. The duke crumpled against the wall under the window.

"Papa!" Isabella screamed, as she stepped into the room.

Stein spun around, shock registered in his eyes at the sight of Paul.

"I'll kill you for hurting him," Isabella said as she ran past Paul, slamming into Stein. He swung his burly arm in an arc and smacked her in the chest with his forearm, sending her reeling to the floor.

"Isabella!" Paul yelled springing forward.

Stein pointed his gun at Paul, freezing him. Stein's jaws flexed, his eyes poured hatred. Paul's forehead beaded with sweat.

"Now, it's your turn," Stein said, steadying his aim, his eyes red with rage.

Isabella let out an ear-piercing scream, jumped on his back, and clawed at his eyes. Stein grunted in pain and twisted madly.

Paul leaped forward, swung the pipe, and smashed Stein's hand with a thud. He yelled and the gun clattered on the floor. Stein's hand hung limp, but he jerked his other arm and landed an elbow to Isabella's ribs. She gasped for breath and slid off his back. Stein glared at Paul with a murderous look.

"You punk. No one will stop me from getting the chair." He pulled the duke's Walther PPK out of his coat pocket with this left hand. He took a step backward, out of range of the lead pipe.

Paul's sweat drenched his body. He madly searched the floor for Stein's gun. He saw it over by the wall. Too far to reach even if he lunged.

Stein clicked off the safety and raised the gun, his face contorted in anger. Suddenly, he started shaking, then convulsing. The gun dropped out of his hand. His head wobbled, and he let out an anguished cry of pain and dropped to his knees. Isabella held the Tazer to Stein's back. His eyes glazed over, and he fell face forward on the floor, his head thudding against the stones. As his body twitched, Isabella stood over him jabbing the metal prongs into him.

"Enough, Isabella," Paul said. He took the Tazer out of her hand, collected the two pistols, and laid them on one of the glass cases, and then wiped his forehead with his sleeve. He found the duke, dazed and disoriented, slumped against the wall by the window. He kept mumbling something Paul couldn't understand.

"Papa, Papa. Are you okay?" Isabella knelt beside him.

The room smelled of gasoline—a smell Paul knew well.

Paul put his hand under the duke's arm and pulled him up. "Help me Isabella. We need to get out of here."

Once he was on his feet, they both tried to lead him downstairs, but he shook them off.

"Get out of here," the duke commanded, pulling his arms out of their grasp. He pushed them away.

Paul saw his glassy look, took Isabella's hand, and backed off.

"What's wrong, Papa?" she asked.

"Get back!" he screamed. His hair fell over his face, his cheek bruised.

It was the first time Paul had ever seen the duke's jacket askew, his shirt wrinkled, or his hair messed. Then Paul saw the box of matches in his hand.

"Get back," he commanded Paul.

Paul pulled Isabella to the door. They both stood just outside on the small landing. Paul wrapped his arms around her and held her tight.

"Papa, what're you doing?" Isabella pleaded.

"Don't do it in here, Frederick," Paul said.

"I must destroy this devil," he said. Taking out a match, he held it to the striker pad.

"Papa!" she screamed.

Paul covered her head with his arms. They turned their backs to the room.

The explosion was deafening. Paul and Isabella were thrown against the wall by a brief but violent gush of hot air.

Paul opened his eyes and looked around. Shards of glass like little diamonds were everywhere. Coughing from the fumes, Paul scanned the room for the duke. All the glass cases were smashed, their contents of books and clothes were just so much debris—like someone had gone crazy with a shredder. Tiny flames licked at small patches of gasoline on the floor, but otherwise the fire was out. Paul moved cautiously toward the center of the room, glass crunching under his feet.

"Papa! Where's Papa?" she cried, hysterically.

"He couldn't have left without us seeing him."

Isabella rushed to the window. At the windowpane, she picked at shreds of a sport coat caught in the crevice between the sill and the casement window.

"No, no, no," she wailed, leaning her head out the window.

Paul caught her around the waist, and dragged her back in. He examined the fragments of cloth and leaned out, but it was too dark to see anything. "I'm sorry, Isabella."

"We've got to help him," she said frantically, grabbing Paul's shoulder, digging her nails into his arm.

He took her hand and they sprinted for the door, then suddenly Paul stopped dead bringing her to a halt.

"What is it?" Isabella said.

"Look at this."

The chair stood unscathed in the middle of the room. Its walnut patina shone as if it had just been polished. He studied it for a moment then started for the door. They rushed downstairs and ran around the castle to where her father lay below the far tower.

It is well that you should often leave off work
and take a little relaxation.

—Leonardo da Vinci, *Notebooks*

31

*T*he police finished their investigation just as the ambulance with the duke's body slowly pulled away sometime after dawn. The officers had listened to Paul and Isabella's story and then inspected the tower. They found everything as they had said, but Stein and his weapon were nowhere to be found. They recovered only the duke's pistol, the Walther PPK, from the rubble and, of course, the chair of Leonardo. With Isabella insisting that Stein was in the tower, the police mounted a search of the grounds and found his car gone. Several officers found their way down to the cellar and came back with the news that the dungeons and the cellar storage room were empty. One officer searching the duke's study found the suicide letter. With this piece of the puzzle in hand, the inspector in charge showed it to Isabella. She covered her face in disbelief, then started to cry all over again. It took him almost an hour to calm her down. The police left after taking fingerprint evidence from several rooms and asking Paul and Isabella not to leave the area.

Paul spent the next several days comforting Isabella. She decided to bury her father on the grounds of the castle he so deeply loved, instead of in the family plot in Turin. The ceremony was simple, and at the reception afterward it comforted Isabella to see so many of his old friends. In the following days, her sadness deepened and she fell into a dark silence. Paul expected it would take time for her to grieve, so he stayed close to her.

The police issued their final report on the duke's death and ruled it an accident. The inspector confided in Paul that his office had done a considerable amount of investigation, and they concluded the suicide note was genuine. The duke had not only planned to commit suicide, but to kill him as well. Instead, he had accidentally killed himself when he tried to light the gasoline. The match igniting the fumes in the air had caused an explosion with enough force to hurtle him out the window. The inspector was not prepared to call the duke's stupidity a suicide.

As for Stein, the inspector could only imagine that he had interrupted the duke's scheme and tried to stop him. So, in the absence of any other evidence, they didn't consider him a suspect. But they still wanted to interview Stein. Their forensics team had determined that someone lying about ten feet from the chair had been injured, possibly some second-degree burns on the left side of his body. They assumed it was Stein. Warnings had gone out to all the burn wards in Northern Italy. They would find him soon.

Paul realized the police had surmised most of the events correctly. Paul thought about telling the police about Stein locking him in the dungeon, but he didn't think it would change their opinions about what had happened. Stein was out of the picture, and so were his crazy plans to forge a da Vinci. Paul's nearly completed painting and the supplies had disappeared. Tosatti probably took them since he had been scheduled to show up that morning anyway. No one was going to admit the things Stein and Tosatti took even existed. It was best for all of them if Stein disappeared forever.

During one of the evenings when Isabella sat staring inconsolably into the roaring fire in the library fireplace, Paul made his way up to the third-floor gallery. The chair had been restored to its place on the dais and he stood gazing at it from behind the velvet rope. He unhooked a length of rope and approached it. He ran his index finger over the carved work on the arm. As he suspected, he felt nothing. He lowered himself into the seat and leaned against the stiff back. Nothing. He smiled. The vision of the piercing eyes in the dungeon darkness came back to him. In a sudden sense of intuition, the answer to the whole riddle of the chair unfolded in his thoughts. Paul was now convinced it had been created by Leonardo da Vinci, and somehow he had imbued it with his artistic power. How? Not even the late Duke of Savoy knew that. But the chair's power came alive when men gave their souls to it. And why would anyone do such a thing? The temptation of possessing the artistic genius of one of the greatest artists to ever live was too great to pass up. Paul had felt the rush of da Vinci's superior achievement. The taste of his own experience still stirred him. But it stayed with him now, more as a warning than a wish. That moment when he had sensed that what he created had elevated him above other men, above other artists, yes, and above the Giver of all gifts himself, was an intoxicating moment. He'd stood, in his imagination, on a mountain of his own making, higher than all other mountains. It was the same mountain Lucifer climbed when he said he would ascend to the most high, and be like God. It was the same mountain Judas scaled when he decided to determine for himself the destiny of Christ. But those dark eyes in the solitary dungeon had set him free. How, he didn't completely understand either, but it was true. *I don't need this to be the painter I've always wanted to be.*

He stood up, walked briskly from the chair, and with one last glance back he saw the glint of the walnut patina, the beautiful intarsia work; he turned and strode out of the room for the last time.

At dusk one evening as they walked along the north wall, Paul took Isabella in his arms and kissed her.

"You want to go home, don't you?" she asked, lying her head on his shoulder.

"It's time for you to leave here, too."

She raised her head, and looked him in the eyes. Her face brightened for a moment, then it clouded over again like it had for the past weeks.

"It would be hard for me to leave Savoy right now. I have so many things to do. The trustees have given me a couple of months to pack and move. There are other legal matters."

"I'm sorry."

"This was all my father's doing. Now I have to pick up the pieces. Why don't you go back to California and see your parents and that will give me time to settle my father's estate. Then I will come and visit you in California."

He touched her hair that took on the hue of spun gold in the sunset. "I can't leave you here alone. You've had a frown on your face for weeks like you've been trying to solve world hunger or something."

The evening cooled as the sun dipped behind the mountains and the sky turned dark. A wind whipped off the slopes and spun across the wall, sending chills through Isabella. She held him tighter.

"You're such a gentleman. I love you and want to be with you forever, but I can't right now." She kissed his cheek with her soft lips. "I suppose you want to take the chair."

He shook his head, "No."

"What?" she said, looking at him quizzically.

"I don't need it."

"Why do you say that?"

"I don't ever want to see it again. It should stay here in Savoy where it belongs."

She frowned at him, "I don't understand you."

He took her hand and steadied himself. This would be difficult to explain, but he must try. "Isabella, both of us have struggled to understand what Leonardo's chair is all about. The chair is not good, and it can't bring anything but harm to those who use it."

"But you have used it, and now you don't want to. Aren't you afraid to walk away from it, that the curse will follow you?"

"No, I have peace now."

She looked up at him when he said that word. "You do seem different lately. What happened?"

"Let me show you." He led her down the stairs, to the court-yard and into the Savoy Chapel. The light was waning through the high windows, but a yellowish shaft played on the central figures of the *Last Supper* above the altar. "Judas has the deeply rutted face. He's the ugly one."

She lifted her eyes. "No, I don't think so."

"Look carefully, he's the one that betrayed Jesus."

Frowning as she gazed up, she shook her head slowly. "No, I don't see what you see."

"Isabella, Jesus had to die. That was why he came to earth."

"You mean like God became man?"

"Yes, exactly." He pointed at the large Judas. "Don't you see Judas smirking? He's holding the moneybag. He just wants everything for himself."

"I don't understand what you're getting at. Paul, I'm tired. Can we go outside?"

He led her back outside and they sat quietly in the courtyard.

He put his arm around her waist. "Isabella, you have to understand this. It's very important. The curse is real."

"Then why aren't you afraid of it?"

"I'm free of it. I know I am."

"Because of a painting?"

"The message of the painting. You must take this seriously. It would be dangerous for you to ignore the consequences of using that chair."

She smiled warmly for the first time in weeks. "Please," she said, tapping his lips with her finger. "I want the same thing you have, just not right now."

"Promise?" he asked.

She smiled warmly at him. "When I come to you in California, we'll talk more about it."

"Isabella, before you come, you must study the painting in the chapel. You can't ignore what I'm saying."

She looked him in the eyes. "You have been wonderful to me. I promise you I will." She kissed him on the lips passionately. "I will never forget you, Paul LaBont."

He held her close. Her eyes were deep emerald pools. He felt lost in them; he wanted this feeling to go on forever. Kissing her soft lips, she touched his soul; his body pressed against hers, he knew the power of oneness was the deepness of two lives meant for each other. As they kissed, they seemed to dance under the carpet of stars; they held each other as the night quickened and the wind whistling through tall pines whispered in his ears that nothing, not time, not distance, could unbind what passed between them.

Nature teaches us that an object can never be seen perfectly when it is too close to one's nose.

—Leonardo da Vinci, *Notebooks*

32

*P*aul LaBont gripped his armrests as the United 747 touched the runway at LAX with a bump. The rumbling jet swept through the wispy fog swirling in its path as it steadily braked and then taxied to the terminal. Even though the journey from Milan had taken longer than he'd planned because of an eight-hour layover in London, it wasn't unpleasant. Every time he dozed off, he dreamt of Isabella and that last shimmering embrace upon the castle wall.

Once he retrieved his suitcase, made his way through passport control and customs, he hailed a cab and headed home. Slouched in the backseat of the cab as they drove down the freeway, the drab sameness of the endless rows of homes struck him. Even the leaden sky seemed drained of life and replaced with a conforming drabness. The bright Italian sunshine, pouring like molten gold from the sky through the wind-blown strands of Isabella's hair glinted in his mind. He sighed and tried to gather his thoughts.

He'd come to California for a purpose, and he'd given a lot of his waking moments the last few days preparing himself for his homecoming. His father would be upset that he hadn't brought home the chair. Paul hadn't even mentioned his plans in his few conversations with his mother since he decided not to bring it home, so his arrival home sans the chair would be a shock. But he knew he'd made the right decision to leave it in Savoy. He doubted his father would be convinced of that, at least at first.

Would he rage and go berserk? Paul only hoped not. He didn't want to add to his father's misery, but he also didn't intend to back down from his decision. He had planned his words carefully; nevertheless, he thought it best to simply be straightforward. Leaning his head on the back of the seat, he let the scenery slip by as the cab sped down the freeway.

Marcella stood on the Laguna shore in the misty fog and watched the waves rise and curl and then crash against the sand. The brisk morning air chilled her face as she continued her walk to the pier, where she turned in the soft sand and strolled home. Her life had settled into a safe routine. After her walk, she retreated to her room down the hall from Vincent and painted. He had agreed that he would not interfere with her work, but she hadn't expected his silence. At first he just stood at her door and watched as she painted, never saying a word. She had arranged her worktable so her back faced the door so when he ducked his head inside, she didn't have to see his expression. She wanted him to speak with his voice, not his eyes. She sensed him, this morning, silently standing at the door as she worked. She held her breath until he left. She'd expected a period of adjustment for him. Watching her paint wasn't easy for him. The fire had stripped him of his abilities, and she knew what that felt like.

But what she hadn't expected was the effect of his silence on her. Quietness at home carried a different meaning to her than it had in the studio in Rhonda's gallery where it allowed her to work uninterrupted. She couldn't help but wonder why he couldn't bring himself to compliment her work. Would he ever be able to? She felt thankful that she knew her worth as an artist. If she were to measure it simply by the dollars patrons paid for her water-colors, she was fast approaching Vincent's category of success. When she showed him a check from Scott from her last show, even Vincent had to raise his eyebrows in surprise. She enjoyed seeing the look on his face. He couldn't argue with results equated in dollars. But his wordless stare at her back each morning reminded her how deeply she needed something from him that money couldn't buy. She sighed as she brushed an aqua sea up to an azure sky on the paper in front of her as if it were an unguent for her soul.

Last week the visiting nurse had taken the bandages off Vincent's hands, and he now had enough flexibility in his left one to hold a book. And what of Vincent's soul? As his healing progressed, would he change? She would have to wait and see.

So, she filled her mornings with art; her afternoons with errands and taking care of Vincent; and her evenings with hope. She hoped for a miraculous cure for whatever ailed him, but she knew that at best it would come in imperceptible degrees. Having Paul home would help. It wouldn't be too many more hours before he and the chair would arrive.

And how would Vincent's magic chair help him? She didn't know what bringing it back into her home would mean. Would it bring a smile to Vincent's face? If it had the power to make him believe in himself again, it would be worth having it around. Like everything else in her life, she would have to wait and see what happened. She smiled as she brushed the sky with sure strokes, and with strong but delicate lines painted a wave rolling on the sea.

Confident brushwork, Scott had often told her, made her paintings stand out. She continued working into the morning with bold, quick movements of her brush. Here, in this one corner of her life, she knew exactly what to do and how to do it.

As the cab rolled through Laguna Canyon, Paul pondered his talk with his father. How could he explain the vision in his cell of Leonardo's *The Last Supper?* Since that encounter everything in his life looked so different, as if colors had come alive in ways he'd never imagined. He'd never experienced such peace before. He knew his art was a gift. And a gift presupposed a giver. An intentional giver. The anonymous universe had not put a desire in his heart to express himself, *someone* had; of this truth, Paul was now certain.

He leaned back in his seat. He was glad to be home, but he missed Isabella. He prayed she would be safe. Praying before had been a mere ritual, but now he knew someone listened. He reassured himself he would see beautiful Isabella again soon.

When the cab turned onto Pacific Coast Highway, he rolled down the window and listened for the familiar sound of the surf crashing against the sand. Everything seemed just as he had left it, but everything had changed.

A little while later the taxi slid into his driveway. Paul grabbed his lone suitcase, paid the driver, and watched as it circled the cul-de-sac and drove out of sight. Home should feel familiar, like a well-worn coat, but it didn't. He walked slowly up the steps to the front door and not having his keys, knocked.

Marcella opened the door and nearly shouted. "Paul, honey, you're home!" She kissed him on the cheek, hugged him, and then led him into the living room.

"Sit down, you must be exhausted," she said.

Paul plopped on the large sofa while she studied his suitcase as if trying to recognize it.

"Did you lose your luggage?" she asked.

"Yeah, you could say that," he said, remembering the night on the road to Savoy so long ago.

"Oh, dear. I hope the chair didn't get lost, too."

"Don't worry, it's not lost."

"Is the airline delivering it? When will it be arriving?" came a deep voice from behind him. Vincent moved around the end of the sofa and sat across from him, his face as gray as the morning mist.

Paul wanted to cry when he saw his father. This man who had been such pillar in his life now seemed like only a shadow of himself. He got up and sat down next to him, and put his arm around his father's stiff shoulders. "Good to see you, Dad."

Vincent relaxed slightly, but his expression didn't change.

Paul couldn't help staring at his unbandaged hands. The fingers on his right hand were thin and disfigured, the left less so. But across the backs of his hands the scars ran deep, like ancient wadis. And his face was gaunt. He had aged noticeably in the weeks Paul had been away, and not so gracefully.

Paul rubbed his forehead.

"Are you all right, son?" Marcella asked.

He nodded and looked at his father. "I have a lot of things to tell you both, but the most important thing you need to know is that the chair's in Savoy where it belongs."

"What?" Vincent said harshly, his face creasing in anger. He pulled away from Paul.

"I thought you said the duke would sell it to you?" Marcella said.

"I lied." He glanced at his mother. "I'd planned on stealing it."

"Oh, Paul. How could you?" She put her hands to her face.

"Mom, it was the only way to get it out of Savoy, believe me."

"So, why didn't you bring it home then?" Vincent demanded.

He turned to his father. "Because I decided that we didn't need it."

Vincent's eyes widened but he didn't say anything. Then he stood and let out a disgusted sigh. "How could you make such an important decision without talking to me?"

He stood and caught his father's eye. "You sent me to Savoy to find the chair. I did exactly what you wanted. And I also found out that we don't need it, so I did what I thought was right."

His father glared at him with darkened eyes.

"What do you mean, 'we don't need it'?" Marcella asked.

"Let me show you what I mean, Dad."

"Show me what?"

"I brought something home that will help you."

Vincent raised his eyebrows. "What? A souvenir? A postcard?"

Paul took his arm. At first he was reluctant, finally he relented. "Please, Dad, trust me."

Paul led him into the bedroom his mother had set up as a studio. He set his father down in front of the easel on a small stool. He found a canvas leaning against the wall, set it on the easel, and seated himself beside his father. Marcella followed them and stood by the door, leaning against the jamb.

Paul found a couple of new brushes and held one out to his father.

"What's this?" Vincent said angrily.

"Vincent, I think you need to listen," she said from behind them.

Vincent took a deep breath. Paul glanced at her and smiled.

"I learned something in Italy."

"A new technique?"

Paul nodded his head slightly. "Not really, it's more what I learned about myself. Let me show you."

Vincent held up his hands as if defending himself. "Paul you know I can't do this—"

Paul put his hand on his father's shoulder. "You need to relax. This isn't going to hurt." He could feel the slight tremors in his body as he waited until his father calmed.

"I can't paint. I can't even hold a brush because of the pain. Why didn't you just bring home the chair like I asked you to?"

Paul sat silent until Vincent relaxed.

His father frowned and clenched his jaw. "So what is it you want to show me?"

"I'm going to teach you to paint." He gently massaged his father's hand, loosening his fingers. He took a number six brush and placed it in his father's left palm.

"I can't do this," Vincent said, raising his voice. Without closing his fist, he catapulted the brush across the room with a swing of his arm. It slapped against the wall and fell to the carpet.

Paul didn't budge. He felt himself smiling inside. He found another brush, placed it in Vincent's hand and locked eyes with his father. "You need to trust me, like I trusted you when I was young," he said firmly.

Vincent jumped up, leaning forward over Paul. "Why should I? You can't even do what I asked."

Paul held onto his arm, stood, and stared him in the eyes. "Because I know what I'm talking about."

Vincent glared and pulled his arm back. He quickly turned toward the door then abruptly stopped. Marcella, with her arms crossed over her chest, blocked his exit. Paul could see the determination in her eyes. A lot had changed while he was gone. Vincent stepped forward menacingly as if he would push his way by her, but he came up short. Neither one said anything for a long half a minute. She seemed to paralyze him with her glare.

He sighed and returned slowly to the stool beside Paul. They were both seated and acquiescently, he held out his hand. Paul took it gently in his.

Carefully taking Vincent's fingers one at a time, he bent them around the wooden handle.

"What's happened to you?" Vincent asked, his voice sounding resigned.

"I found out the truth about the chair, and it's not good." Paul stated, working his father's hands around the shaft of the brush.

"There's nothing wrong with it."

Paul held up his father's hand. "Look what it did to you. And it almost did it to me. And it's killed almost all of those who have used it over the last four centuries."

Vincent pursed his lips and glared.

Paul closed his father's pinkie around the wooden stock of the brush. "You don't have to live in the shadow of the chair, always wondering what's going to happen to you."

"But you know what that means."

"It means you have to become like a little child and accept who you are and what God has made you."

"That's an awfully high price to pay."

Paul sighed. He didn't expect this would be easy. "Peace with yourself and with your Creator is far better than having the ability to paint even the *Mona Lisa.*"

"You wouldn't say that if you'd been where I have."

"I have been there, Dad, and I've come back to tell you it almost killed me, and would have killed you. Is it worth having the world at your feet, only to burn to cinders?"

Vincent studied his hands for a long moment, then spoke. "So with all your changes, you seem to have forgotten I taught you everything you know about painting."

"I know you did. And I'm grateful to you for everything you've done for me." He took Vincent's hand, now closed around the brush, and held it up to a new canvas.

"And how's this going to help me?" Vincent said.

Paul sitting beside his father held Vincent's hand to the canvas. He wrapped his other arm around his father's tense shoulders. He carefully guided Vincent's hand up to the blank canvas on the easel, much like his father had guided him once when he was very young. Together they moved the brush across the clean canvas until his father's jerky movements were transformed into the strong, sweeping strokes with the fluid rhythm of an experienced painter.

Paul could see the pain on his father's face diminish with each silky sweep of their hands. There was no magic here, only a conviction in Paul's mind he would prevail.

"So, what are you teaching me here, maestro," his father asked sarcastically, "that I don't already know?"

"I'm going to teach you," Paul said as he continued the motion of his hand with Vincent's, "to paint from your heart."

He is a poor disciple who does not excel his master.

—Leonardo da Vinci, *Notebooks*

Epilogue

Over the next few weeks, Paul did everything he could think of to contact Isabella. He called, wrote letters, e-mailed, but his calls went unanswered, his letters were returned, and his e-mails bounced. He put several calls into Giocomo Tossatti, the art dealer in Milan, but even he wouldn't come to the phone. After a few weeks, the number to the castle in Savoy was disconnected, and he lost any hope of ever speaking to her again.

Paul moved out of his parents' Monarch Bay home and into a small house in Laguna Canyon. His home—on a shady street—had an airy studio in the back with large windows that opened up with a view of the scrub-covered canyon hillsides. He threw himself into his work. Painting with Isabella on his mind became a heavy chore, like trying to make smooth strokes with leaden brushes. Even mixing his colors—they didn't seem as bright, or as glossy on the canvas, or as reflective of the light as they had in Italy. He wondered if Isabella's grief had driven her away from her own heart. How can someone just disappear?

Paul rededicated himself to his work and painted a variety of landscapes. Some from the memories stored away from his time in Savoy. Others of the coastal hills he could see out his window. One day, unconsciously, he found himself painting a long-legged woman with flowing strawberry blonde hair running through a meadow. He worked from memory as if her image was branded on his mind down to the dimples on her cheeks, for it was.

Late one hot October morning, he decided to escape the still air of the canyon and drive to the beach a few miles away to have an early lunch. Seated on the sun-splashed patio of Las Losos, cooled by a soothing ocean breeze, he sipped an iced tea. After ordering his food, he unfolded a newspaper, spread it out on the table, and scanned the front page. While bringing his glass to his mouth, he began to read an article in the lower quarter of the page. The liquid rolled off his tongue and dribbled down his chin. He lowered the glass, holding it frozen in midair.

Paul couldn't believe what he was reading. An art dealer in Milan, one Giocomo Tosatti, had been commissioned by an anonymous owner to sell a da Vinci that had been thought to be destroyed in 1497 when Savanarolla had the citizens of Florence burn their books and pagan artworks. The lost self-portrait of Leonardo da Vinci has been authenticated as original and would probably sell at auction for upwards of eighty million dollars. While not naming the owner, Tosatti claimed it had been discovered hidden in an ancestral home somewhere in Northern Italy. The writer guessed that it had been found in Florence.

He froze, stunned. The glass slipped from his hand, shattering on the floor with a sharp crash. He shoved his chair back so hard it almost tipped over; he stood and walked out of the restaurant patio to the adjacent sidewalk overlooking the crowded beach below.

Isabella is in Florence.

He knew now what she had been up to these past months. The realization pierced him with a sharpness, penetrating to his marrow. He had to find her and help her before it was too late. He stormed down the walkway to his car. Tomorrow he would leave for Florence.

The End

Readers' Guide

For Personal Reflection
or Group Discussion

Readers' Guide

In the beginning God created the heavens and the earth. Now the earth was formless and empty, darkness was over the surface of the deep, and the Spirit of God was hovering over the waters. And God said, "Let there be light," and there was light. God saw that the light was good, and he separated the light from the darkness (Gen. 1:1–4).

There is no artist that can compare with Almighty God. There is no greater masterpiece than the universe we live in and no greater gift than the simple existence of light. He is the one true Master, for he created everything out of nothing—by the power of his spoken word, all that is and has been and ever will be came into being.

It is no less amazing that God made man in his image, and placed the potential for tremendous creativity and artistic expression within each one of us. But despite these free and glorious gifts, mankind is rarely satisfied. Like Lucifer, who believed himself to be above the One who created him, humanity has long struggled with the delusion that we are greater than our Maker—that we too can be God.

Leonardo's Chair is a story as timeless as good versus evil; tasting forbidden fruit; mankind's fall and God's redemptive love. In the same way that Satan thought himself to be the greatest, each possessor of the chair comes to believe that he or she is the most capable of artists; the master of his or her generation. One by one, each artist becomes intoxicated by the power of the chair, only to be destroyed by the very thing he or she desires most.

There is a critical lesson to be learned from this story—for we all must decide between pride and humility. We must come to understand that though we are of great value, priceless in God's eyes, apart from him we are nothing but dust. "Yet, O LORD, you are our Father. We are the clay, you are the potter; we are all the work of your hand" (Isa. 64:8).

As you study the following questions, examine your own heart and life. Are you serving yourself or serving God? Do you desire "greatness," or to ascribe all glory to him who made you? Consider the question Paul poses to his father: "Is it worth having the world at your feet, only to burn to cinders?"

1. Bartolomeo warns his son to "Stay humble. Never let the pride of greatness lift you up." What suggests that Pierino lacks humility—even before he travels to Rome? How might this character flaw contribute to his feeling of "imprisonment" after two years of painting for the city's most influential citizens? What is always the inevitable consequence of pride, and how does it play out in Pierino's life?

2. Vincent bravely enters his burning home and rescues Marcella. Does it seem surprising, given what we already know about his family relationships, that he was so heroic and selfless? Is Vincent God's answer to Marcella's prayer for help? Why does he foolishly risk his own life to try and save the chair? What do both of these choices reveal about Vincent's character?

3. With both parents seriously injured and hospitalized, Paul considers praying but decides against it. How common is his belief that prayer is only done in moments of "weakness," and that it really isn't "fair to plead with God just when the chips are down"? Is there any truth to this conviction? Why or why not?

4. Paul compares his father's use of the chair to a "crutch," but believes it to be a better alternative than other vices commonly used by artists—such as drugs or alcohol. Is Vincent justified in using the chair if it really helps him paint? Do the "ends" really justify the "means"? Have you ever tried to excuse a destructive habit or bad decision in a similar manner? Why is this type of rationalization particularly dangerous?

5. Does it seem strange that first the insurance company, and then Vincent and Paul learn of the survival of the chair? How is it possible for that information to become public—when the fire provided such a convenient "cover" for the burglary? What warning signs are evident that everything is not as it seems?

6. Despite numerous obstacles, Paul pursues his quest to retrieve the chair. Why is he so determined to succeed? Is he really most concerned with helping his father? What other motives might be spurring him on?

7. What is the significance of Paul's dreams? What do the following images represent: the beautiful woman in white; the swirling pit within of living darkness; Paul's bare, fleshless bones; the flames? Is God trying to speak to Paul through his dreams? If so, why does he seem unable to comprehend the message?

8. As a result of the fire, Marcella must make decisions that change her life. In what ways is Marcella different from her son and husband? Does she have a more sensitive heart for God? How does her simple love of art and beauty contrast with her husband's ambitions and "superior" attitudes? How have Vincent's harsh judgments and criticism affected Marcella's self-esteem and ability to appreciate the value of her own work?

9. The duke's castle is filled with famous works of art—many done on a grand scale—but despite their perceived value, almost all of the works are copies. Where is the intrinsic value really found—in the unique vision, ability, and creativity of the artist, or in the finished product itself? Can a counterfeit piece of artwork—no matter how

skillfully accomplished—be as valuable as the original? How does this principle apply to our own lives, as God's unique creations? Despite our imperfections, what is our true value? (See Gen. 1:27–31; Isa. 64:8; 1 Cor. 6:20; John 3:16.)

10. Is Isabella a master manipulator or merely deceived? What is faulty about her beliefs? Is it difficult to pinpoint where her arguments go off course? Why does her "vision" of *The Last Supper* differ so much from Paul's view? What does her empathy and compassion for Judas reveal about her the true condition of her soul?

11. The duke is desperate to find an "antidote" for the chair's evil curse. He purchases numerous artifacts and researches ancient rituals in the hope of protecting his daughter. What has the duke placed his faith in? Are these effective methods to combat the spiritual forces of evil?

12. The Bible says, "The thief comes only to steal and kill and destroy; I have come that they may have life, and have it to the full" (John 10:10). How does Stein personify the Enemy? In what ways does his influence infiltrate and corrupt the duke's family? How does their association with Stein reflect the similar consequences we experience when we "make a pact with the devil" to attain something we desire?

13. Virtually everyone who comes in contact with the chair attests to its "power." Is it possible for an inanimate object to possess a creative force—either for good or evil? What is the true source of all that is good? By contrast, where does all evil originate? (See James 1:17; Ps. 86:8–15; 91; Luke 10:18–19.)

14. The duke shows Paul an ancient book that chronicles the history of his family for five hundred years. This "Book of Fire" records the horrific, premature deaths of those that used the chair—most perishing by fire. What striking contrast does this tome present to the "Lamb's Book of Life"? (See Luke 10:20; Phil. 4:3; Rev. 21:27.)

15. Isabella finally succumbs to Stein's persuasive temptation, and begins to use the chair. How does she feel about relying on something "so arcane"? How does her disappointment in her own progress and abilities lead to her decision? What is her greatest desire? Like Pierino before her, does Isabella suffer from the pride of greatness?

16. When the duke makes his proposition to Paul: the chair in exchange for a forged da Vinci, Paul adamantly rejects the idea. He doesn't want to be a "copyist"—instead he believes he must hold true to his artistic ideals. What causes his resistance to break down? Is his change of attitude really his own doing, or is he being manipulated? What common characteristics can be seen that often lead to the choice to compromise?

17. When Isabella tempts Paul with "everything you've ever wanted and more," why does he ignore his instinct to run? Why does he give in to temptation—despite the fulfillment of the warnings in his dreams? How is the scene with Isabella and the chair similar to Adam and Eve in the Garden of Eden? Is it coincidence that the decision to stay and paint the da Vinci is now easy—without any of the concerns that had bothered him before?

18. Despite her commitment to her husband, Marcella faces great temptation to turn outside her marriage for comfort and companionship. How are her choices similar to those we all experience at one time or another? Would the world have considered her "justified" in leaving her dominating, depressed, and emotionally abusive husband? Instead, why does she respond to the "still, small voice" that prompts her to return home? How do Marcella's choices make the difference between life and death—both physically and spiritually? How might the outcome have been different if she had refused to make the right decision?

19. Is Isabella right when she declares that all of the tragic events associated with the chair were the result of a "choice" and not a "curse"? If so, what is the wrong choice that so many have made in regards to the chair? Is suffering and tragedy always the result of our actions? What significant issue does Isabella fail to recognize? (See Eph. 6:12.)

20. In what ways does God pursue Paul? When the painting of Jesus reaches out to him, why does he feel marked as a traitor? Is he misinterpreting the meaning of the offered bread? What does Jesus really extend to Paul?

21. The duke believes the chair to be inherently evil and decides that it must be destroyed. Is he right about the presence of evil at work? If so, does he accurately pinpoint its source? Despite his attempt to produce a counterfeit da Vinci in order to save his property, is he really an evil man? What evidence suggests that he has a sincere desire to please God? What is the greatest tragedy of his life?

22. After his encounter with God in the dungeon, Paul is no longer affected or controlled by the chair. What gives Paul new understanding of the chair's power? Why does he suddenly have eyes to see—while Isabella is still blind to the truth?

23. According to his brother, Bartolomeo, Leonardo da Vinci insisted that whomever used the chair should never be far from it, believing that it would remind the owner that all artistic talent and ability is a gift from God. How was his intent perverted? Does the chair represent the designs of the Creator or the Enemy? Is it a blessing or a curse . . . or both? Does the result depend on the spiritual condition of the person who possesses it?

The Journey of Souls Series

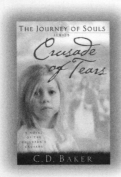

Crusade of Tears

A Novel of the Children's Crusade—Volume 1

C.D. Baker

It's the year 1212, and Jerusalem is occupied by Islam. Christian knights have failed to liberate the Holy City. Who else will the Church send to fight for the faith? More knights? Peasant laborers? Or. . . their children?

This masterfully written novel will transport readers back into 13th century Christendom when 50,000 children, falsely inspired, set out to reclaim Jerusalem. *Based on a true account.*

ISBN: 1-58919-009-2 ITEM #: 103295
5-1/2 x 8-1/2 PB 632P

Quest of Hope

Volume 2

C.D. Baker

This second book in the series provides a wonderful background to *Crusade of Tears*. Starting with the birth of Heinrich, the father of two of the young crusaders, it follows his amazing life during the Middle Ages.

ISBN: 1-58919-011-4 ITEM #: 103623
5-1/2 x 8-1/2 PB 640P

The Ahab's Legacy Series

Ahab's Bride
Book One of Ahab's Legacy
Louise M. Gouge

Before Captain Ahab encountered Moby Dick, he met the woman who would capture his heart—Hannah Oldweiler. This voyage to 19th century Nantucket introduces you to the woman whose spirit and determination matched the man she loved.

ISBN: 1-58919-007-6 ITEM #: 103292
5-1/4 x 8 PB 348P

Hannah Rose
Book Two of Ahab's Legacy
Louise M. Gouge

As the second book in this series begins, Captain Ahab has become the victim of his own mad pursuit of the great whale. Hannah, his widow, and her son, Timothy, seek to distance themselves from the Ahab name by planning a trip to Europe. While visiting friends in Boston, Hannah encounters some prospective love interests, but finds she must first search her heart regarding some important issues, not the least of which is slavery.

ISBN: 1-58919-040-8 ITEM #: 103817
5-1/4 x 8 PB 320P

More Terrific Historical Fiction

Flight to Eden

Cradleland Chronicles—Book 1

Douglas Hirt

Satan has caused the fall of man and now wants complete control of Earth, but there is the problem of the prophecy about a Redeemer who's coming who as the power to "crush his head!" Read about Satan's scheme to pollute the human bloodline and prevent the prophecy from coming to pass!

ISBN: 1-58919-053-X ITEM #: 104176
5-1/2 x 8-1/2 PB 512P

Mysterious Ways

Terry W. Burns

When Amos Taylor steals a parson's clothes, he thinks he's found the ideal disguise to hide his life of crime. Before long the disguise is working too well: local residents expect Amos to serve as their preacher! When revival breaks out, Amos's payoff is bigger than he could have dared imagine— proving that the Lord works in *Mysterious Ways*.

ISBN: 1-58919-027-0 ITEM #: 103664
5-1/4 x 8 PB 320P

Longshot

Mark Ammerman

In the 18th century, a decade after the Great Awakening has swept throughout the colonies, the flame of revival has touched even the Native Americans lands. But some still have not bowed to the Love that tirelessly pursues them. But no man can run forever, and God never sleeps.

ISBN: 1-58919-047-5 ITEM #: 104096
5-1/2 x 8-1/2 PB 320P

Order Your Copies Today!
Order Online: www.cookministries.com
Phone: 1-800-323-7543
Or Visit your Local Christian Bookstore

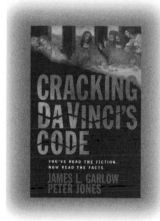

The Word at Work Around the World

A vital part of Cook Communications Ministries is our international outreach, Cook Communications Ministries International (CCMI). Your purchase of this book, and of other books and Christian-growth products from Cook, enables CCMI to provide Bibles and Christian literature to people in more than 150 languages in 65 countries.

Cook Communications Ministries is a not-for-profit, self-supporting organization. Revenues from sales of our books, Bible curricula, and other church and home products not only fund our U.S. ministry, but also fund our CCMI ministry around the world. One hundred percent of donations to CCMI go to our international literature programs.

CCMI reaches out internationally in three ways:

· Our premier International Christian Publishing Institute (ICPI) trains leaders from nationally led publishing houses around the world.

· We provide literature for pastors, evangelists, and Christian workers in their national language.

· We reach people at risk—refugees, AIDS victims, street children, and famine victims—with God's Word.

Word Power, God's Power

Faith Kidz, RiverOak, Honor, Life Journey, Victor, NexGen — every time you purchase a book produced by Cook Communications Ministries, you not only meet a vital personal need in your life or in the life of someone you love, but you're also a part of ministering to José in Colombia, Humberto in Chile, Gousa in India, or Lidiane in Brazil. You help make it possible for a pastor in China, a child in Peru, or a mother in West Africa to enjoy a life-changing book. And because you helped, children and adults around the world are learning God's Word and walking in his ways.

Thank you for your partnership in helping to disciple the world. May God bless you with the power of his Word in your life.

For more information about our international ministries, visit www.ccmi.org.

Additional copies of *LEONARDO'S CHAIR*
and other RiverOak titles are available
from your local bookseller.

If you have enjoyed this book,
or if it has had an impact on your life,
we would like to hear from you.

Please contact us at:

RIVEROAK BOOKS
Cook Communications Ministries, Dept. 201
4050 Lee Vance View
Colorado Springs, CO 80918

or

Visit our Web site
www.cookministries.com